RAYSTAR OF TERRA

Kurt Johnson

Dear Nicola,
Happy Birthday! It's been
a pleasure knowing you and I count
myself fortunate to be amongst your
friends. Health, happiness
and love and
success in this
personal new year!

— Kurt

Bruce E. Mitchell, Editor

Cover Artwork
Diogo Lando, www.diogolando.com

Editorial Work and Interior Design
Perrin Davis, Three Muses Creative, www.threemusescreative.com

Printed in the United States of America.

For Kiran

Foreword

"Star clusters birthed new suns; red giants blazed their dying light; nebulas shrouded the relentless gravity of black holes." So begins Kurt Johnson's first novel, the story of a thirteen-year-old girl living 1,800 years after a galaxy-wide war between Humanity and the Convergence. Even though this "fiction" stretches credulity, Kurt is able to magically submerge the reader into that alternative reality and to assimilate its strangeness into the reader's own consciousness.

What makes *Raystar of Terra* unusual is its seamless development of bizarre relationships, making them believable, even comfortable, by converting the weird "other" into the normal "another" and transforming "creatures" into loyal friends as well as fierce foes. Raystar, a wonderfully innocent teenager, is an outcast on the planet Nem', yet she is also a talisman for humanity, someone who enables the reader to explore the unearthliness of her alien encounters along with the light-filled grandeur of her human potential. Raystar enables the reader to settle in, to get comfortable with the unimagined extremes of foreign worlds, outside possibilities…definable only in terms of themselves. I am reminded of that most famous of outcasts, Ishmael in *Moby Dick*, when he magnanimously said: "Not ignoring what is good, I am quick to perceive a horror, and could still be social with it—would they let me—since it is but well to be on friendly terms with all the inmates of the place one lodges in."

Raystar lives on a farm with her father, mother, sister, and her own synthetic attendant, a remarkably human artificial intelligence. She understands that she, as a human, is an exception on Nem', but certainly not exceptional in the grand scheme of things. She is dwarfed (literally) by enormous creatures much smarter, swifter, and more awe inspiring than she. However, part of her quest for identity is to discover what unique powers she does possess. In that sense, her story is an old one, that of self-realization, but her growth is explored and tested in new realities, new challenges—all while carrying old baggage, the genetic suitcase of her own humanity.

Raystar's family farm is nestled below the Mesas, "three-thousand-meter–high plateaus that blocked out the sky with their square brutishness," that are subsumed every six weeks by "giant, dark walls of angry clouds and bellies gorged with lightning, rumbling from one pole to another." Kurt does a wonderful job of creating a setting full of beauty and threat, one that becomes real in its attention to detail, but also one that mirrors Earth's environments, lands that nourish as well as destroy: "Leggers hunted the animals that lived in the 'natch fields. Legger packs would occasionally take a lone farmer or stray kid. And in really dry years, sometimes they would attack a household." In Raystar's life on Nem', there is danger, dark unknowns that lurk just outside her well-fortified home. Her parents are on constant alert regarding the possibility of their child's vulnerability, yet they cannot totally protect her from risk. They know that some day she must walk alone, in the dry years, unprotected.

Even though *Raystar of Terra* is set in a far-flung, alien universe, it explores close-to-home human concerns: weakness, power, loss, family, isolation, friendship, violence, fear, compassion, and humanism. All of these complex issues are interwoven into the bizarre experiences of Raystar, and perhaps, into the awareness that her story may bring to the reader's own quest for understanding in the hurly-burly of this world's present.

Almost on a daily basis, we absorb negative images of human conduct, rending snapshots in a long continuum of mayhem and violence. In 2016, on the shores of Lake Kentura in Kenya, ten 10,000-year-old male skeletons were discovered, grouped together. All of them showed signs of head trauma, evidence of one tribe's attack on another. By not ignoring what is bad in our history as well as what may be negative or positive in our future, *Raystar of Terra* is a realistic novel, but at the same time, it is also one that is "real" in its wonderful portrayal of a family's closeness, the power of defiant hearts, and the unique pluck of a teenager who refuses to become an alien.

On a personal note, it has been my honor and my pleasure to edit this book. Twenty-nine years ago, Kurt Johnson was a student in my senior English class at Evanston Township High School in Evanston, Illinois. It is not often that a teacher, particularly one so many years beyond the classroom, gets a chance to witness the extraordinary intellectual and emotional growth of one of his or her charges. It has been my blessing to have been a teacher, and to have had the career that was my calling. Often, I reflect back on the ebb and flow of shared experiences in the classroom, but also on the hidden linkages between all of us, the interconnections we just barely intuit in dreams, memories, and feelings. I extend an immeasurable thank you to all I have had the pleasure to know, who have become part of me, and to Kurt…to whom I owe the fulfillment of this long-term, shared journey.

—*Bruce E. Mitchell*

1

Star clusters birthed suns; red giants blazed their dying light; nebulas shrouded the relentless gravity of black holes. This close to the Milky Way's core, it is personal. Every color glared at me from the darkness.

Destruction. Creation.

Gorgeous.

I wedged myself into the crook of my dad's lower arm and raised my face to the cool fall air, feeling the soft grass through my worn overalls. A chorus of insects, common to every life-supporting planet, thrummed, chirped, and cricked around us in a random, 360-degree orchestra.

Dad was a high-collared, broad-shouldered silhouette against the white, gold, and blue smear of 100 billion suns. The waterfall of stars stopped at the horizon, except to the west, where the Mesa mountain range imposed square black outlines on the night. By Core-light, I could see our farm's 'natch fields stretched out, a leafy ocean surging in the wind against the base of the Mesas.

A chill scuttled along my spine, and Dad wrapped his upper arm around me.

I would have dreamed in his warmth and protection until the stars and their secrets faded into the dawn. *THAT wasn't* going to happen. Cuddling, dreaming, bathing in the shock and awe of the Galactic Core—none of that would make me "galaxy-ready," according to Mom and Dad. Relaxation was not preparation. I unclenched my fists and let out a breath, feeling the sting from where my fingernails had dug into my palms.

Mom and Dad were right about being prepared, just maybe not in the way they thought. I needed to be up *THERE*. Not here. School was starting in two days, and I wished I could fast-forward through it. Skip to being grown-up and getting on with my life.

I inhaled the loamy night air. This had been a particularly grueling summer break. I'd wake before the sun and work until sunset. My friends went to camps. I operated heavy farm equipment. They watched vids. If I was lucky, I'd have enough energy to vid with friends after dinner. There were as many vids floating around of me falling asleep, mid-sentence, as there were stars. I don't care what race you are—a head hitting the pillow (I drool when I sleep) always gets a laugh. Work, work, and work, and then it was "early to bed!" or some such nonsense phrase.

In response, for my eyes only, 12:01 A.M. flashed across my field of vision. Ha. You see, every Galactic had at least one synth, or synthetic attendant. I called mine AI, after the Terran phrase "artificial intelligence." He was a fist-sized, diamond-shaped, rusted brown pendant that hung around my neck from a simple, linked, Human-made, and oddly corroded metal chain. AI had heard my thoughts, and he was pointing out that Dad and I were up past midnight.

He flashed soft green, barely visible through my clothes, and emitted of a pulse of warmth I felt against my chest. See, he used temperature and color for nonverbal communication. And he was laughing at me.

I didn't mind his snark. More often than not, he made me smile. He was my conscience, my counterpoint, and if anyone could pull a laugh out of me, it was he.

My friends' attendants weren't anything like AI. While my friends usually had more than one synth, I needed only him. In fact, I couldn't imagine wanting more than one of HIM. AI was able to *do* more than the synthetic attendants my friends had. I'd never felt right telling even my parents all the stuff he could do, fearing he'd be taken from me.

AI was all I had from my organic parents.

A soft breeze replaced thoughts of school (and my bizarre attendant) with smells of fresh-cut fields, the wetness that comes before a storm, and the gentle "sshhhh" of leaves brushing against leaves.

"Mom and Cri would have enjoyed the view. We have not had so much time together as a family this summer." I raised my eyebrows and turned toward Dad. Tucked this closely against him, I felt his rumbling voice vibrate through me.

"Dad, they...."

"Raystar." He lifted a massive hand to me and turned his face upward. He found his thoughts in the heavens, and wind filled the silence. "Galactics have not been kind to your species."

I frowned and looked up at him. He met my eyes with a level gaze. "Daughter, have you not wondered why there are so few of your kind?"

"We got eaten?"

"I would talk to you without humor."

"C'mon, Dad, it's obvious," I grumbled. "We lost the War. It's in the Recorders' history."

"And you believe what is Recorded?"

"I...don't know. Does it even matter?"

Something scraped through the leaves in the field loud enough to be heard over the breeze. I peered toward the sound. Despite the Core's diffused glow, the endless 'natch stalks were motionless, revealing nothing. Blinking, I turned back to my dad.

"More than ever, Raystar, history matters. I wanted this time to discuss your legacy without your mother or sister present."

My legacy? Last night, when Dad and I discussed going star-watching today, Mom and Cri had been in the kitchen, not doing anything particularly important that I could tell. Mom had been working at her console and Cri was lounging at the kitchen table, scrolling through a reader-tablet. So he could have invited them to join us. Curious, I moved a bit away from his side, so I could see him more fully.

"Humans have been a challenge," Dad continued, "for the Convergence, even after 1,800 years. Your kind…." His voice trailed off as he slowly looked around, taking in the changing scene. A glow, like the sun rising at our backs, stretched our shadows outward across the 'natch fields, and then, just as rapidly, shrank them back toward us.

As one, Dad and I turned toward the…light?

"METEORS!" I shouted, pointing at the burning orbs that screamed by, high overhead.

Dad encircled me in a fortress of arms. Bulging through his shirt, his biceps were like stone overlaid with cloth. Three angry blazes cut red gashes across the sky and hurtled toward the Mesas in a triangle pattern. I covered my ears as they tore the air with thundering, supersonic violence. Two staggered flashes washed upward as the rear-most two intruders burned in Nem's atmosphere. Sonic booms cracked the sky.

My dad spun us, so his back faced the light, and covered my eyes with a hand as big as my face. Fast as he was, I saw the third flash turn darkness into day.

The Mesas and our fields flickered in a cartoonish grey and white from the strobe of brightness. Sound followed light, and a double-heartbeat explosion whumped in the distance. The third explosion shook our hill. I clutched my pendant, which housed AI.

"Youu…gett'n this?" My eyes bulged as my dad's protectiveness squeezed air from my lungs.

"Affirmative!" AI whispered, showing a brief replay across a virtual screen. *Who says "affirmative"?* And then the plants shushed and a thunderstorm wind crashed over us.

In the aftermath of the meteor storm, I blew hair from my face and blinked dust from my eyes. Darkness returned, the wind died; we could have sat frozen atop the hill for a minute, or an hour.

"Well," Dad muttered, breaking the spell that had held us. He loosened his arms, and I sucked in a full breath. "That was unusual. The last time I saw anything similar…." He shook his head, as if clearing the thought. Then: "Come. It is bedtime."

I wriggled the rest of the way out of his arms and stared at him, my mouth slightly open. Had the Mesas been nuked? Were fire-breathing monsters going to hatch and UNLEASH A RAMPAGE OF DESTRUCTION ON OUR DEFENSELESS AND UNSUSPECTING PLANET? WHAT WAS GOING ON? Or, was it just, I dunno, "unusual," and now it's my bedtime? Meteor showers happen all the time this close to the Core.

These meteors would most certainly be in the news.

Squinting in the explosion's after-image, our star-lit wavy plant-fields were transformed with ominous, shadow-filled, jagged, things-in-the-darkness potential. The bugs had gone silent.

It was dead quiet.

Dad frowned at the spot where the meteors had vanished and rose with a bit more speed than normal. Even when I'm grown, Gleans will still tower over me. Humans are smaller than pretty much all Galactics. But…I'd never actually seen another of my kind, except on the vids.

Three meters gone, he was a dark outline against the oblivious stars. His legs were two tree trunks wrapped in leather and ending in giant boots. The metal buttons on his overcoat glinted, and his flared collar blacked out the night around his head. The wind streamed his hair over his collar, and his cleft chin was a statement against…something, I suppose. With a pair of swords across his back and a blaster at his hip, he looked more pirate than hero. I just called him Dad.

Even so, I slid to my feet a breath behind him. Golden eyes glowed down at me. Gleans' eyes glowed when they were excited. Mine didn't glow. Cool things that other races could do? I've totally stopped counting. Raystar? Zero. But I didn't like the height gap, and sprawling on the ground didn't seem like the common-sense place to be.

"Dad, you said the last time you saw anything explode like that… whaaaat?" Speaking slowly helps grownups understand. I'm sure *they're* thinking that *we're* just speaking slowly because we're kids. We just want them to understand us.

"Raystar…I…do not believe we are safe. In any case, we must rise early to fix an irrigation controller." His four huge arms created an X-silhouette as he stretched. *Irrigation controller? What?*

Scowling, I folded my TWO arms across my chest and glared into the now completely creepy 'natch fields. *Not safe?*

He laughed, picked me up—crossed arms and all—and set me on his shoulders. "Fierce daughter mine, tonight was supposed to be a history lesson." He sucked in a breath. "Which we must continue another day."

"But, Dad! They were just big meteors. Cool, big, explosive meteors, for sure." I shook my head, "I don't get it. One minute we're star-gazing, the next we're ducking for cover, and now we're running back ho…." His eyes glowed. I coughed, amending what I was going to say, "…Er, leaving quickly. And what's with the controller? They never break. *Dad?*"

'Natch leaves rustled, closer this time, and just right of the path we'd take home. I had not imagined *that*. I peered over his head toward the sound.

"You may stay here and think on that question, if you prefer?" He moved to lift me from his shoulders.

"No, no!" I batted his arms and hands away. It was like swatting rocks. Home was several kilometers away, and I was thoroughly on edge. Besides, Dad was done giving me any more information. Once he'd made up his mind, his thoughts were like giant boulders come to rest.

What could have him so freaked?

Rampaging, fire-breathing monsters?

I spared a parting glance toward the sound of the rustling leaves and caught a pair of silver eyes glowing at me through the foliage. I froze, blinked, and they were gone.

"Dad," I said, "Can we go?"

He reached up a hand, patted my back, and started tromping back home. Dad hadn't seen what I'd seen. I swayed on his shoulders, staring hard into the darkness of the 'natch.

A billion intrusions into my social life later, the "Human specialists" had yet to figure out why I felt like my head was being crushed whenever Nem's planetary Storm Walls scraped the land flat.

The Storm Walls, and my headaches, were a mystery. We knew some of how the tempests were created, but it was like explaining a god's anger through chemical reactions. The Mesa Range was one magnetic pole, and its twin sat on the exact opposite side of the planet. These mountain ranges changed the electrical charge of the air.

The intense ionization of particles made the atmosphere go insane. As in—giant, dark walls of angry clouds and bellies gorged with lightning, rumbling from one pole to another, roughly every six weeks. Unshielded galactic structures were spectacularly transformed into twisted, melted slag, which meant that a significant part of the energy output on Nem' was dedicated to micro shielding. This might seem like a huge task, but Galactic tech—specifically, Galactic nanotech—was integrated into almost every manufactured item, and thus provided mostly sufficient shielding on a nano level.

The Storm Wall was kilometers thick and was really storms within storms—tornadoes, hail, scraping winds, ground-searing lightning. It was the stuff of gas giants, not Goldilocks worlds. And somehow, the 'natch thrived. Nem' was one giant, hairy 'natch ball.

Attempts had been made to dig into the plateaus, but machines and electronics simply stopped working when they got too close to the Mesas. I couldn't imagine why the Convergence had even built cities on this planet given how well Nem' resisted colonization. Or at least, the Galactics' attempts at colonization.

Nearly two millennia ago, Nem' was home to billions of citizens of the Terran Republic. It was different then. *Right?* I mean, why would the ancients want to live through this maelstrom every six weeks?

Most believed the Mesas were Human constructs and the Storm Walls a result of a Terra-forming project gone wrong. But there was little about Nem's history in the Recorders' archives. All I knew was that since I'd turned ten, whenever the storms came, the headaches followed.

We were roughly ten days away from the Storm Wall and its energy was reaching toward the sky in giant, angry, lightning-filled clouds. The week before the Storm Wall was the best time for me, actually—I buzzed with energy, feeling more alive and alert than usual. But when the wall of clouds rose from the bulk of the Mesas into Nem's stratosphere, the fun stopped. If I was outside, blinding headaches would curl me into a shivering ball of kid.

Energy was building all right, but it felt different this time, more urgent. And…I don't know. Different.

I winced, gently rubbing my temples, as I remembered the last Storm Wall. I'd been walking into the house from our farm's central yard. AI had been yelling at me to hurry. Thunder cracked overhead. My vision changed, as if I'd put on silver sunshades, and objects and people seemed to shimmer. *Then* the pain hit.

Just like now.

OK, well, right now there was no pain. Just a SEARING LIGHT SHINING DIRECTLY ONTO MY BRAIN THROUGH MY EYE-BALLS. I crushed a pillow over my face. What time was it? Aren't there laws against light at this hour?

"RAYSTAR! DESTINY AWAITS! Breakfast!" Dad thundered, leaning in from the doorway.

Destiny, my butt. "Ten more minutes?" I groaned. Destiny was NOT awake at this hour.

"Of course." He rumbled. I didn't have time to peek at him from under my pillow. He grabbed my comforter, tugged it over my feet, and dropped it at my knees. Crisp morning air surrounded my exposed legs and....

"Unnngh!" I flopped about, trying to toss the comforter down around my feet.

"Breakfast in five, we leave in thirty." His deep chuckle faded as he walked downstairs. I lifted my head from the bed and the pillow from my face, and watched my door as it slid shut. AI flashed 4:15 A.M. to me.

Questions from last night came to me as I glared at the purple comforter, now warming only one of my feet. I squinted into my ceiling lights. *Why would meteors have Dad so alarmed? And what the great-gravity-well was the rush to fix this controller?* I dropped my head back on the bed and the pillow back over my face. AI chimed, "4:17 A.M."

Yeah, yeah. I thought to him.

Don't hate the player, Ray, AI thought back, strobing brightly enough so flashes of green shone through the pillow I'd wrapped around my face.

I rolled my eyes. *Don't hate the....* That didn't even make sense.

When you live with someone long enough that a pattern becomes common, it takes only a nudge of contrast to remind you that just because you're used to something doesn't mean it's normal. AI was peculiar. Often. I wondered briefly how he'd acted with my biological parents. I guess it didn't matter, at least now, at 4:18 in the flipping morning.

Pulling and pushing myself out my tangle of blankets, I uncurled in a spinning stretch that turned me toward the window. My bangs fell over my eyes, and I poofed them out of the way.

My room had two of the farmhouse's eight outside walls on the second floor, but only one wall had a window. My view framed the flat-topped mountains. The Mesas blocked the sky, but in the orange of morning light, I could just see the source of my second-biggest question. Ancient Human Ruins crisscrossed their base, like a charcoal sketch of my history.

What exactly HAD happened to us? Now, 1,800 years later, Galactics still hadn't figured out our technology. The War had been so traumatic that my kind was talked about in hushed words of anger and fear. If I was any sort of representative of my kind, I found it hard to believe we could be a threat. I'd never met other Humans, and Mom and Dad were at best evasive when questioned about maybe, I dunno, getting offworld and meeting some more of my kind? We couldn't be all bad. Or still be bad? Or whatever.

I wasn't bad. I was a kid, pretty much like a lot of other kids at school. Smaller maybe.

The fact was…today, Humans were weeds growing on the edge of a well-kept garden. We were nothing at all like the billions and billions who had made up the Terran Republic.

For all I knew, I was the lone weed.

I finished my stretch and snapped my mouth shut, lest I yawn myself back into bed.

And what the great gravity well did Dad want to talk to me about last night?

My feet didn't leave my room's thick, white carpeting. Static electricity snapped and nibbled at my toes as I dragged myself toward the bathroom, and I winced with each crackle and bite. My room was a rectangle, with my bed on one end and my bathroom on the other. One wall was graced with a floor-to-ceiling 3-D slow-motion animation of a Glean Dreadnought destroying a Lethian attack formation.

The holo vid was AI's present to me on my fifth birthday. AI didn't have any arms (or any appendages, for that matter). But he had amazing abilities to manipulate computers and electronics. He'd hacked the house attendant and reprogrammed my room's display, effectively mounting it on my wall. After a quick "Happy Birthday to You!" in some ancient Terran tune, the vid showed me gorgeous views of streaking missiles and plasma-cannon broadsides from a gargantuan Glean Dreadnought that transformed a squadron of Lethian cruisers into gold-grey puffs against the hungry darkness of space.

Because it was mounted on the wall, I couldn't watch any other videos. That was OK. I never tired of that scene.

AI had said it was my birthright. I remember Mom hating it immediately and commanding our house's attendant to take it down. But when the house synth couldn't recognize that the holo was even there, Mom went nova on AI. Dad separated the two, which is weird when you think about a fist-sized pendant needing to be separated from a multi-hundred-kilogram mother.

That was the first time I remember my parents yelling at each other. Imagine, five-year-old me, barely up to my parents' knees, cowering, while the gods thundered. That memory is fuzzy with images and emotions, but Dad's final words are as clear as if spoken a second ago, "War. Sathra. It is all she has of her people."

To AI's glee, and Mom's displeasure, I'd set the holo on repeat.

Opposite the battle scene floated a wall-sized image of pre-war Terra: blue, white, green. Planet Earth had sure been pretty. "Homeworld" was framed against the black backdrop of space, and arching red letters flickered, "Live Free or Die!" Even lost as I was in my morning fog, that was grim. I squinted at my feet, shuffled through the staticky, sparkly carpet, and considered that I'd never asked my parents where they got *that* poster.

My shuffle brought me past my lounge chair and alongside my desk, which held my collection of *things* from the Mesa Ruins. Fused lumps of metal and elements of shattered devices that looked oddly new, each with their own hidden history, felt like a connection to my past. To be clear, I'd never gone IN the Ruins. That was craxy dangerous. But I'd been close.

There was a wide swath of scrabble between the skeletal Terran structures and our 'natch fields. It was a tossed salad of concrete, weeds, twisted metal beams, and bits of, well, stuff. I'd never gathered enough courage to cross that chaotic, jagged distance to the Ruins, nor to even go half-way. Between AI flipping out about how dangerous the jagged, hollow-skulled buildings were, and my own imagination, thinking that each dark crevasse I passed or jumped over was a *lair for some predatory drooling denizen of the fallen city*, I limited my collecting forays to the shelter of our 'natch fields. And I was pretty sure there was *something* in there.

Cri made fun of my metal collection. Mostly, I didn't care. My kind had once used, or at least touched, that stuff. Probably. Or not. Either way, I imagined they had, and subsequently, I fiercely protected my collection with socks and T-shirts to keep, uh, dust and unwanted eyes off it. *Whatever. It's way too early to justify myself.*

Besides, my room was nowhere as messy as Cri's. My sister used her drawers to store air and kept her floor warm with discarded clothes. I blew a strand of hair out of my eyes and plodded on. Where was my dumb bathroom? Had someone moved it?

Lights buzzed on. A full-sized 3-D image of me, with frizzy purple hair and oversized pajamas, flickered twice before stabilizing. We stared at each other. I stuck my lower lip out and puffed the same strand of hair out of my eye once again, and my image did the same. If you were a critic, you'd say my bathroom was messier than my room. Combs, brushes, my favorite flower sock, and a green boot were scattered across the floor and counter. The boot, of course, was supposed to be on the counter. There was order here.

"Heya," I waved. My image copied me down to the wisp of hair as it fell back into my face. My reflection was the closest thing to another Human around here, so we might as well be friends. I was tan. I had a dimple when I laughed, and a few more when I *really* laughed. My eyes were brown. Usually.

It was my hair that Mom and Dad said made me different. From what? There were so many races. What was I different from? How would anyone know if purple hair was normal to Humans? And Mom said I was going through a growth spurt, but seriously, how would she know? As far back as I could remember, I'd always been able to eat seconds and thirds. Yawning, I programmed my clean clothes, tossed my nightclothes on the floor, and hopped in the shower.

"RAYSTAR. USE HASTE," my dad boomed, his voice thundering around me. Our house communicator probably did a fine job of transmitting to whomever was up at this hour, listening, my startled shriek and the "thunk" that transpired as I slid in the soap onto my butt. I glowered as water streamed into my eyes. Nova and gravity wells, a little volume control, AI?

My friends had all sorts of cute names for their AIs.

"Okay, Dad, on my way," I replied into the air. AI better give him the message. I rinsed off, stepped out of the shower, and grabbed a drying cloth. A blower lowered and whooshed hot air at me from all directions. I pulled programmed clothes off a rack that extended from the wall. Upright spiky hair, grey coveralls, purple t-shirt to match my hair, and stompy boots, yeah. How had I not been discovered by a video production company was beyond me. My holo and I winked at each other in near real-time. I brushed my teeth and spat in the sink.

And watched in horror as blood made a lazy spiral on its way down the drain.

"AI?" I whispered, tasting the metal in my blood. Yellow scan-beams washed over me, flashing from the pendant I'd hung on my bedpost.

Alpha-wave readings are irregular. Blood sugar and iron are low. And—OW!

"What? What?" I turned to face him, ready for help.

Your HAIR! It BURNS my virtual eyes!

Rolling my actual eyes, I rubbed my tongue against my gums, sucked hard, and spat again. The water was clear.

C'mon, Ray. You gotta tell your parents.

"You worried about me?" I put a finger in my mouth and lifted my lips, searching for blood along my gums.

This is how the headaches start.

I grabbed him from my bed. Pausing at my doorway, I considered his smooth, steel-grey surface resting in my hand. "Am I way off my norms?"

You know your chemistry isn't the whole picture. There are storms in today's forecast.

Ugh. Blood sugar, iron. Was I in denial, thinking I just needed breakfast? Probably. It wasn't even a question that there was something peculiar about my headaches. But…I'd rather be fixing an irrigation controller than going to the doctor.

Lethian doctors.

"I'll get food, and then we'll see. For now, AI, it's our secret." With a shiver, I settled him around my neck. He didn't emit any colors, but he'd turned ice-cold in frustration. Increasingly skeptical about the notion of the Universe leaving my last two days of summer vacation alone, I headed downstairs.

3

Oh, yeah. You have not eaten until you've had a farm breakfast on Nem? Eggs, fried gratcher steak, and hot toasted bread. Breakfast's salty, savory aroma greeted me as I stumbled down our Glean-sized stairs into the utilitarian kitchen, and it made my stomach rumble in anticipation.

Gratchers evolved from Terran pigs. We raised them, along with endlessly forsaken amounts of 'natch. I'd seen vids of pigs. Gratchers were nothing like their porcine ancestors. For starters, their mottled brown skin failed to camouflage their saber-like teeth. Small gratchers were easily 800 kg; herd leaders weighed in at 5,000 kg and left craters where they stomped. Mom and Dad called our big guy "Chunks." Alas, for most Galactics, large creatures weren't a problem. No way was I going near one of those things without a stunner. Pretty much everything in the Convergence was bigger, faster, stronger, or something-er than I.

My parents had "Human-sized" our house with furniture and access to everything that was suited to a being that was NOT three or so meters tall (that would be me). It helped that Cri was "relatively" my size too, for sure. I sat on my high chair—a barstool with a back. Three other Glean-sized chairs ringed the large round metal table. The chairs were arranged in a half-circle facing a flat wall. That wall served as our primary video viewer, but also an interface to the house synth; from there, we could control all of the farm compound's functions.

Mom had the news on, and an uncharacteristically balding Glean in a plaid suit peered, seemingly at me, as he attempted to make a report about 'natch harvests more interesting, with each frown and gesture synchronized to his words.

Ugh. 'Natch.

But wow. I ran a strip of steak through my eggs, slopped it on my bread, shoved it in my mouth, and squinted in ecstasy. Just. Wow! My tongue almost convinced me to forget about the meteors, my blood in the sink, and why I was up at this ridiculous hour without Cri.

"How about chewing?" Mom said, her golden eyes widening, as I shoved another forkful in my mouth. She touched me gently between my shoulder blades. *Seriously, would anyone die if I slouched?*

Straightening, I looked up from my plate and, for her benefit, moved my jaw in vaguely chewy-esque motions. Mom's dark-red skin, jet-black hair, and golden eyes were typical Glean. How they showed up on her was a surprise that made you want to look at her again and again, just to be sure. My sister had inherited *that,* too, and nearly all the remotely male Galactics my age thought *they* were nova. *Pfft.* I didn't need a bunch of boys getting goofy around me.

Unlike my dad, Nent, my mom, Sathra, was "only" less than three meters tall. Her deep-space-black hair flowed past her shoulders and curtained left and right as she moved. Mom's eyes were rounder than mine, and her lashes were so thick and long I imagined I could feel the breeze when she blinked. Beyond that, and their size, Human and Glean faces were similar.

Except for her scar, Mom's features were perfectly symmetrical. The scar cut through her symmetry, streaking from her right eyebrow to her jaw. It could be mistaken for runny make-up, or a tear.

"Raystar," she'd say to me, softly, touching the healed ridge across her cheek, like the memory was RIGHT THERE. It was all I got when I asked her about it. Cri got angry with *me* when Mom cried. Like it was *MY* fault Mom had a scar. When the scar came up, Mom would cry, Cri would glare, and I'd grit my teeth and leave the room.

There was a hard history in my parents that they tried to keep from us. But I noticed. I watched Mom from the corner of my eye, flowing about our kitchen in her bedrobe, not unlike royalty. Whatever had happened to her was still fresh....

Well. If she wasn't going to tell me about it, I wasn't going to think about it, at least for now. I was too hungry to be curious.

"It'ssoommmgood!"

"Architect," Mom breathed. "You should be as large as we are with the amount you eat."

Yeah, well. Too bad. Just keep the food coming. I craned my neck to see if she was making more.

Mom half-turned toward me. "After last night, you and Dad need to be careful. And wear sunscreen."

Sunscreen? I swallowed and shoveled in another mouthful of salty, savory energy. Gratcher. Eggs. Toast. Carbs. Iron. I thought about it. Yes, I needed more food. "Careful of what, Mom?"

"We'll talk when you return. I've told Dad in no uncertain words that safety is essential. I am telling you, no snooping about in the Ruins. Fix the controller and go. Drop EVERYTHING at the first sign of a storm."

I frowned.

Ray, you gotta tell her. AI urged. *You only bleed before really bad storms.*

"What do the Ruins have to do with anything? And what about those meteors?" I asked Mom while frowning at AI's comment. My fork scratched against my plate as I impaled pieces of gratcher and bread and swirled the bite-to-be through the egg yolk, giving the toast time to absorb the juice. I stared sullenly at no-place-in-particular.

"Ray...." Mom paused. "We'll talk, I promise. We'll talk about everything when you return."

I continued swirling. Silence filled the vacuum between us. The vid screen was muted, and in its silence, it lit up the kitchen with blue, flickering light. I glanced at the feed. A young, silver-haired Glean news reporter stood atop one of the towers in Blue River, pointing with two hands at the Mesas while gesturing with her other two hands for emphasis. Her blue suit, red skin, golden eyes, bobbed hair, and face fit her curious eagerness. She was instantly likeable. Her video drones showed smoke rising from the impact site at the base of the squat, dark Mesas. The caption read, "Nyla Jax, Galactic News Network: Mystery Morning Meteors Impact the Human Ruins!"

I blinked.

"Darling, you know the results you get with the nannites."

"I get it."

"And with the Storm Wall building, we need you back before the afternoon."

"MOM," I said, loudly. "This sucks. Not seeing my friends, getting up early…and summer's over! Cri gets to sleep in because she can't do what I do with the nanotech? I mean, thanks. But that sucks too! You and Dad have been trying to tell me something for weeks now. It's about me, obviously. Obviously. Right?"

I shoved in the now-ready mouthful, expecting snark from AI but receiving only mental silence. I felt my friend's virtual eyes going back and forth between Mom and me. He was room temperature and didn't flash any emotional colors—uncharacteristically, he was keeping his thoughts to himself.

Last week, Dad had gone so far as to sit us all down before dinner and start off with, "Raystar, you know we love you." But Cri had shot a furious glare at me and stomped out of the kitchen to her room, thus ending our family conversation. They wouldn't tell me anymore, saying we all needed to be present. There were secrets in the stars, and down here on Nem'.

Right. I should be telling Mom about the toothbrush incident.

"Mom," I blurted, ready to confess all.

Mom was simultaneously putting pans in the cabinet, dishes in the shelves, and food back in the cooler with the coordination and speed only a Glean's four arms can accomplish. Without turning, she interrupted me. "I'm sorry you feel like you didn't have fun this summer."

Finished with cleanup, but not with her thought, she leaned down and placed her two upper hands gently on either side of my head and her lower two hands on my shoulders. The warmth from her touch melted through my clothes. Our faces were close enough to feel each other's breath.

She considered me with her golden eyes. A curtain of hair spilled over her shoulders, cascaded around us, and carried with it her mom-scents of flowers and earth. I chewed my huge forkful, doing my teen-age best to ignore how good all of it felt and smelled. She mushed my cheeks into fish-lips, smiled, and kissed me on the forehead. "I love you so much, Raystar. Maybe you'll see this all differently one day. Until then, sit up straight."

I renewed the glare I'd focused on my plate and straightened up.

I knew she loved me. I was the best with the nano. She was right about the Storm Wall too.

Outside, Dad could be heard giving instructions to Aidee. Extra-ordinary clanking and sounds of twisting metal followed each order. Aidee's name was actually AD9—autonomous drone number nine. I'd never bothered to ask why she was number nine.

She was an egg-shaped, floating, do-everything helper, larger than me by a half. She had multiple extendable arms, storage space, and multiple sensor clusters, all hidden by reflective, sky-blue, Galactic metal. AD9 was a communicator, a drone for managing farm equip-ment, a security guard, a babysitter, and a farmhand.

The hangar lights were bright in the morning darkness, and they threw harsh shadows through the kitchen windows. I looked at my mom and slouched a little, letting out a breath. I was lucky. My friends, they might have more, but none had my family. Even so—is love enough? Where does it stop, and when do I start?

I asked Mom if there was more steak. She sighed, squeezed me with all four arms, and put the last piece of sizzling gratcher on my plate.

I had a suspicion that I should be telling Mom I loved her, too.

As often as I could.

4

Dad froze as my brown, leather-booted foot thumped on the porch leading from our kitchen to the central yard. My hair was jagged; I was a purple comet. He eyed me for a millisecond, snorted and pulled himself into the lev-sled. In Dad's mind, everyone had a place in the mission, and it was all down to execution. The door hissed shut behind him. If he had his way, I bet we'd all be wearing freshly pressed uniforms.

Whatever. It was too early for parents to get to me. Besides, by his own admission, HE owed ME explanations, not the other way around.

The central yard was ringed by our humble (and very square) two-story house, the hangar for our various vehicles, the über-utilitarian work shed, and the gratcher compound. Opposite the hangar, near the force-gate entrance to our property and farthest away from our house, sprawled the gratcher pen. As I mentioned, our house was a standard Galactic square shape—the application of millennia of non-creativity. Even rectangles would be exciting. I'd be completely starred if someone showed up with, like, a triangle. OMG, what would I do with an acute triangle?

I digress.

The small garden outside of our kitchen was guilty of being decorative. It reminded Mom of home, or so she said. It was hard for me to imagine being from any place other than Nem'. But I was adopted. The flowers she planted weren't from "here." Is home where we're from, or where we belong?

Thick, grey walls rising two stories above our house comprised our hangar. The top two floors were off-limits. Our vehicles all fit in the bottom two floors, with room to spare. "We'll show you two one day," Mom would say whenever we asked about the upper levels. I swear, "one day" was like "maybe." "Maybe" is pretty much, like, never! Think I'm kidding?

There were so many boys wanting to kiss Cri. "Maybe," is all THEY got.

If the thickness of the supports and power conduits that snaked upward from the hangar's floor through the ceiling were any indication of what was up there, it was HEAVY and needed a flipping nova's worth of power. Despite our best attempts, neither Cri nor I had figured out how to actually GET up to the third floor.

In contrast to the hangar's puzzle, the work-shed won the competition for the most non-remarkable structure in the freaking MILKY WAY. It was square and filled with tools more neatly organized and inventoried than the stores where the tools were bought.

Finally, the gratcher pen was, hands down, the most organic of our farm's structures. Our gratcher herd of roughly forty of the giant pig descendants needed ROOM. Notwithstanding your race, if you had a nose, you needed some distance from the gratchers' "perfume." The pen had an enclosure that sheltered the creatures from the regular storms, as well as the Storm Wall. A muddy, black field was relentlessly churned by their hooves and mixed with poop and the food they didn't eat. While wind, and perhaps the whine of anti-gravity engines, were the only sounds to be heard in the rest of the compound, a basso profundo "Squea! Squea!" blared constantly from the pen, with the occasional "SQUEA!!" from Chunks reminding all who the boss gratcher was.

Roughly ten meters beyond each building stood blood-red metallic pillars spaced evenly in a circle around our compound. They bristled with sensors. A single, very large autocannon sat atop each pillar. Like angry gargoyles, the cannons tracked everything inbound and outbound. At night, the smoldering plasma visible in their giant twin barrels looked like red monster eyes. The pillars didn't just serve as autocannon perches—they were the force dome generators that, when activated (which was always), created a defensive shield around our compound. The Dome, as we called it, distorted reality around the farm with a shimmering field as thick as I was tall. It was the security of my home.

Inside was safety.

Although Nem' had been settled for thousands of years, its wildlife could ruin your day. Leggers, random nanotech, rats, and, in recent months, *things* coming from the Mesa Ruins made it important to be prepared.

Grownups have incomprehensible stuff going on. Since I'm a kid, I feel like I never know how much I know or don't know. Because, uh, I'm a kid? *Shouldn't* grownups know more?

Nem' was violent and raw. Why hadn't the Convergence, a 1,300-system-strong civilization, made us safe here? We're a key agricultural world. What else should power be for, if not to protect what's important?

Don't get me wrong: our wildlife was absolutely survivable. Go out during the day, AVOID the Ruins, bring along light weaponry and shielding. *Easy.* My parents spent eternities drilling Cri and me, both of us, with and without weapons, so we could even be prepared while unarmed. Having only two hands, I grew up bruised, but fast and nimble. This summer, I was almost able to handle myself against Mom or Dad. Once my adrenaline surged through me, I could predict, almost *see*, where they would be and adjust accordingly. But the training, the weapons—it seemed excessive. At least that *was* my opinion until I could understand the nightly reports about farms that couldn't afford weapons or defenses.

Maybe Mom and Dad *did* have a clue.

Our lev-sled currently occupied the center of the courtyard. Its size, color, and…something else…made it seem out of place against our agrarian ecosystem. Dad had its stubborn nose pointed toward the house, presumably to make it easier to join him in the cockpit.

The lev-sled was a mottled, black-and-grey, elongated hexagon. Its squat form was about twenty meters long and a third as wide, with sides that sloped out from the ground at a forty-five degree angle, rose vertically, and then sloped back in at an equivalent opposite angle to complete its seven-meter height. Glass-steel at the front of the sled, where inside the pilot and three other people could fit, could be made clear or opaque and take on the rest of the sled's pattern.

It was the largest 'natch hauler I'd seen. Our neighbors' sleds had nothing remotely close to its hulking, bullying form. Despite its years of hard farmwork, the excessively thick plating that covered it was razor smooth. You could pound it with the hardest metal and not even scratch it.

Last year, with all my little Human strength, I'd hit the lev-sled using a hammer from our toolshed. I'd been quite surprised by the resulting deep gong the hammer made upon impact. Cri should have been *cleaning* the container bed instead of *napping* in it, and the only thing louder than the reverberations of my hammer blow was Cri's shriek and subsequent swearing.

Ahh. Yeah. I grinned at the pre-dawn sky, remembering.

Dad had strapped in as the anti-gravity pods whined and nudged the sled's house-sized hulk upward. The cockpit's glass-metal faded to clear, and I saw him wave at me to join him or get in the back. Sprinting through the morning darkness, I raced down the porch to the ladder that extended from the sled's sidewall.

As I ran to him, I passed AD9's empty storage dock in the sled's underbelly. Dad had had "her" working on…something…since breakfast. I frowned not because she was working, but because she was working *now*. We'd always taken her when we went into the fields. Dad and I were well equipped to handle ourselves, but out in the fields, two were better than one, and three were better than two.

I grabbed the cool rungs along the sled's exterior, spidered up the six meters to the container bed's rim, and dove in. The farmhouse, stars, and sky spun as I launched myself head-over-boots into the sled's full bed of 'natch. I bounced twice, sinking into the leafy green harvest.

Reality shimmered and tingled as the sled's shields flickered to life. Its plasma autoturrets powered up, their barrels filling with smoldering orange fire. There were eight barrels on the sled. Four were on top, with two on each side at the front and two on each side at the back. The other four were directly underneath, attached upside down against the sled's upsloping plating. With every angle covered by at least two cannons, we were not an empty threat.

Once in the air, Dad rotated the sled toward our compound's exit and through the geodesic force dome encompassing our compound. Gratchers *squea'd* their displeasure as we glided by. I wrinkled my nose as I smelled them, voicing my own complaint.

We passed through our Dome's shimmering, tingly perimeter and emerged into Nem's open air. The breeze from our speed caressed my exposed skin. I faced the new day's sky on my back, my hands laced underneath my head, on an over-full bed of poky 'natch.

The ancients called it *spinach*. Rich in nutrients and protein, 'natch was a cash crop.

It made me want to vomit. It wasn't unreasonable to believe that Humans lost the War because we ate too much 'natch.

Starbats circled above as dawn forced the night's darkness toward the horizon. The starbats' four wings alternated beats, and their flickering red mouth lights convinced naïve little birds to investigate and become breakfast. The little fliers were almost as pretty as the fading stars.

By the time we'd reached the controller, Banefire, the red giant squatting in the center of our solar system, was a backdrop filling half the sky. The asteroid belt around Nem' shimmered with metal. The metal was supposedly the Ruins from a Human battle station that had been obliterated during the defense of Nem'. It must have been huge. I frowned, trying to remember when I'd seen it this defined—it was usually more of a haze than a line. Banefire's malevolent glare reflected off the trillions of metal pieces that wrapped around Nem' like an electron's orbit. It created the illusion of a rainbow-rope that ran from the near horizon to the top of the sky, only to arch down and reach back to the far horizon.

I was lying with my head facing the direction we were headed. Framed between my feet, our town, Blue River, rose like a cluster of needles that stabbed into our atmosphere. The clouds around the city were actually air traffic made up of everything from individual darts to cargo ships. I craned my head back, so I was looking upside down in the direction we were headed. The Mesas, three-thousand-meter–high plateaus, hid the sky with their square brutishness.

The Ruins meshed across their bases like a tattered frock. Smoke spiraled up from one point and drew my eyes down to raging flames laced with blue lightning. Banefire cast a red tint over the green fields and the warped, grey, Human structures. The buildings had been ripped apart. Orange-yellow fire snaked and writhed between the gaping building skeletons and roiling smoke. *Great gravity well. THAT was the meteor impact from last night?*

"A minute to arrival," Dad called.

I filed the image in my "don't get hit by a meteor" folder. *How could Dad not have seen the destruction?* He saw it. Who was I kidding? He saw it. *Right?*

"Dad."

Silence.

"Dad! On our four o'clock."

"The objective, Raystar. The Ruins are not for today. Focus."

Focus? I swear.

The brown patch of dried 'natch we were approaching was no less obvious than the fiery-red crater. The irrigation controller that lay near it was a two-by-two-meter, blue-white metallic box made of standard Galactic self-healing nano alloy. Pipes went in, pipes came out. It ensured the 'natch in its area of responsibility received the right water and nutrient flows.

Only a corner of this one's frame remained. Silver fuzz blanketed what was left of the controller. The mold growth transitioned into a pool of sparkling-blue nanobots that sometimes looked like liquid and other times like fine sand.

I peered apprehensively at the mess and then spared a glance toward the flaming Ruins. *THOSE fires could be put out. Nanotech, however....*

It's the foundation of Galactic civilization. Nannites are mechanical or organic robots. They could be as small as a molecule or as large as a few cells. They are in shampoo to give cleaner, shinier hair; in machines, for better performance; and in vaccinations, for better health. They are EVERYWHERE, and they always worked.

Except when they didn't.

Fear gripped my gut. The first lesson every Galactic learns is that insane nanobots will be the death of the civilization. Our controller was "self-healing." But think about it. If self-healing programming was in the control code, so was reproduction. Which meant the nannites had to eat. When their governing software code was corrupted, the nanobots didn't care what they ate. Metal. Plants.

Galactics.

AI whistled in my head and flashed yellow. *Whoaaaa. That's messed up. REALLY messed up.*

"What do you see?" I asked, frowning at his color. He was genuinely concerned.

Nano behaving badly. I wouldn't get close to it. He sighed. *But I'm just a pendant around your neck. So, of course I'm going to get close to it.*

"Funny," I muttered, "I mean, you know, do you see anything strange?"

It's melted.

"Seriously!"

Chillax.

"No one says 'chillax,'" I mumbled to myself. I brushed purple bangs from my face, never taking my eyes off the goo-puddle as we slowed to a stop.

Dad powered down the sled, walked to the storage compartment, and pulled out the repair kit. He glanced at me curiously as he paced to the rear. The storage area contained a control headband, a vat of replacement nano, and four head-sized cubes of blue feeder alloy. The idea was that the replacement nano would consume the corrupted nannites and then multiply thanks to the feeder cubes. We would be able to regrow the irrigation controller by guiding the replacement nano via the control headband.

I started down the ladder and jumped at the halfway point, tucking into a roll and coming to my feet a short distance from my dad.

Ray, something's not right here. AI paused. *I mean, beyond the melted controller. Which is freaky.* AI was getting hot. He didn't need to get hot; I'd heard him, after all.

"Something" isn't enough to act on, I thought back. He muttered something about *"teens"* and *"bossy"* that I didn't quite catch.

Dad had moved to the edge of the puddle, his boots only centimeters away from the liquid, and stared intently at its gooey, percolating surface. Usually, when people stared like that, they were in conversation with their attendant. Or, uh, thinking.

AI was right. Something was off. Dad didn't think like that unless he really had to.

Carefully, so as not to touch the bubbling goo with his toes or gloved hands, Dad placed the alloy blocks in the center of the puddle. He tossed me the headband. I caught it and in a single motion placed the thin, silver strip on my head like a crown. Virtual screens flickered to life. Instructions, definitions, readouts were all superimposed on my vision, and control was a thought command away.

The interface also linked my mind to the replacement nano and its energy. *Wait for it...ahh!* My awareness expanded, and I was stronger, faster. Mom and Dad said the feeling of heightened awareness was common. The standard Galactic links only gave the user specific control over the nannites. They said the feeling of increased energy was just a kid's imagination. I didn't think so. I could imagine quite a bit, but nothing gave me a thrill like this. What was not up for debate was that my ability to control nanotech was simply beyond that of Galactics, including Mom, Dad, and Cri. If there'd been other Humans around, maybe we could have seen if this was a uniquely Human thing, or if I was just a unique Human.

But if I couldn't fix this, no one else could. It was the reason I was up at this hour and Cri was still in bed. And if I couldn't fix this, we'd have to report this to the government. The authorities took malfunctioning nano seriously. An invasion of technicians and their equipment would be here within an hour if it turned out we needed to report this.

Dad peered at me. "Are you well?"

"Good." I shook out my arms like an athlete and glanced over my control displays. *Are you kidding? I felt GREAT.*

"OK. When you are ready, I shall proceed with the new nanoinfusion. Tell me when you have engaged the repair protocols." Keeping one arm free, he picked up the vat of fresh nano with three arms and held it ready to pour above the alloy blocks.

I reached out with my mind, touching the nano and creating the control link. I could feel the tingling, surging little 'bots in the goo. They oriented on me, waiting for my thought commands. Which was strange.

There should be no "orienting." They shouldn't even be paying attention to me. There shouldn't even be a "they."

As a frown pinched my face, my sight revealed red fingers of color stretching into the pool of blue goo. The "infection."

Stop! AI's voice sounded in my head, for me only. I felt his temperature increasing in alarm. *There's unknown nano here.*

"Dad!" I pulled my mind back and canceled the link's protocol. And yet I still *felt* the nanos' attention on me. I shook my head, trying to shake the feeling. You don't mess around with this stuff. "AI guesses there's some..." I started to say to Dad, worry cracking my voice.

I am not guessing.

"Eh?" I frowned more deeply.

There IS an unknown nano strain in this mix. I'm not guessing. HURRY. Dad set down the vat and stood, feet apart, with his lower arms on his thick belt and his upper arms folded across his chest. He regarded me curiously.

"Calm, Ray, you're talking to me out loud again," AI whispered.

Dad raised an eyebrow and rolled two hands in the universal motion that indicated, "continue...."

"Uh…I. Yeah. AI has detected an unknown nanostrain. And then gave me major attitude. And then…."

"Raystar," he said, pointing at the goo with his two closest hands and with a third at Banefire—which was nearly directly overhead. "Would it be nice to get home early?" he asked.

I looked at the controller, then back at him, with wide eyes.

He smiled and sighed, crossing the distance between us. Bending to one knee, he gave me a hug, simultaneously ruffling my hair with his other two hands. "My twig, invest your energy in the battles that mean something. Synthetics do what synthetics do. We can investigate yours when we return home. It is older than most, and perhaps it has been corrupted." He frowned disapproval at my pendant and then turned his gaze to me. His features were like an ancient Human statue, perfect in their symmetry, except with large, golden eyes.

Corrupted, my virtual butt! Ain't nobody investigating me when we get back home, or anywhere! AI hissed in my brain.

I winced at how hot he'd become, and then turned to Dad. "AI found a separate strain of nano in the mix and advised we not proceed with the rebuilding."

Thanks for the credit, AI muttered.

Dad thought about my comment a moment, then nodded. Why bother with words when you can nod? No matter that AD9 wasn't here—with a massive arm, Dad hoisted the hundred-kilo vat of replacement nano to his shoulder, turned, and thumped back to the sled. A moment later, he returned with a containment unit and three shovel-like scoops, each held lightly in a separate hand. The containment unit was built of nanoresistant alloy and featured a multifrequency energy shield as an extra measure to keep the little 'bots in. The scoops were both to shovel and to prevent leakage from the ground to the containment unit. Two scoops for him, one for me. We looked at the puddle. And froze.

The four alloy feeder cubes were gone. They had been eaten. That wasn't normal at all.

I met my dad's gaze. My eyes must have been huge. Feeder-cube safety protocols should have been active, and no nano should have been able to consume material until I granted permission via the control band. Dad frowned, lifted his hands toward my pendant, and dipped his head toward me in question.

Are we safe to remove the nano? I thought to AI.

Yes. Hurry-the-great-gravity-well up! I'm not screaming "hurry" for you and your dad to make googly-eyes at each other. THIS NEEDS TO BE CONTAINED!

"Yes. And he says we should hurry," I said, wincing as AI shouted directly into my brain. Dad paused and eyed me, suspicious about my internal conversation. Then he started shoveling, two hands on each of his scoops.

AI, why should we hurry? I thought silently, pushing my tool into the dirt.

Ray. Stop with the questions! Just do!

"Just do?" I huffed. Dad looked at me from his shoveling. I shook my head. The day could only get unweirder from here. AI wasn't joking, though. He was molten red.

5

"URRGGNNN!" Dad's four arms surged with a million veins and a stampede of muscles. With two of his arms, he steadied the top of the me-sized container, and with the other two, he grabbed it from below. In a move like he was pulling a tree from the ground, he pivoted and lifted the container above his head. Filled with dirt, it was heavy. Dad staggered to the sled-wall. There, he hung the containment unit in its cradle with great care, like it was an egg.

"One thing more remains," he panted, stomping around to the front of the sled.

We'd filled the container with the unusual nanogoo and a good deal of the surrounding dirt. A great, filthy hole in the ground remained. The moist, black soil was greying in Banefire's late-morning heat. I was sweaty, covered in soil, and ever so grateful for the rising wind sprinting over our expanse of 'natch. With our irrigation controller gone, Banefire's intensity was drying out this section of field.

I smelled dirt, the 'natch, and something vaguely metallic. With my last bit of strength, I climbed up and over into the carrying bed and collapsed. My legs flopped in different directions. The leaves were cool against my neck and exposed skin. Stems pressed against me through my clothes, and my arms ached with exertion.

The thought of our other hundred or so irrigation controllers being infected by the mysterious goo was nova bad. The thought of what it would do to my weekends was terrifying. If only one more thing remained, then I was all about taking care of it. Besides, clouds were massing in the late-morning sky, and I could feel the storm's energy coiling like a spring. And something else. My insides were flopping; anxiety was making me hot. Maybe I was just tired from digging. *Sure, that was it. More like, everything was feeling off and stranger with each passing second.*

We *had* been shoveling longer than expected. I was betting Dad didn't want to face Mom any more than I did, especially since we'd forgotten sunscreen. I was pretty much enthusiastically *for* finishing quickly and getting home.

The sled flowed into motion as Dad brought it around and then stopped so it was perpendicular to the hole we'd dug. Smoldering autocannons whirred, and heat trails followed their glowing barrels in an arc as the four on that side of the sled spun precisely toward their target. *WHAT THE NOVA!?* I buried myself in the 'natch, but not before a pulse of light streamed from the front and rear sled-cannons to our just-dug pit. A series of drum rolls and whumps followed, succeeded by waves of heat.

When the sounds of the barrage were replaced by the rising breeze, I peeked over the container wall. This was the "one thing?"

The hole was shiny, and the molten dirt was cooling into glass. Ozone, burnt 'natch, and something else chemical infused each breath. Dad stood on one side, upper arms crossed, his lower two hands on his hips. His black hair streamed in the wind, and his eyes glowed as he hunted the newly formed hole's perimeter for, apparently, any other dirt that needed ANNIHILATION.

"Sathra, it is as we thought," he said, monotone, into his link. "The controller was infected with an unknown strain. I have sterilized the area...."

Mom said something.

"*Of course* we did not go near the Ruins," he said, not raising his voice, but his annoyance unmistakable. "Her synth identified the infection," he continued before nodding at Mom's reply. Severing the link, he stomped one more lap around the glassed pit, taking his frustration out on the dirt under each boot-fall.

I frowned, turning my gaze to the Ruins in contemplation. *What was as they had thought?*

We were going to have an in-depth, kid-to-parents conversation.

"Raystar," AI chimed, pulsing alternating yellow-orange warnings.

The view beyond my dad, over the fields, assembling above the Mesas, was captivating. A black-grey thunderhead mushroomed and billowed above them in slow-motion. The meteor-crater smoke was no longer visible. Instead, lightning crackled in between the ancient Human structures. I blinked up at the clouds' rising blackness.

"Raystar. You're bleeding," AI said, louder.

Lightning played along the Ruins; it was mesmerizing. *You're bleeding?* His words crept into my awareness and I rubbed a tickle of sweat from my chin. My hand came away grimy and red. My nose was runny, like I had a cold. I sniffed the runniness back in, and when I wiped my nose with my sleeve, the fabric came away streaked with crimson. Blood, in fact, was everywhere; my hands and arms were slick with it, and my shirt was soaked.

In a rush of patting, I felt my body for wounds.

And then the blood *turned into mist*, shrouding my body in red haze. Within the mist, darker tendrils of…my blood…snaked around me lazily, as if caught in some unseen air current. My nose filled with the smell of ozone and burnt metal. Sound faded, so only my heartbeat thundered in my ears. Ripples of energy pulsed from my navel to my fingers, down to my toes, and tingled up my spine. I shivered. Fingers of brown radiated outward from me and the surrounding 'natch—in fact, the entire load of 'natch I was standing on flashed and turned to ash. The 'natch-turned-soot, no longer able to support my weight, dumped me to the bed of our carrier. I managed the five-meter drop unhurt, landing on my feet and hands. I winced as sounds came back in a roar.

My feelings were a storm of confusion. Bewilderment and panic threatened to take over my mind. If I'd learned anything during my parents' training, it was that you can always be afraid, BUT you can't let fear stop you from taking action. I had to move. The walls of the container were five meters up. If I could get my fingers on the rim,

I was confident I could pull myself over. Incredibly, I *knew* I could jump, at least to the edge.

Dad's gaze snapped on me as my jump launched me out of the sled. I landed in a stumble on the top of the cockpit. My blood-mist stayed centered around me despite my jump.

What happened next was in disorienting, high-definition clarity. The millions of pinhead-sized droplets buzzed and quivered. Then, like fireworks, they blossomed into an undulating screen of sparkles. I was surrounded by billions of sparkles.

In the distance, lightning ripped from the Mesa Ruins *toward* the darkening sky. Thunder pounded the air after each bolt connected with the growing black clouds. My vision turned silvery. It always did this before the headaches. I stared at my glowing hands, dimly recalling AI's warning from this morning.

But instead of a crippling headache, I felt AMAZING! The silvery view that normally heralded a headache's arrival formed controls and symbols overlaying my vision. I didn't understand the language, but it reminded me of an incredibly complicated control headband. Did I mention I felt amazing?

Dad's eyes grew wide and blazed gold light as he took me in. A seven-meter jump launched him from the smoldering pit to the sled. He spread his arms into a wide "X." His jacket flapped and his black hair swirled around his head, revealing only his glowing eyes. Three hundred kilograms THUNKED to my right.

"Rayst..." he reached out tentatively. My sparks greeted his outstretched hand and swirled up his arm. Our eyes met in panic, and as one, we watched as bits of his jacket eroded like dry sand in the wind.

Metal squealed and the containment unit's klaxon blared, signaling a breach. Dad and I jerked toward the alarm's scream. *Impossible.* Something had escaped the container from the inside out. Those containers were tough—shielded, reinforced Galactic-alloy tombs for whatever was placed inside. *Apparently not.*

A silver *claw*, complete with talons the size of Dad's hands, curled over the edge of the container wall. Metal nails scraped against the galactic alloy. A blink later, a second claw slammed down on the wall's rim, gonging and vibrating the entire sled.

What heaved itself up and onto the lev-sled's container wall was... ME.

"F..." Whatever AI was going to say was drowned by the scream of twisting metal as the THING bent the sled's walls as it ascended.

IT-ME (as I named IT) was the color of the blue nano feeder cubes. It balanced impossibly on the edge of the container's wall, like it was glued there. Spiky hair crowned a duplicate of my face. Silver eyes, with pupils too bright to look at directly, shifted to take in my dad and then flicked to me. Oversized, talon-tipped hands spread on either side of it as it crouched and fixed me with a stare.

I had seen those eyes before. *Last night.*

"RRRRRaaaaaaaayyyyyssttrrrrrrr," IT-ME croaked. My shimmering halo coalesced in front of me, rippling as an unseen force crashed into it. Dad staggered back a step. This morning had edged beyond extreme.

IT-ME raised and swung its clawed arms toward me. Sputtering lightning formed between its outstretched talons.

The lightning coalesced into a crackling ball and streaked toward my face, leaving a comet's trail of sparks in the air.

"We're going to dieeeeee!" AI screamed, flaring into a yellow, fist-sized, cowardly star.

Power coursed through me, and my corona intercepted the streaming lightning. Sound and color flower-petaled the walls of the lev-sled outward, scattering the surrounding 'natch to the sky like a green, nutritious tornado. Dad was thrown airborne and thumped on his back some ten meters away. Barely an instant later, three hundred kilograms of giant, angry Glean flipped to its feet. From the folds of his farmer's jacket, Dad produced FOUR enormous plasma pistols. He crouched low and spread his arms in an X.

Orange bolts thundered from each pistol's cavernous maw, impacting IT-ME dead-center. Instead of a gratifying explosion or much-wished-for obliteration, the creature simply froze, paralyzed, and fell like a tree into the container bed. The bed gonged with IT-ME's impact. My nose filled with ozone, incinerated 'natch, and slagged lev-sled.

Even though IT-ME was on the other side of the sled, I was close enough to the plasma wash that I should have been singed. But my corona had simply grown brighter and energy surged through me, pinpricks against my skin. I felt no heat. I felt....

HUNGER.

The *thing* staggered to its feet and turned its head to me. The swirling sparks around me intensified, concentrating into balls of light around my fists. Unbidden, my hands unclenched and raised in the direction of the creature. IT-ME's silvery eyes grew wide as it took in the glowing orbs of lightning centered in each of my palms. Spiderwebs of light flashed from my hands toward it, becoming brighter and thicker as the net of silken light made contact and stuck. My control overlay revealed that IT-ME's body was a lattice of red crisscrossed lines. I didn't understand the symbols, but I *knew*. I knew that if I pushed my energy toward those lines, I would destroy its *shield*. I was hungry, eager, greedy.

I WOULD CONSUME IT MOLECULE BY MOLECULE, AND FEED ON ITS SUBSTANCE!

What the nova was wrong with me?

CONSUME! DESTORY! ABSORB!

I raised my hands, gathered my desire, and gave into my NEED. Blue-white arcs played between my fingers and the shell of my corona. I grabbed IT-ME. *CLAWS OF ENERGY* formed at my gesture, stabbing through its shield. It writhed. I shivered. "PREY!" I screamed to the sky.

Wherever my claws dug into its substance, it turned to ash. As it turned to ash, energy thundered through me.

And yet.

I could feel IT-ME pulling at me, leaching MY energy! But panic gave me strength, and I threw another storm of lightning at the creature. Electric tendrils stabbed through IT-ME's ribs and then through its back, until a web of coruscating, blinding arcs surrounded IT-ME, pulling it to me like a fish in a fisherman's net. I clawed into the cracks of its shields, prying and popping them apart. Consumption, absorption! Life-essence raced through my being, filling me like no food I'd EVER HAD! MORE!

.I leaned back against the thing's tug at MY life and PULLED. Images flashed across my mind's eye. A dirty, rust-colored room. Pain. A blurred figure looming over me. A boy with freckles and brown hair, strange brown eyes. Human. Familiar. They were gone in a disorienting blink. I staggered in momentary confusion, and through the distraction, heard AI.

"Ray! Come back!"

Fool. I ignored AI and shoved more energy into the seams of the creature's defenses. Armor cracked, seams spread wider, and I entered. I was through. IT-ME's panic surged around me.

I pushed aside the tiny, horrified part of me and SCREAMED MY ANGER TO THE SKY! Lightning pounded the ground around the lev-sled in response. Clods of soil and grass rocketed skyward, paused, and then fell to the dirt with dull thumps. IT-ME pushed against my grip, its counter-force a pressure on my palms.

I PUSHED BACK HARDER, DRIVING MY CLAWS DEEPER.

What was left of the creature exploded through the air and cratered into the field. A circle of brown, dead 'natch instantly spread out from where it landed. The 'natch crumbled to ash just as quickly as it had with me. IT-ME morphed into a silver sphere and levitated a meter above the ground. Dad had maneuvered below where I stood atop the sled's cockpit. From around the sled's container wall, he launched a barrage of head-sized orange plasma bolts at the creature from his gigantic pistols. But the destructive globs only blossomed loudly and prettily against IT-ME. The creature's shield absorbed Dad's fire.

It ignored my dad.

"RRRRYYYYSSSSSSTTRRRRR!" IT-ME crackled, then tore off toward the Mesa Ruins and the approaching storm in a silver streak that sucked 'natch into the air in its wake.

I LITERALLY hissed with energy, HUNGRY STILL. I turned my gaze slowly toward Dad. He looked up at me, eyes wide, now seeing something different in my expression.

And then the moment of power was gone.

The unintelligible display overlaying my vision flickered and disappeared. A nanosecond later, my corona vanished. The sled's walls were bent and torn. Regular, natural lightning arced from the clouds down to the 'natch field around us, sending geysers of dirt and green into the air. I was mortal again, and flinched with each lightning punch to the ground as it boomed and then—a second later—echoed off of the Mesas kilometers away. Dad turned in the direction the creature had vanished, his giant plasma pistols smoking in each hand.

Exhaustion crushed me to the floor and I tumbled from the top of the cockpit to the ground. I lay crumpled on the earth, my hand a few centimeters from my face, dimly aware that there was no blood on me. Dad lifted me, cradling me gently in all four arms. I blinked into his worried golden eyes and curled my knees to my face. My corona's disappearance marked my headache's grand entry. I gripped my head, as if I could squeeze the pain out. Rain poured down. I threw up. On Dad. On me. On the sled.

And then, thankfully, I passed out.

6

"Raystar. Nem' to my Raystar."

Mom. My room. My bed.

She cradled me. I was warm. Oh, Architect, I was hungry. Someone hadn't removed the nail from my forehead. But Mom caressed my temples with a deliciously cool towel. With effort, I willed my eyelids open and, like rusty shutters, they responded, pouring painful light into my brain.

She wore a worried frown slightly offset by a faint smile, no doubt from my waking up. Her scar shone purple against her red skin, and she idly traced the line with a finger. My hand brushed against the wiry fabric on her arm as I grasped her wrist for comfort. If I hadn't already been squinting, I would have frowned. *Why was she in her combat suit?*

Nonetheless. She was warm and all around me, and that was what I focused on. It was good to be small sometimes.

"She looks fine," someone yelled, their tinny voice in my ear. In both ears. I felt like I had ten ears, and they were all being yelled in. And then what could only be my sister's finger poked me between my eyes. "Mom, she seems OK. See? She's moving. Can we do something else now?" Pain crashed through my forehead.

"Cri, be gentle. She's had an episode. Have you seen the lev-sled? Architect be praised, she and Dad are OK."

"She *always* has episodes," my sister grumped.

I shuddered as events replayed with motion-picture speed. That thing had been spying on us the day before. I was sure of it! *It ate our controller!* Panic swelled up my throat. *It said my name!* I'd sparked out, or whatever I'd done. *WHAT HAD I DONE?* Mom called it an "episode." None of my "episodes" had ever involved seven-meter claws of lightning—pretty sure I would have remembered that. I shivered, remembering the power I'd held, the delicious thrill of it. And the hunger. IT-ME, the creature, had been helpless, and I had wanted to eat it. Eat. It.

I blinked against the light and turned my head to see Cri staring at me. She would have been a perfect mini-version of Mom, down to her silver combat suit. But while mom's smile was filled with sunshine and sunflowers, Cri's expression held the threat of cruelty just underneath, just within reach of each smile, or joke, or word. Straight-faced and magazine-gorgeous, she slowly reached out a hand to poke me again while trying to distract me with her "innocent" eye contact.

As if I wouldn't notice her flipping Glean-sized hand coming toward me.

"Touch me, you die," I mumbled, raising my shaky arm to ward her away. "Mom!"

Cri smirked. "Big words, Twig."

Ugh. Here we go.

Cri ran her upper hands through her long black hair. Waves of her lustrous strands flowed through long fingers, and as it did so, it changed to purple.

"What's with your hair?" I muttered, dropping my arm back on my stomach.

She posed, batting her lashes over golden eyes, "Do you like? Purple is the style now."

"I have no idea what you're talking about."

"Since you're getting so much attention from *my* parents, I thought I'd change my hair to something they'd notice me for."

"Cri Ceridian!" I felt Mom tense and arched my neck to look up at her. Mom's scar was deep purple, a sure sign of her anger. "Apologize, at once!"

My sister returned Mom's glare with blazing eyes. Which actually didn't look uncool against her red skin and purple hair. Finally, she lowered her gaze and turned to me.

"Please don't be mad at me, Mom. Please." Cri, said, looking furtively at Mom. Then she turned her gaze to me and gently placed a hand on my shoulder. "Sorry."

Whatever. I didn't need her attitude. It was her same old jealousy. And of what? Her parents hadn't put *her* up for adoption. I shrugged her hand from my shoulder.

Cri's recalcitrant expression turned into a glare and then a "see what happens when I try to be nice" look aimed at Mom.

Mom sighed, "You two are a pair of leggers."

Leggers hunted the animals that lived in the 'natch fields. They looked like woolly, hairy Terran spiders—but were about two meters tall. Standing on six legs (thus the nickname), they had two front appendages for grabbing and a circular mouth for gnawing what they grabbed. Eight unnervingly Human-looking eyes were sunk into the tops of their heads, and they could see in nearly all directions. Wealthy farms could put up protective-force fences against them, but for most, adequate legger defenses were well out of the budget. Legger packs would occasionally take the lone farmer or stray kid. And in really dry years, sometimes they would attack a homestead.

When a female would lay her eggs, she'd do her best to irritate her mate to death. If he turned his back, she would trip or poke him. Who knows how they, as a couple, registered pleasure, but it was believed that they enjoyed this back-and-forth game. Of course, there is such a thing as taking a game too far. In this case, the loser became dinner for the hatchlings. Leggers were the ultimate frenemies.

Mom noticed my expression. A curtain of her jet-black hair fell around me as she tilted her head to me, and I breathed in her smell of flowers, like spring. "Little Twig, we've got to be more careful."

"Not little!" OK, I was a lot of little. Fine. "And how more careful? That, that creature! How could that have been predicted? You and Dad aren't telling me things! What's going on, Mom?"

"Hush," she said, putting the cool towel down and caressing my face with her other hand. "Yes, we have waited too long to talk with you," she said, nodding, "but I swear on my lineage, Daughter, that creature is not something we knew about. We must concentrate on recovering your strength. Resting."

"Mom?" Dizzy, I wriggled out of her lap and swayed unsteadily, daring Mom or Cri to help me. *And how do I get some food?* Hunger was burning in my stomach. "How exactly am I supposed to 'rest'?" I grabbed my hair, as if I could pull understanding from my head.

Cri flopped down on the only chair in my room, landing rudely on a pile of my clothes that had been resting there. She squeaked. Her eyes grew big, and she pulled out from under her butt a green boot that matched the one on my bathroom counter.

Huh. I would have never checked for it there.

I was thankful. A boot in her butt was OK by me.

"This room's a gratcher pen," Cri grumped, her teen voice crack-ing. She chucked the boot onto my bed in annoyance and grabbed a panel reader resting on the chair's arm. Light shown on her face as images flared to life. She was no doubt going to start vidding with her friends. About me. But that wasn't what made me frown. The back of the reader was polished Galactic alloy.

And in the reflection I saw myself.

My hair was the deepest shade of purple I'd ever seen. But it was my eyes that got me. "Hey!" Cri yelled as I snatched the reader from her and held the back up to my face. I put my hand against my forehead and pushed up my bangs. My pupils had no brown.

"Take it easy? Mom, I'm NOVA FLIPPING PURPLE!" I stared hard at my reflection, "My eyes are purple! My hair is purple! What is going on? School is starting tomorrow!"

Cri gasped at my swear, but Mom didn't blink. She just nodded and listened as I raged on. "I hate this! Why does this happen? How am I supposed to take anything easy? I get headaches from storms, *something* just tried to kill me, and...I AM PURPLE!"

"How?" I asked in a smaller voice, looking at her. Uugh. I could feel my eyes welling up. I was not going to cry. Cri had moved behind me while I'd been ranting. My shoulders started jerking as the frustration inside of me shook its way out. Tears came down. "What's wrong with me, Mom? Why am I like this?"

Cri put her arms around me, and Mom put her warm arms around both of us. Their pressure felt good. My family felt good.

"Shhhh. Oh, Raystar, it's OK. C'mon, shhh," Mom said, rocking Cri and me back and forth together. Cri pinched my cheek softly. I looked at her. She winked, pointing at her purple hair.

I snorted and laughed, but was shaking mostly.

"Raystar," Mom said, holding Cri and me back from her embrace. I stuck my lower lip out and poofed up my bangs, as well as the strand of Mom's hair that was lying on Cri and me. She looked at me, concerned, and wiped the wet streaks from my cheeks. "We will figure out what's going on. I promise." And then she smiled. In that moment I was the center of her universe.

"I bet you're hungry. Let's get some food."

My stomach growled its agreement.

We three girls spilled into the kitchen and froze at the strange scene. Dad sat at the kitchen table, glowering. He hadn't changed his burned, dirt-covered clothes or removed his four plasma pistols (visible in their straps across his chest and holsters at his hip). Two hands pushed around virtual hologram images of our fight from this morning. He played them forward, then back, and then forward again, from different angles. The images blurred and fizzed into static when he scrolled to the creature emerging from the nanocontainer. *IT-ME.* His two other hands drummed aggressively on the table—*thrump, thrump, thrump.* In the middle of the table was a jar filled with a clear liquid. There was a familiar shape in the jar. I clutched at the emptiness in my chest.

Dad must have taken AI while I was unconscious.

"Thank the Architect! Ray, your dad's insane and is torturing me!" AI vocalized from the jar. A small ruby pinpoint glowed at his center; he was not happy.

Mom and Cri gasped. Mom moved forward. "Nent?"

Dad jumped, bumping the table and nearly tipping over the jar with my pendant. The images flickered and faded.

"Show me the attack sequence." Dad had a great command voice. I would have shown him the images, as would most normal beings not as giant and angry and Glean as he was just then.

"Well, ginormous alien, as I told you before, I would show you only with Raystar present."

"Stop. Calling. Me. That," Dad snapped, gritting his teeth.

"Alien? It's what you are."

Mom, Cri, and I looked between my pendant and my dad. Today was way in the Do-Not-Repeat-Ever zone.

"You!" Dad gasped, "are not even alive!" He was strangling the jar with two hands as his lower two hands braced him against the table. AI glowed the color of lava, and the liquid bubbled over the top on to Dad's fingers. He thunked the jar back on the table, waving his massive, scalded hands in the air so quickly that they created a breeze.

"Dear Nent."

"You're an alien. Ai-leee-en," AI sang.

"People!" Mom thundered. It was a Glean thing, commanding attention with thunderclaps of sound. AI and Dad paused, and Dad put the jar down. AI turned a smug green and did a lazy swirl as liquid sloshed around the jar.

"Thank you for interceding, Lady Sathra. Your husband placed me in nanosolvent in an attempt to break my seal and access my personality and lifecores. I have failed to convince him that he cannot. More important than his thuggery is that I *am* an independent life form. His actions break multiple Republic treaties."

"I have transferred relevant sections of said treaties to the house attendant for your review. Beyond breaching covenants regarding torturing allies, he is being a jerk," AI paused and briefly turned red. "And *is* a jerk. And most likely will always be one."

Cri caught my eye and mouthed, "Lady Sathra?"

Today was not becoming unweirder.

AI was showing remarkable restraint. If I was dumped in acid designed to eat at my brain, I would be furious. I've known AI my whole life; his behavior was odd. Diplomatic. Like he claimed as much power here as Mom or Dad. And I didn't think he was being snarky when he addressed Mom as Lady Sathra. My headache roared back, this time from the implications of how little I seemed to know about all these familiar people around me.

AI had been with me every day of my conscious life. He was a weight at my chest and a thought in my head. If there was anyone I could say knew me, it would be AI. And if there was anyone I thought I'd known, he'd be at the top of the list. Our togetherness made it easy to forget how different he was.

"Nent," Mom dipped her head toward AI. One of her hands extended and turned over, long fingers drifting toward the jar, "Please remove, ah…him from the solvent."

"Sathra…." Dad stopped midsentence, sighed, nodded his head, and took AI out. He even rinsed and dried him before returning him to me. "My apologies to you, AI, and to you as well, Raystar," he muttered as I draped AI around my neck. I felt better as his familiar warmth and weight returned.

"Whatever, alien," replied AI. Dad's eyes glowed. Mom wasn't finished.

"AI, *protocols* have been observed. You are a guest, and this house has come under outside threat. Aid us with your response." And after a millisecond's pause, Mom dipped her head and added, "Please."

"Of course, Lady Sathra. I should love to play the remaining images for you," AI said sweetly. Mom nodded. Dad clenched his fists. Cri giggled.

The images restarted, and the four of us got to see, from various angles and with full sound, exactly what had happened.

The creature launched meteors of energy at me. The lightning claws I generated were nearly as long as the lev-sled, and somehow AI had gotten an excellent view of my craxy face. The part where I threw my head back and screamed toward the sky, uh, certainly conjured up words like *insanity* and *unstable*. My hands twitched as I recalled the glee I had felt when tearing down the thing's shield. And satisfaction of eating…it. "Not normal," I muttered silently to myself, over and over, while I rocked slightly.

The room was quiet as my claws ripped into IT-ME and the resulting explosion threw it into the fields. Dad's plasma pistols made a great light show, but had no effect. The creature raced off. Lightning scattered clods of dirt around us. I collapsed. The images vanished.

Everyone let out a collective breath and turned to me.

"Hi." I leaned against Mom and waved a hand from my hip.

"The creature is a nanoconstruct," AI continued, not letting silence get a grip on the room. He emitted molten red light that cast shadows on the walls and made us, despite the whiteness of the kitchen's illumination, look like we were staring into a campfire. "My scans indicated it's composed of Human tech. It's a strain of nano not in any of my databases, but at its core, it's Human-tech nonetheless."

Dad thunked down in a chair by the kitchen table and stared down at his four hands spread out, palms up. The muscles around his jaws bulged, and he alternately clenched his hands into fists.

"What I was able to scan of the creature, it resembles, well...Raystar." My parents gasped, and AI continued. "One explanation is that it self-assembled in the Mesa Ruins and was out searching for consumable material. Self-assembly, as you're aware, can happen when enough nano aggregates in a single place that it can spontaneously activate. I'm surprised this doesn't happen more, given what's in those Ruins. But that does not explain the resemblance between them."

Outside, Chunks squea'd, ominously annoyed at something.

"As to Raystar...," he let the sentence hang, flashing cool blue. "Please understand that Raystar's parents bound me to...." Somehow, AI saw the looks on Mom and Dad's faces. "...silence on certain topics. I will not discuss what she did."

"Bound you...you mean, you promised *them*?" Mom whispered, looking down at her hands. "But *we're* her parents."

"I'm not going to be mysteried to death," Cri exclaimed, "*What* is going on?" Even though "mysteried" wasn't an actual word, my sister was spot on. We needed answers. "Is Twig a mutant? A Human mutant? A Hutant or Mutan? Part machine? *What is she?*" Cri continued, her lower hands posed on her hips as she gestured with her upper arms.

I reeled as the realization that AI had known my parents slammed into me. *He knew them. He must know what I was. What I AM.* Thinking that *THING* and I were somehow connected put a giant knot in my stomach.

"Cri!" Mom hissed to my sister, her eyes blazing. Startled, Cri took a step back from Mom, who turned to me and took my hands in hers. "Raystar, you are a perfectly amazing and natural Human child. Our beautiful child! But the purple in your hair and eyes is the sign of an ancient and rare gene." She looked down and then back at me. I had never given my purple a second thought.

"Toward the end of the Lethian–Human conflict," she continued, "Humans integrated advanced nanotechnology with their own biological structure so only they could control Human technology."

"Soooo?" I gestured vaguely at myself.

Dad stood up, towering over all of us. "Daughter," he paused, "For whatever reason, those of your kind with the gene have purple hair. And over the years, hundreds of years, Humans with this control gene have been"—he paused—"disappearing. You have this gene, and *something else*." He waved to where the images of me had hung in the air.

"THAT'S what you wanted to talk to me about last night!" Then I thought about it. "Uh, the gene, or the 'disappearing' part?"

"Human tech is largely a mystery. Elements within the Convergence believe that examining Humans with this gene is essential to unlock the ancient technology," Mom said. My thoughts surged at the implications. *Who were my parents? Why was I adopted?*

"It is my belief, Lady Sathra, Commander Nent, that this construct was sent after Raystar. It knew her name," AI said. "It looked like her." I felt his scowl and disapproval aimed directly at my parents. The ruby at his heart pulsed and increased in brightness with each word. "*You've let her be discovered.*"

Mom put two hands over her mouth and braced herself against the table as AI's accusation hit her.

Dad simply processed it. "An assassin," he hissed though his teeth. Straightening, Dad turned his massive bulk to Mom. "Sathra, I spoke to the embassy after our return from the fields." Then, more quietly, he added, "Your brother is there, in Ever."

Mom gasped, touching her face. Her scar.

"Offworld help had already been requested and should be making contact with us today." He glanced outside the window, frowning at a thought, and turned back to us. "My estimate, if we are lucky: We have three days before vid-sats route the images to the NPD."

NPD—the Nem Planetary Defense? Help had already been sent? What did the Glean Embassy have to do with this? And Mom never talked about her brother. How did he fit in? I had questions. And then yesterday's events came together with those questions in a sudden punch to my gut.

"Dad…what if…our help already tried to get to us?"

Mom and Dad stared at each other as they followed my thoughts. Dad broke the silence with a whisper. "The meteors."

"Will someone tell me what's going on? An assassin? Hunters? Genes?" Cri stomped a foot, looking at each of us in turn. "What's the big deal with…oh."

Those meteors were ships. One—or all—had crashed in the Mesa Ruins.

AI projected the images he'd recorded that evening. The Core had been as beautiful as ever, and then three meteors had cut across the blackness. AI magnified the images. At the heart of each fireball was a ship. Just like my 3-D battle scene, plasma streaked back and forth between the two rear ships and the front ship. A glowing missile trail arced from the lead ship to one of the rear ships, and the ensuing explosion whited out the view for a moment. The remaining pursuer accelerated to collide with the lead ship, and they smashed into the Ruins.

Mom straightened up. Her black hair flowed around her face, hooding her glowing eyes. "We are not even remotely prepared for this," she muttered to herself, absently tracing her scar line down her cheek with one finger.

A low rumble shook loose dust from the ceiling and rattled my teeth. Was she talking about the assassin, the meteors, or the quake beneath our feet?

8

Quakes don't give time for dramatic pauses or questioning looks. Our kitchen cabinets vomited dishes. Dad drew and flung two of his four pistols to Mom before any porcelain hit the floor. Mom, her eyes glowing, caught them over Cri's head just as the dishes reached the ground and shattered. She clicked them to her combat suit at her hips while activating the blank wall next to our kitchen table with her free hands. At Mom's command, a 3-D image of our compound appeared, rotating slowly three centimeters above said table. She spun it with a hand and the image shifted, tracking the motion outside.

"The perimeter defense has been overridden," the house synth calmly chimed—in the same voice, incidentally, that it used to ask if we wanted our milk warmed.

View screens showed a black, vaguely oval predator descend and squat in our courtyard. Weapon clusters broke its smooth lines, but there was no mistaking that its viewport, armaments, and sensors were pointing at our kitchen door.

The cruiser's engines rumbled dust toward the gratcher outbuilding. I'd never seen a cruiser this close, except in vids when the bad guys were about to lose spectacularly. Panic churned in my stomach, and I wanted to run.

Our gratchers squea'd, bucking at the dust streaming around them. They shoved their toothy muzzles in between the slats of the fence and then pulled back when their bravery wore off.

Except for Chunks. A mountain of territoriality, he braced himself against the exhaust while his responsibilities squealed behind his sheltering hulk. Can gratchers squint? He turned his massive, bristly, tusked head left and then right, judging. With wild eyes, he analyzed the cruiser and the squad that spilled out of it.

"Stay by Mom," Dad ordered. He moved to the kitchen door, turning sideways so as not to stand directly in front of it, and looked back at Sathra. Cri squatted with her back to the wall and pulled a plasma pistol out of her shirt. I blinked, wondering only for a split second where it had been hidden. I bumped my back against the wall, wondering why I hadn't brought mine. I curled myself around AI and waited.

"Mom?" At Cri's whisper, Mom held a finger vertically to her lips and shook her head, her other hands moving over the wall controls with trained familiarity. She hadn't taken her eyes off what she was doing.

The image of the yard shifted to reveal four Lethian security officers standing two-by-two behind their leader. They wore matte-black uniforms with giant red NPD letters marking their arms, chests, and backs. Combined with their flowing white hair, they looked pretty cool—at least on the vids. Lethians are as tall as Gleans, but while Gleans weigh 200 to 300 kilograms, Lethians were usually only a kilo or so over 200 kilograms, and, like me, they had only two arms.

Their skin was the same color as a storm cloud. Two vertical slits held approximately similar positions on their faces, like thin, Human noses. Their mouths were almost like ours, except their black lips curled down at the end, locking them in a perpetual sneer.

Their eyes were also black (and directionless). Only by the turn of their heads, and the context of the conversation, could you tell if they were looking at you. From the kitchen vid, however, we could clearly see where the leader was looking.

He was repeatedly poking one side of the doorframe (we may be the only Galactic house fitted with a doorbell designed for Human fingers). Frustrated, he poked harder at the tiny button.

"Rearm perimeter and interior defenses with Alpha priority, auto target on my mark," Mom commanded, frowning. Somehow, our guests had disarmed our defenses. A separate wall image showed dozens of green dots lighting up along our force fence, the first level of the house, and then a huge green dot on the hangar.

The line down Mom's face was livid, like a fresh wound, and through clenched teeth and a quavering voice, she looked at Dad and said, "I will not let them take her, Nent."

Dad returned her challenge with wide eyes, "And you believe I *will*? *This* is not the time for *that* discussion." He dipped his head and gestured with two hands at the door.

After repeated thumps, each successively harder than the next, the doorbell chimed. The Lethian leader straightened and struck a serious pose.

"Systems rearmed, Lady Sathra," the house attendant intoned, its voice surrounding us. The dots turned red. Mom nodded to Dad; each had unconsciously slid their hands to the plasma pistols resting at their hips. Dad straightened, opened the door, and stepped outside. We held our breath and followed him via the holograph. I didn't know our compound had this many auto cannons.

"Mark," Mom breathed.

"Confirmed. Targets acquired," replied the house synth. *Targets acquired?* Sure, we had tested the house defenses over the years. But we'd never actually pointed them at anything! I swallowed, but my mouth had gone dry.

The lead officer frowned. His face looked like someone had wrapped grey skin around a skull and pulled it so tight there wasn't enough flesh to create lips, so the teeth were always exposed in a permanent grin.

"Master...," He made a show of peering at the virtual display his synth had created. "...Nent Ceridian. I am Jurisdictor Godwill. I am here to discuss this morning's events." He peered around Nent into the kitchen. "You have a Human, yes? I will inspect it."

Jurisdictor.

And I had seen him before. The image from my battle with IT-ME. *He was the blurred figure!*

We were so completely head and body in the Architect's giant gravity well. Every parent told his or her kid some version of "Jurisdictor's gonna do something horrible if you don't…" at some time or another. It was a surefire way to get a child to go to bed, do homework, eat more 'natch, etc.

"…I'll give you something to inspect! Freaking idiot, we should have annihilated their grey a…" AI paused a moment and then muttered something I couldn't catch. "…from Terra to the black hole they crawled out of." Mom and Cri both glared at me, eyes ablaze.

Wide-eyed, I shoved AI into my shirt. He shone like the sun through the material and continued muttering about some "stupid plan." I clutched my hands around him to hide his glow.

My dad nodded formally. "Jurisdictor," he then said through a huge, white-toothed grin, "our Gathering always welcomes Lethian delegations. One wonders how Nem's police are involved, however?"

Because, you see, Lethians were the leaders of the Galactic Convergence. It was only accidental or convenient that they headed up the Nem' Planetary Defense.

The Jurisdictor paused, "What?"

Dad took a step toward Godwill. His eyes shone like twin suns, illuminating the deck and casting Lethian shadows on the walls. Godwill's team shifted their rifles indirectly toward my dad, and the house's autocannons shifted directly toward them. "Godwill. Leave."

"Come now, Commander," Godwill said softly, ignoring the disrespect he'd been shown by being deprived of his title. He took an equal step toward my dad. His dark grey face and enormous black eyes contrasted with Nent's red skin and glowing golden eyes. "Living this close to the Ruins, you saw *something*. Vid-sats documented your lev-sled headed straight toward them this morning. Your pet was in the back." I heard Mom suck in a breath. I blinked. *Commander?* My ignorance seemed to be the only certainty, the only constant in my world.

"Jurisdictor. My *daughter* and I were fixing an irrigation controller. There was a storm. We returned. I remind you that you are on Glean territory. You know the Republic War Treaty as well as any junior officer. With witnesses, I direct you to leave."

The War Treaty—an 1,800 year old agreement between the Terran Republic, its allies, and the Convergence. The terms of surrender were essentially that the Lethians could do nearly anything with Humans, but their allies were full members of the Convergence. Their homes and property were nearly off-limits to Convergence control. Gleans had been amongst the closest of Humanity's allies. My Dad *could* legally kick him out.

"Listen well, Glean," Godwill spat, "only a micro storm saved your Human. We had hoped that the lightning damaged you and your creature as much as it did our vid-sats." Godwill paused, inhaled, got control of himself, and then bowed his head slightly, all the while never taking his eyes off Dad. He made an effort to purse his lips, but it didn't seem like there was enough skin, so he snarled, "You will receive a directive tomorrow. I will expect you at NPD headquarters. Bring your sled's navigation records, along with any additional items listed in the Directive. Good evening."

My dad was still as he watched them go. OK, maybe his fingers twitched a bit above his plasma pistols. Cri and I breathed a sigh of relief as the NPD force turned and headed back to their cruiser.

"INSPECT THIS, LETHIAN SLIME!" AI yelled from underneath my shirt. AI flashed as if a star was around my neck, and the entire room was cast in shadows from his anger-red, nova flash. Mom jumped and had her pistols out in an eye blink. The shadows her pistols cast against the ceiling were HUGE. Cri ducked and I grabbed AI through my shirt. *What on Nem' was wrong with him?*

"LONG LIVE HUMANITY!" he yelled again, this time through the house speakers. A section of fence blinked yellow on the holograph and then alarms went off. The gratcher pen opened.

"Man, I mfknkms hate those mufmf guys!" AI's muffled voice continued from between my hands.

Chunks, our bristly, smelly, 5,000 kg gratcher meteor, smashed into the police cruiser again and again. The cruiser swayed under Chunks' repeated ramming. His deep squeals were matched only by the sound of bending, grinding Galactic alloy as it surrendered to his massive tusks. The cruiser's struts and lower armored sidewall buckled inward, and the police cruiser listed toward Chunks. The engines, which were on, kicked up a dirty plume at this new altered angle.

Jurisdictor Godwill stumbled backward and tripped into my father's arms. Godwill's officers screamed and ran in a mob toward the house. Chunks heard their panicked cries and turned his giant head toward them. If his look was a word, it would be "I'M HUNGRY!" (OK, that's two words.) He bunched his hind legs underneath himself and bucked his head up and down. Eyes wild and wide, he thundered toward the terrified NPD team, squealing as only something ten times your size can do.

"Sathra!" my dad yelled, pulling everyone inside the house.

"Gratcher neutralization!" Mom shouted, and Chunks and the herd fell instantly asleep. The control units on each collar blinked yellow. Of course, Chunks had been charging at the time, and as he went limp and tumbled, his bulk carried him forward in an avalanche-style roll that ended with a ground-shaking collision with the house. More dishes spilled out of the cabinets and dust poofed from new cracks in the ceiling.

"Suckers," AI whispered from my shirt.

9

Chaos, thy name is: five Lethian officers, my Dad, a floor full of broken dishes, and a hostile, 5,000-kg predatory pig. Said officers, and Dad, had spilled into the kitchen, crunching and sliding on the broken dishes, in their haste to escape the now-comatose Chunks. One officer lost his footing and skidded on his back to land at Mom's feet. Mom had stepped in front of Cri and me, her hands on the plasma pistols Dad had thrown her. The pistols were huge.

In the enclosed space of the kitchen, a shot from either pistol would have likely given us more than sunburn. Cri stood a little behind and to Mom's left. I was behind her and to her right.

You need to shut up! I thought furiously to AI.

The Lethian officer looked up at Mom as he tried to regain his breath. Then he became aware of her charged pistol, aimed at his head, and crab-walked slowly across the floor toward his team. Dad's back was against the door, and he'd drawn one of his guns and pointed it down.

I HATE Lethians. I'm sick of this horrible planet, AI's reply floated back to me. I could feel him clenching his virtual teeth and becoming warmer. *But yeah. I could have handled that differently.*

The NPD officers had recovered from the shock of pig-ocolypse and stood stalwart. Two faced Dad and two faced Mom.

Godwill shot a disgusted glance at his squad and then looked at

Mom. "Lady Ceridian," he bowed, "I apologize for our..." His eyes lifted. He spotted me. And froze.

"PURPLE!" Godwill gasped, pointing at ME. The NPD team, as one, whipped around. For one very long second, no one moved. His bulging eyes became even wider when he saw Cri's hair. She hadn't changed it back to black from this morning. "And the....," he paused and looked to me, and then back to my sister.

"*It's*…infected a Glean," he whispered to himself, his voice raised in a creepy, mad-scientist way.

"Leave, Godwill. Now." Mom's complete lack of emotion was a promise of violence. Dad opened the door and motioned the NPD officers toward the courtyard with his pistol. Chunks' snoring and our breathing filled the air between us as we all eyed each other.

"FOOLS!" Godwill shouted, breaking the momentary pause. His eyes were crazed as he glanced from Mom to Dad. "It's purple! You have lost control of your Human!" He wiped a fleck of spit from his mouth with his sleeve and then made a small, circular gesture to his guards that ended with a finger pointed at me. The two nearest officers stepped toward me. "*It* must come with us. And your daughter, we must inspect her as well."

Cri gasped at that. I was terrified. I knew I was different, but today was just one difference after another. My dad's words from a moment ago were loud in my memory. *Hunted*. It was too much. My heart raced. My eyes welled over. *NO*. These jerks were not going to see me cry.

In a blink, Mom's other pistol was drawn and smoldering air-distorting orange wrath. Godwill frowned at her and then Dad, as he realized that he and his men had dropped their rifles in the courtyard. Under Chunks. He motioned to his officers to stand down and became still for a moment. I saw his transformation. His giant eyelids slid down and up as he regarded me…and switched to Plan B.

"Little Terran," he said to me, dipping his head in a single nod, suddenly composed.

"Leave. Now," Dad said, pointing his guns directly at Godwill. But Godwill's skeletal gaze didn't move from me.

"Until the next time, Raystar."

My name from his lips froze me where I stood.

The Jurisdictor exited our kitchen. Ignoring my dad, his four officers formed up, two-by-two, and followed in his wake. Their white ponytails waggled along the black and red of their NPD uniforms as they discreetly stepped around the snoring Chunks and entered their cruiser.

Looking more like a cracked egg than an oval, the cruiser took to the air uncertainly. It trailed heavy smoke as it turned toward Blue River and disappeared in the twilight. The house perimeter autocannons, every one of them, tracked the ship's departure.

I wondered what they were talking about on their ride home. How their cruiser got trashed by a gratcher? Or were they plotting how to capture one purple-haired Terran? He'd known my name the entire time! I was hunted, and the hunter had made himself known. Was that thing in the fields connected to Godwill?

"Purrrrrple! Eeeek! Huuuman! Weee're all going to dieeee!!" AI squealed at the retreating cruiser, from under my shirt, making us all jump. Then, in a normal voice and a brief flare of green, AI crooned, "By the Architect's galactic butt! Those Lethians deserve everything that's...."

"You set the gratchers loose on them?" Mom interrupted, glaring at me. The door was open and her hair spread out behind her from the incoming breeze. Her eyes glowed like twin suns. I scrambled backward.

"Mom...I...."

"Yeah, what in the great gravity well? You autotargeted them with our house defenses?" My dad turned his glowing stare to me as well.

"Could you be any more CRAXY? You mocked Godwill?" my sister shouted. At me!

"Uh," AI chimed from under my shirt. I fumbled with the pendant around my neck like it was on fire and held AI at arm's length. Mom, Dad, and Cri's eyes burned after it.

"Yeah! What's your major malfunction?" I said, heaping it on. And then I thought to him, *What WERE you thinking?*

Raystar. For over a millennia, Lethian doctrine is to "disappear" Humans that manifest. You have manifested dramatically, AI returned.

So what? Hide me! You focus them on me? That's DUMB! I snarled. I imagined a future on the run, living off of the land, being chased by leggers, evading NPD cruisers, craxy nanoconstructs, and being on GalNet's "Most Wanted" list.

Forget any free weekends this year. Playtime was over. Giant doors were closing, and any semblance of a normal kid's life was being sealed off behind them. My hands balled into fists. I struggled to breathe.

Ray, get a grip.

Answers, AI…I am not doing this anymore. I needed information like oxygen.

You haven't been ready for answers. No one has. You've been too young, and your parents…they've strayed. I had no idea what he was talking about. The tightness in my chest pushed a storm of emotions through me and I gasped for air.

And became aware of…the growing silence in the room. My family had paused their interrogation of AI and was watching me. The conversation with him was in my head, so they only saw my fury with each thought.

"Explain yourself, AI." My dad stepped toward me, gently removing the pendant from my outstretched hand. In contrast to his calm, his eyes were on fire. I blinked up at him.

"Lethian doctrine is the removal of Humans expressing the control gene. This isn't over. You both know this. He knew Raystar's name. This is endgame," AI said as he swung slowly from my dad's hand. "I bought us time to identify a solution. A solution YOU BOTH SHOULD NEVER HAVE NEEDED! That thing in the fields this morning, and now a Jurisdictor? Why are we even on this stupid planet? I didn't cram myself into this ingot to babysit you both while you get lost in each other's teenage Glean passions! Grow the gravity well up!"

"LADY. COMMANDER," he continued, his voice dripping with sarcasm. "You've both lost control! Raystar is our responsibility and this is how you discharge your DUTY?" Mom and Dad looked at each other with guilt. The four of us, as one, blinked. Eye glows flashed out, replaced with the calm of Glean gold.

And then, to me, he thought, *Raystar, you're getting a nose-bleed. Calm, Raystar, calm.*

I swiped away the drop that had reached my lip before anyone else saw it. *What is "endgame" supposed to mean? Answers, AI. You, everyone, is keeping secrets. AND YOU KNOW MY PARENTS! I need to know what's happening!*

I'm here to help you. You don't see it now, but you will. I promise, Raystar.

Pfft. I rubbed my blood between my thumb and forefingers, feeling it spark. Whatever this thing inside me was, it was active, just underneath, waiting for my emotions to release it.

Mom sighed, regarding AI. "He…it," she made a small cutting motion with a hand as if waving away a fly. "Nent, we must occupy them with compliance to their rules. Create time for us to get offworld."

"Uhng! I don't understand," Cri threw her hands up and thumped down on a chair.

Nent placed AI on the kitchen table, and sat down with his head in all four hands, black hair cascading around his fingers. "I can stall them for a week, maybe two," he mumbled to the ground.

"You called the Embassy," Mom said to Dad. "I haven't spoken with my brother in…a long time." She straightened up, touching her scar absently. "My movements will be tracked, yet Ever is safe for me. This threat is directed solely at Raystar. I will vid you from the Embassy."

Cri stared at our parents, her mouth open in disbelief. "Mom. Dad. *What* are you talking about?" I wanted to tell her to say it slowly, so the grownups could understand the weight of this question, but I was locked in my battle with burning eyes. Mom looked at my sister, then me, and sighed.

"Darling Cri," Mom said, "Our time on this planet is finished. Until we know what action to take, we must act as if the NPD visit was nothing more than a scary interruption." she said. "When I return from Ever, we will have the information needed to determine our next move. In the meantime, you two will go to school as if it is the most natural thing in the world."

Cri wrinkled her face and tilted her head skeptically at Mom.

"This is because of her?" my sister asked, refocusing her attention on me, an accusatory frown gathering like a storm over her softly pulsing eyes.

Mom and Dad had moved toward each other, missing her question. They lit up each other's faces with their deep gaze, and Dad took Mom's four hands in his. "Love, I believe this is as much and as good as we can do right now." They reached out to Cri and me and pulled us into a hug. I grabbed AI as eight parental arms wrapped us in a Glean embrace. In our familial hug, they missed Cri's words:

"I don't want to leave."

10

The *chirrups* from the little bugs every world has were noticeably absent. They'd greeted me every waking morning since I could remember. Our house was *quiet*.

Ray, c'mon. Breakfast. School, AI prodded.

Arg. I rubbed my face with my hands. Waking up was dumb.

To my right, the Glean Dreadnought annihilated the Lethian ships for the millionth time. Opposite, Terra spun lazily in her blue, green, and white glory. Terra. Lethia. Neither of them should have been my problem. I pulled my blanket up and around my head so only my face was exposed. I'd seen my first space battle two days ago. Right above my home. Something had attacked me in the fields. I was being hunted. The NPD wanted me. Me. And my DNA was…what? Nothing made sense, and yet, too much was happening too closely together for this to be coincidence. The secrets I'd wanted so fervently to find had tracked ME down.

Everyone—well, maybe not Cri, but everyone else, including now apparently the flipping Jurisdictor of my planet—knew more than I did about ME.

For the first time in my life, I felt isolated. Alien. Desperately lacking in information. Whom could I trust?

I frowned. One person was at the center of all of my questions.

Answers. Now.

AI acknowledged me with a mental nod, as if he'd been expecting me to eventually get to him. I could hear my pulse. Sparks crackled from my hair to my hands with each stress-filled heartbeat. I recognized that surge of energy coursing through my body.

You're different from other synths. What. Are. You?

The conversation must have looked odd. I'd jumped out of bed, AI clenched in both hands. I was glaring at his metallic, uh, self. I could have sworn he sighed, collapsing his virtual shoulders in a shrug.

I'm two things, he said, after a moment. *I'm your ally. And I'm your... friend. I can't give you specifics, in case, you know, Godwill manages to ask you questions, um, directly. Like through torture or something.*

What? How could he joke right now?

Tell me something not out of a spy vid, AI. Besides, Mom and Dad are getting us offworld. I waited for him to continue. He didn't. *AI. I need more.*

Yesterday, he had been my best friend. He'd been given to me by my Human parents. Today? This INGOT was holding out on me. Why? A spark jumped from my hair to the 3-D battle scene. It crackled and with a puff of metallic smoke, flashed off. My biological parents, my...DNA, he had known about these things all of my existence.

And he wasn't telling me.

WE CANNOT GO OFFWORLD, he replied. *Ray, trust me. We need to get you to....*

"I've trusted you my WHOLE LIFE!" I shouted, ignoring his cautionary yellow glow.

I returned to communication by thought. *Not go offworld?* Static snapped, singeing the clothes covering my desk and making the shag carpet smoke. *You've been holding out on me, for what, thirteen years? Trust you?*

Calm down, Ray. Calm down. Your parents have it wrong. You're an easy target offworld. Lethians will find you up there easier than on Nem'.

That didn't help my stress at all. *The Convergence wants my DNA?* I thought back to him.

Not the Convergence. The Lethians, the Empress.

Riiiight.

Yeah. And there's only one place where you'll be safe. It's a hail-Mary play, but safer by far than offworld.

Unngh! He could be so annoying! *Can you just talk normal? Like, without all these flipping up-the-gravity-well expressions?*

There's a deserted Human base, underneath the Mesas. We need to get you in there.

I blinked, not expecting that. On one level, it made sense that there might be a Human base there, because Nem' was, after all, a Human world originally. But for that base to be a safe haven after all these years? And how would he know? Dad was right—AI needed to be inspected.

C'mon, AI.

It's true, Raystar. I've been searching for the key protocols, and I found them. They're here on Nem', in Blue River.

Seriously, why am I listening to this? Tell me something useful. My tone was full of contempt.

Ray, you gotta believe me. The base is called New Mars…you'll need a DNA control key to get in.

I could do without any more talk about DNA.

Oh, AI thought.

What? I responded.

Maybe Godwill has it, and that's why he's made his move? I pictured the Jurisdictor's skeletal grin, his last look at me as he called my name, and shuddered.

Last chance, AI. My whole life you have been spying on me. For whom? Keeping secrets from me. WHY? You're supposed to be my FRIEND! If you know all this stuff now, why didn't you tell me before? When it mattered!

"WHEN YOU MATTERED!" I was shouting now. Wisps of lightning crackled from my legs, melting brown circles into the shag carpet.

No. Seriously, Ray. I'm….

I began to hyperventilate. The smell of plastic filled my nose as I stomped to my bathroom and dropped him in my toilet.

Waiiit! Talk to the Elio.... I flushed. He'd turned bright yellow as he started to go down, and I saw the light follow him into our waste processor. As he disappeared, the toilet, the bathroom, and I returned to darkness.

With a buzz, the 3-D image of me flickered to life. My bedhead crackled with sparks and a thin line of blood traced from my nose to my lip, glittering with electricity. My eyes were huge and my chest heaved. I didn't look unstable. Not at all. Right?

Who was I kidding? I would never have a babysitting job again. I imagined what my parents' friends might say: "Raystar, don't worry about the damage. Why, we hired an interior designer just last week, and the burned furniture is a reminder that this remodeling isn't a next-year project. Besides, our littlest thinks you're simply, how do you say? Nova! So...Here's the tip. We'll be sure to call you...if we ever become suicidal."

Whatever. I batted the sparks away, smoothed my hair down, and used my wrist to wipe the blood from my nose.

"There," I said, "better." *It was, right?* My pajamas fell off me as a rack extended from the wall with my school clothes. If I rushed, I could make it down before Cri and actually get some food.

And if AI had a nose, he'd smell how done I was with the mystery. ALL DONE with his mysteries. His maddening presence in my life. Flushed down a toilet. Gone.

Thirteen years of companionship, gone. Pff. It was clearly a fake friendship. But I couldn't dismiss how he'd comforted me, perhaps even more than Mom or Dad. He was in my head. When I was fever-sick, he'd tell me stories of Earth. When I was sad, AI helped me think through the sadness and, failing that, he'd tell me some stupid joke. So many times, I'd laugh despite myself. And if I did something amazing, or that I was proud of, he was there more than my parents to witness my achievement, to congratulate me, and to urge me to be proud of what I'd done, nearly the moment I'd done it. I had an unconscious running dialogue with him.

It wasn't there any more. AI wasn't just in my head, I realized. He was in my heart.

Oh my god.

"Raystar!" Dad shouted, startling me out of my horror. "Mom has left for Ever and I've made breakfast!" The house amplified his already way-too-loud voice. I felt weak. *What had I done?*

Dad smiled at me as I thunked down the stairs to the kitchen. He didn't catch my deepening despair.

My purple hair flopped over my face and the additional weight pulled me toward the table. *Gratcher. Eggs. Uhg.* The smell wasn't delicious any more. It was just familiar. I thought of Chunks. He'd beat the…heck out of the NPD cruiser and pretty much saved us. Wow.

I can't eat gratcher anymore. I ate everything around the steak and pushed the plate away.

"AAAIIIIIEEEEEE!" Cri screamed as she leaped down the stairs, sliding to a stop at my plate. Her black hair swished from her momentum. Dad's giant guns materialized in his hands. I jumped, coughed a spark out like I was choking on electricity.

"Thanks!" she said, grabbing my plate, oblivious to her options for destruction. After finishing my food, she grabbed the plate Dad had set out for her with a hand and shoved its contents in her face with the others.

The first day of school made her hungry. And loud. Not in that order. She sucked down her food.

She shouted "C'mon, Twig!" and grabbed my hand with one hand and our lunches in two other hands. We rocketed out the door, into the courtyard, to our darts. "I'm not going to be late because of you."

"SQUEAAAA!" Chunks thundered. Cri stopped dead in her tracks and I smashed my face into her backpack. Chunks looked down at us with lidded pig-eyes and snuffed again. I rubbed my nose. Ow.

"That gratcher is CRAXY," my sister whispered, leaning toward me before backing a meter away from the gratcher pen.

I looked at Chunks while he regarded me. He was big and ugly, for sure. I was a weed. A hunted weed. Something clicked, irrational as it was. We were what was left of Terra.

Huh.

I reached into my lunch, grabbed the cake Mom had made for dessert, and, breaking it, tossed half through the force fence. His eye, high up in his giant head, tracked the cake's arc. He looked back at me and lowered his head, reaching his slimy tongue out to taste the cake bit where it landed. It vanished delicately into his huge, toothy mouth. On a hunch, I reached my hand between the bars, the other half of the cake resting on my palm.

I moved slowly.

"Raystar, what the..." Cri whispered frantically.

"Shssshshshsh!"

Chunks glared at me. And, after a moment of insanity during which I wondered whether my hand would stay connected to my body, he ever so gently reached out his tongue and removed the other half of the cake.

"Thanks, Chunks." I breathed, leaned in, and patted his muzzle. He snuffed, glared at me, and trotted back to his herd. He could have eaten my skinny, kid arm. I whooshed out the breath I'd been holding.

"Are you out of your flipping mind?"

I walked past her, calling, "We're going to be late. C'mon."

And yes. I *was* out of my flipping mind.

I had just flushed my best friend down the toilet.

11

Cri landed at the school's Vehicle Containment Pad—the VCP—a moment before me. Her dart's red-environmental shields created a teardrop envelope around the blue fuselage—an engine, a two-person seat, and a glowing-blue control console. She pulled her helmet off and tossed her silky, long hair out of her face. Her anger from last night forgotten, she grinned at me.

"YEAH!" She pumped four fists in the air, and her eyes glowed on the down motion. "YEAH! Raystar! Are you kidding? That was NOVA!"

I wasn't Twig anymore? I settled my dart, my own shield melting into air. When *my* helmet came off, my hair exploded, all purple and spiky. Yesterday's encounter with the NPD was on continuous replay, interrupted only by commercials of me flushing AI down the waste chute of my life.

Still, the ride to school had been a needed distraction. We'd covered the twenty green, 'natchy kilometers from our farm to our school (on the outskirts of Blue River) in two blinks. At one point, I'd flown so low and so fast that the compressed air *in front* of my dart had parted the 'natch around me and sucked it back and out of the ground, creating a fountain-like trail of twirling leaves.

AI never let me go flat out on my dart.

Raystar, you'll have your entire life to destroy yourself horribly. Slow down and start tomorrow! he'd say. And then he'd keep muttering as he took control of our dart's speed. *And let me know so I can be somewhere else.*

But I'd flushed him. He was alone with the poop now.

"Finally got the old grumper to relax?" she said, leaning in to fist-bump my two hands with her upper two.

I stepped out of the way.

"Shut up, Cri," I said as she stumbled past me. She turned, confusion in her golden eyes.

"What?" she frowned.

I gritted my teeth and pushed past her down the path to the Blue River Educational Facility.

"You shut up!" she called after me.

Pfft.

On the way from the VCP to the Blue River Education Facility, our ears filled with the low roar you hear when approaching a stadium. The muted volume becomes sharper and louder as each detail of sound competed with another. Standard Galactic came through our nanotranslators, but our ears heard low voices, high chirps, laughter, people's names. Just regular conversations in kids' lives.

The cacophony of the thousand or so of my classmates corralled together in the courtyard sounded more like a mob of ten thousand.

The Facility was a series of tall, grey octagonal slabs stacked into an inverted pyramid. It was dark enough at the base so that no grass grew, and the building glared disapprovingly at the students from its towering height. A grass play field flowed out from school's giant doors. Play equipment stretched upward, maybe three stories tall. The jungle gym was a forest of multicolored beams and various levels of platforms that grew just by the schoolyard entrance.

The Facility's perimeter shimmered with a force fence similar to the one that guarded my home. After yesterday's incident with the NPD, I wasn't so sure the fence was to keep strangers out.

The Facility was positioned at the far eastern end of the city of Blue River. The metropolis rose skyward, a wall of Galactic-blue optimism extending into the heavens. A glittering crystalline collection of reflective spires pierced the clouds, and in the afternoon, they cast multi-kilometer-long shadows over the school and back toward our farm.

Cri caught up to me at the playground. I didn't give her a chance to talk as I shoved and navigated through the chaotic throng of students. I was headed over to a dense section of pipes, beams, blocks, tubes, and swings. Its geometric tangle was, as always, doing its job of pulling delighted cackles and screams from the kids.

Our destination was one particular tree-like climbing structure that was set apart from the mass of yelling, wheezing, and whistling children. It was our usual before-school meeting place.

I felt a series of rapid thuds underfoot and a Crynit, large for his age, thrummed up to us on fifty blood-red, grasping claws. His mottled, navy blue, segmented chitin hadn't yet taken on the pure black of a grownup, and he was only a bit under three meters long. He'd tied red, blue, green and orange sashes to each of his legs, and they flowed like colored water as he moved. Nonch was his name.

"Human," Nonch said, bobbing his head. Nanotranslators smoothly ensured all Galactics understood each other. Four black eyes underneath two even larger orange eyes regarded me with a predatory lack of expression. Two feathered sensor stalks dipped slightly toward me. As he spoke, sword-like mandibles as long as my forearm and an inner, fang-lined mouth pulsed slightly. Suddenly, his six larger serrated arms extended, cage-like, around me. Their incredibly sensitive manipulator claws reached out simultaneously, the colored cloth tied to them fluttering less like decorations and more like hunting trophies, or scalps of a rainbow.

He was being so formal.

"Shells!" I laughed and stepped into his cage of arms, encircling him in a careful hug. My friend was not soft. Blood—mine—would be spilled if either of us hugged a nudge harder. While my arms didn't wrap fully around his smooth carapace, he was warm to the touch. I called him "Shells." Not all Galactics were into nicknames. I think he called me "Juice-bag."

"Nonch! Nice colors!" Cri said. Nonch bobbed his head at the compliment, glancing sideways at me before turning his head to my sister.

"Thank you, Cri, Sister-of-Raystar. Broodmother has created many eggs. We celebrate." I peered closely at his sashes. He, or some other Crynit, had actually created the silk scarves. The patterns were beautiful. It was heartening to see such a fearsome individual take an interest in, well, beauty. While many species came to Nem', Crynits had settled on the planet after the War. They'd *fought* us. We were gone.

They were here.

I remember meeting Nonch in class for the first time, when I was five. He must have been a little over a meter long. He raced around me, darting close to touch me with his sensor stalks. I giggled uncontrollably, and then, as five-year-olds will do when spinning, fell on my butt. He climbed over my knees and touched my hair. I can still feel his claws poking through my clothes, but with his immature weight, they only tickled. I laughed and grabbed him, and felt his cool, hard carapace. It felt like a shell, except smoother. "Shells," I had giggled, and lo, the name had stuck.

"Good health," I said, squeezing my friend once more. He bopped me on the head with his sensor stalks, two big feather dusters as long as my arm, that sat above his array of eyes. It was our secret high-five.

I released Nonch, who'd frozen in a J-like shape (probably not wanting to accidentally spill my "juice" with a sudden movement.) Cri fist-bumped two of his claws, and her two other fists touched Jenna's.

"Cri!" Jenna and my sister grabbed each other in a four-armed Glean hug. "I am sooo unstarred to be here!" Releasing Cri, she turned to me and rolled her eyes. "Raystar."

Her black hair was dyed green and cut short. The multicolored beads she'd woven through her jade strands clinked as she moved. She was wearing blue pants with rips above the knees and thighs and a faded shirt that matched her hair and exposed her belly button. It wasn't that she was some sort of fashionista—it was that she was the loudest, the flashiest, the first to laugh, the first to criticize, and the first to draw attention to herself with everything she did.

I'm sure I'm not being nice thinking all this, but then, Jenna hadn't been very nice to me. What I wore, what I ate, and even my hair was a constant source of sarcasm and slights. "Ew, Human food! How do your parents stand it?" The worst was her nickname for me. "Hey Purps!" she'd call. *Yeah.*

Cri would sometimes tell her to stop, I think mostly because she wanted to talk about something else. I hadn't told either Mom or Dad about the slights or the nicknames. Maybe some of that was fear that there was truth to them—that it was a burden making special Human food, or that maybe, they didn't like the color purple. I wasn't feeling like a champion right now, after what I'd done to AI. Maybe I deserved the ridicule.

My hands clenched as I thought about all of the things I wasn't, and what I was doing wrong.

"Jenna," I smiled. "Hope the classes aren't as hard for you THIS year as they were last year. I mostly didn't enjoy seeing you struggle."

She frowned back at me. Cri moved between us.

"Don't mind Raystar, Jenna, she's universally angry." I glanced at my sister. Last time I checked, her house had JUST BEEN INVADED TOO! A retort pointed at my sister was just about to explode from me when a hand closed around my arm, pulling me gently to the side.

"Friend, mine," Nonch said. "You insult?" I stared into Nonch's two orange eyes. He lowered his voice and cocked his head to the side. "School has not even started and you are troubled?"

Cri and Jenna had moved on and were laughing and pointing at someone else.

"Shells," I leaned in and he obligingly dipped a sensor stalk toward me. "I'm up the gravity well. REALLY."

He was about to reply when Jenna exclaimed, "You see that new kid? An Elio—uh, yeah, an *Elion*! What a freak. I mean, that fur, and those huge nova-craxy eyes." Jenna leaned in, a hand covering her mouth, and whispered to us, "They drool when they're hot!"

Nonch twisted the upper part of his "J," bending around me to see our new classmate. We all looked over, as out-of-the-corner-of-our-eyes as possible. Which was silly, given how the thousands of kids around us pretty much ignored the thousands of kids around *them*.

The Elion was covered in long, thick, white, puffy fur. His eight stubby, blue legs—each the circumference of my thighs—supported his meter-round torso. Two huge, wide, verdant eyes glanced around, nervously. His arm claws weren't visible. Our gaze met for an instant, and I grinned at him. All my troubles were forgotten in a blink. *I mean, look at him!*

"I wonder if all that fur is clean?" Jenna sniggered.

"School hasn't begun and you're starting in on people? Seriously, Jen." I frowned at Jenna. I glanced back at the Elion.

He was walking toward us in a spidery manner and growing, well, fluffier with each step. Like a pillow—a big, comfortable pillow with blue legs. That you wanted to *crush* to you, and wrap your arms and legs around, and just roll around in before you fall of the cliff of consciousness and into the canyon of sleep. Pillows…good.

I snorted, thinking about my summer. "We all drool, Jenna."

"I—," she started.

"Jenna knows what freaks are," a voice chimed behind us. "And the Elion is a small freak-star next to your freak-nova Human. Except, perhaps, for the hypocrisy of the false sister of the Human."

We turned toward the voice to face three Lethian boys who had just come to a stop behind us. I knew two of them—T'jarl and Fell. I'd met them both the same time as I'd met Nonch.

T'jarl had been my friend for a while, until he realized he wasn't Human or that I wasn't Lethian. I blame that on the growth spurt. His, that is. Galactic records show that comparatively, Humans don't have growth spurts. We're small, and then as everyone gets larger, we get comparatively smaller. T'jarl and I had never been great friends, but as kids usually do, we would throw balls to each other with the expectation of catching and receiving.

Fell was different. His expectation was mostly to have you catch what he threw with your face. *Perma-jerk.* Found something unexpectedly slimy in your lunch? Got a nudge that rebounded you off a corner of the hallway as you were rushing to class? Felt a toe at the back of your ankle as you're taking a step over the spring playground mud? *Yeah.* I'd had foodless lunches, bruises, mud on my new clothes, you name it—pretty much since I could remember—because of HIM. He was the stereotypical bully.

But the third boy. *My.* He was tall. Serene. Galaxy knows how he could feel so comfortable dressed in midnight robes cut with a deep red sash and trimmed with gold. It was a level of detail most farmers on Nem' simply had never thought of, let alone had been able to afford. It certainly wasn't what I had grown up with. He glided a step past his entourage and half-turned toward Nonch.

The two shared a heartbeat's glance, and I swear, NONCH DIPPED A SENSOR STALK AND HE NODDED. *What in the great galaxy's gravity wells was that about? Auuuuggh!*

The morning had been going so well. My heart thudded, and I forced myself to breathe. When Mom had told me to "act normal," I'm sure she didn't mean through unusual levels of bullying. And yet, here we were, in the first twenty minutes of school. WITH THIS! My normal.

"Mieant, don't you have someone else to bother?" Cri said, folding her hands across her chest and propping her lower hands on her hips. Few kids messed with Cri. She was big. And craxy, too. She wasn't used to being picked on. Jenna, in contrast, looked pleased that someone had complimented her.

Mieant, who stood taller than Cri, returned her gaze and smiled haughtily. "Bother?" he retorted. "It is my race that unites the Convergence. It is your races that are being united." His parents were part of the Convergence hierarchy, or something like that. What they were doing in Blue River was beyond me. But two years ago, they'd arrived.

And Mieant had immediately sought me out and introduced me to actual antagonism. I don't know why he hated me. I got along with other Lethians, Gleans, Crynits—in fact, there really wasn't any species I didn't get along with, now that I think about it. If it was just straight bullying, I'm not sure I'd have felt so affected. But he was one of the cool kids, one of the popular ones. In fact, we should have just called him The Most. He was always the most athletic, the most fashionable, the one with the best grades. It seemed the only thing he was bad at was being nice to me.

"Freak!" Mieant turned his attention back to me, disgust turning his already downward-pointing mouth into a snarl. "What say you? Rumor is that the attacks are because of you."

Seriously. I had not done anything to him. Yet his gaze was so intense, so filled with anger that seemed to show up only for me, that I unconsciously took a step backward. I had done nothing wrong. This was my school. My world. I had as much right to be here as anyone else.

In fact, I had been here first.

I sucked in a breath and took one and a half steps toward him. This was not stressful at all. No. Not at all.

"Broodmother says the attacks are because of old machines. Human machines," Nonch nodded and looked between us, his colored sashes flowing with his movements.

Attacks? I eyed at Shells and he LOOKED AWAY.

Mieant laughed at my bewilderment, and his black hair waved in slow motion. He'd be awesome if he wasn't such a jerk. But wasn't that most peoples' problem?

After a moment's silence, my entertainment value was spent. Without a backward glance, Mieant strode away toward a group of Lethians as his "troops" followed him. Jenna's big golden eyes got bigger as she watched him leave.

"Plllthhhsssssppbbbbb!" I wheezed, leaning over with my hands on my knees as my breath exploded from the container of my chest.

"He's sooo nova!" Jenna sighed. Cri nudged her shoulder, sending her hair beads in a clinking frenzy as they tumbled around her face.

"He is rude. Ignore him, Raystar," Nonch said, taking my arm with his larger arms and flowing beside me. He looked at me intently and then at Jenna and Cri. "I am sorry. Silent I was going to be, but silent I was not. About the attacks and correlation to your kind."

"Well, *I* still think he's cute," said Jenna, straightening her clothes.

I squinted at her. She did not think in straight lines. But Nonch's comment...

"Nonch, what about the attacks? And the machines?" I asked, turning to him. "And what's between you and HIM?" I might have said it a bit imperiously.

"I...."

"Nonch?" I gaped at his hesitation.

"I was to be silent on this matter." As Nonch spoke, he bobbed his head. His feathery sensor stalks made him look like a giant, dangerous flower assortment. He peered from under a stalk (much as I did with my strand of hair when I wanted no one to notice my glance) first at Cri and then back to me.

"The matter of him?" I asked, frowning. I pointed at flipping Mieant to let him know that I knew they'd had a private moment! I was completely unstarred by not understanding whatever-the-flip that was about.

"Raystar—ally! I have not chosen him as my mate!"

"WHAT?"

My friend looked at me, his sensor stalks flopped back against his head. "I am without things to say. My feeling is I am communicating poorly. Or, as you Humans say, 'uh.'"

"What?" I sputtered, "We don't say 'uh' for things like that." I frowned. "Mostly."

He eyed me, skeptical.

"So what WAS that?" I pressed.

Nonch glanced at his scarves. With that, the morning chime, a deep, belly-vibrating note that held for two breaths, gonged, and the giant navy blue metal doors, large and thick enough to repel an invasion, slid open. A swarm of kids pushed us toward the entrance, and my friend and I were separated in the rush.

"At lunch, Nonch!" I shouted over the crowd. "Don't hold out on me!"

I turned and smashed into the soft, fluffy fur of the Elion who'd sidled right up beside me. I take that back—it was, in fact, the softest, fluffiest fur I'd ever smashed into. He was about my height, and my face had bumped into him right between his wide, emerald eyes, each of which rolled toward me.

"Mffmff," I said, looking left at one green orb, then right at the other, as I disengaged.

"Human," the Elion said in a sing-song voice. "I am Alar. Urgent talk."

I puffed a strand of his white fur from my mouth and flipped my tongue against my lips. Oddly, it had no taste. "I, hullo. I am Raystar?"

Claws extended from his so-soft fur, and he straightened me up, patting my hair and picking another strand of fur from my forehead. "Apologieth for thurprithing you, Raythtar-Human. We remember your peoplth kindneth, and time ith thort."

His giant, luminous eyes blinked. He frowned and continued, "Well, technically, time ith not thort. It flowth quickly and directly. In contextht with thpeed and obthervathion, acthually."

Alar placed one of his stick-like arms, one ending in a sharp talon, gently on my shoulder. "But temporal dithcution and contemplathion are not my purpoth. The Avenue will not open for you."

"I don't understand." I said, turning my head from one of his giant ocean-green eyes to the other. The sea of kids surged around us, bumping and nudging us apart. "Alar, what are you talking about?"

"Come to uth, tho you may follow the Avenue."

A troop of laughing Gleans and Lethians—older girls—pushed their way between us, and just like that, Alar's soft, furry, fluffiness was gone.

The second gong chimed.

I blinked at the emptying schoolyard, startled at how quickly noises like wind and blowing leaves could fill the vacuum left by people. The school's huge doors pivoted to close in a slow-motion finality, so I took off in a run toward them.

It would not do to be on the wrong side of those doors.

12

It seems like school should have evolved into something amazing over the millennia. *RIGHT?* I wanted knowledge pills, mind grafts, or just learning through osmosis. How 'bout direct-beaming knowledge? How about plugging in? Or standing near some beacon of learning and absorbing society's knowledge? Upload flipping civilization, and LET ME GO PLAY! Now *that* would be science fiction!

Nope.

We still sit in desks, we still read stuff, and we still listen to linear, verbal diatribes by evangelical grownups (i.e., TEACHERS).

Nonetheless, I loved school. I asked questions, and I got answers. Teachers appreciated me. I wasn't Human, I was a STUDENT. *Do you understand?*

Out of breath, lost in reverie, I reached my locker on the fourth floor. My mind gnawed on Alar's cryptic statements. *My people's kindness? Follow the avenue?* "Avenue" was an old way of talking. We used air cars, so the address system in Blue River—no, everywhere in the Convergence—always included all three dimensions. There was an X-axis (left–right), a Y-axis (forward–backward), and a Z-axis (how high–how low).

Avenues? Like streets? That was—Human? Was the Elion referring to a Human structure? And what door? I crammed my lunch and school bag into my locker. I didn't know much about Elions. And by much, I mean ANYTHING. There were so many races in the Convergence, but I dimly remembered some connection between Elions and Humans during the War. Library time was needed.

The third gong sounded.

Nova and great gravity wells! If I didn't sprint, I'd get my first detention in my first class! Mom would kill me.

Class was several levels down, but the real issue was dodging the floating, scuttling, and running students while sustaining any sort of speed. At one hallway intersection, my heart nearly exploded when I thought I caught sight of Jurisdictor Godwill. Meeting him…was not comprehensible. I spun around a corner and raced down the hallway that I knew would get me right to the classroom door.

Again, out of breath, I skidded into class and flopped down into a preassigned chair that glowed green as it recognized my presence. Green. I sucked in the faintly chemical air of the classroom, relieved that I wasn't late.

The crescent-shaped classroom was terraced and resembled a small auditorium. Rows of desks descended to a large multipurpose podium, behind which was a projection imager. The walls of the room were Galactic metal blue, and the floors were made of some soft, short, dark-grey carpet. Silvery light bands crossed the length of the room's ceilings.

If nothing else about school had changed, the desks sure had. They floated and morphed their force supports to accommodate various Galactic body shapes. There was a console interface that allowed us to query the GalNet, see our individual holo-screens, and watch whatever the teacher was showing us.

My classmates were filing in; nearly all of the forty seats contained a student. Nonch, seated two rows behind me, was talking with his friends.

Jenna clapped her four hands as she made eye contact with one of her friends across the room. She bounced in her seat and mouthed, "Nova!" *Keep the glucose away from that girl.*

On my right was the Elion. I blinked. He looked hot, and he was beginning to pant. His blue tongue had a mind of its own; it perched on the side of his mouth like it was assessing where to find the next coolest place in the solar system. He seemed not to notice me.

My need to talk to Alar was suddenly stifled—as I realized Mieant was seated on my left. OF COURSE he was seated next to me. Feeling my gaze, he turned and smiled.

"Human," he hissed at me.

"JERK," I hissed back. Twisting back to my workstation, I grabbed for AI and grimaced as my fingers clutched in the space above my heart where he usually hung. *Who was the jerk?* I bet Mieant didn't flush his friends. My stomach twisted with betrayal and guilt.

My workstation, an empty-hearted surrogate for AI, scanned me and projected my morning's lessons in the direction I faced. I angrily swiped through them, not really looking at anything.

A gentle, bony weight on my right arm made me jump.

"Let uth talk at lunch, Raythtar."

I looked to my right and found myself about to fall into the Elion's two, huge, sea-green eyes. I had no idea what he was talking about, though—none.

"What avenue?" I whispered to him.

Alar tilted his body in a slow, wise nod. "Yeth. You underthtand. We remember your peoplth kindneth. We REMEMBER, Raythtar," he said, shaking me gently for emphasis. I gritted my teeth, because 100% of nothing was all I understood.

"Ahhhh," a voice intoned. It is how I imagined the Architect would sound—a voice from everywhere. The voice took on a directional perspective and the class turned toward its source.

The voice continued. "Alar. What an appropriate start to our first lesson in Galactic History. Humanity's kindness. But were Humans indeed kind? A cynic would say that history belongs to the victors. What say you, Raystar?"

Our teacher had entered the classroom, unnoticed.

Except this wasn't a teacher. She was the tallest Lethian I had ever seen. She wore her short-cropped black hair like a crown. Her hair highlighted her grey skin and black eyes. Her graceful arms folded across her midsection as she flowed toward the center of the room. Her white robes cascaded from her shoulders and billowed behind her, curling in the air centimeters above the ground. As she came to a stop, her robes flared like the wings of a mythical flying creature coming in for a landing.

Principal Entarch.

She gestured vaguely to me. My workspace lit up with a blue glow, as it projected sound to the room.

"I...." I was unprepared, is what I was. "Principal Entarch, that's not tru...."

"Galactic history has been witnessed," she interrupted, cutting the air with her hand. "With our Recorders, there is no interpretation of history. The Human Worlds, for instance, were destroyed because of their unlawful attack on the Convergence."

"So history belongs to the Recorders!" Mieant cracked, and the class laughed with him. At least he was a universal jerk. I did like that about him.

"You, Asrigard, I can see why you aren't on an offworld school. Please either contribute per your status, or be silent so as not to disgrace your parents further." A nanosecond's silence washed over the room and was then replaced with an enormous shuffle, as we all turned toward Mieant. His eyes flashed, and he looked down.

Principal Entarch nodded, and floated her gaze across the room, daring us to say anything. Alar's space lit up as he was recognized to speak.

"Humanth were drawn into a war. There ith no reathon the Terran Republic thould ever have been attacked. The Convergenthe..."

"Alar," Entarch interrupted. "Did Elions have Galactic Recorders documenting your species' involvement? There is no truth without witness, and without Recorders, there is no truth. The Convergence had the Recorders." I turned toward Alar as he collected his response. He wasn't going to give on this point.

"Know your enemy and know yourthelf, and you can fight a hundred battleth without..."

Kurt Johnson

"SILENCE. YOUR PEOPLE...."

But Alar didn't stop. "...Dithathter," he finished.

Quiet echoed through the classroom. Super-huggy-green-eyed pillow vs. Lethian Principal.

"...Were primitives 1,800 years ago," she finished over him, drawing a gasp from the class.

"But we thaw what happ...." Alar was flustered. His tongue was hanging out further than before as he panted. Kids tittered and giggled. His eyes darted toward each laugh and comment.

"They are vermin," Entarch said quietly. Notes that were about to change hands were dropped mid-aisle. Jokes froze on kids' tongues. Sleepy heads jerked up and riveted on our principal. Then, as one, the class turned to me. As far as I knew, I was the only one of my kind on this 'natch-riddled rock. There was no "they"—just me. My cheeks grew hot and I looked down.

"Elions may be the Galaxy's traders today," Entarch continued. "But eighteen hundred years ago, your civilization had barely reached your planet's moon. Recorded fact. *And* these facts about where we came from, our civilization's march to progress, and the friends and foes...."

She turned her space-empty gaze at me. "It is to these facts that we will now turn our attention. I will be your history teacher this season. Please follow now as we move to Section One of our curriculum."

"Pppppllllllthhhh!" Alar shouted, or slurped, or panted. His claws stretched out, grasping at anything close for stability and caught my desk. He was strong and tilted my desk beyond its anti-gravity compensators' stabilization capacity. I hopped out before I became the first Galactic kid to be squashed by a desk. The kids closest to Alar scrambled away, shrieking. Alar was seriously upset.

No, he wasn't.

He was wide eyed. His tongue was sticking out, like it was tasting life, and his claws extended at all angles from his body to keep him sliding him to darkness. This was not the innocent, curious creature from this morning. It was a plea.

For life.

"Contain yourself, podling!" Principal Entarch said sternly, pointing at him.

The class was laughing. What I had taken initially for anger, I knew was fear. Alar's emerald gaze searched for help. We made eye contact; realization hit my gut like a meteor.

"He's overheating—Nonch! Jenna! Let's get him outside!" I shouted. Nonch flowed toward the quivering Elion and grabbed him with his six powerful manipulator arms as I moved around him, grasping for whatever I could catch on to. I narrowed my eyes. Jenna looked nervously away, rubbing her palms against her clothes.

I grunted. Alar was too heavy for Nonch and me, and the rest of the class was useless. We weren't going to save him! I strained to lift Alar from his crumpled space, when suddenly his weight disappeared. I lost my grip and fell back into a desk.

Mieant lifted my end of my friend, and he and Nonch were carrying Alar. I pushed myself up and ran in front of them to open door after door after stupid door until we reached the playground. We crashed into cool, fresh air that swirled around us, like Mom's hugs, like water after a long run or the best coolness after the thing that's totally stressed you out.

"Nonch! Water! Wet towels!" I yelled, waving a hand in the general direction of the school. Nonch melted away as only a Crynit can do.

"Mieant, we need to cool him off!" I took my sweater off and put it under him. Which was useless.

I caught Mieant looking at me, a mix of thoughts in his glance. I crossed my legs, and after some grunting, managed to position most of Alar's head and upper body on my lap. Alar's huge eyes focused on me with a strange intensity, but he was still unable to talk.

Nonch flowed back to us holding a drinking container with water and soaked towels. Mieant poured the water into Alar's mouth, and he gulped it down. On a hunch, I placed the towels on his tongue to reduce his temperature. Some animals don't sweat, and instead, pant. I figured with all that fur, THAT was how Elions regulated themselves.

Principal Entarch strode through the doors, standing at the top of the stairs that led down to the play ground.

"I said…," she boomed, and was then interrupted.

A hologram containing a mountain-sized, purply-scarred Elion flashed into existence above where I sat with Alar. I froze, my mouth open, and tilted my head back to take in the giant form. *Great gravity well. Just how big do Elions get?*

"SCHOOLMASTER," its voice thundered throughout the courtyard, "YOU HAVE IGNORED ELION BIOLOGY. YOU HAVE HINDERED AID IN A TIME OF NEED. MY REPORT TO YOUR SUPERIORS AND THIS GOVERNMENT REGARDING YOUR IRRESPONSIBILITY HAS BEEN FILED. KNOW THAT DIPLOMATIC EXPULSION AS A THREAT DOES NOT WORRY THE ELION. WE WILL NOT BE COWED BY SUCH AS YOU."

Then, to my horror, the giant Elion turned to me. "THANK YOU, RAYSTAR CERIDIAN."

And the mountain bowed.

A hush, like the one that comes after a bad, bad, BAD, inappropriate joke, when no one knows how the flip to react, fell over the playground. I closed my mouth and gulped as I looked up at Alar's, uh, parent. Several classmates took an unconscious step back from the image, or me, or both. Alar's parent was neither cute, nor cuddly.

"Are you threatening me? In my school? I will…" Principal Entarch started. But the image had flickered away. Not used to being casually dismissed, Entarch clenched her fists, breathed in, and lowered her head for a pause. Then she raised her head, slowly, and *stared* at me. Pretty much every kid stared at me.

"Your kindneth will be remembered, Raythtar," Alar whispered, jarring me out of the terror of the principal's glare as he backhandedly tapped me with a claw. I blinked. Whispering had been no small feat, given the towels on Alar's tongue. I looked up reflexively and met Mieant's equally surprised eyes. He stood and backed away from us, uncertain.

"Mieant," Principal Entarch said, turning to him and ignoring me.

"I commend you on your quick thinking. You have saved the Elion's life!"

I didn't need any credit for this, but wasn't *I* the one who had initiated saving Alar? Wasn't that obvious? I played back the recent events, trying to see what I might have done to anger her—or anger anyone, for that matter. I bent over and gave Alar a small hug, hiding the surge of expressions that would reveal too much of what I was feeling.

Four security guards arrived and gently lifted Alar. Behind them, a dark figure floated in to stand at the side of the doorway. Jurisdictor Godwill. His black eyes reflected daylight from the shadows and bulged from his skeletal head, as, hands behind his back, he took in the playground scene. As his gaze landed on me, a corner of his slightly open mouth turned upward in a smile, exposing bone-white teeth.

Security took Alar away, presumably to the nurse's office. Entarch glanced at Godwill for a microsecond and then turned to the rest of us. "Back to your classrooms with you."

Did I mention that roaches also still existed? We made like them and scattered under her burning glare.

I kept my gaze on the ground as I passed through the doorway by Godwill.

13

"You didn't have to help," I whispered.

Principal Entarch's topic today was the Human–Lethian Wars' final decades and the collapse of the Human defenses. Star systems rotated slowly above her as she explained how the defeat of Nem' was key to the Lethian victory, and how Humanity was CRUSHED.

He blinked.

"You didn't have to help!" I yell-whispered.

Mieant turned toward me, eyes wide in annoyance, "You know NOTHING," he hissed.

I regarded him and shrugged. "It was still cool of you. You don't suck...." I blinked and considered my next words. "So bad."

Our desks both lit up in blue. "Does either the Human or the Lethian have a question?" Entarch asked. Like 'natch rippling in a gust, the class rustled and turned its attention toward us.

"Raystar continuously talks to me," Mieant mumbled, looking down. *JERK.* I kept my gaze on my terminal but clenched my hands into fists. My workstation's blue turned yellow. I shook my head in disgust. I had been "bubbled." When the blue field that allowed us to talk flickered to yellow, we were essentially cut off from communicating with the class.

Principal Entarch closed the distance between us in several flowing strides, coming to stand at the first row of students, regarding first Mieant and then me like distasteful art at a museum.

"You, Asrigard, should know better." Mieant met her gaze. Whatever he'd been thinking flared his nostrils and drew his eyebrows into a frown. He didn't look contrite. The two stared at each other a moment longer before he looked away.

Entarch's pupil-less gaze shifted minutely as she turned her attention to me. I shifted nervously. Talking in class has never merited this level of attention. "You, Raystar Ceridian, will serve solitary detention over lunch." Kids sniggered. Why shouldn't they? The first class of the whole flipping year wasn't even over.

I groaned. My chance to talk with Nonch or Alar over lunch had been eliminated. To further make the day less nova, I was bubbled in every subsequent class.

My last class let out, and I slumped against my locker. Kids streamed around me, making me feel like I was in slow motion and out of step with the world. Some that recognized me would quickly avert their gazes. Others chittered to their friends and attempted a subtle point in my direction. *Like I couldn't see them. Pfft.*

Saving Alar had only gained me the Principal's anger. The giant Elion, Alar's parent, *knew me*. Alar's cryptic statements were a puzzle piece that, like all of the others, suggested that this was a big puzzle.

And between the meteors.... I frowned and corrected myself. *...Between the crashed starships two days ago and the events leading up to now....* The thought of finding the other pieces of this puzzle made my heart thump with urgency.

Once I'd retrieved my supplies from my locker, I picked up my pace. I'd been walking slowly, not only to think, but on the offchance Nonch might find me. We usually bumped into each other after school, but he was nowhere to be found. Hope of catching a minute with him before we all left for home faded with each step across the playground.

I waited for Cri at the VCP. Despite the fact that I'd been upset with her earlier in the morning, her company would have been a comfort.

She probably would have told me that grownups didn't know what they were doing, and that being bubbled by Principal Entarch was totally nova. I smiled, imagining her saying that and the accompanying fist-bumps. Five more lonely minutes passed. With a sigh, I left a message on her dart that I'd waited, mounted my dart, and flew home.

Let's see. School Day 1? Miserable.

Oh, and I also had a meteor-load's worth of homework.

14

Banefire, angry and huge, looked like it was boiling the ocean as it set. Pink, orange, and purple clouds the size of mountains were streaks of foam against its horizon-spanning background. And the thousand-meter tall Galactic-alloy buildings scattered sunbeams through streams of air cars and billowing factory smoke…so, so far below us.

At this height, the thrush of the wind crowded out nearly every other sound. Far below us, Ever, the sprawling, glittering prism that was Nem's capital city, was a whisper. My stomach lurched, my inner ears grew heavy, and I fell forward over the balcony toward the streets below. I grabbed the kitchen table and turned away from the 3-D holo vid in an attempt to manage my vertigo.

The experian that Mom had thrown over the balcony accelerated with vomitus speed, leveled, and then spiraled back to our height atop one of the spires that marked the Glean Embassy. Experian drones slightly larger than a Human hand transmitted 3-D images (everything except for smell) back to their designated holoprojector. Our experian drone provided a view of our capitol and the eighty million or so Galactics that walked, drove, and flew in Ever's ecosystem. In a blink, we were above the Embassy, soaring toward the clouds and the birds above the city.

"Sqwaaaargk!" The drone tumbled, and our view flashed from city-to-sky-to-city-to-ground-to-city-to-ground-to-sky for several moments before stabilizing. A storm of red, green, gold, and yellow feathers flashed into our view like confetti.

Well before the War was over, Humans had seeded the galaxy with what I'd affectionately labeled as bioterrorists—rats, gratcher, and spinach, oh my. The most prolific and profoundly annoying of the bioterrorists were the parrots—aka *flips*. After 1,800 years, flips had expanded throughout the Convergence and now lived, well, wherever they could possibly live. They had perfected reproducing, flying, pooping, and eating as loudly as possible. From level flight above their target, they'd "flip" into a dive and, zooming at incredible speeds, knock their prey senseless and out of the sky. Sometimes, when too intent on their target, they missed. Misses inevitably ended messily.

"Ooooookay," Mom said.

Just like that, Ever's forest of kilometer-high spires, clouds, and swarming traffic shimmered and was replaced by a grey, oval, stone conference table that could seat thirty Gleans. It was huge. Mom sat at the head of the table. Behind and above her on the wall was the Glean Unity Creed: "Peace, Love, Family, War." Empty, high-backed chairs rose like black monuments on either side of her, each emblazoned with the creed.

That last word didn't translate into Terran. It wasn't really "war"; it was more like, "aggressive defense of Peace, Love, and Family." Mom's white suit and charcoal turtleneck contrasted with her red skin, golden eyes, and jet-black hair.

"Those flips," she sighed, shaking her head while smiling at us.

"You girls would love it here," she continued, and then, more to herself, "I wanted us to have at least a weekend in Ever before school started…."

"Love to you," Dad said, breaking her reverie. He folded his four hands to his heart and then his forehead, and last, extended them toward his wife while dipping his head at the last gesture. They had been apart for only a day. Mom's scar flushed purple and her eyes flashed gold at his words.

"Love to you," she returned before following Dad's gestures.

Dad cleared his throat and, without ceremony, said, "Raystar was bubbled today. All day, in fact."

I rolled my eyes and thumped my head on the kitchen table. Fabulous start, Dad.

"I saved an Elio–," I murmured.

"What?" Mom placed her hands on the grey stone table as she leaned forward. "Which teacher?"

"No teacher. Principal Entarch," Dad said, shaking his head. "Raystar and two of her friends. The young Asrigard, in fact, saved an Elion's life, and…."

Mom flushed, her scar turning dark and angry at the mention of an Elion. I gritted my teeth. They were not *two* of my friends. Only Nonch was my friend. I winced, noting that with AI gone, I was down to one friend.

"Well, something more important happened to me," Cri interrupted.

I lifted my head and eyed her. Dad turned to her and blinked. *Nova, what was her problem?* She returned our looks with an eager head nod.

"Yeah," she said, looking at me like her competition. "I got expelled."

"WHAT?" we chorused.

"I was leaving school and I had to go to the bathroom. I came around a corner and found three older kids who had Mieant surrounded." She paused, looking to each one of us. "They were pushing him. He was pushing back."

We stared at her. Mom waved impatiently with her two lower hands for Cri to continue.

"I heard Raystar's name. The kids were shouting about Mieant's parents being 'Human lovers' or something. I didn't get involved then, uh, 'cause I really had to go. When I came out, though, the kids were hitting Mieant. He saw me. We made eye contact." She straightened. "I couldn't *not* get involved."

Mieant was a jerk. I hadn't ever thought of him as someone who needed saving.

"And then…?" Mom asked.

"Well, uh, then the fight was broken up." Cri looked down. She peered up at Mom, and then Dad. "By Jurisdictor Godwill and school security."

"Godwill!" Dad thundered. "What was he doing at school? You see, Sathra, we must make all…."

Mom silenced him with a pointed stare and thrummed her fingers on the stone table.

"What happened then?" Mom asked softly.

"Godwill took the two of us to the Principal's office. He told her that we'd been caught fighting." Cri paused. "What could I have done, Mom…Dad? It's not like the Principal would believe me over the Jurisdictor."

Dad placed a giant hand on the back of her head. "No," he said gently. Proudly. "You did fine, Cri."

"Did you talk with this Mieant-child?" Mom asked.

"Uh," Cri paused, "A bit when we were waiting outside the Principal's office. He said he was surprised I helped him. He thanked me, a lot." She looked down, smiling slightly as she remembered. Her face turned a deeper shade of red. "Yeah. He thanked me a lot."

"Curious," Mom said, pushing her chair back and staring into the clouds through the window. "The Asrigards. I could not imagine them being targets."

Behind Cri and me, my three-hundred-kilogram giganta-Dad clomped back and forth across the kitchen floor. He stopped, surveyed us, and then looked at Mom.

"Sathra, Lethians are fighting Lethians." Dad shook his head slowly. "Attacking us? Understandable. Inevitable. Antagonizing the Asrigards by attacking their son? These tactics do not make sense to me. I should make contact with them."

"Is revealing ourselves wise, darling?"

Dad stared at Mom. "Without allies, we are powerless." He hesitated. "Without knowledge, we are powerless. If we gain allies or knowledge, our tactical situation is improved…."

He let his thought trail into silence, and Mom nodded. Before I could ask what the flip they were talking about, Dad continued. "What news from your brother?"

Mom stopped thrumming and looked at her hands.

"The debate is as fresh as it was thirteen years ago. His opinion of us has not changed." She paused and sighed. "But he recognizes our commitment. Perhaps he grudgingly accepts it." She paused again and tilted her head, considering. "Or perhaps not."

"He warned me that the Convergence is mobilizing on a scale not seen since"—Mom's golden eyes took me in—"the War. New alliances are forming. Old ones are being destroyed. Raystar's guess was correct. The aid my parents sent us was eliminated." She moved a hand to her heart as she spoke. "We cannot proceed in ignorance any more. We must gain understanding."

"Mom?" Cri questioned in a small voice, looking from her image to Dad. "What are you talking about?"

Maybe Mom didn't hear her biological daughter's question. She took a deep breath and fixed her husband with an eyes-wide stare. Placing her hands evenly on the stone table, she said, "And I fear there is much more," she paused. "The Ninety-Eighth and Three Hundred and First Battle Groups are being sent to Nem.'"

Dad rocked back. "Two entire battle groups?" he whispered to nobody in particular.

Cri and I both glanced at each other. My bubbling in school, the fight with Mieant, Cri's expulsion—all these big events were washed away by the magnitude of the news. Along with my belief in coincidence.

Twelve thousand ships were coming to Nem'??

"What does your brother instruct?"

Mom inhaled. A moment later, she responded. "He has sent our current status to the Great Gathering. He believes Mother and Father will act, but only after they have weighed outcomes in the context of why we came to Nem' in the first place."

She looked at me, then at Cri, then back to Dad, and then continued. "Given the distance, any help they would send is a month away. The

Convergence fleets are two weeks from Nem'. While we have our own ship, Brother advises us to stay on Nem' and remain in Blue River."

Dad blinked, considering.

"Love, that makes no sense. Why does he think that makes sense? Staying here is not an option," he said. Then he tapped the kitchen table softly with his lower two fists. "Do we even have two weeks?"

Mom stood and smoothed her suit. "I do not believe so." Her eyes flashed gold as she made a decision. "I will return tomorrow."

"Lady Ceridian." A deep voice interrupted our conversation. The voice's source was out of the experian's viewing range. "The Heir requests your presence."

Mom looked hard at Dad, tilted her head to us, and then looked back toward the doorway—where, presumably, the attendant who was speaking to her stood. *The Heir? Of the flipping Gathering?* Dad's face collapsed from his planning look to his resignation-about-something-horrible-about-to-happen look.

Cri missed his expression. I'm neither arrogant nor trying to put her down. I am saying that my sister was frowning at her hands as she twiddled all of her thumbs (which, at least from a multitasking perspective, was a nova more impressive than I could do), and I think Mom and Dad's last words had flown over her head like a starbat.

Mom looked toward the voice and then turned her gaze back to us.

"Brother calls," she sighed as she rose, smoothing out her white suit as if preparing for battle. "Be safe. I will be there in the morning. I love you all." The holovid flickered and then was gone, leaving only the kitchen wall and silence.

Cri dropped her mouth open so wide a gratcher could have fallen asleep on her tongue. She stared at Dad.

That made Mom, the uh, Heir's sister. My parents were nobility. Nothing made sense. I needed to think, but I was too staggered by the revelation. *They had kept this from Cri and me?*

Dad pulled out a chair, placed his hands on both of our shoulders as he sat, and said, "My daughters, we need to talk."

15

"I AM ASCENDANT!" Cri yelled, bounced, and twirled around the kitchen, ruffling my hair as she spun past me. I batted her hand away and pulled my knees to my chin.

"Yes," Dad made hushing movements with all four hands as he set out food for us. "Yes."

The puzzle pieces were impossibly jumbled. My parents hadn't lied, but I sure felt my place in the family was uncertain. That they had kept a secret like this for so much of my life hinted at a much flipping larger purpose. That I'd been kept in ignorance for this long cracked the foundation of my trust in them.

"Jenna is going to be soooooo jealous," Cri said, excitedly.

"Ab-so-lute-ly. Not." Dad accentuated each syllable with a poke at the table.

Cri stopped mid-spin, rebellion in her eyes.

"No." Dad's voice was firm.

"But–," Cri said.

"NO."

I needed AI. He had huge amounts of real estate in my head and my heart. I could have talked with him about this, worked things out. I don't think we realize how much space our friends and family have until they're gone. And they can leave so quickly. I angrily rubbed my eyes with my palms.

"Daaad!" Cri whined.

"You must not tell anyone," Dad rumbled. I didn't look up, but I'd bet his eyes were flashing.

I tucked my head in between my knees and closed my eyes, trying to shut out their noise. I was dependent on everyone for safety, for information. No one was dependent on me. Two days ago the only threats I faced were the bullies at school, or the headaches from the Storm Walls, or possibly dying of boredom. I couldn't let fear make me an unthinking beast.

Because whatever I was, I had power of my own, even if I didn't know how to control it. Information was power. Tomorrow, then, I'd go to the library and do research. I grimaced. If I'd had AI with me, I could have done a lot more tonight. Add him to the list, then. I needed to get him out of the waste recycler.

"Fine," my sister huffed and plunked down in the chair next to mine at the table. Then she turned her glare to me. "Raystar's not Ascendant, is she?"

"SHUT UP!" I exploded, my chair clanking to the ground as I stood over her.

NOVA! I couldn't think with her talking about Ascendants. I couldn't keep a straight thought in my head whenever she said that word, and she must have said it a million times!

Cri frowned, but then a slow half-smile crept onto her lips as she looked up at me, returning my gaze. "Feeling left out, Twig?"

"Apologize," Dad said calmly, "to your sister."

My heart pounded against my ribcage, and I realized I'd forgotten to breathe. I let the air and angst out with a soft exhale. I looked from Dad to Cri. "Sorry," I paused. "I'm going upstairs."

I stacked bread and cheese into a napkin and walked toward the stairs, but Dad caught my arm as I passed him and gently guided me back to the table. He set the chair upright and met my gaze. I sat down.

"Please, listen, Raystar." I looked at him and he continued, nodding at me. "When we adopted you, we, the Gathering, decided that your care could only be trusted to the Ascendant line. Mom and I. Nobody on Nem' knows who we are. We did this for your safety."

"My safety," I said, blankly.

"Yes. Your genetic makeup is…" he paused, considering his words, "a threat to the Convergence. And perhaps more." He sighed and waved vaguely at the kitchen table for me to sit, as if giving up on some internal struggle. "We are all in danger. You both must understand."

"I'm Ascendant, and now Raystar gets all the attention," Cri muttered. Dad looked at her under lidded eyes.

"In order to understand Raystar's status, context is needed. Some you may know."

"Ppppppplllllllllfffffff!" Cri rolled her head backward. "History? Seriously, Dad?"

"Cri, shut up, I swear I'll…."

"Enough," Dad huffed. "Now is the time for understanding."

He rose to begin the lesson. "Humans are confusingly, creatively, brightly alive. Your free will and concept of self-determination terrifies the Lethians. They have led the Convergence for millennia, and we all have grown accustomed to accepting their rule. But they were unprepared for Humanity. When the Convergence came across the Humans 1,800 years ago, completely predictable demands were made by the thousand-world-strong Convergence to your newly discovered race—demands that had been made and met countless times before.

"Join, or be conquered. Given how small Earth's influence appeared to be, the Humans' response was…unexpected.

"Human space was comprised of loose associations and trade agreements, but under the Convergence threat, alliances and treaties became laws, political structures became rules, and the Terran Republic was born. Your kind's resistance inspired the Gleans, Elions, Charians, and Machines to join the Republic as allies. Each species was unhappy with the Convergence in its own way. With these new allies, the Humans' seat of power converged on the remarkably beautiful planet, Earth, in the Sol System. Terra.

"And so, Humanity turned its creativity and technical prowess, to...war." Dad paused and looked at me seriously.

He continued, "If the Lethians were terrified of your kind's ideas, Humanity waging war was an entirely different level of fear. Had they studied your history, they would have seen a species with the will for genocide. They would have seen a species that NEEDED an adversary, that needed a unifying challenge to avoid its own self-destruction.

"The Lethian–Human conflict became a fight that Galactics wished had never started. Upstart Humans mobilized; gathered Gleans, Chars, and Machines as core allies; and waged WAR. Humans are devious...and craxy.

"Lethia, thinking they could cow the new Republic into submission, destroyed seven Terran worlds. They were nuked in cold blood—their surfaces incinerated—and billions of Humans and Galactics alike vanished that day.

"On that day, 'NEMESIS' appeared on every visual display across the Convergence that was wired to the Galactic Net. Overnight, trillions of Galactics became students of your ancient tongue, Latin. The fact that Humanity had the ability to distribute the message everywhere, and invade every Galactic home—even the bank accounts—with that message was terrifying.

"And then Humans introduced planet-sized, Apocalypse-class battle platforms. Planetships. These massive battle stations rode Lagrange pathways into Lethian systems. Using a mass conveyer to destabilize each system's primary star, thus triggering a nova, entire star systems flashed into nothingness.

"Humans seeded known space with their mysterious nanotechnology. The nannites destroyed existing machines or transformed them into weapons for the Humans. Imagine our lev-sled suddenly activating and attacking us. Nothing could be trusted. Furthermore, Humanity keyed control of its technology to Human DNA. The result was that only Humans could control Human tech, whether it was Human-made or converted."

Dad looked at me. "Humans, like you...." He paused and then continued, "To see your kind so small and comparatively weak, turn so incredibly deadly, was a lesson to foes and allies alike."

I gulped. Cri raised her head and looked between Dad and me.

"But in the end, those combined forces were overwhelmed by the thousands of years of fully developed production capabilities of the Convergence. Our superior tactics and technology were fought to a standstill by sheer numbers.

"In the final century of the war, the Humans surprised the Convergence yet again. The Terran Republic's leaders approached their allies with a plan that, in typical Human fashion, didn't make sense. Humans would relinquish their worlds, destroy their fleets, and join the Convergence—only if the Glean, Charian, and Machine spheres of influence were integrated as is. The Convergence could rule, but Terran allies were to suffer no consequences.

"Historians believe that the Terrans realized the ridiculous futility of going against the united power of the Convergence. The Surrender was accepted, and the Terran Republic fleets stood down. Two planet-busting core imploders were placed on Terra's north and south poles to ensure good behavior. As the story goes, the ink on the Surrender Agreement had only just dried when the ruling Lethian High Commander, with the sanction of the Lethian Empress, detonated the bombs.

"But the remaining Terrans kept their promise. Lethia could not completely eradicate Humanity for fear of reigniting the war—this time, with its own allies. Because who indeed can trust a double-crosser to lead?

"A century into looting Terran-Republic planets, a Recorder reported to the Convergence that the math was wrong. There were nowhere near enough Humans. Concern mushroomed to panic when further investigation revealed that the decimated planets had been abandoned. The enormous ship graveyards were husks of older-generation battle tech.

"Where had the Humans gone?"

"Dad," I said, in a small voice, "are those fleets coming to Nem' because of *me*?"

"It is not unreasonable to believe you are tied to this," he said, gently placing a giant hand on my back. "But I think not. One battle group is massive overkill. Two suggests some other objective."

Her thoughts of nobility replaced by a frown, Cri stared at me, "I don't get it, Dad. Why is she even *with us*?"

I sucked in my breath. However rude and jerkish Cri was being, I wanted to know the exact same thing.

Dad gathered us to his chest. He wrapped his arms around us and patted our backs comfortingly. "Cri. Raystar is your sister. *Why* we are together is less important than the fact that we *are* together. Mom and I should have told you both sooner. We should have."

"But why, Dad?" Cri persisted. "Why are we here? Why is she with us?"

"Humanity's old allies—the Gleans, the Charians, the Machines—recognized the power in the Human technology, and Lethia's desire for that power. We take it upon ourselves to shelter key Humans that have the potential to manifest the control gene. We hide them out of the reach of Lethia.

"Over the last several decades, across known space, Human tech has been reactivating—though it was once thought of as eradicated, or at least nonfunctional. The Convergence is finding that Humanity's ghost is alive and doing…something. Mining factories, constructed by self-replicating nanotech, are churning out raw materials. Random clusters of nannites, disguised as rocks, or toys, or almost anything, suddenly become explosive, or take over, say, the controls of a ship…." He let the thought hang there.

I thought about what Nonch had said about his Broodmother. That the Human machines were waking up. I needed to talk to Nonch.

Dad spoke again. "The technology only responds to Humans with the control gene. Raystar has remarkably undiluted genetic code. She CANNOT fall into the wrong hands. Your mother and I volunteered to hide her."

Cri looked at him like he'd grown a third eye. "But what about me?"

Two giant hands caressed her face. My dad's gentleness seemed impossible, given his size. "We thought this world could be home. For you. For us. Away from the Gathering's demands and intrigue.

"Sathra's Brother," he paused, scowling, "will be the next leader of the Gathering. With that obligation removed, we could raise a family, you two girls could have a normal childhood, and then when you were both older...."

I felt his hand stop patting my back. Instead, he poked at the base of my neck, where AI's necklace usually hung.

"Raystar?" he said. He pulled back so he could look into my eyes. There was concern on his face. "Where is AI?"

16

Dad listened with a veneer of calm. It was an illusion. His eyes blazed; there was no mistaking his anger and disbelief.

"You flushed him?" Cri squealed. "NOVA!" She stood to high-five me but then sat back down quickly after a sunbeam-hot glare from Dad.

I looked at her helplessly. The shame of public discovery was crushing. I had intended to find him, just not like this.

"Sit. As much as I do not like that creature, you have no idea what you have done," he said, pointing to us, then at our chairs. "Wait." He rose and left the kitchen. We looked at each other, and Cri made a move to rise. He poked his head and an arm in again, eyes blazing, and pointed at each of us, "Stay!" And then he left the kitchen again.

Cri leaned over to me, "That 'ingot' totally deserved it, Ray! Totally a starred move! You may not suck so bad, Sis'!"

I leaned away and frowned at her, raising my eyebrows. Any other day, I would have been happy to have her compliments. Weren't two civilization-crushing fleets headed our way? Hadn't Dad just told us that Lethia was collecting purple Humans?

Could she *be* that obtuse?

I watched her call up her attendant and message her friends, despite Dad's express orders NOT to tell anyone. I blinked. She *could* be that oblivious. As Dad stomped back into the room, her virtual screen vanished and she sat up straight, blinking innocently. He held scanners and two neon-green environmental suits. One suit had two arms—the other, four. They were both kid sized.

We were going to go hunting for AI. In the waste recycler. We trudged after Dad in silence, following him downstairs into our large, orderly basement. Concrete floors dry and clean of dust were lit by cold light strips that vanished down multiple hallways. The basement was huge, with neatly stacked pallets and occasional sealed doors guarded by biometric scanners that came alive with red lights as you approached.

Dad marched us to a yellow-and-red diagonally striped door marked "BIOHAZARD."

I gulped.

He unsealed the door. In an instant, my knees went weak and I retched. Our helmets' air scrubbers didn't protect us from the stench that leapt like an escaping prisoner out of our waste recycler. Cri gagged beside me and gave me the stink eye, just to make sure I understood this was my fault.

I knew it was my fault.

We waded into the squishy content of that dark, square room, tripping down to our hands and knees on submerged pipes. We tried in vain to clear our faceplates but only succeeded in smearing grey-brown muck over our field of vision.

But I gulped down my gag reflex and searched with all my heart.

AI was not there.

17

Fresh morning air stroked my cheeks with cool fingers and almost removed the memory of the waste recycler's stink. I puffed strands of purple hair from my eyes and shuffled by Chunks on my way to my dart. Chunks *whuffled* a gigantic sneeze that blew dirt into the air as I approached. He shook his mountainous, bristly head, wriggled his nose in my direction, and eyed me suspiciously. *Everyone's a critic.*

I tossed my extra 'natch sandwich through the gratcher pen's force bars. His giant pig eyes followed it as it landed, tumbled, and unraveled at his feet. He dipped his enormous head, and the sandwich vanished with a swipe of his tongue. He *humphed* and walked back to his herd.

Friends were in short supply.

Banefire marched upward, dominating nearly a third of the horizon with its furious red aura. Green 'natch fields waved in the breeze. Mom would be back from Ever, our capital city, by the end of the day, and I'd feel a lot better with all four of us together. Cri was sleeping in. I shook my head. I actually didn't mind her making the most of being expelled. Nova, I would.

Dad was scheduled to go into Blue River to meet with the Jurisdictor later in the morning. The idea was to file a complaint about the NPD's unlawful entrance into a Glean's government-protected property. The NPD would have to respond to it, and thanks to the resulting raging paperwork battle, we'd get more time to figure out our next steps.

Grownups had forms and lists and lines for everything, so it seemed like a good plan. I swallowed, rubbed the sweat off my palms, and fired up my dart's engine. The two-seat air cycle hummed to life. Blue and red displays blinked on and the silvery environmental shield shimmered into existence around me. My helmet was snug and comforting. I looked around at the compound, inhaled, and lifted up toward the blue sky.

I spared a glance toward the Mesas. Smoke curled lazily up from the crash site, now nearly invisible against the dark, grey clouds that had begun to concentrate around the tops of the flat mountains. The Storm Wall was building.

Thousands of flips wheeled low over the 'natch fields. They were yellow, red, purple, blue, and green. The flock moved as a two-kilometer-wide organism of color. Suddenly, those lower to the field parted like waves splashing against a rock. The rest of the flock followed suit and split in two. I squinted to see what had alarmed them. In the dense, thick greenery, large, dark shapes moved, occasionally flicking hairy, spidery legs in the air toward the flips.

Leggers.

That was crazy. They hardly ever came out during the day. I shivered and checked my dart's battery. I leaned down, accelerating. My flight to school was fast and lonely and scary.

I landed on the VCP, powered down the dart, and locked its systems. *AI would have done that automatically.* Alone, I walked to the schoolyard.

The roar of kids washed over me. My friends were at their usual place next to a tall jungle gym across the field. Nonch bobbed and weaved his six arm claws as he spoke to Jenna. I wondered, as I trudged toward them, what could have him so animated? Crynits' natural weaponry and armor made others nervous, so they tried not to get too excited in public.

"Raystar!"

I turned and saw Mieant running toward me. He was dressed in all black with a shoulder-length grey cape, presumably to ward off the morning chill. At the speed he was running, it flared behind him, looking like the wings of some giant aerial beast.

Great. Being chased, caught, and presumably pummeled by the most fashionable, popular kid first thing in the morning was low on my to-do list. I launched myself toward my friends.

We were covering serious ground by the time he caught me. I hadn't ever run *this* fast before. His long hand nudged my shoulder, and I stumbled and faced him in a low fighting stance. "Mieant!" I panted. "What?"

"Raystar," he wheezed, one hand on his knees and the other held palm open toward me as he lowered his head for breath. His long, black hair curtained around his grey face. "Raystar, I," he gasped, breathing hard, tucking strands behind his ears so we could see each other. "I wanted to thank you. Your sister, actually."

It was a trick. I blinked and straightened slightly from my crouch. As he stood to his full height, I saw that the shadows on his face were bruises.

"She pulled them off me." He straightened his cape unconsciously and looked down at me, still breathing hard.

"She's expelled because of you."

"I know. I know," he said, moving his hands in a calming gesture, his chest heaving as he sucked in air. "I've told my parents what happened, and they are coming to school to talk with Entarch about the incident. To speak on your sister's behalf."

I blinked at him.

"I owe her," he said. "I do not like you, Human. But you are different from what I thought." He leaned in; I didn't pull back.

In a low, urgent voice, he said, "Have care, Raystar. Something is happening. My parents are worried. I will inform you of anything I learn. Oh," he paused, looking at me almost shyly. "Please say thank you to your sister. Um."

And he walked away. I blinked again.

"Pllllthhhssssssppbbbbb!" I expelled the breath I'd been holding. I bent over, hands on my hips, and allowed myself to relax for a flipping, hyperventilated second—when suddenly, knives poked at my shoulders, hips, and calves.

"Aiiiyee!" I screamed, rolling forward to rise and spin into a fighting crouch. My hair sparked and crackled. Energy surged through me. *No no no no. I couldn't spark out!* I fought toward calm, thinking that if the day continued like this, I would blow up or grow a third arm.

"Ease, Raystar! I was surprising you. Be at ease, friend." Nonch's orange primary eyes, underlined by rows of space-black orbs, regarded me. His claw arms were spread out low, signaling no threat and his hundred feet thrummed as his close to three-meter-long, midnight-blue, armored length flowed backward from me. He cocked his head and his feathery sensor stalks brushed sparks from my clothes.

"NOVA! Flip! Auugh! Architect's gravity well!" I yelled. I stepped to him and pushed. "Shells! Don't sneak up on me like that!" I shoved him again with both hands and put my weight into it, so his hundred legs rippled to one side to keep him from falling over.

"*Never* sneak up on me like that!" I punched him, learning the hard way that the Human fist was not the weapon of choice against impenetrable Crynit chitin.

Nonch weaved nonetheless, startled at my intensity. Jenna laughed, but then tilted her head to one side and considered me as I waved my bruised fist in the air and scowled at the pair of them.

"Was that…did your hair just spark?" she asked, leaning in for a closer inspection.

I smoothed down my hair. "No!" I said.

Static electricity hissed and popped. Twice. Jenna raised an eyebrow.

"Well, you should wipe your nose, or go see the nurse. Your blood is disgusting," she said, making a face. I rubbed my nose with my sleeve, and she grimaced. "We saw Mieant chasing you. You two were flying. I didn't know Humans could run that fast!" Jenna continued. The multicolored beads woven into her green hair clinked and flashed the sun.

"What did he say? He looked friendly. Wait," her eyes got huge, "you're not...you have a crush on him! I knew it! Raystar's craxy in love! You've been pretending to hate him. You even darkened your hair color. Cra-cra-Ray-Ray! I bet you flushed your synth because your dad said you couldn't see Mieant. Hey...Ow!"

Nonch bapped her on the head with a sensor stalk. "Do not be low intelligence, Jenna. Of course Raystar does not want to mate with Mieant. I am correct in this, yes? Raystar?"

"I...ugh," I pulled my hair and sucked in a deep breath. Insanity. "You know Cri's been expelled?"

"She told me everything," Jenna huffed. Nonch raised both sensor-stalks and scuttled around so he faced me.

"Some older kids attacked Mieant and she pulled them off him. Mieant wanted me to thank her." I said, not telling her quite everything.

Nonch rolled back a meter and clacked his armor. Jenna squinted at me and shook her head. "It doesn't make sense."

"Look at him in class. His face is bruised." I frowned. "And you know Cri's at home."

Nonch clacked his armor again, nodding. "This does not make logic. Lethians should be attacking Raystar, not Mieant. That is curious. Especially given his family." *Yeah. Attack me! Of course, that made sense.*

Jenna frowned at Nonch. "I told you..."

"You are not the master of me, Jenna." He turned his full, weaponized, navy blue and orange head to her, flaring his sensor stalks over her to make his "not-my-boss" point. "You requested I remain quiet on this topic. However, I cannot. Broodmother asks me to stay away from Raystar, and I will not." He looked at me and reached out to touch me on the shoulder with a blade claw. "I cannot be away from my friend. And I must share what I know. The time of truth and revelation is approaching. The Human machines are waking."

Why would Jenna not want him to talk to me? "Nonch, about that...," I started.

Jenna giggled nervously, interrupting each of us with a hand to our respective shoulder-ish spots. "You guys need a life. Human machines? No offense, but that was a bajillion years ago. Guard attacks? C'mon, it's day two of school. Can we talk about something different? Like Mieant and Raystar?" She made a kissing noise.

Nonch looked at her like she was a bug before turning back to me.

"Truth and revelation?" I asked. "Nonch, what in the Architect's nova does that mean?" I rested my hands on my hips.

"Broodmother says it is like the old times, but not. Lethians will send ships to destroy the machines, and the Humans controlling the machines. It is as the Lethians have always done. But THIS time will not be as it has always been." He looked at me.

"Nonch," I waved toward the kids on the playground and leaned in, letting my frustration come out. "It may not be apparent, but I'm the only flipping Human around here!"

"Anger, friend Raystar. If I was intent on ensuring your anger with me, I would have chosen different tactics than information sharing."

I ran my hand through my hair and took a deep breath. Purple strands flowed through my Human, brown, kid fingers. "Shells, I'm sorry for losing it. For pushing you. Listen, Mieant mentioned his parents are coming to talk to Principal Entarch. He said something strange was happening. I should be careful. And Nonch, we need to talk about this machine thing your Broodmother keeps referring to." I wondered if Nonch's Broodmother was aware of the two battle groups on their way to Nem'.

Jenna interrupted us. "What we need to do is sit together at lunch today. I'll make sure Mieant is at our table." She turned to go, waving two hands randomly in the air. "And you guys seriously need to talk about something else."

Nonch and I watched her walk away. She disappeared into the crowd, the sound of her beads quickly fading into the roar of the kids. We turned toward each other.

"Nonch, let's go to the library before lunch. We can talk there. I could use some help researching information about," I gestured to the air with both hands, "everything."

The deep chime signaled the start of the school day and set off the mad rush through the school's military-sized doors. The crowd moved around us, and we were pulled apart.

I looked at him as his figure retreated. "If you want to help me, that is."

"You should be certain of me, Raystar. Let us meet. I will share information that I believe is important. Between then and now, Raystar, have care, take care," he said, bobbing his head. The current of kids swept around us, and he turned and thrummed away.

Careful sounded good. Information sounded better.

18

Principal Entarch wasn't in history class. Neither was Alar. Nurse Pheelios was our sub.

She stalked across the platform at the front of the class, much like Entarch had. Except, well, she floated. And she was round. And black. And had whip-like arms.

Pheelios was a Sylltha. If Gleans were the giant, high-gravity citizens, Syllthans were their wispy, low-gravity opposites. Originating from gas giants, they were lumpy, soft, vaporous intellects. While they had evolved sentience, they hadn't become spacefaring until they were discovered by the Convergence—much like the Elions hadn't been truly spacefaring until they'd met the Humans.

Syllthans couldn't manipulate heavy metals so they couldn't build spacecraft. Instead, they bartered the mining rights of their gas giants in exchange for environmental suits and interstellar passage. Syllthans needed Galactics to build suits so they could manipulate the world around them, or even just to leave their planet and exist on other worlds. That evolutionary dependency made them perpetually mean. I wondered, *Does being independent make you nicer?*

Given my developing awareness of the galaxy's obvious and emerging threats pointed at ME, I could relate.

But my sole experience with Syllthans was Nurse Pheelios. Trips to her office, for everything from a headache to a scrape, were filled with so much pain that I would usually forget the reason I had gone to her office.

Syllthan environmental suits were round and black and had tentacle appendages that could hold, tow, grapple, slice, or defend. Behind her suit's round, clear, metal view surface was the darkly colorful, swirling essence of our nurse. She pivoted in the air to face us.

"Sweet children. Principal Entarch is focused elsewhere. I am proud to be your teacher today. I know each of you intimately, as I have cared for your bodies. And now I get to touch your minds." *Yuck. Just, yuck.* "My people, we come from gas giants, where matter and thought are not so far apart in weight. With me, you can let go of your mass. Together, we will free ourselves from gravity and nurture our thoughts. I am honored to be your very personal guide on this journey."

I shivered and spared a glance to Alar's empty desk. Day two, and we'd already lost a student. I hoped he was OK. He was too fluffy and cute not to be OK.

Frowning, I shifted my gaze to Mieant. He sat, back straight, and stared impassively at Nurse Pheelios. His bruises darkened his face like a bad makeup job.

"I understand from our honored principal that you spent yesterday's class talking about our purposeful enemies. Like gas eludes gravity's grip, let us turn OUR enlightenment to our borders, and the outward expansion of our dearest, most beloved Convergence. Let us contemplate our immediate future, and our accidental enemies."

As she said this, a 3-D star map flared to life behind her, rising from the floor to the ceiling and spanning the length of the platform. The Milky Way rotated slowly, a giant starfish with gracefully curved arms. Green lights twinkled toward the Core, marking the Convergence. Our thirteen hundred lights in the darkness were an uneven sphere toward the middle of one of the Galaxy's arms. A strand of lights extending from the sphere toward the far end of the arm presumably represented the Terran Republic's inward expansion, and subsequent absorption, into the Galactic society. Red dots created an edge along the most Coreward edge of the Convergence. Pheelios directed the map to zoom in, and the line blurred into a jagged blur of green and red systems.

"Before we begin, I want to confirm that you, brilliant children, have received your assignment for the end of the week. I am challenging you to originate a model of governance that can assimilate a wide variety of races into a single system. Your minds, your different types of lovely bodies, the smells of your cultures, how you use humor, how you wield anger—I want you to apply yourself to understanding how each of these variables can be integrated into a single, unified system. I shall ensure that you have the proper framework to complete this inquiry. Do you understand the timeline, lovely, sweet students?"

The silence was broken only by the rustling of clothes as some kids, including myself, shivered. Ick. Dozens of eyes, sensor stalks, and other sensory organs stared back at her blankly.

"Oh, class. Tender children. Silence will not do. Indicate 'Yes' or 'No,' and your desk synth will record your answers."

Like a choreographed drum roll, a classroom of claws, spikes, hands, tentacles, and appendages thumped their desk synths in response.

"Wonderful," she said in the silence that followed. "I shall proceed. As you know, Humans were the last challenge the Convergence crushed. We destroyed their arrogance, their presumption, the thought that their monkey lifestyle could ever...." *Right.* This story, I'd heard a million times, and it didn't seem nearly as true as it did two days ago. I couldn't let myself be distracted. I needed a plan.

Because, you know, there were TWELVE THOUSAND ships coming to Nem? That was nearly ten million in crew, plus who knows how many marines, to presumably occupy my planet. *WHY?* There was so much I didn't know. *Nova.* I didn't even know what I didn't even know.

I was meeting Nonch at the library next period. There had to be news that would shed light on who or what the threat was. I mean, what if it wasn't me, but something particular to Nem? That thing that attacked me, for instance? Maybe IT-ME was the reason two battle groups were in transit?

"Raystar?" I blinked upon hearing Nurse Pheelios say my name. "Lovely Human, are you paying attention?"

"I...," I looked wide-eyed at Nurse Pheelios, who had turned to me some moments before. Students giggled. *What had she been talking about?*

"I am pleased, soft child, at your attempt for attention. Tell me of the Rass, little one. How are they different from what the Human threat had been? Educate us with your insight, my delicate Human."

I wriggled at her ick and remained silent. I had no flipping idea what the nova she was talking about.

Mieant's desk lit up green, indicating he had an answer. Pheelios pivoted to him. "Mieant? Will you contribute to our exploration?"

"With your permission, I am sure my answer contributes more to our group's knowledge than," he paused for effect, "the Human's." Students tittered.

"Of course, young Asrigard. It is expected that you would lead this class in that knowledge." He nodded like an arrogant jerk at the compliment. Then the façade vanished, and he winked at me. I blinked.

Since when was I on the same team as the coolest kid in school?

"We encountered the Rass nearly one hundred years ago," he started. "Unlike the Humans, they made no attempt at diplomacy. They simply destroyed our scouts and initial diplomatic missions. From a military perspective, they have proven more than equal to the Convergence in technology and capability. Reports suggest they have greater numbers than we do, and we do not know the extent of their sphere of control. All contact has ended violently."

"Your mind, Mieant, is the dessert I should not eat before dinner. Little Human, sweet Raystar, will you add to the Asrigard's dish, or leave him alone for us to consume his thoughts?"

She was the worst substitute teacher in the world.

I stared at her blankly, not knowing how to respond. She continued, "No? Can anyone tell me about Rass bodies...? Their physiology? Let me expand your understanding about their vessels in contrast with your own delicious bodies." Her creepiness resumed, reciting the same old gratcher excrement of insults about Humans I'd heard a million meters before. *Original, she was not.*

My sleepy overcame her creepy. I snapped my head up somewhere during Pheelios's lecture to wipe drool from my mouth and rub the crick out of my neck.

I glanced over at Mieant. What he'd done was kind. Was he setting me up for something? His bruises argued against it. I wished that AI was there. I moved my jaw from side to side, wondering how long I'd been asleep, and tapped my desk's console to message Nonch:

>still meeting @ library 4 recess?<

Within a second, I received my answer and turned my attention back to Nurse Pheelios. Having concluded the first part of the lesson, the nurse was wrapping things up. Her cloudy essence swirled behind her suit's faceplate.

"You have your assignment, children. Since there are no questions, we shall adjourn after a brief word from our special and esteemed guest, Jurisdictor Godwill, head of Nem's Planetary Defense force."

On cue, the same squad of four NPD officers that had invaded our house, led by Godwill, marched into the room, down the stairs, and up on to the platform. I froze while my heart pounded against my ribcage. Without pause or hesitation, Godwill nodded to the nurse and turned to face us.

Fear made it impossible to move anything else except my eyeballs. I was seated way too flipping nova close to the front of the classroom.

"Students. I'm sure your gossip webs have made you aware of the vicious attacks in your school." He paused. His eyes scanned the class, touching each of us, but not making direct contact. "Be assured that we are questioning students who have either witnessed or been involved in the incidents. You will receive red or green notifications on your synth. With a green notification, you are free to leave once school is finished. Otherwise, you must report to Principal Entarch's office."

Mieant's desk lit up with a question. "Will our parents be contacted if we have a red notification?" he asked.

Godwill flowed three steps forward, off the platform, and through the first set of desk rows to stop precisely between Mieant and me. The skin around his mouth was pulled tight in a half-grimace; his eyes bulged large from his skull as he studied us speculatively.

"Mieant Covent Asrigard, isn't it? I've been told your parents are SO very important," Godwill gritted his teeth as he spoke. His spit flecked onto Mieant, my bully-turned-ally.

Mieant swallowed.

Godwill grabbed Mieant's face and pulled him out of his desk. "The question is, *are you*?" He shoved Mieant back into his chair, and the class gasped. Mieant did nothing, just looked down.

Godwill surveyed the class. "Is who your parents are the thing that makes you important, Asrigard? I am the law on this planet, child. Your parents have no power here. I will have them, I will have you. I will have whatever I want, whenever I want it." He leaned into Mieant's face, almost kissing his cheek with his pursed-lipped anger. Mieant squinted away, waiting for the touch.

His skeletal, Lethian, cold-grey face whispered into the teen's cold-grey face. "If you receive a red notification, I expect compliance."

Godwill rose, discarded Mieant, and turned his gaze to me.

"You…," he said softly. Leaning over slightly, he reached out with a cupped hand toward my face. Paralyzed, I didn't move. I couldn't move. I wanted to *RUN. TO SCREAM.*

Galactics were so used to their size that they assumed everyone was as big as they were—and often didn't realize that I was much, much smaller than them. I braced myself for pain. His fingers traced a warm, dry path from my forehead to my cheek and then down my neck to my collarbone. His fingers were cool and smooth as they slipped a fingernail's length under my shirt. I wriggled away, so his fingers lay on the muscle between my shoulders and neck.

"Little Human female, this pleasure is once again mine." He made a show of thinking about his next words, even managing to purse his lips. "Your adoptive parents are Ascendants. Yet you are not of the Ceridian bloodline. "

The class gasped again as his hand traced my flushed profile. "Raystar…of Earth. No," he paused, taking a moment to consider his next words. "Terra. Raystar of Terra. THAT is a good name."

He leaned in close, so only I could hear. His breath smelled slightly of musty caramel. "Raystar of Terra, I trust you are staying out of trouble. But should you receive a red notification, I am sure we will work it out."

He remained that way a moment longer, until, not unlike a hunter that sensed its prey nearby in the 'natch, he stood and looked to the door. Alert and intent, he flowed out of the classroom, his security team close behind.

I shivered. All eyes in the class were on me. Spiders tingled up my spine, and my heart was slamming against my rib cage. I could still feel fingers sliding against my skin. I dropped my gaze, listening to the *whump-whump, whump-whump* of my fear.

The end-of-class chime shattered the classroom's shocked silence. Students filed out with barely a whisper. I was rushing to the classroom's threshold when a cool metallic tentacle wrapped around my bicep and spun me around with enough force to make me wince.

"Raystar? Sweet Human, you have a red notice. Do not leave the school grounds," Pheelios said, her voice filled with honey.

Since AI wasn't with me, the school systems placed my notifications on whichever synth I was registered to at the time. I could see that one of the vid-screens at my desk was glowing red. I'd never thought to check my desk synth for the notification.

I nodded to the blackness behind the Nurse's faceplate. She released me.

Right. I rubbed where she'd gripped me, sure there was going to be a bruise.

Nova and gravity wells. No way was I flipping staying after school a minute longer than I could draw in a life-giving breath.

19

The entrance to the library was inside the school, a bit past the main doors. Its enormous entryway descended two levels. The stairs were as wide as a terraced hillside sinking into a dark canyon's depths. Rows of thick, grey columns stretched up to meet the vaulted ceiling. As one moved further in and down, darkness pooled above in the unlit ceiling as light glowed up from the base of the pillars. When we were younger, Cri and I would play hide-and-seek around the column bases, endlessly entertained by the giant shadows we cast in all directions.

Our library networked to other libraries across the Convergence's 1,300 worlds. Two days ago, I would have said all of civilization's knowledge was available here. Even given my new perspective, thinking about the lifetimes of information accessible in this maze of aisles and workstations made me wish I could live long enough to read, see, and experience it all.

The Galactic net, or GalNet, accessed everything! There were actors, actresses, sports, tragedies, humor…things happening out there that I would never hear about or see. THIS knowledge sat, accessible to little me, right here. For free. For nothing. My imagination was my guide, and the Universe knew I had so many questions.

My one, tiny existence, here, now.

There were trillions of lifetimes of people and places, out THERE.

I took a long, deep breath of the familiar, slightly chemical school air and descended into the forest of columns.

Metallic-grey walls reached down from the ceiling and met dark, ghost-grey carpeting. Blood-red sails, I guessed three meters wide at their bases and six meters long to their tips, hung down from the ceiling's blackness at two-meter intervals. Between the columns and the sails, the library's cathedral effect stretched off into the distance.

The sails were sound dampeners. Two people could speak a meter away from you in almost total privacy. Clusters of tables were surrounded by high-backed chairs that morphed to your body type, and the sails enabled study teams to work together at the tables without disturbing the library's other patrons. Equipment was stacked neatly by each cluster. There were control headbands, low-end synths for research projects, and actual writing tablets, too.

Synths?

I paused by the pile of school-owned synthetic attendants. Not all personal synths were compatible with the school's computers. Some didn't have enough memory or some other issue, so the school maintained these spares to augment our studies. If it weren't for the locators built into each device, I would have taken one to compensate for the loss of AI.

I found Nonch curled into a ball in front of a vid-screen. The workstation cluster he'd chosen was a bit away from a light column. The shadows he cast were dark, tall, and exaggerated against the shelves around us. Soft blue light reflected on his dark, armored form and lit his orange eyes in iridescent shimmers. His six arms were swiping, poking, and scrolling with blinding speed. Without pausing, he turned his head to me and nodded. Crynits were the elite marines of the Convergence Navy; given this impressive display of multitasking, it was apparent why. But despite how sharp and knifey my friend was, I couldn't imagine him harming any sentient.

"Showoff," I said, approaching. He tilted his head, uncurled, and, with his hindmost legs, activated *another* vid-screen. I laughed and sat down next to him. He re-curled and faced me. "Shells, thanks for helping me." I paused to consider for a moment. "Why *are* you helping me? You don't even know what I need help with!"

He stopped his search. "My people have been on Nem' since the end of the war. We saw Humans leave. Now, *things*—machines, dormant for thousands of years—are waking up.

"In contrast with the stories we have been told and the Recorded History, I have only seen honesty and kindness from you. You are in need. I cannot believe that the 'awakening' and your troubles are unrelated, Raystar."

His empathy released waves of emotion. The last few days' events had blown up, one by one, each core belief I'd had about security, family, the sanity of the universe.

His simple act of compassion meant the world to me, and my chest threatened to burst. Nonch reached a sensor stalk to my face. His touch felt like a feather duster as he gently traced the wet line down my cheek. Which I promptly wiped away with the back of my sleeve.

"Sodium."

"It's a tear," I sniffed.

"Perhaps," he said, touching the moisture with his hand claw. I suspected he sensed it on a chemical level and wondered what he was getting from my tear. "Or maybe it is called life."

"Pfffft!" I huffed, turning to the vid-screens lest I leak any more. I told him about the battle in the field with IT-ME, Godwill's home invasion, and flushing AI. And Alar.

"Your experiences are," he paused, "varied." I snorted and started researching Nem's history. There had to be something about the Mesas I could use. "My experiences are not so diverse," he continued.

I stopped and peered at him, sensing something different. His face was colored by the blue-shadow of screen lights. "Uh."

"You are aware that Crynits are feared?" He registered my raised eyebrow and encouraging nod to continue. "Are we only weapons? Humans have created things, protected their allies. Lethians have united and ruled. Gleans have loved and nurtured. Each race is known positively. Not us. No, Crynits are destroyers. Not known for intelligence. We are destroyers, not creators."

"Hey," I said, pulling his blade arm toward me. "What's going on?"

"I do not like being a Crynit."

I froze and looked into his giant orange eyes. After a moment, he continued. "I feel we could be more; we could be lights and leaders, not the fear in the darkness. "

Nonch met my dropped jaw with an impassive face. The smell of fresh rain expanded around us. It was the memory of sunshine on a stormy day, when the fun is nowhere to be had. He saw me breathe in and nodded.

"Nonch, you are *my* light in the darkness. I'm sorry you feel this way. I have only seen you as strength and inspiration."

"I have sodium too."

"Oh, Nonch." I reached out to hug my friend, trying to find an un-armed part so he could get the best part of a hug—the friendly pressure. The scent of rain grew sharper, and after a moment he pulled me off him. "But I don't understand why you feel this way? Your people are vibrant. Important."

"We dig. We hunt. Broodmother says it is how we have stayed safe since integrating into the Convergence millennia ago."

I blinked. How unexpected, coming from a Crynit. *Safe from what?*

"I have a request of you, Raystar. Please, tell no one my thoughts." I nodded solemnly.

"Telling no one. That is not the favor I ask," he added, studying me. "When the time comes, I will ask my favor of you. Will you do your best to grant my request?"

I swallowed. Open-ended favor granting invited a lot into my future. "If I'm able," I said in a tiny voice, concerned about my promise and ability to follow through on my commitment. "I will, Nonch."

My friend's segmented body lowered, visibly relaxed with grati-tude.

"Thank you, friend! When the time is right, Raystar, I will ask. Prior to your arrival in the Library, I started a general search on 'Hu-mans.'" An arm blade swiped at two images. The floating pages con-densed into balls of pale blue light. He flicked the first one toward me. The headline hovered, slightly transparent, above the light-ball. It read, "Foundationalist Movement Pushes for Full Integration of Humans into Weapon Reclamation Project."

I grabbed it and, with a flick, cast the image in front of me. I snuck a glance back at my armored friend. It had never occurred to me to wonder what life was like back at his hive. I was full of questions. *Did they play? Have friends? What* did *Crynits do after school for fun? Did I know anything about anyone around me? Auuugh!!*

This favor, it was important to him. Which meant, of course, that it was probably impossibly hard. *Yay.* As much my own chaos was screaming for my mental attention, I wasn't going to leave him hanging. I'd already flushed AI out of my life.

Let yet another friend down? I would not do that.

I squeezed his sword arm, sucked in a breath as I committed myself to my promise, and turned back to the news images. Ships, people, places I'd never seen blurred across my screen as I sifted through the data Nonch had collected.

The Foundationalist Movement came up again and again, in increasingly disturbing ways. There were more videos than I had time to go through from hundreds of worlds where there were Human populations. They showed Humans—millions of "us"—being lined up and loaded onto titanic transports. My people all had purple hair, but I didn't see any with hair as loud or vibrant as mine. Were my ancestors such idiots that they had all their hopes colored a recognizable purple? Maybe it was simply the age of the vids—somehow time had faded the color? It was a hopeful yet impossible thought. One headline from fourteen years ago caught my attention: "Foundationalist Movement Announces Major Breakthrough in the Human Technology Reclamation Project!"

The Convergence was, or perhaps the Lethians were, fixated on the concept of getting access to Human tech. I frowned as I read further, correlating the information there with what Mom, Dad, and AI had told me over the past day. The concept was this: Through extraction of Human DNA, a key could be created that would allow the Convergence to make use of the ancient Human tech that was nearly everywhere and learn what my ancestors knew. It wasn't clear why we needed to be collected though. The Humans in the vids looked panicked. I read on.

A more recent headline read, "Previously Unknown Human Base in the Elios System Discovered!" My questions were having whole question families. The baby questions were then growing up and raising more questions.

Human technology was clearly a priority for these "Foundationalists." Were the Foundationalists behind the fleets? Were these fleets coming here for me? *I* couldn't possibly be the reason. And how were the Elios involved in this?

Further into the article, I spied a youthful image of Kaleren and Freela Asrigard. They were holding hands and standing on a massive, worn bridge that arched over a bottomless, jagged-cliffed canyon. The background was foreboding: storm-grey clouds, ice-covered mountains, and lots of wind-swept snow. Behind the Asrigards, rows of Elions in battle armor, lined up in four-soldier-abreast columns, stretched back to the beginning of their half of the bridge.

Alar was cute and fluffy. Grownup Elions were huge. Not pillow-like at all. These Elions were armed, mountainous, stick-legged spiders covered in white fur. Each had eight legs, with six arm appendages covered in armor and weapons of various shapes and colors. Behind the Elions, blanketed in snow and ice, I could barely make out a time-worn installation. I squinted at the pixilated images and realized that they were Human structures!

A column of Convergence troops, at full attention, stood facing the Asrigards, the Elions, and the Human base. One figure, covered in its own combat armor, stood at the head—apparently trying to negotiate access to the Human installation. The Asrigards and the Elions were clearly blocking the way.

Wait. I started making connections. Kaleren and Freela were Co-Governors of Quadrant Four. This quadrant. They led the Integration Party movement, which favored improving Human integration into the Convergence. The Party argued that peaceful dialogue would provide more willing access to currently inaccessible Human technology; thankfully, the Integration Party controlled a majority of the government across the Convergence.

I paused. *Asrigard? Mieant's parents managed a quarter of Convergence space? Why would they be stationed here on Nem', in this great green expanse of 'natch? How in the Architect's gravity wells could I be so flipping ignorant about everyone around me?*

"Shells. Wow. Thanks!" I lifted my head from the news feeds and focused on him. "Broodmother has talked about the Awakening, the attacks on people here in Blue River. She believes somehow this is linked to Humans. How?" I took two of his blade arms in my hands.

"You."

"Yes, help me…uh. What?"

"She believes the end of the Human winter is linked to you." I looked into his eyes, waiting for him to continue. "You are the only Human on this planet. Long ago, Nem' was a key Human world."

"Yeah, so?"

"Our hive is under the city. Under Blue River. Even under this library." He poked the carpeting with his blade claws. "The planet has become noisy. Our rangers, the ones who patrol our hive, see machines, for lack of a better word. Things that WERE rocks are growing legs and move toward the Mesa Ruins. Things that were metal scrap are reforming into discs and flying off in apparently random directions. These devices move with purpose. My Queen's thought is that now that you are becoming a mature Human, something inside of you is triggering their awakening."

"These…" he paused, "*things* are attracted to Galactic material. Energy sources. Entire farm compounds are vanishing. High-end equipment—simply gone. People, too."

I thought about the controller incident. About the GNN news reports.

"I need information, Nonch." And maybe protection, I thought silently. "May I meet Broodmother?"

He faced me—black eyes underlining two giant orange orbs, mandibles, claws, all sharp edges, all pointing toward me—and became still. Without changing his gaze, he reached a blade arm out and nudged the other newsball, floating it off to one side. At his touch, it drifted through the distance toward me.

"What?"

"Read."

It was a roster of Nem's military and police command. It showed all the government employees in a tree format—where and how people were connected to their bosses, and their bosses to their bosses, and so on.

"Gee. It's an organizational chart. That's great. So what?" I shrugged, nonplussed.

He pointed to a name, listed as the head of the Nem' Planetary Defense: Jurisdictor Xzaris Alenion of Broodmother Krig. A Crynit. There was no Jurisdictor Godwill. None at all.

"Move!" I pushed him aside and expanded the news vid to full size. "Where! Where did you find this?"

"I accessed the Convergence archives instead of the local files on Nem'. Godwill does not exist."

"What of Jurisdictor Xzaris?"

"We do not know." His head dipped, and his chitin-plates rippled down the length of his body, "Broodmother knows where all of her Crynits are on Nem'. Xzaris disappeared two weeks ago. She fears the implication." His sensor stalks waved.

We looked at each other with big eyes. Well, his were always big.

"Nonch. My mom comes back from Ever tonight. I'll have more information from, uh," I thought of Mom's Brother. "…other sources. Would Broodmother help me? Us? Would she meet my parents?"

His arms spread wide and he wrapped them around me, pulling me close in a hug.

"It is a curious thing, this hugging, that you do. Broodmother is amused by this habit I have taken from you. She says we should only 'hug' when we are hunting."

He released me and uncurled from his ball. I turned my head up to look at him from where I was sitting, now suddenly below him. "Crynits have long memories. Broodmother has always been convinced that Humans, even with your scattered numbers, are dangerous. Your kind destroyed untold millions of us. My Mother feels this awakening heralds a new time of destruction."

"Shells," I whispered. "It's me. Raystar. I haven't done anything."

He put a blade arm on my shoulder. "You are my best friend, Raystar. It is a secret the Recorders do not reveal that during the War, Lethia held our hives hostage to ensure we fought Humanity and its allies with commitment. They placed 'planet-buster' devices across our worlds, even in our hive ships. It is a fact conveniently overlooked by the Convergence."

"Nonch! Listen! Ask Broodmother if she'll meet me and my parents! An information exchange. We will help each other."

"Gleans. They fought us too."

"Shells! Stop with this 'we fought, they fought.' *Augh*. We have things in front of us, right now, that we need to do something about. Our now is not our history!"

"Raystar, *our* history is why *everything* is happening right now." He dipped his head and spread his arms wide and low. "History is why you and I are friends. Our past is ours to curse and to thank for our today." He raised himself again and stared down at me. I puffed purple hair out of my face and slouched.

I was out of ideas. Waiting for Mom, I guess, was all I could do.

"But I will see if Broodmother will meet you and your parents."

"Yeah! Nonch!" I sprung up and smacked him on the back.

"Silent about this we must be."

I nodded, grabbed the news orbs, and threw them into the information recycler on the desk. Next to the recycler was one of the sphere-shaped library synths I'd seen before. I blinked at the beginning of a plan and pocketed the synth.

Nonch gently and firmly held me by my shoulders, turning me to face him.

"To clarify, Raystar-Friend. My intention, my hope, is that we must be silent about what I said. About me not wanting to be a Crynit. About the favor I will ask of you."

Things were looking up. Given my parents' Ascendant status, a meeting with Broodmother gave me hope we might find an ally. *I had taken action and had caused something to happen* instead of the reverse—being happened to. While I didn't have anything close to the answers I needed, the answers *were out there*, and I was a tiny step closer to them. We do our best with what we have. There's no going back.

I gulped, looked up into my friend's orange orb-eyes, and nodded.

The lunch bell chimed. Nonch and I left the library separately.

In addition to the pain, I get nauseous during my headache episodes. Like now. No, this was worse. Boiled 'natch. Warm, soggy, green, and stringy, it oozed from between the two pieces of bread that I was holding.

Raw 'natch has the smell of earth, forest, life, summer. What wafted from the grey plasti-wrapper was dirt-like, for sure—dead dirt. The smell curled fingers of nausea around my belly and crawled up my spine with a shiver. Imagine the piles of decaying plants we recycled at the farm's gardens after a long summer of sitting in the sun. Now mix that with gratcher manure.

I had a sandwich full of it.

Jenna gasped as the smell reached her; it seemed even her multi-colored beaded braids shook in disgust.

Startled at my lunch destiny, I fumbled my sandwich. It pancaked on the cafeteria table with a wet smack and ended up half outside its wrapper. As one, my friends and I stared, horrified, at the green rivulets that trickled across the white tabletop. They moved tentatively, as if they were exploring their best path from the table to the floor.

Jenna covered her face with her upper hands, moved her lunch tray away from mine with one of her lower hands, and stretched out her fourth hand, fingers spread and palm toward me. Nonch wrapped his appendages around his head so only his eyes were visible and flattened his sensor stalks along his back.

Mieant scowled and raised an eyebrow imperiously in my direction. "No wonder Humans lost the War." *Ha, ha, never heard that one before.* But I agreed with him. Today he wore frayed dark blue pants, a rough-spun manila tunic, and big, industrial, stompy, leather boots. The sleeves flared out slightly, giving him a farm boy look despite his aristocratic bearing. He pulled his nearest sleeve clear of a green river that was heading from my sandwich toward his fashion statement. I grabbed a napkin and wiped the 'natch juice into larger smears, all in a futile attempt to do something about the smell. It was a losing battle.

We scuttled to a different table to escape the 'natch spill. Hunger makes me irrational. I salvaged what I could of my lunch and brought it with me to the new, clean table. I was ravenous.

"Purps," Jenna said, smoothing her hair and pointing at my sandwich with a hand. "It must be hard for your parents. Cooking different foods for you, especially when it's like *that*. I don't know how Cri puts up with it," she muttered, looking away.

My cheeks flushed hot. I hated being called that. Dad usually packs great lunches. "We…," I began.

"…Will begin," said Nonch as he placed his blade arms gently on the table in front of Jenna and me, his razor-sharp blade making a soft *tack* as it touched the table's surface. I looked down, trying to get hold of my embarrassment and wounded pride. Nonch continued. "Raystar and I went to the library. It seems the Jurisdictor was correct about your parents' importance, Mieant Asrigard."

Mieant's frown deepened as he played with his water glass.

Jenna looked from Mieant to Nonch. "I don't understand."

"It must be hard for your friends to have to constantly explain things," I blurted, my face warm with anger. Jenna sat up straight, her mouth in an "O." Her eyebrows came together as she turned hard to me.

"Wait. Wait!" Mieant put his hands up to both of us. His gesture agitated the 'natch stench back into the air and I grimaced, wondering if my parents had been making different food just for me all these years. "It's no secret. Anyone who cared to search would know that my parents are in the government." He looked down. "And they run this Quadrant."

Jenna turned and grabbed him with all four hands. Her beads clinked. "NOVA! Ohhh my Architect! I knew there was something different about you!" Her voice rose as she hugged him. With two hands framing his shoulders and two more around his face, she looked like she was going to pull him in for a kiss.

"I...there is nothing different about me," he sputtered, plucking her hands off him one by one and tilting his head at an angle away from her lips. "And I didn't sit with you because we're friends!"

"Is that Human food I smell?"

We turned to face T'jarl and Fell, the boys who were with Mieant on the first day of school, plus another boy I'd met only once before.

"Darien," Mieant said to the boy who'd asked the question, rising fluidly. Darien had a huge chin, typical black Lethian eyes, and large ears, giving his head an oversized appearance. "Ease your adrenaline," Mieant continued.

"You, Mieant? Sitting with my Jenna? And the Human?" Darien looked at Jenna appraisingly and winked, and then he took in the rest of us. Jenna sprang away from Mieant, and Mieant's scowl, which I'd most likely started by dropping my sandwich, blossomed into full-blown anger. I was grateful he wasn't directing it at me.

"OK..." I rose and lifted my hands, palms out. My life is a stream of interruptions. The dim hope that dropping my 'natch sandwich was the worst thing that could happen to me today, poofed away as I registered the premeditation in the boys' eyes. This was a setup. Behind me, Jenna stood and scooched away from the table. Nonch uncoiled and began swaying slightly as he took us all in.

"Why—you like this *creature*?" Darien spat at Mieant while pointing at me. He stared at each of my friends in turn before shoving Mieant's shoulder.

Mieant returned the push, and Darien stumbled. "I was talking with her abou—" He snapped his mouth shut as he reached the same conclusion I had. *This was a setup.*

"You eat with this beast," Darien said before turning his scowl to Nonch. He stuck his chin out and jeered, "Crynit. Is a Human the only friend you can find?"

Meanwhile, Fell turned a haughty expression to Jenna, looked her up and down, and laughed, "And you? I thought Darien was your premate?"

I rolled my eyes.

Jenna began edging away from us and toward Darien. "I'm ONLY friends with her sister. Raystar is crushing on Mieant. It's a disgusting thought." She turned a speculative gaze at me and sniffed, "He's so out of your league."

What?

Nonch tilted his head toward Jenna before refocusing on the Lethians, his arm claws slightly spread. Like Lethians, Crynits don't have pupils, but they do have a center of focus. With large orange upper eyes, four smaller black eyes, and mandibles as large as my forearms, they had as close to 360-degree vision as you could get. When all *that* is pointed at *you*? You felt their attention.

In contrast to my friend, the Lethian boys looked like wispy clones of one another—white hair, giant black eyes, downward-turned smiles, and even the same navy blue jumpsuits. T'jarl took note of Nonch's pose and took a half step back.

Fell fixated his strange, pupil-less glare on me. I could only imagine the legends created by early encounters between my ancestors and Lethians. While they weren't as big as a Glean, they stood taller. They weren't skinny, precisely. More like sinewy and lanky.

Our increasingly loud conversation was attracting the attention of our bored fellow lunchmates. A few had risen and were eating their meals standing up while watching us.

Darien looked at Jenna, laughed, and turned back to Mieant. "So you want to play with these *others*?" He waved vaguely at Nonch and me. "Is that why your family's not on Solium4?"

"Do not ever talk about my family, Darien." Mieant's scowl transformed from a thunderstorm to something much more menacing. His long, grey fingers curled into fists. "You know *nothing*."

I picked up my soggy 'natch sandwich. It felt more like a bag of lumpy pasta than a nutritious meal. Right now, at least, lunch was the most important meal of the day. I took a bite.

"OK. C'mon, guys, let's move," I said to Nonch and Mieant, spitting flecks of green with my consonants. I nodded as 'natch juice plopped to the floor by Darien's feet. "Just want to finish my lunch...."

Oh. I *might* have added, "...Away from you jerks."

Darien narrowed his eyes as he moved to block me. He leaned his big head in and croaked, "What did you say?"

I looked up at him. His obsidian eyes glared at me from a half a meter above my head, which goes to show either how short I am or how tall he is. I was looking up at his chin. His navy blue jumpsuit ended at his collarbones, and in the moment, I could see a vein pulse under his grey skin. As he turned his head down, I smelled the sweet caramel breath of a predator. I frowned, contemplating which smelled worse—predators, or people who'd just eaten 'natch. But he didn't know I was weighing different types of bad breath, and I wasn't about to tell him.

The kids around us gasped and *ooohed*. Tiny Human versus big Lethian. I bet they were placing bets with their desserts.

"Oh," I said as I gently placed my palm on his chest and shoved. I'd been beaten up before and school security had responded within a minute. I could take a minute of it. Besides, I was pretty sure this fight had been set up well in advance. The choice was to play his game or figure out how to turn something, anything, to my advantage. "You mean the part about lunch? Or the part where I said you and your friends are ignorant, unintelligent—" Nonch caught my gaze and made a "get on with it" motion, "—jerks?"

"Human," Darien moved against me, pushing me back, "you were simply adopted for, what? Money? You are an unwanted—"

Well said. I pivoted on one leg and twisted my body, whipping my arm upward. And released a 'natch-a-pult at his head.

My wet, green comet left a trail of stink as it flew at Darien and smacked into his mouth. I grabbed a lunch tray from a gawking student and launched myself after my stinky green projectile. Darien furiously scraped 'natch from his face and opened his eyes just as the lunch tray connected.

Several things happened at once. The tray broke. Darien shrieked. His feet slid out from under him on the slippery 'natch, and he fell onto his butt. Students screamed in delight, some shouting "Raystar!" while others shouted, "Food fight!"

In a blink, the air was crowded with arms, tentacles, and grabbers winging edible missiles at random targets.

Lunchageddon was upon us!

Nonch flowed toward me, slapping vomit-colored noodle soup out of the air with one claw and deflecting a dessert with a tray held in his other. There was a splat behind him. He twisted and peered curiously at a student who'd lost balance and face planted on his armored back.

Mieant vaulted over a chair that skidded his way and grabbed Fell by the shirt. With a heave, he threw him into T'jarl, and they dominoed into a cluster of other students busy hurling their lunches by the fistful.

We had an opening. I slapped Nonch's carapace and jerked Mieant's shirt. Remarkably, we coalesced into a team, and my friends followed my charge out of the cafeteria. The doors hissed shut behind us, cutting off the screams of joy and the chant, "Raystar! Raystar! Raystar!"

Nonch held a blade arm up to me and made a fist. I punched it with my own.

"*That* was nova," Mieant said.

21

"There they are!" As one, we turned toward Jenna's voice as her traitorous timbre seeped through to us.

A dozen school security guards in light body armor jogged past us and into the lunchroom chaos.

"Raystar! Raystar! Raystar!" sounded as the doors to the cafeteria swished open. Lunchageddon was still calling my name. "I didn't do it" was not going to be an option.

Principal Entarch marched up behind four more security guards. Straight backed, she stopped a meter behind her Lethian entourage with her chin up and hands clasped behind her back. Her black eyes considered us impassively. Only her flaring nostrils gave any indication of her rage.

Jenna walked a little behind her, to her right. Her beads jingled with each step as she struggled to match the principal's strides.

"Raystar! Rays…." The doors finally swooshed closed behind the guards and silence fell. I tried to gulp. There was no moisture in my mouth.

"Raystar," Entarch said, halting in front of us. I shifted my gaze away from the Principal and glared at Jenna. She was supposed to be Cri's friend! Jenna smirked back.

"I would expect nothing less of you," Entarch burned her words into me. "But you, Broodmother Krig's spawn? My, my, my. And the Asrigard." She leaned down, laid a finger on Mieant's chest, and pushed. "You four"—her eyes turned to Jenna—"are quite the catch."

Jenna's eyes flashed golden and then grew huge. "I, but…I brought you here!"

"No one likes a traitor, Jenna." Entarch poked Mieant's head with each word. "Not me. And, I would expect, not your friends, either." She marched past us in the direction of her office. We were expected to follow.

We did.

22

I imagined the bridge of a starship looking like this. Dark. Vid-screens with various control images. Symbols lighting up the blackness and the crew's faces with a red glow. The crew communicating silently with each other except for the occasional "shields at 70 percent and failing fast!" that needed to be screamed to the captain.

We were seated against the wall and faced the multi-level amphitheater of the Blue River Educational Facility's control room. From here, we could observe the administrators as they watched the school's environmental readouts and monitored student activities. I hadn't realized how many cameras there were.

I glanced at Nonch. In this light, his immature, violet carapace looked black. The reflection of muted green and red lights shone against his armor. Jenna's head was in her hands, and the glow of her eyes lit up her legs and feet with each alternating thought. I hoped she was revisiting how turning us in was EVER a good plan. She, I didn't care about.

"Shells. You OK?"

Nonch reached out a sensor stalk and bopped me gently on the head.

Right. He was either furious or terrified. I suspected that Brood-mothers became grumpy when their kids didn't listen to directives. Uh, like, "Don't be around Raystar." Or maybe, "Don't tell Raystar our secrets." Or how about, "Don't start a food fight with Raystar." I sighed. Had I done *anything* good for the people around me?

"A synth from the library is missing," I heard one Glean tech announce. Gloom was momentarily replaced by panic. I craned my neck to spot the owner of the voice. The Lethian staffer she was talking to swiped across her vid-screen; she didn't look like a shining example of alertness. After acknowledging that a library synth was missing, and dutifully shouting it into the air, the Lethian yawned and called up her own attendant to check a personal message. Yawning again, she shifted her attention unenthusiastically toward the approaching supervisor. "It's on the school grounds," she said.

With stilt legs, a belly bulging over his belt, and long lanky arms, the Lethian supervisor glanced at her screen, swiped several information globes from her vid to his, and shrugged. "No matter. It's a low-quality unit. I'll have the cleaning and maintenance crew hunt for it in this evening cycle." He turned to go and said, over his shoulder, "Good work."

The tech yawned, made sure her supervisor was gone, and then switched to a different view.

I reached into my pocket and felt for the synth I'd pilfered. I needed it now more than ever. It was great news that the monitors couldn't track it very well, and even better news that the school security staff just didn't care.

Light glared from across the room, and Principal Entarch flowed imperiously from her office toward us. Her robes swished as she moved; her hands were behind her back and her chin angled upward. Mieant followed her like a wilted 'natch stalk. I made the decision right then and there that my starship would not include a Principal.

Mieant slumped into the chair on my other side with a thud.

"Raystar," Entarch motioned to me, turned, and strode back to her office.

Nonch's sensor stalks and a blade arm nudged me as I walked by.

"You have done nothing wrong," he said, so quietly it was almost inaudible. "We are friends." His blade arm extended to its fullest and touched my shoulder until I walked out of his reach. I glanced back at him, attempting a smile.

"You probably think your lunch incident was simply children's immaturity," the principal said over her shoulder as I followed her. I didn't think that at all. I was sure we had been set up by Jenna and Darien. I just couldn't understand why.

"A food fight," she continued, "Easily enough dealt with. But had you not been there, it would NOT have happened. Time and again, you Humans bring out the worst in Galactics. Now, we *finally* approach a time when your species' disruption will be no more."

That didn't sound like a reprimand.

Going from the dark control center to her bright, white office made me squint and shield my eyes momentarily. Blue seams outlined the white alloy plates that made up the floor, ceiling, and walls. Multiple white, curved chairs sat in front of a giant crescent-shaped desk. She sat behind her desk. I sat in front of her desk.

On the wall behind her, images of me lying on my back in the levsled flickered to life. The fire from the Ruins was on one screen. Closeups of Dad and me shoveling steel-blue goop into the containment appeared on another. My farm compound flickered on yet another. These were vid-sat images. There were no pictures of the food fight.

A thin smile slid across Entarch's face as she watched me in silence.

Oh, no.

The pure black column standing to the right of her desk—somehow, I'd completely missed it—suddenly shimmered and took form. Jurisdictor Godwill uncrossed his arms. *How had I not seen him?* Principal Entarch leaned back in her chair, nodded to Godwill, motioned to me with a hand, and smiled. "I believe you know each other."

I jumped up. He approached, raking over me with his black gaze. His eyes were too big for his skeletal head. He shot me a malicious, crooked smile that revealed his bone-crunching teeth.

"Raystar of Terra."

"That's not my name, Jurisdictor, sir." I was sweating. "I am Raystar Ceridian."

He stood in front of me, took my face in his hand, and made me look at him. Only Mom was allowed to give me fish lips. My face got hot. "You are no Ceridian, little Human."

I put my hands to his and eased my contorted face out of his grip. He chortled merrily. "Raystar of Terra, do you understand that I can do whatever I want? Get whatever I want?"

He met my glare with a smile.

"What?" he asked, mock care on his face. "Your parents will save you? Your mother? In line for the Ascendancy? They should be worrying about their *real* daughter," he chuckled.

Godwill pulled me close, and I smelled bittersweet caramel on his breath—the smell of predator, of meat. His skull face morphed as his downward frown stretched his lips into a mound. He puckered and kissed my forehead.

I nearly vomited. My heart pounded and my stomach crawled into my throat. Godwill put a hand on my head and moved it down over my hair to my neck. He grabbed my hair at the base of my neck and jerked my head back so I could only look up at him.

"I want this!" He slid his other hand around my face, to the back of my head. His grip tightened, and he pulled. I screamed as hair was pulled from my scalp. I grabbed at the stinging flesh where it had been and simultaneously twisted out of his grip with all the strength I had.

"Now, as to the matter of the lunch incident?" Principal Entarch said, glancing at Godwill to see if he wanted to be part of the next conversation. He jerked his head at me, and then pointed to the door with his chin. He carefully dropped my red-tinged purple strands into a specimen bag and then turned to me, his face now expressionless.

"We will discuss your future later, Raystar. Tell Broodmother Krig's offspring to come in," Principal Entarch said, waving to the exit. I glared at her. At Godwill. I wiped my nose, hoping for the energy to destroy them. My sleeve came away dry. I had cursed my nosebleeds and sparks at the least useful times. To have them now would have been nice.

"Raystar of Terra," Godwill shook the bag holding the clump of my hair. "Leave us. Or are you volunteering more samples?"

I sprinted out of Principal Entarch's office, my hand to the back of my head, and boiled on the inside at the absence of my stupid sparks.

"RAYSTAR!" Entarch called after me. I skidded to a halt at her office door. "Do not forget. You have a red notification. We will continue our conversation after school."

Godwill beamed at me.

I ran.

Upon my approach, Mieant sat upright from his slouch. Whatever he was about to say froze on his lips when he saw me race by, holding the back of my head. Nonch flowed from his curled position and extended his arms. I dodged around him. I needed to get away. *No one could help me!* Jenna shrank from me, and her seat-chair morphed around her new pose.

The Principal's office was on the top floor of the Blue River Educational Facility. I sprinted down to my locker, gravity carrying me faster downstairs than my coordination could keep up with. I stumbled forward, but I didn't care. *I had to get the nova out of here.* Huffing, I threw my locker open and shoved everything into my backpack, which already sagged under the weight of last year's books and papers.

I wasn't actually sure why I was taking any of this stuff, but I couldn't think clearly. *Maybe not at all.*

The synth I'd stolen from the library was cold against my palm. I lifted it close to my face and used the locker door to shield what I was doing from cameras or any students. "Unit," I spoke softly, out of breath. "Erase primary identity and register yourself to me, Raystar Ceridian."

"I acknowledge that you are Raystar Ceridian. I am Synth Library Unit Five-Oh-Six. What is the purpose of your request?"

"I've lost my synth. And need a replacement for the day. You can resume your regular identity tomorrow. I need class assignments and curricula sent to my GalNet address for access at home as well."

"OK Raystar, this is within my parameters. I have made the changes." *Yes!* I squeezed the synth. A red notification blinked to life on my virtual screen, and the synth buzzed to life. "You have a red notification, Raystar. Principal Entarch is requesting your presence at her office after class."

Perfect!

"Thank you, synth. I'm aware of that notification."

"I am pleased to help." Wow, AI was never like this. He would probably tell me he wasn't a personal organizer and that I should use my brain to remember my appointments. I put my hand on my chest, where he used to hang above my heart. I missed him. *Terribly.*

"I have an additional request. My family has been having issues with drought and a subsequent reduction in 'natch production. I would like you to research solutions, either technical or biologic, that could improve yields, assuming that the dry situation will be here to stay."

"That is within my parameters as a Library Unit," it said, sounding pleased to have a task so well suited to its design. "I have multiple levels of research access and clearance and will send my results to your GalNet address within the week."

I had no idea what its reference to "clearance" was about. I shrugged. I wanted the synth to be active. Now that I knew how much spying the school administrators could actually do, my little research project might convince them that all was well for the time I needed to get home.

It was, after all, true that our fields were suffering from drought. School administrators would see the diligent Human researching how to help her mom and dad feed the family. I hoped.

"Thank you," I said, and I shoved it back in my pocket. My next class was Advanced Math. My stomach was knotted with hunger and the idea of going to the principal's office again after school. Godwill terrified me. I needed to go home. To be with my family and talk to them about this.

"RAYSTAR!"

I spun and slammed myself against my locker; my heart had sprung loose and was pounding around in my chest. A group of kids traipsed by, their clothes mottled with food stains.

Wide-eyed and panting, I shoved my back against the locker. One of the kids, a Glean, held a fist out to me. I stared at it, not understanding. He smiled at me.

Oh! I fist-bumped him. He nodded, lost in a reverie of lunchageddon.

"Totally nova! How you stood up to those Lethians. And the food fight was completely STARRRED!" another one said, making arcs in the air like explosions.

"Heh! I got your dessert!" a girl chimed to the second kid. She winked at me. "I bet him my dessert you were going to kick butt!"

"Yeah, uh," I gulped. "Thanks!"

They turned and continued down the hall. I turned and headed toward the VCP.

Wait.

"Hey!" I spun and shouted after them. "Where are you going?"

"Lower level. Athletics," the Glean I'd fist-bumped replied. *Perfect.*

"I accidentally took a synth from the library but have to get to my math class," I gestured with my thumb toward the level above us. "It's on your way. Could you, uh, drop this off for me?" I pulled out the synth and bounced it in my hand.

"Sure! S'long as we get another food fight!" That got a laugh from the kids. I walked toward them.

"Thanks! Uh, hey, can you just, you know, set it on one of the workstations? Principal Entarch is pretty upset with me. I don't want her to add 'stealing from the library' to the list. It will be hard to get you that food fight from permanent detention." I handed him the synth and raised my eyebrows.

"Nova!" he said, pocketing the little device. The kids turned the corner and their voices faded. I let out a breath. The school administrators in the control center would "see" me walking to the library. And then when I didn't show up for detention, they'd "find" me studiously researching away.

I rummaged through my backpack for my helmet and put it on. It was all I had to hide my purple hair from the cameras. Turning in the other direction, I sprinted toward the VCP, my dart, and open air.

I'd be long gone before they found me missing.

23

My shoes thunked on the metal deck much too loudly as I half-ran, half-jogged to my dart at the far end of the deserted VCP. The wind that raced across the landing pad carried the smell of rain and 'natch, and the promise of escaping the claustrophobia of school. This place had been my freedom. Now it was just walls and threats. Hands shaking, I unlocked my air scooter and stowed my backpack. The dart's nose faced home.

I was about to straddle it when I heard a noise. I crouched and spun. *It sounded like thudding feet.*

The VCP was empty.

Cool fall air washed across my exposed skin. Paper scraps blew erratically across the deck. *The unmistakable sound* of someone in *heavy boots thudded toward me from across the VCP.*

My gaze fixated on the sound coming from the center of the VCP platform, I activated the dart and grabbed the handlebars. Antigrav thrusters came awake with a whine, and I shoved my hip against the mid-point of the air bike. I grunted, pivoting the dart to face the center of the VCP platform.

The thudding drew closer. Those were boots. Lighter than Dad's, but big nonetheless.

Panicked, I threw a leg over my seat and grabbed the dart with my thighs. *Don't panic.* AI would have said that to me.

Acceleration pushed me down on the seat as I launched backward and up. My imagination was thrashing wildly. I expected a taloned grip on my shoulder digging through my clothes and hooking me off the dart. I imagined the dart tilting as I fell, and then jetting skyward, abandoning me as I smashed to the VCP's hard surface.

Instead, I rose through the air with bone-crushing speed.

Only when I was a hundred meters above the VCP did a figure materialize, not three meters from where I'd taken off!

Jurisdictor Godwill. He turned his eyes up to me, black orbs in a grey skull. No smile, no sneer. Expressionless, he just watched me. He held a pistol in one hand.

I spun the dart toward home and opened the throttle. Shields flashed around me as the speed increased. *Stay cool, Raystar*, I said to myself, looking back at Godwill's shrinking figure.

Frosty. Gotta stay frosty. I didn't even know what that meant. It was one of AI's phrases. But I needed to keep my wits about me or risk raving, screaming, unthinking panic. As I shot away from the VCP, I saw five oval cruisers parked on the playground. They were motionless. *Godwill wanted to catch me alone or he would have alerted them.* Somehow, he suspected I wouldn't show up for detention and had seen through my misdirection.

What if...I'd been caught?

My knuckles were white from my fear grip on the dart's controls. I wiped sweat from my palms on my jacket and pushed the dart to unstable speeds. My heart was going to launch itself thought my chest. *Frosty. Gotta stay frosty.*

Dark green 'natch blurred beneath me as my speed outran my panic. Not meant for performance, the dart tilted dizzyingly each time I craned my neck up to the clouds or behind me to see if I was being followed. No one behind me. No friends. No enemies.

The giant flock of flips from yesterday was gone. With only a few days to go before the Storm Wall, they wouldn't be caught in the open. I didn't know where they had gone, but guessed they took cover in the tangle of pipes that was the Blue River's industrial sector.

For now, it was me with me. I was alone.

On cue, thunder vibrated the air—a low, rolling sound that stretched from horizon to horizon. Ahead, the Storm Wall rose, startling in its sheer height and breadth.

This close to the start of the Storm Wall's cycle, opaque dark clouds churned and boiled, backlit with random flashes of rainbow lightning as the Wall grew wider and taller. Its vertical shape was seemingly held upright by the enormous Mesas. Ionized clouds spread out on either side, rising higher above the mountains than at the horizon. The energy sent my mind buzzing with excitement. This Storm Wall cycle felt different. Purposeful. Connected. Even so, I shuddered at the thought of getting a headache while screaming through Nem's atmosphere.

Leaning low, I accelerated, intent on the shimmering, defensive dome emerging on the horizon.

Home!

I'd never seen our compound with its defenses active. The "farm" illusion I'd lived in for the past twelve years was a reality of crackling, angry force fences and buildings bristling with cannons. Their barrels glowed orange and left trails of heat as they scanned the air and land. They were novas against the almost black Storm Wall. Atop the tool shed sat the mystery of whatever was in the top story of our hangar. A giant, dual-barreled turret over six meters long glowed with twin orange suns. Its massive form was meant for much, much more than police cruisers. Or leggers. *It was a flipping atmosphere cannon.* As in, capable of blasting through the atmosphere to destroy orbiting, shielded spacecraft. Unless Mom and Dad were planning on cooking all the 'natch on our farm at once, I was pretty sure our farm didn't need planetary defense armaments.

My thoughts tripped over themselves to pick up answers as I stared at the immense cannon. Only three days ago, Dad had been trying to tell me something. The night of the "meteors"...or, as I knew now, my first view of a dogfight.

But how much earlier had that help been sent? A month? A year? And how long did it take to fuel, stock, and staff twelve thousand ships and their crews? Under no circumstances did sending two battle groups seem like a last-minute, leave-for-the-weekend thing. How long ago had this swirl of events been set into motion? I remembered the article about the discovery of the Human base on Elios fourteen years ago and dug my nails into my palms, frustrated at how quickly the list of what I didn't know kept growing.

Then there was AI. He'd been given to me by my parents. By his own admission, he knew things about me that he'd promised my organic parents that he wouldn't mention.

One of AI's final thoughts had been to take shelter in the Human base in the Mesa Ruins. I glanced at the dark mountains and their crown of thunderheads. Lightning flickered silently in the purple-black clouds, sometimes reaching tentatively down to the jagged bones of the Human city to dance amongst its exposed metal. That's where he said I'd be safe?

Riiiight.

Both my dart and I were recognized by the house's artificial attendant. *Mom was back!* Her golden aircar was parked next to Cri's dart; by the looks of it, Mom had only just returned.

I tingled as I pierced the farm's geodesic dome-shield. I tipped my dart sideways, decelerating hard. The dart's gravity dampeners screamed. Chunks *squea'd* loud enough to match my dart's howl as I arched over him toward the parked vehicles. Despite the day's events, I couldn't keep the giant grin from my face as I slid into my landing.

The kitchen door opened, and Mom, Dad, and Cri piled out. Mom was in a suit. Dad's grey overalls were smeared in brown and black oils, no doubt from the lev-sled. Cri was in her favorite white and blue pajamas. Her slippers were cartoon leggers, six fluffy legs splayed in multiple directions as she walked. I didn't anchor the air scooter, so as I leaped off, and it drifted slowly in the opposite direction.

"MOM, DAD!" I yelled, dropping my backpack and throwing my helmet off as I ran.

"Ray!" Mom said, opening her arms to me. I collided into her, and she picked me and whirled me around into a giant hug. She smelled of sunflowers. I buried my face in her neck.

"What happened?" Mom squeezed me to her.

Dad put a heavy hand on my shoulder and looked at Cri. "Get Mom's things out of the car and let's get Raystar settled in the kitchen." He turned to Mom. "We should not speak outdoors." Mom blinked and nodded.

Cri followed us in the house, shouting in no particular direction, "Aidee! Bring Mom's stuff from the car!" AD9 detached herself from the nook on Mom's aircar.

Compartments slid open and Aidee reached in to pull Mom's bags out. She hovered past us and vanished into the house to put Mom's things away. Cri smirked at Dad's frown and shrugged.

No place like home.

24

"Darien is a worm," Cri said, interrupting my retelling of the food fight. Then she shaped her hands in the whisper position around her mouth and my ear and hissed, "He tried to kiss me last year. You should have broken that tray on his face…twice!"

"He kissed you?" Dad asked. Cri whirled toward him, eyes wide.

"We can hear you, Cri," Mom said, hands on her hips. "Raystar, what happened? Did this Darien boy kiss you?"

"No! I wasn't interested!" Cri protested to Dad.

"Mom…" I tried to get in.

"AND SO NOW HE'S KISSED RAYSTAR?" Dad thundered.

"Nobody kissed me!" I shouted.

"I'm Ascendant. They *should* try to kiss me. Not *her*," Cri muttered.

"Nent! I leave for a day and this?" Mom pointed to Cri with one hand and to me with another.

"I…" Dad looked to Mom, eyebrows raised and all four hands palms up.

"Nobody kissed me!" I repeated.

"Well, I think you'd remember if they had," Cri said, wisely. Bug-eyed, I gaped at her.

"YOU DON'T REMEMBER?" Mom asked, incredulous. "Raystar Ceridian," she grabbed my ear and pulled me over to the kitchen table. I winced as my head tilted and followed my ear. "You are not old enough to do any of this," she said through her teeth.

"Ow! Mom!"

"Do. You. Understand?"

Architect. What was wrong with these people?

"Godwill and Principal Entarch…."

"They ki–?" Dad began. He looked at Mom, who gave him the parent-to-parent "calm down, I got this" sign with her hands.

"Dad…," I said.

Dad ground his teeth and stomped out of the kitchen into the courtyard. "Aidee! Unmount the atmosphere cannon. Affix it to the bed of the…" The door whooshed shut behind him.

Four hands wrapped around me. Mom pulled me close. I could feel her muscles beneath the scratchy fabric of her suit.

"My baby," Mom breathed, holding me to her. "No one will touch you."

"Eww?" Cri said, "Can't believe you kissed Godwill. And he wants to, like, kill you. That's galactic-level ick."

What? I mouthed to my sister, wondering if I'd flown home to a different family.

And then, loudly, I exclaimed, "Mom. Stop! Listen!" Mom paused for a millisecond and unwrapped me from her hug. Her scar was dark purple and her cheeks, wet with concern, were drawn tight from my outburst.

"No one kissed me! No one kissed anything! There was no kissing." I waved my hands straight out, "None. Whatsoever!" I motioned sideways with the flats of my hands. Mom looked to Cri with the beginning of a "but" forming on her lips. "NONE," I emphasized.

"Why didn't you say so?" Cri said, exasperated.

I massaged my temples and then looked up to my mom and sister. Outside, metal screeched as the atmosphere cannon was removed from the roof of the toolshed. Mom frowned at me.

"Why are you home early then?"

"I'm in trouble," I said, wondering where to begin. Cri moved to a chair. Mom was silent, inviting me to continue. "Godwill took a sample of my hair."

Mom gasped.

The doors whooshed open and Dad strode in. He had found his calm in the courtyard. Through the doors, I caught a glimpse of the atmosphere cannon being mounted into the lev-sled bed.

What do you know? It fit. The lev-sled's front and rear plasma cannons nestled perfectly under the giant twin barrels. I gulped as recognition settled over me. The lev-sled looked just like something I'd seen in action vids.

All these years, we'd been harvesting 'natch in a Glean assault tank.

25

Mom and Dad sat quietly around the kitchen table as I recounted my day. Cri sat on the table, her legs swinging idly, and the furry legger slippers swayed like ropy hair below her feet. Mom gasped upon learning that there was no record of Godwill in the library. She started furiously looking something up on her data pad.

"The Foundationalists would not move against us," Dad said as he stood and commenced pacing.

Foundationalists. The organization that was wrecking my life. Hearing the word from Dad made it tangible, ominous...closer.

"The cruiser on our doorstep earlier this week was intended to gauge our reaction. Cri's expulsion was maneuvering." Mom's eyes flashed gold at Dad. "Taking Raystar's hair was a direct attack. They ARE moving against us." She looked down at her laced hands, "AI was right about our distraction."

I winced at the mention of his name.

"We've extended too much trust to AI, despite his origin and our circumstances," Dad said, grinding his teeth, and then took a millisecond's glance at me. "We have not relaxed our vigilance. He has not ever been correct about you and me, love."

"Love?" Mom looked at him. "LOVE?" She shouted, throwing her pad to the floor. Pieces skidded to the far corners of the kitchen. Cri and I shrank back from her, eyes wide. "Was that not AI's primary concern? *Our love?*" Mom's scar shone black against her red skin and golden eyes. Veins pulsed along her neck. "Is that not why we've failed?"

"Sathra. Peace," Dad said, pumping his palms downward. "I–"

"You WHAT?" Mom yelled, glaring at him with twin suns. Cri and I pressed our backs against the kitchen table in unison.

Dad dropped his hands to his waist and lowered his voice. "Sathra-lea, our love is not the problem. We. Have. Not. Failed."

Mom blazed on and took a step toward Dad. He took a step back. She drew two small plasma pistols from her jacket and held them up. Then, she produced a curvy sword as long as my arm that had been hidden along her thigh. "No? Then why do I have these with me always? We, in spite of these," she turned, her eyes blazing and her scar livid, and gestured at me with the sword, "have not kept HER safe."

I blinked and looked from Mom to Dad and moved slightly against Cri so I could feel her warmth against me. She pressed back against me.

Dad dropped his hands to his waist and stared at his wife. "Sathralea."

Mom reholstered her plasma pistols and sheathed her sword. She moved to Dad, wrapped her arms around him, and pulled him into a hug. He looked down into her gaze. My parents were cracking. Because of me. They were fighting because of me.

Cool things other species could do? I've stopped counting. Individuals Raystar could destroy through association? The body count was increasing.

"Uh," Cri said, mostly to herself. Mom heard Cri, though, and a change flickered over her expression. She pulled Dad's face close and kissed him, patted his biceps with her lower arms, and pushed herself away.

Mom looked at Dad intently across the short distance between them and considered her next words. The depth of their history, accented by a slightly sad smile, overflowed from her gaze. "Commander," she intoned, "This is not the time for us to have *this* discussion."

Dad blinked, and in that instant, he was replaced by someone else.

He'd been called "Commander" now several times. He drew himself up, and I realized it wasn't a nickname: It was a title.

Nova and gravity wells. Did I know anything *about my parents?*

"Mother and Father have not decided on a course of action," he started after a millisecond's pause. "And what of Raystar's meeting with Broodmother? And the Asrigards? Sathral–."

Meanwhile, in siblingville, Cri stepped away and frowned at me under heavy brows before looking back at Mom and Dad. I was so caught up in my parents' imminent destruction that I'd almost missed my sister's glance. She seemed to be constantly mad or unhappy with me lately. Frankly, I didn't need the stress. Or the guilt. Or whatever she thought I was doing wrong. I looked back at Mom as she spoke.

"We cannot wait for others to save us," Mom said. She punched the table softly with a fist, as if the table was whatever she was thinking. "Brother is disappointingly consistent. Godwill is an impostor, which suggests a deeper and broader infection. There is more here than a 'hunt' for our daughter." She slowly shook her head and dark black hair cascaded around her face. Her anger turned her scar a deep purple. "These Battle Groups are in transit. We have, maximum, five days before their arrival. Certainly no more than that."

I glanced at my sister in the silence that hung after Mom's words. Cri, who had taken a perch a little away from me on the kitchen table, peered between Mom and Dad. Though she was bigger and stronger than me, I sensed she wouldn't cope well with change. She swung her feet, and her legger slippers limply trailed fluffy red and yellow arms within the back and forth motion.

"Where will we go?" Cri asked. She was a child of Nem'. This was her world. I'd foolishly thought it was mine. She and I had watched vids about other planets and space habitats, had even played that we lived on them. But neither of us seriously considered the reality or possibility of living somewhere else. I mean, what were the schools like? Grocery stores? Would I need new clothes, based on the atmosphere? How long would it take to make new friends? How would I keep in touch with my old ones? That last question was more Cri's problem than mine.

"What about the Gathering?" Cri asked, hopeful. Mom and Dad exchanged a thought in a microsecond of eye contact. Dad shoved his lower hands in his pockets and folded his upper hands across his chest. He hunched over slightly.

"The Fleet is on the other side of the Convergence, and until it reaches its next waypoint, it is not an option," Dad replied, turning his eyes to Cri.

The Glean Gatherer Fleet moved from system to system. It was a mobile homeworld comprised of hundreds of thousands of home-ships and an innumerable swarm of public and private starcraft of all sizes. Long considered one of the wonders of the Convergence, it was essentially a smaller version of the Galactic Core made up of starships instead of stars. And because it was the Glean homeworld, nothing remotely threatening was allowed close.

"But what of, uh, your Mother and Father," I asked. My parents frowned. I had to ask, though. I mean, they *were* Mom's *parents*. They ruled the Ascendancy with more power than even the Heir.

An ugly question flashed in front of me.

What did Heirs do? Actually?

"Darling," Mom said to me, "It is not that it is a bad idea. It is that space, time, and odds are against getting to their safety."

"You mean, *me*, getting to *there*, safely?"

Mom and Dad were quiet. They traded a glance and an invisible message before turning back to me.

"Wait," I said, eyes getting big as I stood to face them, "The Ascendancy's not safe if I'M there? Is that what you–"

"STOP!" Cri yelled. "I'm sick of being mysteried! WHAT THE NOVA IS EVERYONE TALKING ABOUT?"

"We will go to the Embassy. We will go to Ever." Dad ignored both of our questions and nodded to himself. "And we must leave now." He turned to Mom. "Your Brother will furnish clothes and supplies when we arrive?"

"Predictable," Mom said, tracing her scar. She turned to Dad. "Do you think we can act normal *enough* to deceive Godwill for just one more day? The Asrigards are attending the Facility tomorrow for some announcement."

Cri looked between them in amazement as they ignored her.

"Let's send Raystar to school and then depart when we pick her up. The misdirection will work. They would not dare attempt anything with thousands of students and cameras, and...." Mom continued, talking to herself now, "if I was Godwill, I would expect us to leave tonight."

Yeah, except after today, going to school was the worst idea in the world. *The worst.*

"Can't they take her at school whenever they want?" Cri asked, resigned to not having her question answered. She turned her eyes down and swung her feet again. I thought I saw a corner of her mouth turn up into a smirk as she thought through THAT scenario.

Dad frowned and looked out the window. Mom spun and, with a curl of her wrist, activated the control wall. "Show us visuals of defense sats and NPD aircar traffic within 300 kilometers."

The house synth created a 3-D holo of Blue River, the Mesas, and the surrounding countryside. Mom grabbed the image and positioned it so we were looking down at Nem' from orbit. Three red dots shone in the space above Blue River.

Defense sats had both space-to-space and space-to-ground weapons. Their armaments ranged from directed energy beams to missiles. Three of them were arranged in a geosynchronous orbit and could cover us for more than a 700-kilometer radius. They were essentially right above us. She grabbed the holo again, and the continent raced toward us as the view magnified.

Blue River looked like a swarm of insects as regular traffic flowed in and out of the city. A major airway followed above the high-speed land train and disappeared in the general direction of Ever. The expected number of NPD cars, represented as smaller red dots, wove in and out of the traffic. But the additional dots located at the edge of the map were alarming. Assuming those were NPD cruisers, they could effectively intercept any traffic to the capital.

"They can take *us* any time they want," Mom sighed. Her scar was a purple streak across her face. I imagined it pulsing with a mother's will to defend her own, but it didn't sound like her anger was directed only at our circumstances. I remembered their fights. *Was I a wedge between them?*

I looked from Mom to Dad. They'd never told me how they'd met, and I was feeling like that was important. I was feeling like *I* was the source of the anger they pointed at each other.

"Even with AD9's assistance, our ship will not be ready until tomorrow evening. I…it needs fuel." Dad looked chagrined. Mom raised an eyebrow. *Our spaceship was out of gas?*

"What if we didn't go to Ever?" I asked. My family, in unison, turned to me. "Uh. AI mentioned a base. Under the Mesas." Mom and Dad exchanged a glance. Cri stopped swinging her legs and looked at me. "A Human base," I continued, now in a smaller voice.

"There is no base under the Mesas," Dad said. Then, looking at Mom, he waved three hands at me. "See? The *thing* filled her head with these notions. No. We need to get to Ever, then offworld." He turned to the window.

"Ray," Mom said gently to me, "do you believe AI?"

I met her gaze squarely. "I'm having a tough time with everyone's truth." I pointed at the display, the satellites, the security forces blocking our path to Ever. Before she could follow up her frown with words, I added, "But given that the Mesas are inside the ring of ships and satellites, it seemed unpredictable enough to bring up."

"Even if it were true," Mom said gently, "it's a Human base. Could WE get in?" She pointed to herself, Cri, and Dad. "How would YOU get in?" She moved closer to stand in front of me. *Uh.*

I looked up at her as she continued.

"We have resources offworld. Tremendous resources." She put her hand on my head. *Yes.* My stupid nova head had flushed AI, who probably could have answered all of our questions.

"I will leave first thing in the morning to file the official protest as part of the Glean Ascendancy," Dad said, deciding. "The protest, plus

Raystar being in school, will signal we intend to stay in Blue River."
He turned away from the window and faced us. "I will," he paused, a
crooked smile hanging on his face, "emphasize not only our intention
to stay, but our ability to enforce our will."

Mom nodded. "And tomorrow, we can take Raystar to and from
school."

Gee. That would be new. I couldn't wait to show up in a tank.

Dad nodded and gestured to the oil on his clothes. "I must change.
Synth," he commanded, "prepare a shower and get my uniform ready
for tomorrow."

I didn't even blink. I didn't know my parents anymore. It only
made sense that nobility would have uniforms. Whatever disguise
and camouflage they'd wanted to create here on Nem' had certainly
kept me from the truth. *Sure. Why not have a uniform?*

I bet he looked great in it, too.

"Affirmative, Commander," the house answered back. I blinked.
That word again. Dad's shower could be heard turning on. He tousled
our hair and made his way upstairs.

"So," Mom said as she smoothed her suit and looked at Cri and me,
"do you have homework?"

As one, Cri shook her head and I nodded. We glared at each other.
I shook my head and she nodded. Cri threw her hands up. "Raystar!"

"C'mon, ladies. Knowledge is power," Mom said. "Architect knows
we need all the power we can get." She sighed, ushering us toward the
stairs.

I can't believe that on the eve of my destruction, I'm doing flipping
homework.

Pfft.

Homework is heavy.

I lifted the reader from my face and opened my eyes, wincing at the pain. I'd fallen asleep on my back while reading. The homework-filled data tablet had been resting on my chest, and it awakened me as it hit my face.

Nurse Pheelios's assignment was to do a report on a governmental structure that could assimilate multiple views. Seriously, why not just tell us to write about the Convergence?

I sighed, rubbing the bridge of my nose. Assuming I lived long enough to turn my homework in, there was no way she was going to get that answer from me. Because facts were facts: The Convergence *had not* united its members.

Someone thumped softly on my door.

"Come in."

My mom entered. Her scar was now vivid purple and looked like war paint against her red skin. She gazed at me intently with golden eyes.

I sat up and smiled.

"Hey, Mom, what's up?"

She grabbed my chair and shook it, dumping its contents to the ground. Mostly clothes, but my Human junk, er, relic collection also clanked to the floor. I blinked. *What was it doing there? And what was up with Mom?*

"Mom?" I said, swinging my feet down so that I was sitting across from her.

"Dad told me about what you did. With AI," she said. Her lower two hands gripped the chair. She crossed her two top arms.

I froze and looked at her.

"AI was given to you by your par…your biological parents."

I stayed perfectly still and quiet.

"He was your friend. You have no idea how many times he stood up for you with us, how he taught us about Human behavior."

"Mom, I…"

"And the disrespect you gave? He was a sentient! *Is* a sentient! Are you better or worse than the Galactics who look down on Humans?" Mom was trembling; the arms of the chair bent under her grip.

My face flushed. I hadn't seen it that way. I hadn't considered that he was a Galactic. "I didn't know," I mumbled, lamely.

"Raystar Ceridian, do not insult my intelligence or yours. Did you have conversations with him? Did you confide in him?"

"Yeah," I whispered. Salty memories rolled down my cheeks freely and plopped on my pajama leg.

"Did he give you comfort when you were scared, give you joy when you interacted? Could you depend on him?"

"I—."

"So why does he need a title, or a certificate, or someone else to say he is a real person? Do you need someone to tell you someone is real? That they have a spirit? Are you so blind?"

"Mom," I sniffed, wiping at my face, "I'm sorry! I was angry. Scared. Mostly angry, and I…"

"What. Do. You. Think. I. Am. Now?" she said, her tone flat and cold. "What should I do to you, given how angry and scared I might be?" She rose and headed to the door. Halfway across my room, she turned back to me. "Raystar, I say this once. Never in my dreams would I have thought I'd have to tell you at all."

I stared at her, miserable, and licked salt from the corner of my mouth.

"We do not abandon family. It is the core of our strength. You are my daughter. A Ceridian. *We do not abandon family. Ever.* Find AI. Find him alive, or find his husk. *You are accountable.*" Her eyes were solar flares that lit up the walls as she turned and exited my room.

I started shaking and rolled into bed. I couldn't stop the tears. I wadded up my blankets and hugged them with my arms and legs. Between sobs and memories of all of the conversations I'd had with AI— his help, his humor—I wondered what I'd ever given back. I drifted into a turbulent sleep.

27

"No gratcher," I said, waving away the heaping forkful Dad was tilting toward my plate. Mom and Dad frowned at me. "More eggs and toast, though. Please."

Mom scooped eggs and toast from her plate to mine with a curious look. Nodding my thanks, I resumed my slouch. The eggs smelled good. I hadn't been eating enough lately, and could feel my energy levels dipping low. I could feel the Storm Wall's pressure on the back of my head, the headache just hovering at the edge of my awareness. But it was nothing next the tempest of guilt I was experiencing. Mom's words thundered around in my conscience. *AI was gone because of me.* I loaded my fork, blowing my drooping hair out of the way, and shoveled it into my mouth. I chewed and swallowed.

"One moment, Sathra." Dad's charcoal uniform was lined with microstreaks of silver. As I'd thought, he looked good in his uniform. His medals read "Commander." I blinked, wondering what he had commanded. His grey cape was connected across his collarbone by a brooch inscribed with the Ascendancy Creed: "Peace, Love, Family, War."

He was a vision of grey, black, and silver, all contrasted by his red skin, golden eyes, black ponytail, and cleft chin. He was meeting with Godwill as an Ascendant, so of course he needed to be formal. Dad raised his jacket tails and strapped a sinister-looking flat pistol to the small of his back. Next, he clipped a long, slightly curved sheathed sword to his waist and its matching sibling on the other side. I stopped chewing long enough to note that his belt had two additional empty scabbard attachments.

Humming, he grabbed his smock from the wall. We'd given it to him years ago; from the front of it, the hologram of a younger Cri and me, eating pancakes, grinned back. "Hungry!" was printed above the image. He fastened it around his back with his lower hands while cracking replacement eggs into a pan for Mom.

I watched them from my shelter of purple hair. Despite the conflict between them, they were a team. *A good team.*

We do not leave family behind.

"Where are your pulsers?" Mom asked, taking the plate he offered and resting a hand lightly on his belt. He leaned down and kissed her on the forehead.

"Weapon detectors," Dad grumped. "I'd have to take them off and put them on again going into the NPD building, and then on the way out. If I suddenly need to be in a hurry," he straightened, "it is best to have just one."

"Ah," Mom nodded and turned to me. "Ray, about yesterday."

"AI?" Dad interjected, looking at me. Finding me expressionless, he turned his glance to Mom, "OK. I'll get Cri ready. Wish me luck."

When Dad left, Mom turned to me. "Anger. Raystar, you're smaller than almost all Galactics. You're a child. You don't have the rights of an adult. Anger clouds your thinking, makes you destructive. Hurts your friends." She took my hand in two of hers. I blew my hair out of my face and turned to her.

"Now, more than ever, beautiful child, you cannot afford cloudy judgment."

"I was so wrong, Mom. I'd do anything to have AI back," I sniffed, feeling my eyes burn. "I don't know what to do. For him, for me, for any of this." I waved my hand at the world.

"We're a team, Ray. We won't give up. And that means looking out for your people." *My people?* I hadn't thought of it that way. "You didn't find AI in the waste unit," she continued, "but he has many capabilities, even the ability to move. And he is old."

I squashed a rebellious tear with an eye blink and the back of my hand. He could move? "Why's old good?"

"He's a survivor. If you didn't find him, he is still somewhere," Mom said, nodding. Then she added, "Probably."

"Oh," I frowned, chewing my lower lip, "so he's either unable or unwilling to communicate?"

"Yes. While you and Cri are at school, I will see what resources you can use to find him."

"Wait. What?"

"We do not leave family behind," Mom said, raising her eyebrows to communicate a we're-not-going-to-have-this-conversation-again look.

"Yes, I got that," I huffed. I did actually have that part. "But what did you say about Cri?"

"Principal Entarch called us last night. Her investigation cleared Cri of wrongdoing. Entarch said Cri was to be commended on her bravery and would be welcomed back to school today."

I frowned. "Great timing?"

"Indeed," Dad said as he thumped down the stairs. "They steal hair from one of my daughters and then invite the expelled daughter back to school?"

Cri thudded down the stairs a moment after Dad. She wore tight, black leather pants, a ripped T-shirt, and a jean jacket with dulled spikes around the sleeves and collar. And she had a tattoo on her neck: "Peace, Love, Family, War."

"What on Nem'?" Mom said, taking in her eldest daughter and glancing at Dad.

"Don't make me change!" Cri said, grabbing my plate of unfinished breakfast and placing a hand on Mom's arm.

Mom shook her head and looked at Dad, incredulous. "What is *that* on her neck?" She'd said "that" like you'd say when you spotted a leggy insect on the bathroom wall and pointed it out to the person who's going to get rid of it for you.

Dad grinned. "It is good?" Then he saw Mom's expression begin to change. He raised his four hands toward her. "Wait! It is not permanent." He frowned. "I think."

"Explain." Mom said, moving to Cri and tilting Cri's head to expose her neck.

Dad replied, "I had leftover military nanoink. We need to create our own advantages, however we can. We'll be able to watch them at school." He then turned to the control wall and commanded, "Activate 'Eyes and Ears.'"

The house synth complied and two images flickered before resolving into focus. The first was a map similar to the terrain view Mom had called up. Icons that were clearly Blue River and our school appeared. Dad swiped the image, and we scrolled over farmland until we reached symbols that showed our compound and the Mesas. A tiny green light winked at us from the compound symbol.

"It's a tracker, Mom," Cri said, shoving my food into her mouth. Her head was still tilted sideways.

"And..." Dad waved to the other image. It was the four of us, there in our kitchen. Cri was making a face, pulling the hair out of her mouth that had gotten tangled in her fork. Mom was glowering—albeit less so—at Dad. I was staring open-mouthed at myself. I closed my mouth.

Dad beamed at his ingenuity. "The ink is both the tracker and the vid broadcaster!"

Mom looked at him, shaking her head. "A tattoo?"

"Why not? Our children are brawlers," Dad said, punching two fists together. "Cri has taken on guards, and this one," he pointed to me, "started a riot. The clothes, the nanoink, they are perfect."

Technically, it was a food fight.

Mom closed her eyes, put a hand on her temple, and nodded to herself. "I'm going upstairs to change. You two be ready. We leave in ten." Dad, victorious, walked to his office and started giving commands to the house synth.

I looked at Cri. "This is a horrible plan."

She met my gaze. "You've got your sparky nanowhatever"—she touched her tat—"and we've got 'Eyes and Ears.' It's just another day of school." She grinned. "And it could be our last day of school! Think of that!"

"Cri! That isn't even close to good!"

"Ray," Cri took my hand, "just one day. I finally get to do something cool."

"Cri, we can't mess this up. I don't want to go to school."

"It's always about you," she said, her gaze hiding emotions just under the surface. She dropped my hand.

"I don't want anything to be about me. I don't want to be scared anymore. I want to do my stupid homework!"

"Pfft," she said. Whatever thoughts were there before went deeper, and her expression flickered to mischief. "You realize we're being dropped off and picked up in an assault tank."

I rolled my eyes. She smacked my back as she passed me and walked into the courtyard.

"C'mon! What can happen?" she asked, over her shoulder.

You never ask that.

Never.

28

"It is a tank." The Glean NPD officer's helmet squeezed his cheeks together and pushed his wet lips forward. On the viewscreen, he looked like a red snapper.

"My husband took the aircar."

"Your spare car is…is an assault tank?" His fishlips sputtered.

"Officer Jalusk," Mom snapped her lipstick shut and puckered at an image of herself in a smaller viewscreen off to one side, "we're going to be late for school." Satisfied with her reflection, she turned back to the Glean officer and arched an eyebrow at him.

"I…," Jalusk sighed, "one moment." The screen flickered to black.

With the atmosphere cannon reinstalled on the lev-sled, Cri and I had access to the spacious six-person command center nestled in the tank's belly. Cool air flowed around us. The military seats were firm but wrapped around our bodies. "Pressure gel," I think it was called. In the event that we had to turn quickly and the inertial dampeners—which negated the effects of gravity—failed, the gel would keep us from turning into Galactic paste.

The gel was the military's Plan B to keep a crew safe, but the chair wrapped around my kid body and was a joy to wriggle into.

It was comfortable enough that I could forget I was in an assault tank. The cannon was made to fit into the space that I'd been calling a container bed. I recalled one of the books Mom had made me read.

Glean tanks were modular. Mom and Dad had ordered this one with a land-to-space armament—like they'd been expecting trouble *years* ago. Or maybe the atmosphere cannon had been on sale. Perhaps an impulse buy as they left the assault tank store?

Nova. I knew they loved me. I knew it. But I didn't know anything else about them. And thus, I didn't know anything about me. I winced at that realization. *Who was I?* Or maybe *what was I?* was a better question.

Command displays provided a 360-degree view of the world. Although a short corridor connected the cockpit to the command center, we witnessed the exchange on our own viewscreens. Cri and I traded grins and carefully put our feet up on the console. You know, carefully, so as not to shoot anything.

Hovering at one kilometer above Nem', we had a gorgeous view of a perfect fall day. Blue River stretched upward in front of us; our school was a grey octagon below. Yellow and orange flips swirled around the tallest of the city's spires. Despite our height, we were still below the tops of Blue River's buildings. Clouds roiled by, creating patchwork views of the landscape—which included five jet-black NPD cruisers that ringed us like bees around a flower. The atmosphere cannon and shield generators added size and purpose to our "ride." The tank was a predator among bullies.

Officer Jalusk's image reappeared, all business. "Our pardon, Lady Ceridian. You are cleared for landing." The NPD cruisers broke formation and returned to where I'd seen them parked yesterday.

"Oh, they're letting us through!" Cri said, clapping. I frowned.

"Because assault tanks can go to a school unsupervised?" I said, turning to my sister. "This is a bad plan."

The ramp extended from the belly of the tank with a whirr. A group of kids had seen us land and were chattering as they gathered at the VCP ramp. I could see Nonch and Mieant in the crowd. Nonch's midnight-blue segmented length contrasted with the kids' various colors. Mieant's olive shirt and pants looked vaguely like he was ready to walk through a jungle. Jenna was there too, except off to one side. Her silver outfit reflected light, and she looked ready for a rave.

"Raystar! Wait," Mom called. I turned to her, one foot on the ramp, the other on the VCP. Cri was ahead of me and turned as well, frowning quizzically. Mom strode down the ramp, and behind me I heard the kids' *ooohs*. Especially the boys.

I blinked and looked at Mom. She had changed before she took us to school. She wore the pure white cape of the Ascendancy draped around her neck with her skintight silver combat suit. Her determined stride made the hilts of the plasma pistols at her hips sway with each step. I saw the boys in the crowd, smitten, and wondered how long it would take for their intelligence to find its way back to their brains.

Mom's black hair streamed behind her as she sauntered up to me. Her eyes glowed, and she smiled at each of the kids as she approached.

"Hold still," she said, as she grabbed my head with one hand. She licked a thumb and scrubbed something off of the side of my mouth. She looked at me and gave me a huge hug and wet kiss.

"MMMUAH!"

"MOM! *Agh!* What are you…"

"Stop squirming," she muttered to me and herself as she turned my head slightly to wipe lipstick from my cheek. After a critical evaluation, she straightened. "There. Perfect. OK, see you both this evening!" With that, she strode back up the ramp.

I turned, slowly, and trod down the ramp, lost in my horror.

To my additional horror, Jenna was vidding the scene. She held a camera remote in one hand that projected a virtual screen. With swipes and turns of her wrist, she sent an orb-shaped experian drone that dutifully twisted this way and that for the best angle as it maneuvered in the air. My classmates ignored her, as they were in various states of laughter after having witnessed the scene with Mom. My face burned at each finger pointed in my direction, each laugh at my expense. I hurried toward Nonch, Mieant, and Cri.

"There was nothing on your face," Nonch said, looking to each of us as I approached. "I saw. There was nothing on her face?" His last sentence hung in the air.

The long ramp pulled back into the tank the moment my last foot touched the ground. With hardly a gust of air, the giant assault tank lifted, pivoted in the direction of home, and raced off.

Mieant smiled at me with honest appreciation. "Brilliant," he said, "Your mom's outfit was designed to…uh…draw attention." He shifted awkwardly and shot a glance at Cri. "And your mom…" He wheeled on Jenna, who was directing the drone at him. "Get that away from me!"

"I'm in the school news club!" Jenna fired back. She glared at each of us, but she knew how we'd react when she shoved the experian in our faces.

"You!" I took a step toward her. She pointed the drone at me.

"Do it, Raystar. You're brave enough when your friends are around." She took a step back and the experian recorded it all. The crowd of kids began walking toward the playground in smaller groups. The tank was gone, and my prior embarrassment was well documented. *Ugh.* I couldn't wait for her stories.

"You *were* my friend," I said to her.

"*Hardly.*" The sneer hung in her voice as she turned to my sister, "Cri, let's go. Why do you hang out with her? C'mon. I want you to meet Darien. I think we're, you know." She crossed her fingers in the international symbol of boyfriend–girlfriend. Mieant choked.

"Jenna," Cri said, taking a step forward to stand at my side. She pointed at me, then back to herself, "Uh, sisters? And after what you did yesterday?" Her solidarity felt great. Maybe she did like me still.

"Yesterday? I didn't want Darien hurt," Jenna huffed. She turned to Mieant. "And *you.* I don't get you. Today you're friends with a Human and a Crynit. It's like, out of the blue, you leave your *real* friends behind!"

Mieant considered her and said nothing.

"Jenna, what do you want?" Cri asked. "If it's nothing, then go."

"Pfft. Darien says you're all trouble." She spun and marched down the ramp, her glass beads clinking as she stomped away from us.

"I am confused," Nonch said.

"Darien's using her." Mieant motioned for us to follow. "I bet he's been asked by Principal Entarch to stir something up."

"Whatever," Cri said. Then she added, "You're kidding, right?"

"We were approached several times to, ah, help students understand how to behave. You remember Alar? The Elion? Principal Entarch wanted him to feel unwelcome. *Very* unwelcome," Mieant said. He caught my gaze, and raised his hands to me. "I was not a part of that, though. But as you see, Alar is not here."

"One moment," Nonch interrupted, reaching out and holding the three of us with a blade claw. "My lack of comprehension is troubling. Just now, your mother embarrassed you," he said, turning to me.

"The school is covered with vid-cameras," Mieant explained. "Lady Ceridian is Ascendant and Heir to the Glean Gathering. By showing how much she loves Raystar, in front of all of those cameras, she was both protecting Raystar and diminishing the Human threat."

"Love is rubbing saliva on your child?" Nonch tilted his head and glanced between Mieant and me. Mieant winced and pinched his nose.

"No. She displayed the act of wanting your child, a person you care about, to look good in public. And that particular act is typical with messy children." Cri snorted and then looked at me with a smirk. "The type that can't take care of themselves."

"She made Raystar look like an immature child, so whoever watches the videos would have difficulty believing she is a threat?" Nonch persisted.

"Not 'immature child,'" I coughed, "but yeah." Now that he'd brought it up, it was obviously a ruse on Mom's part. But I took it to the negative. I'd wanted Mom to have done that out of love, out of concern for me. As current and past events were unraveling, it was hard not to suspect that Mom's show wasn't for me, but instead for the "duty" she and Dad talked about so much.

"This surprised you?" he asked me.

"Um, I thought it was an irritating-mom thing," I said, glum that I'd missed what it was really about.

We moved to go. Nonch held us in place. Mieant looked down at his shirt, at the spot where Nonch was holding him. Of the four of us, Nonch was the most formidable. I saw him for a moment from the perspective of Mieant, who arguably was as alpha as any kid could be. Nonch was nearly three meters long, armored and armed. His head was adorned with four black eyes, two orange primary orbs, and mandibles. Nonch was an apex predator, through and through.

"Shells?" I asked, touching his knife-smooth arm blade.

"The question is, what threat does your mother see that we do not?"

29

The ramp from the VCP to the playground was empty. The usual ca-cophony of children was absent. Preoccupied with Nonch's question, I didn't notice the quiet until we were amongst the kids.

"What's happening?" Cri asked, standing on her toes to see over the crowd. Being Human, I rose only to my classmates' elbows and mid-backs.

"Find a spot. Students, find a spot and be silent!" a school secu-rity guard shouted. The Glean guard towered over the students, and, with two hands, he cradled an assault rifle across his chest; its barrel was down. Because, you know, we kids might giggle, or make a mess, or not do our homework...all sorts of military-grade crimes could come from my fellow pre-rebels. "The Greeting Ceremony will begin shortly!"

Paranoid, I tore my gaze from the overarmed security guard and peered between elbows and backpacks to see if anything else craxy was there. Indeed, an unusually large number of school security guards were peppered throughout the crowd.

A shadow passed over me, and I looked up. The five NPD cruis-ers we'd encountered when Mom dropped us off hovered at evenly spaced intervals around the perimeter of the school grounds. And as I dropped my gaze, I noticed orange heat shimmering from their plasma cannons. They were armed and hot. None of this was right. *This was a bad plan.*

"Hey!" I pulled my friends close. "Nova, those cannons are active! We need to leave," I said, pointing at the cruisers. "C'mon!"

Cri grabbed my arm. "Stop it! Seriously. Oh. Gravity wells! Look over there!" She pointed. Dozens of experian news drones flitted about, all focused on one area of the crowd. I gritted my teeth and shoved her hand away, and she glanced down at me with a frown. "It's a Global Network News crew over there. Whatever this ceremony is, it's going to be on GNN!"

Mieant stared thoughtfully at the experian's lights just a few kids away from us. "My parents said they were coming to talk to the principal about the guards' attack on me and Cri's role in helping me escape. And"—he waved generally to the crowd, the security, the hovering police cruisers—"apparently other things as well."

"Didn't you talk to them this morning, before school?" Cri asked, turning her gaze from me to him.

"We vidded last night." He shrugged at the normality of it, "They were out of town."

"Oh," Cri said, thinking. She smiled and grabbed his arm, "Wouldn't that be nova if it were your parents? I'll be the first Ceridian Ascendant to meet the Quadrant Governors!"

"Cri!" Panic rose from my belly. I was sure one of the cruisers was tracking me. I pulled Cri's other arm, hard. "What the nova? We're supposed to be in school. And make it through the day. Only that!"

She spun, grabbed me under my arms and around my ribs—which hurt—and picked me up so I was eye level with her. I wasn't prepared for her fury. Her eyes blazed.

"YOU," she said through clenched teeth, "SHUT UP, and do what I SAY for a change!" My teeth rattled as she shook me with each word. She'd never done this before. "Not everything is about you! DO YOU UNDERSTAND ME? SISTER!" she yelled. Now other kids were staring. I flushed with embarrassment.

"Cri...," I started.

"SHUT UP!" With that, she threw me backward. I didn't fall completely but stumbled through the crowd, bumping kids as I windmilled to keep my balance.

And stumbled into the news crew's lights!

"This is Nyla Jax, independent GNN news investigator, here covering the Quadrant Governors' major policy statement this morning. The Quadrant Four Co-Governors have chosen the Blue River Educational Facility to make their…*OOOOF!*"

I lurched into the petite, silver-haired Glean. The center of my back connected with her stomach, and the vid drones captured a tangle of Human and Glean tumbling to the ground. I squinted against the lights, arched my back, and pulled a round tube, wide as my fist and as long as my forearm, out from underneath me.

Turning my head, I faced Nyla's golden eyes. Her mouth was pursed into an "O." Her surprised expression fled like my dignity, and she snatched the thing I'd been holding, which turned out to be her experian controller and voice recorder. "I'll take that. *Ar.*" She shifted. "*Oh.*"

I pulled my arm out from under her leg and she lifted me off of her stomach. I grunted as we accidentally elbowed each other.

Finally untangled, Nyla stood, straightened out her pantsuit and then her hair, and fixed me with a stare somewhere between curiosity and "stay the great gravity wells away from me." Then she turned to—I swear—the largest Glean I've ever seen. Dressed in leather crisscrossed by thick belts studded with pockets, this giant looked the part of an old-fashioned fantasy monster. He was holding a camera that was likely as big as I was, but against his hulk, it looked like a ridiculous toy.

"She's the tiny one…Nyla," the Glean said, regarding me through a pinched thumb and forefinger from where he towered, practically a kilometer above me.

Nyla's eyes widened as she took me in and jabbed a finger toward his camera. The mountain called Nolan looked at the blinking green light on his recorder and muttered something to the device. Whatever he'd said turned it off. Vid drones ceased hovering around us and retreated to their charging station.

"NOVA. *You're* the Human! What's your name? Where's your synth?" she asked me as she pushed a card into my hand. "I tried transferring my contact information to you and you don't seem to have one." She frowned. "No matter. That's my card."

"I..." I stuttered, standing and dusting myself off. She folded my fingers around her plasti-paper card and took a step back. Kids had cleared a ring about two meters around us. My friends hovered at the perimeter, wearing worried expressions; well, all except for my Sis'. Cri glared at me, because somehow this random collision with the GNN reporter was supposed to be *her* interview. *WELL, MAYBE SHE SHOULDN'T HAVE THROWN ME AT THE REPORTER.* I seethed at the violation, the break in trust, the....

"C'mon, don't be shy," Nyla encouraged me. I blinked, looking at her anew.

"Her name's Raystar, Ms. Jax. I'm her sister," Cri called out, worming through the ring of students. Nyla turned to Cri and then back to me.

"Raystaaaaar?" Nyla prompted me with a small wave of her hands, expecting more.

"Ceridian. Raystar Ceridian. She's my *adopted* sister," Cri said, standing a little in front of me.

"Fascinating. An adopted Human," Nyla said, her pretty face crinkling into a slight frown. "Nice to meet you, Raystar," she added, reaching out a hand in greeting. Cri intercepted and shook it, prompting the GNN reporter to raise an eyebrow.

"I'm Cri. Cri Ceridian, Ascendant of the Gathering," Cri said, gazing into Nyla's eyes. The reporter's expression shifted, as if she saw something in my sister's gaze she wasn't comfortable with. But Nyla's hesitation shattered as she realized what my sister had said.

"Novas and gravity wells! Nolan!" The petite reporter clapped and looked up at her giant coworker and then back to each of us, like she'd just found a large pile of unclaimed money. "Well, Cri Ceridian, Ascendant, we at GNN were not aware that Nem' was home to this level of nobility. Unless you go to offworld schools?" Nyla paused, "Wait, that can't—because the Human, er, Raystar, goes to school here." She frowned at us as she made connections. Suddenly, Cri was an attention-grabbing, overexaggerating teenager instead of a breaking story.

I edged away while Cri beamed at the attention. "We live on a farm about twenty kilometers outside of Blue River. We go to school here."

"A farm." Nyla's expression shifted to blank. We were no longer a pile of money. "Well, Cri, we, uh, must be off. Today is a busy day, but I'll be sure to interview you when I come back for a piece I'm doing on the school attacks," Nyla said.

She thought Cri was lying. I looked at Cri, who had a completely happy, twisted grin on her face. Nyla's disbelief was fine by me, though; I continued to edge away from the two of them. The fewer people who knew about us, the better. And if Cri didn't notice Nyla's disinterest and thought she'd secured a future interview, well, that was fine by me, too. Today wasn't a publicity stunt. It was a day to survive, and then escape.

Anyway. I was boiling over at what Cri had done to me, and these assessments were struggling to find a place in the storm of my anger. Cri and I were going to have words.

Nyla moved off toward the center of the crowd. Waves of kids and security guards parted in front of Nolan like meteors being parted by a juggernaut's gravity-bow wave.

"Was that wise?" Mieant asked me as we waded through the sea of kids. Nonch arched his head over Mieant's shoulder to hear my response.

"NO!" I yelled, turning to both of them. "*Wise?* You don't have anything to say about Cri throwing me?" I turned from them to stomp off into the crowd and bumped into Cri. She was in her own world, no doubt daydreaming about her interview, when I collided with her.

She had humiliated me. *MY SISTER.* In front of all my classmates. It wasn't enough that I was already picked on, that I was already smaller than everyone else, that I was the only one of my kind in this school.

But to have my own family turn against me, publicly? I snapped.

She had been about to say something to me. My open-handed shove caught her in the chest while my left foot hooked behind her right ankle. I followed her down, landing my knees on her chest hard enough to knock the wind out of her. I pushed my elbow on her throat with my weight and cocked my fist above her face.

Cri had as much training as I did. She was stronger and had four arms. I couldn't take her in a fair fight. *Yet.* I was fast, and lately, I had *become* stronger, and life wasn't *fair.* She moved her arms and made to buck me off, but I leaned my weight on my elbow as I touched my forehead to hers. I stared into her eyes and snarled, *"Do you understand me? Sister?"*

Frustration from the past week was coursing through my veins, making me tremble. It was whirling around inside, boiling up and threatening to spill out, all while overwhelming my sense of control. Cri's eyes widened as she looked from my face to my fist.

Sharp hooks pulled both of my shoulders back, gently. Nonch.

"Peace, Raystar," he said. "Peace."

I rose from Cri. She jumped to her feet as she rubbed her throat. Mieant was at her side, speaking in rapid, low tones and ready to hold her off me. Nonch moved me farther from Cri.

"What were you thinking, Cri?" I shouted at her, shaking.

She coughed. I could see tears welling up. "This whole thing is about you, Raystar! *Raystar's small. She's so smart. Mom's always like, 'Raystar's so alone!' Raystar needs to be protected!* Dad's not taking ME ON WALKS AT NIGHT. WHAT ABOUT ME??!!" She yelled the last part, leaning forward and slapping her chest for emphasis. Mieant caught her shoulders, and she let him pull her back while she glared at me with burning, wet eyes.

"What?" I said, dropping my arms to my side, staring at her. "Mom and Dad love you! I AM the adopted one! And not a day goes by, Cri, when I'm not trying to fit in. NOT A DAY! Each morning I see"—I waved my hands at the crowd—"that I'm not one of them. I don't want to be the alien!" My eyes were getting moist now.

"You're ruining my life," she half-sobbed, her gaze revealing the admission's surprise to herself. Mieant put his arm around her, and she leaned into him.

Her words stabbed the belief that had kept me whole. That I had a family. That I belonged.

"We'll catch up to you," Mieant said to Nonch as they walked away into the crowd. He turned, talking softly to her.

I was drained, exhausted. A random backpack hit my shoulder, knocking me off balance and into Nonch.

"You are salting, Raystar," Nonch said. I leaned into him.

I closed my eyes hard, took a deep breath, and opened them. *Stay cool.* Right. I let my breath out and became aware of something crumpled in the fist I was wiping my eyes with.

Nyla's card.

Nonch's arm claws shielded me from the buffeting kids as I uncrumpled the card and memorized her information.

Nyla and I would talk again.

30

"Enemies? Friends? How can we tell the difference except over time?" Nonch said as I stuffed Nyla's card in my pocket. I squinted up at him.

"If enemies are friendly for a short time, are they our friends for that time?"

Security had herded the students into a U-shaped formation around the Blue River Educational Facility's doors, with the open end pointed at the doors. We were a churning mass of different sizes, shapes, and colors. Thunder boomed in the distance, from the Mesas...the Storm Wall. I felt the vibrations in my belly and in the soles of my feet as the rumble moved across the sky. The Facility, an upside-down, octagonal pyramid, was lit from underneath. The lights flicked on, giving the appearance of a ship landing in the night. Technically, it would have been landing on kids in the night, but it still looked like a ship landing.

If we were going to see anything, we needed to move forward. I looked around at the very active plasma turrets on the force fences.

I didn't want to see anything. Leaving immediately sounded great. Still, if we were not going to do that, we should definitely understand what in the GREAT GRAVITY WELLS was going on here. I grabbed Nonch's arm claw and pulled him with me, and he followed with the same sensation as when you pull something heavy with wheels. It takes a bit to get it started.

"And if a friend is friendly for a long time," Nonch continued, "and then becomes an enemy, is she only then the enemy, or has she been a hidden enemy all along?"

"Shells, seriously. My head hurts." I could feel the pressure of the storm. The familiar ache. The fight, or argument, or whatever, with Cri would have given me a headache anyway, even under non-Storm-Wall circumstances.

Nonch spoke again. "How do we ever know, except through each encounter, measured moment by moment?"

"Moment by mom...*wha*?" I looked back at him. His orange primary eyes were more iridescent than normal, and his sensor stalks fanned out. He always looked like that when he was really into a thought.

"When we first met, I was directed to be your enemy."

I snorted, turned my back on him, and resumed pushing my way through the students. We were five when we'd first met. "You should have told me then."

"There would be no way I could have told you when we met. It would have defeated whatever plans I—*ah*. Sarcasm. I am ignoring your comment. At that time, Broodmother indicated that Humans were deadly. To be feared above all others. That Humans' size and apparent weakness were deceiving."

"Right," I said, but I was thinking about AI. I'd sure acted like his enemy. How had he treated me?

"Even to those unfriendly to you, Raystar, you show kindness, restraint. It is not true the other way around. I have witnessed others be horrible to you, because you are a Human."

My eyes unexpectedly burned. They *had* been horrible to me. "Please, Shells, enough with whatever you're doing," I struggled for words. "I'm living my life. I know people don't like me, so, uh, what's your point?"

"Raystar," Nonch said, then stopped. I jerked to a halt and faced him. I didn't need to analyze my feelings, didn't need to open up holes in my life and let the fears inside out. I was confronting enough of the world outside of my head. Then he continued. "If people are friends and enemies at the start, because that is what they are, and only time is the revealer, I fear that we are in a time of revelations."

That wasn't ominous or anything. He leaned into me, and I blinked as I imagined the last view his prey saw. But he touched my head with his two sensor stalks and said, "I have been your friend since the start. You have been mine. I will stand by you. Remember."

Nova. I swallowed.

"Something is going to happen with my people," he said simply. I stopped the other thoughts in my head, the thoughts of Godwill, of the autocannons, of my sister's pettiness, and faced him fully with my mind. And listened.

"Nonch?"

"Broodmother has hinted about something and told me about other things. That we should not be slaves to the Galactics."

"Shells," I whispered, leaning close to his midnight-blue, armored head and resting my hands on either side of his mandibles. "Why are you telling me this?"

"Because I fear, Raystar," he said back. "And I do not want to be part of it. Do you remember my favor?"

I swallowed and gave him a slow micronod.

"Take me with you. I know you are planning on leaving Nem'. It is the only option to you. I do not want to fight. I do not want to be part of an uprising. I am Broodmother's heir. Central to her plans. She will make me into a warrior, and I will not do what she requires."

"Raystar! Nonch!" Mieant's familiar voice called through the cacophony of students.

Nonch gently wrapped his feathery sensor stalks around my head and whispered, "This is your promise. This is my request." And then he let me go and thrummed back a meter, giving any who would care to see us the appearance that we were having a normal conversation.

"There you two are! My parents are just through that crowd," Mieant called out. He and my sister were weaving their way toward us. He waved a hand toward a denser part of the crowd, and he and

Cri were clearly walking together *as a couple*. His arm was around her waist. He glanced at Nonch and me and said, "What were you two talking about? It looked serious."

My eyes grew wide, and then I frowned at them both. "Not as serious as *that*." I pointed at their embrace and turned my hands upside down in a "what the nova?" shrug. No way was I sharing Nonch's conversation with anyone. Mieant returned my frown and Cri glared at me.

Nonch stared at them a millisecond longer and then rose to his full, nearly three-meter height. His hindmost sections supported him. He looked like a giant, deadly, midnight-blue caterpillar reaching for a leaf as he peered in the direction Mieant was pointing.

"They are indeed here," Nonch said, his words breaking us out of our four-way staring contest. He extended a blade claw toward the thickest portion of the crowd. Mieant and several security guards followed his gesture, thinking he was perhaps pointing out the Quadrant Governors in a menacing way. They started pushing their way toward us.

"You have to meet them!" Mieant shouted over the noise and sprinted in the direction Nonch had pointed, pulling Cri with him. The bombshell Nonch had dropped on me had disconnected my brain from my legs, and I stood there, staring at my deadly, centipedish friend who had just entrusted me with his life. The Crynits were going to do *something*. He was a part of it, but he wanted out. I was the out. Somehow, my thirteen-year-old self was an antigravity well that excluded things like playing, cupcakes, and birthday parties and only attracted craxy Jurisdictors and freedom-loving Crynits.

He was my friend. I had flushed my other friend down a toilet.

I'd promised Nonch.

Soft feathers with the density of a good pillow bapped me on the side of the head, gently but effectively breaking me out of my freak-out-to-be. I blinked as Nonch regarded me, tilting his head to one side, while pulling his sensor stalk back for another bap, if I needed it.

"We should follow them," he said. "We will talk more at a different time."

I nodded.

"We should follow them, with haste," he said again.

I nodded again. My body was nearly left behind as Nonch jerked my arm in pursuit of Mieant. We wove our way through the children. Our sprint caught the attention of school security, and they gave chase to the blazing-fast Crynit pulling the purple-haired Human through the crowd of oblivious students.

"Stop those kids!" one guard cried.

I dodged elbows and shoulders and was about to yell to Nonch about how dumb this was when we spilled through the crowd. Nonch let me go, and I tumbled and landed on my stomach in the dust of the playground.

"Mother! Father!" Mieant shouted.

Strong hands lifted me to my feet. They belonged to the Lethian woman kneeling in front of me. Her huge, black eyes took me in, and a small line of worry creased her brow. She looked...the downward smirk that edged most Lethians' lips didn't appear on her face. It was as if joy had liberated the corners of her mouth, and the beginning of a grin was just waiting to be released. As I regarded her silver hair and large, pupil-less eyes, she reminded me of a radiant, silvery moon. Hers was a face filled with hope. Trust. A belief that the starting point between two people should be that they wished goodwill upon each other.

She looked...kind.

"Are you harmed?" she asked, brushing grass and dirt off my shirt. I was winded, but I couldn't stop staring. She raised her hand to someone behind me, her palm extended. "We are safe." The school security guards had reached us and were huffing and puffing at the perimeter of the crowd.

Mieant ran up to where his mother knelt and I stood. "Raystar," he said, pointing from me to his mother. "Mo-, uh, this is my mother, Freela Covent Asrigard, Co-Governor of the Solium4 Quadrant. And this is my father, Kaleren Covent Asrigard, Co-Governor of the Solium4 Quadrant. As well." At this, he gestured to the tall Lethian man striding toward us.

Freela rose, as graceful as if wind was lifting her up, and took two steps back, timing it perfectly with her husband's approach. Apparently, the Lethian colors were white and black. Freela wore a white jumpsuit with a high collar. Her overcoat fit her like a dress, coming to an end above her knees in a black band that flared outward. Her knees were colored brown from the schoolyard's dirt, from when she'd knelt to pick me up. In a mysterious synchronicity, they both stopped, shoulder to shoulder, at exactly the same moment.

"It is a pleasure to meet you, Raystar Ceridian, Ascendant. Perhaps for the wrong reasons, we have heard much about you," Freela said, smiling. *I was Ascendant too?*

I knew I should try to close my mouth.

Kaleren quickly added, "Of course, we are happy to meet you, for all the right reasons."

Kaleren was dressed in black. He wore an identical jump suit and overcoat, which ended at exactly the same spot as Freela's, except the swath of color at the bottom of his was white. Like his wife, he didn't have the usual Lethian perpetual frown. He smiled, and there was clean humor just underneath his words.

I liked them.

"Forgive my stare, young Ceridian," Freela said. I blinked at how nice they were being. My mouth was still open, and my tongue was drying out. "You must know we are aware of what your coloration means. You are much more vivid than images."

"Freela, now is not the time," Kaleren said, touching her elbow lightly and gesturing to the news vids and throngs of people around us.

"She is the reason we came to this…," Freela edited herself, but her reference to the school, to Blue River, and maybe even to Nem' was unmistakable. "It seems right to at least acknowledge my staring."

Mieant frowned at their exchange and coughed politely. They paused, looked at him, then me, and then as one turned to my sister, on my right. "You are Cri."

Cri's eyes had become huge golden plates stuck on either side of her nose. They flashed, and in an unexpected attack of manners, my sister replied, "A pleasure to meet you, Co-Governors."

185

"You have our thanks, Cri Ceridian, Ascendant and Heir, for coming to our child's aid."

"You are welcome," she managed to get out. "They were pounding him. I grabbed the first kid and…" she made fists with two hands and pantomimed. A shadow fell over Kaleren's complexion.

Freela frowned. "Indeed? My son is not without his own skills. I am only happy for his health, and your safety. We will find the creatures responsible for this."

"Enough, Freela," Kaleren whispered.

"Nonch, of Broodmother Krig," Freela said. They turned to Nonch and dipped their heads to him. "Extend our congratulations to your matriarch on her broodship's productivity." Nonch clacked his armor in response. "We know of her uniqueness and hope she recognizes that the attention we have had to give to our distractions is in no way intended as an insult. We should have contacted her sooner."

Nonch froze, and after a millisecond, his sensor stalk twitched. He spread his arm claws low and scuttled back from them. I smelled citrus and was sure it was coming from him. There was so much to Crynits—they had a language that was physical and olfactory—that I didn't know. I'd never seen my friend behave that way.

Kaleren's gaze landed on each of us as he said, "I will make an invitation to your parents. However, since we have you here, let your parents know that we wish all of us to converge at our residence within the week. There is much to discuss."

"Us too?" Cri asked, tentatively. I looked at my sister, trying to understand why she felt so left behind in terms of attention. Mom and Dad loved her like oxygen.

"Of course, young Ceridian. I won't trouble you with the specifics, but if your parents ask, let them know that we consider it of great importance that you all attend."

"Governors," one golden-armored solider, a Crynit, interrupted, "You are at risk of falling behind this afternoon's schedule. We must return to Ever this evening."

Freela nodded to the soldier and looked meaningfully at Kaleren.

She said, "I don't know why the Heir decided to come here from Ever. This shortens our time here today." Kaleren looked from Cri, to me, and finally to his wife, pausing on her for a long moment. Like that meant something.

"Indeed," Kaleren replied, turning his thoughtful gaze to me once more.

Everyone talking in code was hurting my head. Or maybe it was from being tossed to the ground not ten minutes ago.

I looked around. We were midway through the playground. A forest of play structures rose around us, and the imposing upside-down pyramid of Blue River Educational Facility scowled from its heights. Blue River's giant doors hung open like a cavernous maw with a throat leading into darkness. Oblivious, kids hung, sat, and swung on the playground's structures like the Terran monkeys AI had told me I reminded him of. The ones not on the equipment had formed a large U shape. The school doors sat at the open end of the U, and we were about halfway between the doors and the curve of the U.

Principal Entarch strode from the blackness of the school's interior toward a podium just outside the doors. There, apparently, she had initially planned to meet the Asrigards for the greeting ceremony. Nyla and her GNN crew had taken up the best position for shots, and a swarm of video drones hovered above the reporter.

Roughly three hundred security guards had formed in fifty-by-fifty blocks behind the Principal. She needed them all, I guess, to keep order.

To minimize food fights, perhaps?

I gulped as our luck became obvious. If we had stumbled through the crowd closer to the doors, we'd have wound up amidst the guards. Everything would have been different. Chance and luck, once again, had determined our destiny.

Mieant's parents had assembled thirty Solarian4 Quadrant guard escorts. The Lethians, Crynits, and Gleans who made up their security detail wore golden armor, complete with scratches and dents—the symbols of their victories. Weapons clusters poked up from their backpacks like stubby wings. Shield generators bulged like rectangular muscles along their arms and legs, and each wore clear force shields around their faces. The fact that the faceshields were active left no doubt that these soldiers were battle ready. Under Banefire's glare, their golden armor took on a reddish tint.

I sighed. We were supposed to go to class, have a normal day at school, be picked up, and then leave. The day wasn't going in that direction. I ached for normal normality, instead of this abnormal normality. I watched as the school's doors closed, ponderous and final as a glacier. The Quadrant Guards reformed in a diamond shape around the Co-Governors, as they'd adjusted their formation slightly when we'd spilled out of the crowd. Their formation was precise, and their training was amazing, given the chaos of kids around them.

Seeing her honored guests mingling with a pack of kids, Principal Entarch descended from her pedestal and strode toward us. She wore the billowing white ceremonial gown I'd seen her in on the first day of school. Its dramatic effect was reduced as she pulled it tight around her body, as if chilled.

Every step radiated control and confidence. If she was upset by our interruption, she didn't show it. Nyla's news team followed in her wake, and the swarm of experians scattered to the air above, positioning for the best views.

"Co-Governors," Entarch said, bowing her head as she stopped in front of them. Her voice rang across the field, amplified by the sound drones that whirred over the crowd. The kids' chatter dropped to a low murmur. It was incredible that this many children could be this quiet. The Quadrant guards parted as she stepped inside their perimeter. "I welcome you to our school!" she exclaimed, gesturing expansively. "I invite you to see beyond this formality and experience Blue River Educational Facility as a perpetuator of open discourse!"

It was strange that she only used one hand. Her other was buried in her gown.

Freela returned her gaze with a hint of disdain as Entarch continued. "And yet, formality can be the combination lock of friendship. With the right protocols, everything is open."

Entarch blinked, glancing between Freela, Kaleren, and me. "Ah," she sighed, "I see you have met our Human. And her friends." She turned back to the Asrigards. "I assure you, your son's socialization goes well beyond this group of"—Entarch struggled for the words—"special students."

A relative silence froze time under Blue River Educational Facility's oppressive shadow. GNN experians rose from their charging stations and hummed quietly as they zigged and hovered around each other to get the best angles. Somewhere, a bug made a small *crick* Sound, but aside from the drones, and maybe the background sound of thousands of kids breathing, the silence was oppressive.

"Nonetheless," Entarch continued, looking at the vid drones. "While I had planned time for you to see your son in his classroom environment, I am so happy you have had a chance to meet in advance of our discussions."

Unconsciously, Cri, Nonch, Mieant, and I stepped closer to each other.

"Thank you for the kind words, Principal. My son and Cri Ceridian," Freela said, glancing at Mieant, then Cri, and then slowly back to Entarch, "are the catalyst for our meeting today. But not the sole reason."

"Of course, Co-Governor Freela. I am relieved we were able to solve the mystery of the incident concerning your son. Violence at the Blue River Educational Facility is not tolerated. Our report, which we sent your staff yesterday, is on our agenda for discussion. But we do not have to stick to protocol. Shall we proceed indoors?" At the word "indoors," Principal Entarch looked at me again. I returned her gaze with no small amount of fear and anger. This wasn't *just* awkward. Something else was happening here.

Kaleren gestured in my direction. "Actually, Raystar Ceridian is the second reason we are here." A thousand faces turned toward me. My eyes got huge. Unconsciously, I smoothed my purple bangs out of my eyes and tucked my hair behind my ears while simultaneously trying to make myself invisible.

Nyla's news drones whirred in a renewed frenzy as they focused on Kaleren and then on me. One brave student yelled, "Food fight!" I shrank into my friends, feeling Mieant and Cri's warmth and the sureness of Nonch's hard shell at my back.

Principal Entarch opened and shut her mouth. Uncomfortable, she moved to adjust her robe, and something glinted underneath. "I look forward to hearing your purpose, then, Co-Governor."

Kaleren smiled and turned to Nyla and her GNN team. He spoke. "We have treated Humans poorly. Our war with them was nearly two thousand years ago. Their technology haunts us. It is far past the time we take an inclusive approach with this notable Convergence species." He turned back to Principal Entarch, who had taken a step closer to where Kaleren and Freela stood. The Quadrant guards faced the crowd, a golden wall of armor and weapons.

"Principal, I apologize for hijacking your Greeting Ceremony, but I will be brief. Today, I have signed into Quadrant Four law the Human Inclusion Bill, designed to pave the way for full integration of Humanity into the Convergence!"

I had no idea what that meant, but it sounded good. No one cheered. Why should they? I was the only Human on Nem'. But that a law had been passed gave me a flash of hope that there were large enough populations of Humans in Quadrant Four, at least.

Kaleren had turned directly to the GNN drones, and Freela motioned for Nyla to approach. Entarch grimaced and moved, curiously, behind Freela and Kaleren, both hands in the folds of her robes.

"Nonch." I patted his armor. "We have to go. Now."

Mieant turned to me, frowned, and pointed at his parents' thirty giant-sized, golden honor guards. *Like I hadn't seen them.*

"You getting your paranoid on?" Cri said, taking Mieant's hand. She turned to him. "Let her go, if she wants. I'll stay with you."

My bug eyes must have made her laugh. *And what's with her holding hands with Mieant?* Going to school was a bad idea. My paranoia was unstoppable. I looked back at the cruiser I had thought was tracking me earlier.

It was still there, tracking away. If anything, it was closer.

Nova this. I was out of here.

31

"CITIZENS, REMAIN CALM. AND DO NOT MOVE!"

The collective throng of kids, reporters, Co-Governors, security, and Quadrant Troops gasped, and turned as one in the direction of the amplified voice.

Jurisdictor Godwill emerged from the school gates opposite the giant doors. In full NPD battle armor, followed by a squad of a hundred combat-ready, NPD-uniformed soldiers, he marched toward us. His troops stepped in time behind him, and the thundering crunch of their boots echoed though the assembly. Godwill carried his helmet under his right arm, like he'd done it a million times before, and his combat armor was turtlenecked around his jaw. His half-grimace, too-big eyes and protruding cheekbones exaggerated his skeletal visage.

The sea of kids parted like terrified waves off of a ship's bow. His soldiers included Lethians and Crynits, with the Crynits making up the flanks. One Crynit in particular stood out. Over six meters long, it bristled with weapons along its back and stood off to the side and slightly behind Godwill, waving its five claw arms as it breathed and loomed over the other soldiers. The Crynit's segmented armor was midnight-blue, and there was a familiar starburst on each segment along its body. The yellow star shapes were abraded, as if someone had made a half-hearted effort to scrape the images from the armor.

"It cannot be," Nonch whispered.

"What?" I returned, my gaze riveted on the giant Crynit.

"We are in grave danger, Raystar." A note of panic cracked my friend's voice.

"*Pffft.* Look around us, Shells." I waggled my hand at the cruisers, the school security guards, the Ceridians' elite guard, Godwill's small flipping army, the auto cannons on the force fence.

"You do not understand!" he hissed. "That is Sarla," Nonch whispered, gawking at the giant Crynit by Godwill's side. He turned to me. "We run into the crowd, then into the school. We must not be here a moment longer!"

Godwill's soldiers wore scarred and dented armor, proof that they'd seen and—more worrisome—survived lots of combat. Combat armor was made of a nearly indestructible metal. Inside, the armor provided insulation that absorbed electricity, diffused heat, and repelled the cold. It was layered with shield generators that could deflect, at least for a time, most anything that came at the person inside the armor.

The dents meant that these troopers had faced combat even AF-TER their shield generators had given way. And that giant Crynit—that one had the most-worn, battle-scarred armor of all.

I looked at the golden Quadrant Guards and then back to Godwill's small army. I'm sure the Ceridian elite guard had better ammo, fresher energy packs, and the most modern weapons, but the numbers were against them.

"Explain yourself!" Kaleren exclaimed, stepping toward Godwill. Freela stepped with him. Their troops, in unison, armed their weapons and activated their suit shields. A shimmering orange glow interlocked with each additional suit, forming a wall around their squad, the Co-Governors, and Entarch.

"We are so up the gravity well," Cri whispered, pointing. The school's force fences were active. Auto turrets pivoted inward and tracked back and forth across the crowd.

Augh! Hadn't I been pointing that out since we arrived? I scowled at my sister.

"WHAT CAN HAPPEN?" I exclaimed and punched Cri's shoulder, referencing her glib comment. "You NEVER ask that!" I braced for her return punch, but she flashed me a worried glance and nodded in agreement.

"Shut up!" Mieant coughed. "Be ready to run."

"I am Jurisdictor Godwill," he asserted as he marched up to where Kaleren, Freela, and the principal stood. He stopped at the guards' perimeter, his own soldiers fanning out and around the Quadrant troops. He glanced at us, not five meters away, and then back to the Asrigards.

"Move, now," I whispered. As one, we took a step toward the crowd. Then another. There wasn't much further to go before we could be hidden in a mass of wide-eyed, multicolored kids.

"There is no Jurisdictor Godwill," Freela said, frowning slightly. Principal Entarch had moved directly behind the Asrigards. The principal looked terrified. I would have believed her shocked look if I hadn't witnessed her and Godwill teaming up against me in her office yesterday.

She's faking fear! My heart beat faster as adrenaline surged through me. *Why was she acting?*

GNN drones swarmed around us, vying for the best angles. Out of the corner of my eye, I witnessed the auto cannons on the force fence swivel as they tracked each drone.

"Nem' is under the care of Jurisdictor Xzaris Alenion, of Broodmother Krig," Freela continued. "I will say this once, Godwill, or whoever you are. Stand down. Command your"—she looked at the NPD soldiers—"troops to drop their weapons and surrender."

Godwill laughed, his lips peeling back like a receding tide to reveal a red mouth and glistening teeth. In the silence, broken only by the wind and a thousand kids breathing, his laugh carried threats and cruelty.

I looked at Entarch. She was sweating. The mask of false panic she'd worn earlier had been replaced by the concentration of a performer waiting for just the right time to act.

I caught Godwill giving her the slightest nod.

She shifted her hands in the folds of her robe, and as they moved, they revealed shapes. I recognized them from our kitchen this morning. Her hands closed around them.

No.

"Principal Entarch–!" I screamed.

Kids shrieked and crawled, hopped, flowed, flew, and ran in all directions. Godwill's closest troops turned to me, to us, rifles lowered. The Jurisdictor pulled a long, sleek pistol from his suit and sighted it at Mieant's parents in a relaxed shooter's stance. Mieant's parents heard my shout and got a step away from the principal.

Entarch drew two swords. *My dad's swords!* It could not be. *How did she get them?* Question after question overwhelmed me as the scene unfolded in excruciating, slow-motion detail.

The principal raised her hands above her head like a bird poised to fly, angling the swords downward at Kaleren and Freela's backs. I tried to move towards them, but my mind hadn't left the question of what happened to my father. He was my rock. *What if he was gone?* I stood rooted and straight, oblivious to the tumult around me, and watched as the Asrigards tried to take a second step away from danger, each looking over their shoulder, their eyes widening.

The principal began her downward lunge. The swords lit with blue electricity.

"MOM! DAD! NO!" Mieant yelled, his voice cracking with sheer panic. Nonch and Cri grabbed him around the waist and ankles.

With Entarch's reach, there was no missing. Her downward arc slid the swords through Mieant's parents so they protruded, glistening, from Kaleren and Freela's stomachs. Blue sparks erupted from their bodies, and they arched their heads toward the sky. Their arms fell back, and their hands froze into talons as the current flowed through them. Like falling trees, they collapsed, forcing Entarch to release her hold on the swords.

Those sparks. They looked like....

A few of the Asrigards' troops turned inward to give aid to Freela and Kaleren, and their action broke the interlocked force shield.

Something ripped the air like fabric, only a million times louder. An orange plasma bolt lanced from Godwill's gun and impacted Principal Entarch in the chest, carrying her ten meters back into her security. Her troops lost their resolve, dropped their weapons, and ran in the same direction as the kids. Which was anywhere, and everywhere.

Mieant's parents were shrouded in blue microsparks that looked exactly like what I'd manifested two days ago. Only IT-ME had similar powers, and more concerning than that—if it was the same nanotech as mine, it could do ANYTHING.

Like eat the Co-Governors!

I gritted my teeth as Cri's words from this morning penetrated the chaos of my thoughts. *What can happen?* The sparks that crackled over Mieant's parents were definitely similar to what I had seen, what I had done. *Which meant I was probably the only one who could do anything about them.* But questions about Dad had to wait. *I needed to act NOW.*

"Go!" I screamed to my friends, pointing at the school exit. Then I turned and ran toward the fallen Kaleren and Freela.

"Weapons free!" Godwill commanded. "Take them!" Who he meant by "them" wasn't readily apparent, because while most of his soldiers began to open fire on the Quadrant troops, the remainder seemed bent on attacking anything running and not lying prone on the schoolyard. Unimaginable streaks of sound and light raced between the elite troops. For a moment, the Asrigards' team had the advantage. Their training and their equipment showed as they blazed into Godwill's legion.

Which was three times their number.

I dove toward the Co-Governors and slammed myself facedown on the ground. Both sides were firing at point-blank range. A ceiling of energy bolts tore back and forth at waist level, above me. I was in the midst of covering my head and spitting grass out of my mouth when Mieant grabbed my ankle.

"I'm coming with you!" he yelled through the howling fire. I had no idea what I was going to do. I only knew the direction I had to crawl toward.

"Stay down!" I shouted back to him.

As I turned my head, I caught sight of why Gleans and Crynits are such terrifying soldiers. Cri rolled underneath two guards' rifles and stood between them. Unarmed, she ripped the plasma cannons from their grips with two hands; with her other two arms, she grabbed the soldiers and flung them into their squad members. She repositioned the confiscated guns without blinking and started shooting at the feet of Godwill's troops.

Nonch curled into a ball and took a direct plasma bolt to his carapace. He uncoiled and sprung in a three meter arc *over* several NPD troopers' heads. When he landed, he drove his blade arms through their armor and into their legs. Invisibly fast, he grabbed a rifle from a downed trooper and twirled it like a staff. He cracked faceplates, knocked troopers over each other, and paused to fire only when necessary. Soon, he had four rifles. His remaining arms were cutting and whacking as he and Cri fought their way to the school's doors.

I scrambled forward on my stomach, somehow managing to squeeze between a Quadrant trooper's feet, until I reached the Co-Governors. My father's swords crackled and hissed with microsparks. Mieant's parents were paralyzed, their backs arched and their hands frozen into claws. *They were alive!!*

The arcing electricity reached tentatively out to me, and I felt a tingle. My body recognized it as familiar. This was uncontrolled nanotech, Human creations looking for a master.

"Do something!" Mieant shook me.

My hands simultaneously closed around each sword's leather pommels. Energy coursed through me. I ignited in a blaze of white-blue light that cast eerie shadows off the soldiers, the students, anyone standing nearby. The flash of my light stopped the running students, soldiers about to fire, and everyone who saw me. Everything froze, for the briefest second.

Pressure built, like I was holding my breath for too long, and then blasted from me with a deep bass *thrummmmmm*. An invisible force rushed out in an expanding circle from the epicenter. *Me!* Anyone within ten meters was thrown backward and to the ground. Experian drones exploded or were thrown from the sky. They clanked off the troops' armor like giant hail balls. Kids who were further away reeled into each other as my power plowed into them.

With newfound, fear-driven strength, I pulled the swords from Kaleren and Freela and dropped them in the grass. Mieant's parents slumped and then writhed in shock, their hands on their wounds. Microarcs cascaded from me into the grass.

Mieant, his eyes wide in fear, crab-walked backward, away from me. My glowing nimbus of electricity reflected in his blackness, casting him and the surroundings in cool, blue light. *What was I?*

Across the playground, Godwill stood, observing the chaos, observing me. He laughed, madly. "YES!"

Control screens slid over my vision. I still couldn't understand what they meant. As before, I was hungry, but unlike before, I was not angry. The soldiers around me moved in slow motion while I moved at regular speed. They flickered green and red, depending on whether or not they were shooting at me. Mieant's parents were shrouded in a green glow, with glaring red slashes where the swords had cut into them. My singular thought was: *Save Mieant's parents.*

Make something good happen.

I put my hands on their injuries. My displays shifted as profiles of their bodies floated in front of me. My reflexes knew what to do and channeled my energy into their wounds. *They could be healed.* I closed my eyes, concentrating, *willing* their flesh to come together. My nano arced and danced through them, mending Freela's internal damage first and sealing her flesh so there was almost no trace of Entarch's surprise attack. She flickered entirely green. My cloud of shimmering dust motes rose from Freela and settled like an iridescent fog over Kaleren.

I WAS healing them!

A weariness that had crept into my awareness when I'd finished with Freela turned into excruciating pain as I applied my energy to Kaleren. It felt like the aches I'd had in my shins when I was much smaller. Except it was in all of my bones, a deep agony, so far inside of me as to be unreachable, despite how much I massaged my arms and rubbed at my legs. Weakness sapped my muscles. The energy needed to stop Kaleren's bleeding and repair his torn muscles and organs pulled from me more than I had.

I was consuming myself to create the energy needed to heal Kaleren.

I will do this, I thought to myself as the pain made me grimace.

"The Human!" Godwill bellowed. The last of the Co-Governors' elite Quadrant troops smashed to the ground not a meter away from me, taken down by blaster fire. I looked into the soldiers' anonymous reflective faceplates and saw my purple hair and glowing purple eyes, crackling with sparks and energy. I was terrifying. In the faceplates' reflections, I saw a corona of nanosparks around me. I saw Mieant's grief, terror, and surprise as he dragged himself away from me, unsure of my part in either helping or destroying his parents. *Great nova and gravity wells.*

Godwill's remaining forces leveled their plasma cannons at me. And opened fire.

The swirl of micro-sparks around me coalesced into a hard shell that glowed bright and fierce upon the plasma bolts' impact. The first shots filled me with energy, which I directed to Kaleren. His wound closed.

But the full onslaught of the remaining troops' blasts was too much to absorb. Pain was running like fire through my bones and my nerves, and it pounded on the back of my skull. I was going to explode—I couldn't contain this much energy. My cursed, unreadable displays were turning red. The energy I was taking in from the plasma fire was going to erupt from my chest. *One of these flipping controls had to be an overflow type of thing to get rid of excess energy,* I thought. *Unless of course some moron Human weapons engineer had, in a fit of perverse humor, camouflaged the overflow energy button.*

Displays that pulsed with each plasma bolt certainly were correlated to my pain. One tendril of my sparks snaked through the air toward a fallen guard, who, in my overlay, glowed soft green. The dead guard's body was fuel. My nano wanted to use that organic material to replenish me, to convert his biomass into a more useable form. His suit was nanoenergy; his body was made of organic replacement parts I could use to reconstruct Mieant's parents. I remembered how I'd taken energy from IT-ME during our encounter. *If I didn't take it from this soldier, where would I take it from?*

It made sense.

NO! Architect, what was wrong with me? I was not going to EAT someone in public. I WAS NOT EVER GOING TO CONSUME SOMEONE! I stood to run and tripped on Freela's leg. Plasma bolts thundered against my shield, pounding me to the ground with sledgehammer force. The grass around me burst into flame, and I staggered with each impact. My hands skinned on something hard as I fell to my knees. My arms were weak, my elbows gave out, and I crashed, face first, into the hard dirt of the school playground.

Light around me flickered. My corona died.

I'd healed Kaleren, though.

"Hold!" Godwill shouted. Footsteps approached. Combat boots stepped into my field of vision. I tried to be angry, to feel something. My sparks, my energy, whatever it was, had departed. The boots disappeared, until I felt one across my ribs, lifting and flipping me over like a sack of wet 'natch.

Godwill's emaciated face appeared. "Raystar of Terra," he said, smiling through his NPD helmet. "Destiny awaits."

His rifle's butt hovered above me. It was covered in blood, grass, and dirt. My eyes focused on "Made on Solium4" engraved on the metal. He crushed it down. I saw stars.

Then, blackness.

32

"Unexpected. Irresponsible," a bass voice on my right rumbled each syllable with precision. *Ponderous. Deliberate.*

My brain pounded against my skull, attempting to beat its way out. *Where it would go?* I don't think it cared. I couldn't tell if my eyes were open or closed. I tasted blood in my mouth. My face hurt. My hunger was agony, something multipronged and sharp twisting in my gut. I deduced that I was lying on a table. The air tasted faintly chemical and familiar. *I must still be at school.*

"The Asrigard threat is eliminated. I have their spawn. We have YOUR challenger's daughter, and the Broodmother's heir. It is what Humans would call a triple play," said a voice above me and to my left. After a pause, I felt a hand, palm down, pat my stomach. "And of course, we have our key objective. The others are the perfect hostages if the 301st Battle Group arrives before the 98th."

I struggled to remember while trying not to give any sign that I was awake. Principal Entarch had tried to kill the Asrigards. *Nova.* With MY DAD'S swords! How did she get them? Were my parents OK??? *Flip.* I had to think rationally—with my brain, not my heart. But I KNEW the Asrigards were alive. At least, I knew they hadn't died from the swords. I'd saved them.

"Your love of these creatures' expressions is not something I understand. Nor do I understand why you sound so pleased." I knew that tone. *Someone was about to be grounded.* Right-Ear Voice continued,

"It seems to me that were you in control, were that even REMOTELY the case, today's events would NOT HAVE BEEN VISIBLE TO THE PLANET'S NEWS AGENCY! No. I believe you are obsessed with these Humans and...." A sausage-sized finger nudged my head, and my headache fell from the shelf I'd put it on and shattered into a billion icicles of pain. "Your obsession is becoming a deficit."

Meaty fists pounded the table by my head. The hand was removed from my belly.

I heard a groan to my right and turned my head, slowly.

Darkness turned to shadow, which morphed into grey, fog-shrouded shapes. The lumpy blur on the table beside me was Mieant.

Left Ear Voice dropped to a furious whisper, "I, despite what you believe, do not work for you! YOUR attitude will not please the Empress. YOUR premature presence on Nem' has only flipped our plans into the gravity well! Why you are EVEN in Blue River instead of your embassy is beyond me!"

"That fool of a principal had too much information." Left Ear continued, "She is eliminated. We even used the Commander's swords as the murder weapons! The Human's friends are children! THEY will be eliminated. And what did the newsies actually see?" Left Ear wasn't whispering anymore. "They witnessed *this* Human finish off the Co-Governors with her Human nanotech after they had been impaled!" With each syllable, a slimmer finger poked my other shoulder.

Poking a Human is apparently proof that you're saying something important.

"We have hostages," Left-Ear-Voice continued, "We have footage showing a Human planning and attacking the government, and now that we have the Co-Governors, the Integration Party is leaderless."

"You try to make gold out of gratcher excrement," Right Ear Voice said. "Your Empress does not inspire fear anymore. Lethia is not the power anymore, and every Lethian should be terrified of what is really coming. Inside the Convergence, war gains a grip it will not release. Outside, in the darkness of the Core, we face extermination," Right Ear rumbled. "I GIVE YOU TWO DAYS to douse the chaos you have created with order. I want THIS population ready for MY occupation. We must be in place to have control before the 98th Battle Group arrives. Stop playing with children. Despite my reluctance to involve you, your Empress convinced me that you have the skill needed to achieve our plans." Right Ear Voice poked my shoulder. *OW.* "Children take no skill." Right Ear Voice's tone dipped low. "I will occupy this miserable planet. Or I will destroy it. Pick carefully where you are at that time."

Heavy footsteps thudded away. A door whooshed open and closed.

Nova. This was more confusing by the minute and more dangerous by the second.

Warm breath touched my cheek and I shivered in surprise. "Your kind," Left Ear whispered, "is a plague!" And then, Left Ear flicked my forehead. Right between the eyes. You only flick someone out of spite. My headache flared. I saw red. I scrunched my face and curled around on my stomach, the position of my birth. Again, doors whooshed open and closed. Mieant and I were alone.

Get up. Ungh. Yeah. That was what I needed to do.

I uncurled and forced my eyes to open. My sight came back to me like when you have your eyes open underwater. I recognized the cold, metal counter across from me, and a plain and empty blue desk. The nurse's office. I swung my feet down, fighting the dizziness that rose from my belly to my throat. The doors whooshed yet again. In slow motion, I turned my head to the sound. Dizziness spun me as I lost my balance and cracked my head against cold metal.

As I fell off of the bed, I said things my parents say when they are angry. I landed on my side and elbow. My hands scrabbled for purchase as I pulled the thin bed sheet down over me, a ghost in hiding.

The door whooshed closed.

Someone was in there with us.

33

"Raystar, poor dear. Let me help you," a modulated female voice said as a coil wound around my good arm like a tourniquet. The tentacle's band cut into my muscle and lifted me effortlessly toward the black orb floating in the center of the office.

Nurse Pheelios. Another manipulator tentacle snaked around Mieant's slowly moving form like a python coiling around its prey.

"I...." Headache. My arm ached. My side ached. I was collecting aches.

"I understand," Pheelios said, her voice sweet honey. "I understand your body's need. Yes. Nurse Pheelios understands your flesh and bone. Do not think that because I am of the air that empathy and understanding are not achievable." A tentacle caressed my hair and slid down my cheek. Terrified, I strained my neck to move away, trying to keep my eyes on it. She rested the tip of it against my cheek, and a spark of electricity arced to my face. "Or that I am powerless to do anything about it."

I groaned, twisting to escape her rock-hard grip.

"So fragile. And yet it is WE, beings of air, that are trapped in your world." She sent another jolt to my chin, and I shuddered away from her. "Fear not, little Human. The Universe is smiling down on you. I do not normally dispense intravenous medication." Another manipulator snaked through the air toward me, like a mad vine. Except it was a vine holding a syringe.

"I will end your pain. It would please me to end it for you."

WHAT THE NOVA?

I never asked for any of this. *Never.* I wanted to play. To send silly vids of kids drooling to my friends. To go to the library and learn about the stars. My anger sparked to life.

"Beware, Raystar!" Mieant shouted, and with Lethian strength, he ripped himself free of the nurse's tentacle. He stumbled from the bed toward Pheelios. Her free arm whipped through the air, cracking against him. Mieant fell to one knee but managed to rise and lock his hands on the front of her environmental suit. His weight pulled her to the floor.

A million thoughts crashed inside the chaos of my headache. Only one made it through. *SOMEONE was fighting for me.* "*We don't leave anyone behind,*" I heard Mom say.

Mieant struggled with the nurse, but one of her tentacles formed into a point. In the flickering office light, it paused like a scorpion's tail in the air above his face and stabbed through his shoulder. The force of the blow drove him down, and her tentacle pinned him to the floor with a metallic clank.

Mieant screamed.

Blood pooled around his arm. It smelled liked steak. Suddenly, I was hungry, ravenous. Distracted by his scream, Nurse Pheelios's grip on me loosened as her other manipulator snaked around him. He struggled against her as she immobilized him. And then she withdrew the tentacle from his shoulder and paused above the hole she'd made in his shoulder. *Considering.*

Decision made, she pushed her metallic limb back into the bloody wound. He screamed, his voice cracking.

NO.

The room flashed white. Shadows rose like dark ghosts against the illuminated office walls. Pheelios...chairs...tables...everything showed up as elongated shadow-puppets.

Confused, Pheelios rotated her viewport to face me. I saw through the black glass a swirl of clouds as she took me in and jerked backward, in the direction of the door. She lashed at my face, and her tentacle hit my cheek. I crashed into the table, seeing stars momentarily, and the world went white. I heard a hum like a swarm of insects that increased to a deafening buzz. Sparks, like ants, crawled and flowed from my arms, hair, and hands.

HUNGER growled in the deep pit of my stomach. I hadn't eaten today. But NOW I WAS HUNGRY and FURIOUS!

I hadn't asked for this. I'm not a crusader. I'm a kid. Sleep in. Have sweet-milk. Get a new toy. Have a sleepover. Be liked. Have Mom and Dad give me a hug and tell me I'm great. That they loved me. Isn't this what all kids want? Isn't that the gift of childhood? To be free under the umbrella of our parents' shelter?

There was no umbrella for me. My parents were clearly in danger. Mieant's parents had been killed. And he'd just been injured trying to help me.

Fury whitened my vision. Energy coursed through me. It wasn't like healing Mieant's parents; this was like filling the jagged hole of loneliness with nuclear energy.

Pheelios turned to face me and began floating backward toward the door. I stretched out my hand, and lightning arced from my palm. Fingers of energy caressed everything in the office and then followed my will, screaming and crackling with a deafening hiss as they converged on the nurse. Strands of my power danced around her, zigzagging to the door. Acrid smoke grew from where my lightning had fused the door's seams shut.

Nurse Pheelios whipped two tentacles at me from opposite directions. I saw them, in slow motion, as they curved toward my temples.

My halo of electricity intercepted her appendages and, in a blaze of white energy, drove them down and away. I melted them to the Galactic-alloy floor. She strained to re-form her truncated tentacles, but like a balloon tied to a string, she was anchored to the floor. *Welded to it.*

I walked toward her, my rage a burning pressure in my chest. My energy cast black shadows against the wall that shifted their forms with my every step.

She turned the faceplate of her suit toward me. I have no idea what Syllthan emotions look like. I wasn't too sure of my own emotions right now. Inside the suit, a swirl of dark gases tornadoed around some bulbous form. *Was that fear?* My lightning danced on her metal shell, probing. I *felt* the seams of her environmental suit. They would crack open like my favorite red fruits. The suit's energy source was warm and delicious, just waiting for me to reach it. I could smell the rare chemicals of her gas-giant entity. *No more waiting.* I tapped the window a few times to see if she swirled any faster.

"Raystar! Stop! I will tell you what you need!" The suit's remaining arms wriggled, but she was anchored to the floor. She swirled faster.

I didn't want what she could tell me.

I wanted *her*.

Frustration, anger flowed from me in a mist of micro-sparks, and where they touched her suit, the suit dissolved. Streams of light pulsed back toward me, and I felt like I was stepping into a warm bath. *MORE!* I hugged her suit, my face pressed against her faceplate.

One of my sparks found a way inside. I heard a crackle as my currents shorted her vocal circuits. I laughed. My body surged with power. *I WOULD UNMAKE THIS ENEMY.* Another spark was inside. The atmosphere seal popped; her "air" escaped from her suit. My aura congealed around it, and I felt a rush as it became *part of me!*

Far away from this ecstasy, a scared, saner Raystar recoiled, horrified in her understanding of where these actions were taking her. *What I was doing??*

A millisecond later, my sparks flooded into the chamber of Pheelios's suit, and my avatars covered her writhing body. From my toes to the top of my head, I thrummed with life. I screamed, craxy and joyful. I could feel it, my nano, rending, tearing at a molecular level, unmaking Pheelios's cell walls and bringing her matter into me.

I absorbed so much from her that suddenly, new controls flashed on, overlaying my vision. As before, I couldn't read the language. Mieant's puppetlike profile was silhouetted with a green glow, and a red glare marked the wound on his shoulder. When I looked around the room, I saw outlines of power sources, metal seams—a million pieces of information. I knew, for instance, I could create claws and rip through the Galactic alloy in any direction. And there were capabilities even more destructive that I dared not access.

MORE. HEAL. FIGHT. ESCAPE. The thoughts came to me. Microsparks flowed from my body like a fuzzy, silvery gown out and over everything in the room, ceiling included. It looked like a sparkly fantasy scene that would delight young children. The jagged, half-moon husk of Pheelios's suit gonged to the ground.

Armored fists pounded the door. With newfound control, I pulled in my power. Mieant groaned, and I knelt by him. The tentacle pinning him down was gone; his blood was gone; there was no hole in his shoulder, just a tear in his clothes. I blinked, realizing that I'd healed him. He opened his eyes, grabbed my arm. I lifted him like he was weightless, righting and supporting his body as his legs wobbled.

"Raystar, what...." My friend's black, pupil-less eyes took in the nurse's empty suit, the wreckage of the office, the burn marks. "Pheelios. She's...where is she?" he whispered. Then his eyes grew huge, panicked. "Architect!" He scrambled away from me, falling backward on to one of the tables.

"Mieant...." *What? What was I going to say? Don't be afraid. Please?* The pounding increased. "We have got to go NOW!"

The doors exploded inward. Godwill and his security team poured into the Nurse's office. Two guards grabbed Mieant and flung him onto the table, slapped a collar on his neck and injected him with a syringe similar to what Nurse Pheelios had held. Mieant didn't even have time to yell.

The Jurisdictor took the office's destruction in with a glance. He raised an eyebrow at the empty, corroded environmental suit and drew a slim pistol from his belt and pointed it at me. I raised my hands, calling for my power.

Nothing. Not even a spark.

Godwill looked at me curiously and pulled the trigger.

Being unconscious was getting old.

I opened my eyes AGAIN and concentrated on making sense of what was in front of me. Grains of golden sand made up my view of the ground. My neck hurt. With extreme effort, I moved my hand to the circle of fire around my throat. *A collar.*

The avalanche of images, sensations, words, screams, smells, crashed like broken pieces of my life on the floor of my mind. *Remind me not to get shot by a stunner again.*

Peace, I told myself. Disconnected from my thoughts, I picked up a fragment of memory. I tried to keep my breathing calm, to not judge or interpret any individual moment, but instead to simply focus on reassembling pieces into a view of reality I could act on.

Humanity, or more specifically, I, had been framed for killing Mieant's parents. Actually, it was worse than that. My Dad's swords had been used to attack them, which meant my parents could be tied to the assault. *Were my parents OK?* Fear knotted my gut, and I started hyperventilating. Freela and Kaleren had been alive before I was captured—I had healed them.

Peace. I told myself again. *I had to confront these facts and questions, and not panic. I had to THINK! FOCUS! ACT!*

Nurse Pheelios. I had killed her—out of self defense, true. But I'd CONSUMED a sentient being. A citizen of the Convergence. And I'd loved the power and life it gave me! In that moment, I'd been made aware that I had a set of capabilities that I had not yet accessed. *Nova.* I wanted that power, that invincibility. I wouldn't need anyone. But I had to learn to control it. I mean, what if Mom or Dad had been accidentally consumed in my body's quest for energy? I shuddered, remembering the HUNGER, the rage. *What were the ancient Humans like?*

Had my organic parents given me away because they came to realize I was deadly? I closed my eyes against the wave of fear and uncertainty. What I'd done was in the past, and I was going to have to deal with the consequences of my choices and actions. I was terrified. Alone. But I could be those things and still take action. *OK. Breathe.*

I turned my attention to my surroundings. Dull blue metal bars marked the perimeter of my open-air enclosure. The sky was dark, so it was either early morning or night. Lightning strobed and wound silently through blackness, illuminating the roiling Storm Wall. *OK. The Mesas were over there.*

Judging from the increased pressure on the back of my skull, I guessed that a day had passed since I'd been captured. The Storm Wall would soon reach its crescendo atop the Mesas and begin its planetary journey to the sister Mesas on the other side of Nem'. Wind carried occasional fat drops of rain, but nothing constant.

I pushed myself to a sitting position. *Bad idea.* Dizziness and nausea swept from my belly to inside my head, and I threw up, retched, and threw up some more. Whatever Godwill had stunned me with had made me feel pretty unstarred. When there was nothing more to come out, I curled up into a ball.

Between dry heaves and wracking cramps, I became dimly aware of a thrumming vibration through the ground. Recognizing the pattern, I lifted my head, hoping to see Nonch.

The enormous Crynit from the school attack was centimeters away from the bars, regarding me with—I'd learned from Nonch—curiosity.

"Jurisdictor," it said in a light, whispery voice, "The Human is having seizures."

Nonch had called her Sarla. She tilted her massive head to the side, listening for a response.

"Understood. I will report again when it has been subdued and transported."

I'd only just understood the implications of their conversation when fire erupted from my collar. I spasmed as the electrical charge surged through my nerves, and I fell back into unconsciousness.

35

Something poked my back, above my kidneys. I didn't move.

"Is she dead?"

"When she receives the DNA solvent, she will wish she was."

I sat up slowly and opened my eyes. My sore muscles ached, and I had a severe crick in my neck. Turning toward the voices, I found myself squinting into white light.

"Ahhh. Nem's only Human awakens." Someone chuckled behind the blazing whiteness.

Godwill.

"Jerk," I muttered, weakly, and tried to shift and get my knees under me.

"If your adults had the same fire, your ancestors must have been as formidable as the legends say they were," he laughed. After a silence, he continued. "But that is how your world, and your people, died, Raystar of Terra. In ignorance of their place in the galaxy. Alas. For your species, extinction is the only seat reserved for you. But. There is time enough for some final moments of entertainment." And at the word "entertainment," electricity spread outward from my collar. I shrieked. My hands clawed air while my muscles spasmed.

"The collars cause pain. It is a good discovery, Raystar. You will learn that they also cause relief. See?"

I felt nothing. Panting, I looked at him in confusion.

"Here's the pain." The shock hit me again, this time for so long that when it disappeared, I remained on the ground with my back arched, trembling, before my muscles unclenched.

"The moments when you feel nothing are an immense relief, wouldn't you say?"

He shocked me again. Then nothing. He was right. Nothing became relief.

"In your time remaining," Godwill chuckled, "you will thank me for 'nothing.'" He laughed. "It is a play on words. A Human way of speaking, often for causing humor."

Shock. Nothing. On and on and on it went, and then, thankfully, a lot more of nothing. The lights shut off, and I was alone in darkness. Cold seeped up from the floor and into my bones.

I closed my eyes. For a moment, I was grateful for the respite of nothing. But in the darkness of my mind and the silence of my cell, a fire ignited, a mental resistance to their torture.

Heat.

The fire in my mind blazed, chasing the cold of the floor out of my body. It crackled and hissed with promises of action as it grew in strength.

I had been treated to enough insult and cruelty to fuel my internal fire for lifetimes to come. Since I could remember, I'd tried to ignore the sleights of the Galactics around me. I'd pretended to be just another Galactic. I *wasn't*. They didn't want me. I saw my life painted red by the angry firelight in my mind, and it quickened my pulse.

I was the alien. My people were the destroyers.

I poured more anger into the fire, and it soared into the heights of my psyche, turning my thoughts into the deep orange, red, and sooty black of *rage*.

Is this what my ancestors felt when they first encountered the Convergence?

Maybe the Galactics had it wrong. I wasn't JUST their last Human.

I was their last Human *ENEMY*.

So be it.

36

"It is not that simple," a voice said above the clicks, shrieks, and snaps of a million creatures.

"Oppression is not complicated. You antagonized her at every opportunity." I lay still, having awakened halfway into an *interesting* conversation.

"That was school. Look around. This is a different circumstance."

"Oh. How you act on your beliefs changes with your circumstances? Or have you now changed your beliefs?"

"Speak plainly, Crynit."

"What are your motivations? If we find an opportunity to escape, Mieant, which side will you be on?" Nonch's voice was low.

I heard a laugh and a sob.

"My motivations matter very little. My parents were just assassinated!" I heard grief in the voice. There was silence. Mieant took in a ragged breath and continued. "We've been kidnapped. Where does what I want appear in any of this?"

"Your parents have not been confirmed dead."

"Crynit, you know nothing! Where is your all-powerful Broodmother? Or Cri and Raystar's parents? If I were the Jurisdictor, I would have removed them all simultaneously. We are lost. Alone." A starbat let out a series of whistles somewhere nearby. Thunder rumbled in reply, its low growl vibrating the floor against the length of my body.

Mieant continued, "You wanted to know why I didn't like Raystar. Will you let me answer?"

I groaned. Cri had given me her list of reasons she didn't like me. Now I'd have another list. My thoughts from the torture cell whispered, *See? They hate you. YOU are the alien, the outcast, the outsider.*

"I had everything on Solium4," Mieant went on. "Everything. I remember the day my parents learned of some purple-haired Human girl who manifested mysterious abilities. To say they were excited is to say the Galactic Core is merely 'filled with stars.' Mother and Father felt this was THE opportunity to befriend a "genetic key" and gain Human cooperation in harnessing their ancient technology. And, for the greater good of all in the Convergence, to diminish the rising strength of the Foundationalists."

He sighed.

"Solium4 isn't just the Quadrant Capital. It is the heart of the Convergence. I had worked *hard*." He sounded like he was clenching his laser-sharp teeth when he said that last word. "...To achieve an apprenticeship with a Master. I had the beginning of a high-end clothing line, a black-hole-tight marketing plan to get it distributed on key major planets and even in shows in other quadrants. All without my parents' help!"

"I had wondered how you produced the streamers for me. They were indeed beautiful."

"Ha! That's nothing compared to what I had! I could have made arm bands for you that would have honored your Broodmother, with colors and patterns never seen before!

"Nonetheless, I am still grateful for—" Nonch said, but Mieant interrupted him, intent on his thought.

"My friends, my dreams, even my fabrics, are on Solium4. And I'm here. The glorious 'natch capital of the galaxy. When I met Raystar, I could not see how she could help anything, even herself. I was furious about the waste of my life, and the jeopardy my parents had put themselves in by placing their hopes with her."

Armor clacked. I opened an eye. I wasn't on sand anymore. I focused on the weave of the green bedding I lay on. I wasn't angry. We were all just creatures, I guess, trying to do our best with the gap between what we're given and what we want. *Fashion, huh.* It certainly explained his looks. I'd written it off to his parents being wealthy, but had he actually been making his own clothes?

And I could see how unfair it would seem to him. His parents, the Quadrant Governors, moved here for some reason to do with me. That they would move here because of me, that in itself was difficult to imagine. "People" wouldn't even open the door for me.

And yet, an Ascendant family, as a result of a decision made by the *Glean Gathering*, had adopted me. There were other parties involved too. I thought sourly that my circumstance was like a Galactic "adopt Raystar" agreement. But the implications were that I was important to something.

Yet, no miraculous Human tech had manifested itself, with the exception of my new powers. Godwill and his soldiers had neutralized them easily enough. Lightning flashed in the background, and in the darkness of the Storm Wall, it was impossible to tell day or night.

"Nonch, my parents said we'd only be here for two cycles. Instead, I'm growing up here!"

"I am growing up here, too," Nonch replied, a chill in his tone.

"That is your destiny. Mine is not on this planet. This galaxy is so much bigger than you planet-bounds can imagine. My old life was shredded for this small creature that hides in the protection of her sister." There was silence, and then he continued. "And I have seen her do *things*, Crynit. She is not what she seems!"

I cracked open my other eye.

My face rested on my hands, and I had pulled my legs toward my chest. Nonch was curled in a wall around me. His armored midnight-blue segments were hard, but warm to the touch.

Mieant sat cross-legged in front of him. His olive explorer's outfit was torn and singed. There was a hole where Nurse Pheelios's tentacle had stabbed him. I winced at the pain in my back, shoulders, and hips. My collar dug into my neck. No stars, no distant planets, no exploration, no nothing was my destiny. Godwill was going to kill me.

"Lethian-Mieant." Nonch sighed, after a moment. "Ordinarily, I would say that Broodmother would have found us by now. However, this camp must be somehow shielded from our Hive's sensors, or Broodmother would have come to get me, at least. I agree with your assessment. We are on our own. Orphans. But consider—your parents, my Broodmother, and Raystar and Cri's parents. The probability is high that they will all be permanently missing their offspring if we do not take action ourselves."

"You want me to trust you."

"If we do not trust each other, Lethian...."

Silence.

Nonch continued, "I do not think Godwill needed to go through the trouble of bringing us to this dusty camp to eliminate us. He could have done it at any time previously. A much larger thing is happening. We are caught either in its focus or in its wake." As he spoke, Nonch dipped his sensor stalks alternately at the words "focus" and "wake."

"What do you mean?" Mieant's frown creased his forehead, and the edges of his mouth turned downward in a very Lethian expression.

"The son of the Quadrant Co-Governors? The Asrigard Heir? The only Human on Nem'? And I, Broodmother Krig's offspring? Imprisoned together?"

Four species. Except for me, the kids of the leaders. *Yeah.*

Mieant grunted his agreement after a moment. "Nonch, what Raystar did in Nurse Pheelios's office was...terrifying," His voice lowered to a whisper. "She is not telling us everything. Can WE trust HER?"

"Cri approaches," Nonch said a moment before I heard her footsteps. "We will discuss this at another time."

"OK. Bad news," Cri announced as she approached. Her black hair swished behind her shoulders, and her expression, so much like Mom's, lit up when she saw Mieant. Something clanked in her hands, and her eyes glowed with excitement. "I found us food canisters."

"Why's that bad?" Mieant asked.

"The Twig can't eat it," she said, pointing to me and raising an eyebrow. "It's synthetic. She's allergic."

I winced at my nickname, but my stomach pinched and grumbled at the mention of food. Amidst my OTHER pain, I hadn't realized how hungry I was. Most Galactic food was created from chemicals. I couldn't digest it. Usually, only the newer races in the Convergence, those without hundreds of years to adjust to the additives, had that problem. Humans had been in the Convergence for 1,800 years. But maybe with my nanotech, I could consume it?

Right. Along with everyone else. It was a terrifying thought.

I didn't even know how to, uh, activate me.

"I got water, though," she said brightly, holding up several grey metal cylinders hanging on a chain.

I opened my eyes. Being helpless was no longer an option. Everyone here was here because of me. Groaning, I pushed myself up into a cross-legged position. My friends and sister turned my direction.

"Mieant," I said, scooting stiffly to sit facing him, "I tried to save your parents. They're alive. Or at least they were before we were captured," I said, looking directly into his eyes.

He dropped his gaze and swallowed.

"Here," Cri said, handing a canister of water to Mieant and Nonch, and then to me. And then she did a double take. "You got blood." My hand shot to my nose, and I felt a crusty line tracing around my lip and down my cheek. I rubbed dried blood from my face with my dirt-crusted sleeve. We sipped in silence, no one really looking at anyone else.

"Principal Entarch used Dad's swords," I said, still staring at nothing.

"Architect!" She gaped. "Do you think he's OK? How did they get them?" She began hyperventilating. I watched as Mieant rose and wrapped his arms around her. "If they have Dad, then we can't be rescued! And...and...Mom must be in terrible danger! and...OH NO," Cri was devolving into sobs that jerked her shoulders and made her matted hair fall around her face.

"We know nothing conclusively, Cri, Sister-of-Raystar," Nonch said calmly. She peered up at him in between strands of black hair. Her eyes didn't glow. "As Mieant and I had discussed, we believe there is no coincidence that the four of us, given who our parents are, are imprisoned together. While we do not know their status, it is reasonable to assume that they do not know ours. That we are alone and must depend on ourselves in what time we have left. That is our only truth and perhaps, our only hope."

Mieant nodded his assent, pulled Cri close, and whispered something to her.

"Where are we?" I croaked after a long moment. To my surprise, Cri sucked in a breath and disengaged from Mieant. She pushed her hair back behind her ears and straightened her ripped clothes—gestures that reminded me of Mom. Thinking of her, my head began to ache and I thought I tasted blood in my mouth. I willed both sensations into my subconscious. I had to lock them away to have any chance of functioning.

"The camp is rectangular. There's a large building that way, two smaller buildings like this one in a row in front, and on the other side of these is a cruiser landing pad." She sniffed, took in another breath, and began to assemble a map on the concrete using 'natch leaves as building markers. The camp was laid out like a lowercase "t", with the three buildings making the cross, the larger building the base, and the landing pad the top. "I think the other buildings may have prisoners. One's a bathroom." She paused. "The Storm Wall makes it impossible to tell the time, but I think I can see Blue River's lights against the clouds in the distance. Which means it's probably early evening. And there are at least thirty guards—Glean, Lethian and Crynit."

"Wow." I blinked at my sister. "That was, uh, amazingly thorough, Cri." She frowned at my compliment.

"Crynits working with Jurisdictor Godwill!" Nonch hissed.

Mieant laughed bitterly. He waved upward. "Out there, everyone has a side. Even sides have sides, and there are few reasons to be friendly, even to your own species."

Nonch responded with silence and a stillness that revealed nothing of his thoughts. Maybe not for long. Based on what he'd hinted at, change was coming to the Crynits.

"OK," I said, taking a sip. The water tasted like metal and lemon, and something soft dislodged from inside the container and touched my tongue as I drank. I sputtered it out, shuddering, and rubbed my lips against my sleeve. "We need a plan."

"Yes. We need to understand the purpose of the buildings, the ways in and out of the camp," Mieant added.

"Patterns," Cri said, "the guard patterns, shifts, things like that?"

"Glad we have all watched action vids," Mieant snarked. "Cameras. We need to find all of the cameras."

I placed a hand on Nonch's banded, armored back and heaved myself up. *Ow.* Stretching, I surveyed our enclosure. We were on a concrete slab. Four pillars supported a flat roof. Our rough green bedrolls spread over various parts of the floor. It was too dark to see any cameras, but it was a sure bet we were being monitored. I had seen enough action vids to know that.

I turned to Cri. "So they just let us walk around?"

"I did," she shrugged. "I walked over there." She pointed to the large shadow across an expanse of the camp's yard. "Pretty sure these collars let them know where we are, and given that they can turn them on and off whenever, I don't think they worry about us trying to run."

The collars would need to be removed. But we were sorely lacking information. *Right. First figure out what we were up against, then figure out the collars.* I breathed in and lifted my gaze. Through the darkness, I could make out vague, squat shapes. From one building, taller than the others, light seeped through blind-covered windows.

Something was vaguely familiar about the location of the camp.

'Natch! I inhaled its richness. I'd lived my whole life around it, in it, with it. Knowing it was nearby was oddly comforting. I took another deep breath and took in my companions.

Nonch, who'd proven loyal in entrusting me with his life-threatening secret, stood silhouetted against the low light. He was a beacon of stability and common sense. His midnight blue-banded plates dully reflected back the camp lights, and his top two orange primary eyes were iridescent in the darkness. Mieant, my bully-turned-reluctant-ally, was talking softly to my sister, his head against her forehead. I had saved his parents! Maybe now he believed me. His more rigid posture suggested a willingness to at least hope his parents were still alive. I sighed. I knew him better now, knew how intertwined our fates actually were.

Cri. Big Sis'. Dimly, I remembered a time when she could do no wrong, and now? I shook my head. Now? I could do no right. I watched her, nodding occasionally to whatever Mieant was saying. She had her lower arms around his waist. Their intimacy wasn't hidden, and there was no way to mask what was growing between them. The four of us were prisoners together.

Relationships are like clouds. But instead of being created by wind and heat, we're shaped by time and circumstance. Only two days ago, we were different people with different views about each other. The people we collect in our lives may not be the ones we thought we'd have, or even wanted. We can treat them well, or discard them. Show them love, or hate them.

But they're all OURS. In the hardest of times, what do we owe them? What would we do to see them safe?

My eyes burned. I rubbed doubt and uncertainty away.

I'd do anything for my friends.

It was time to explore and see what we had to work with.

37

The shadow that rose out of the morning darkness blocked our first exploratory steps into the compound and towered four meters above us. Five black-chitin, blade-sharp arms sprung around us like a ribcage. Cri was to my left and Mieant was to my right, and its claw arms could touch them both on their outside shoulders.

"Aiiieee!" We jumped back; the terror was shared between the three of us. Nonch opened his arms into a spiky net, keeping us from tumbling to the ground in a jumble of panicked legs and arms.

The creature's head dwarfed my upper body, with mandibles perhaps as long as me; death weaved slowly, back and forth, in front of us. The massive Crynit hissed and clacked. She was easily twice Nonch's size.

Sarla.

Her head lowered toward me, and she my brushed my face tentatively with her sensor stalks.

"You do not look like a destroyer of worlds, little one," the giant Galactic near-whispered as she clacked her arm claws together slowly, like fingers drummed on a table in contemplation. Her voice, rich, feminine, cool, and bemused, vibrated through me. My heart stopped. I tried to restart it by hyperventilating.

She turned to Nonch. The two Crynits froze, quieter than we who lay breathless in Nonch's net of arms.

"Sarla the Betrayer!" Nonch hissed, but he lowered his sensor stalks in a sign of submission. A direct conflict between Sarla and Nonch would be eye-blink quick. And we'd be less one companion.

Fresh earth and sugar wafted through the air.

"Child," the Crynit said, gently, tapping him once softly between his two orange eyes with a blade claw, "you know nothing." Sarla turned back to me and pointed with the same spear-sized append-age. "This tragic creature is your undoing. This Human should never have been saved. Tend to the Brood, young Nonch of Krig, instead of throwing your talent and our hope into the grindstone of WAR." Her husky voice cracked with emotion at the last word, and her long shape shook.

"You abandon us, and tell me to tend to the Brood?"

Sarla hissed, arching above us and flaring her arm claws for a dead-ly downward strike. "Broodmother is blind, and her path is madness. She will bring Crynit deaths on a scale seen not for two thousand years!" Sarla paused and dropped a razor-sharp claw hand within centimeters of my face. With barely contained rage, she hissed, "Be-cause of these Humans!"

My eyes were, I'm sure, crossed as I stared at Sarla's death-dealing fingertip hovering a blade's width from my nose. "I'm just a kid," I breathed out, my fear making breathing difficult. Looking up at Sarla, I mumbled, "I didn't ask for any of this."

Sarla turned her enormous head to me, her hot breath blowing strands of hair from my face. Slowly, she withdrew her claw hand. Two snaps of her mandibles later, she turned and *thrummed* away into the darkness.

Seconds, minutes, hours passed. I don't think any of us knew how long we'd stood there hyperventilating, each of us trying to get our own version of a heart back into its right spot in our chests.

Mieant was the first to rise out of Nonch's arm claws. "Architect. He's big," he breathed.

The sound of his voice startled us all into movement.

"She," Nonch said as he lifted us up. "Sarla is a she. The largest of us are female."

"She smells good, like…sweetness and earth," Cri said.

Nonch spun Cri to face him, with two arm claws poking her gently in the chest. His iridescent orange primary eyes eerily focused on her. "That is the smell of death, Cri Ceridian. If you smell that around my kind, beware."

Cri gulped.

"Nonch," I placed my hand on his arm claw, pulling him away from Cri. "What did Sarla mean? About Broodmother and her madness?"

He hesitated, glancing furtively at Cri and Mieant, and then straightened. "She believes Crynits need to be on a different side. That we chose the wrong side 1,800 years ago. The other Broodmothers do not agree."

"But there's no, uh, war, right now…." Cri's voice tapered off at the last word. She looked at each of us in turn, her eyes big with worry as she moved more tightly against Mieant.

"Cri, Sister-of-Raystar, two Convergence Battlegroups are in transit to Nem'. We"—Nonch waved to the complex in general with his six arm claws—"are in prison."

He had a point.

Mieant coughed and changed the subject. "Maybe we should wait until the sun's fully risen. You know. To explore."

A pair of Lethian guards walked by. They heard Mieant and chuckled.

We looked at each other and straightened up. I'd learned at school that you don't show fear to bullies. This could be a bit different—I mean, these bullies had actually kidnapped us. And they had plasma rifles. I let out the loud breath I'd been holding and smiled after them. One guard frowned. I could put on a brave face.

Because after Sarla, they were not even remotely close to scary.

And we needed to see what this camp was all about.

"So, what? You use smells for emotion?" Mieant asked as I started us off toward the closest of the four buildings. We'd walk around them and be able to see the camp perimeter, check out our captors, and assess the uses of each of the buildings.

"It is much more than that. Pheromones. Highly coded chemical messages. In the hive, it is much more efficient than assembling lines of words."

I looked at Nonch. My friend since forever was turning out to be much more than just a pretty face. "What do you mean?"

"Our pheromone messages are higher-level concepts. If I say, 'run' to you, you understand the action, but there is no context. Our messages are the equivalent of 'run to the hive center as the Broodmother calls.' One smell for ten Galactic words, but they happen at the same time."

"Wow," I rubbed my shoulders, "That's…amazing."

"Can we use it somehow?" Cri asked. "As a signal?"

"Yeah!" I whispered. It was brilliant. "A timed message? So if we're close, we know to take an action. If we're separated, we'll know that certain actions have been taken, and it's our turn."

Nonch clacked. "It is possible."

"It would need to be contextual. And we need to agree on a smell."

The odor of fresh-cut 'natch suddenly wafted around us. We looked at each other, then at Nonch. His sensor stalk twitched.

"Smells like 'natch," Cri said.

"Yes, will it suffice?"

"Sure," I replied. "What does it mean?"

"'Natch."

I looked at him and shrugged. "Well, now it means 'danger,' or 'go,' or 'yes.' We have to interpret it contextually." Nonch didn't reply. Mieant nodded.

"So, if the response is 'no' to a question, we don't smell anything?" Cri asked.

"Exactly," I replied. It was a start. "We need to have a simple code between us *before* we run into trouble."

"Up ahead, look at that," Mieant said. We'd approached a green rectangular building made out of corrugated metal. It had a gently pointed, A-frame roof and looked exactly like the sheds on our farm. *Food? Supplies?*

But Mieant was pointing past the shed, toward the perimeter of the camp. A force wall sparkled occasionally as Nem's insect population incinerated themselves on the otherwise invisible wall. The wall shimmered between six-meter-tall poles about as thick as my body. The poles were spaced every ten meters. Small auto-cannons mounted on each pole pivoted with 360 degrees of freedom. Red sensor clusters glowed in the morning light. Autocannons swiveled toward us as we approached. Below the sensor clusters lay a round shield casing, from which poked a single barrel.

"And? We're walled in? There are guns pointing at us?" I asked, tired of guessing at what he found so interesting. I'd expected defenses like this. Collars or no, it would be much easier to manage us with a physical fence. The autocannons, albeit smaller than those on our farm, would help as well. Why not have all three? Mieant put a hand on my head and moved my head down so I was looking at the ground three or so meters from the force wall. "Oh."

Cloud-grey metal beams twisted from the ground, emerging like a drowning swimmer's hand clawing toward the sky.

Nonch flowed up to the metal and bit it.

"Uh," Cri said.

Nonch turned back to us. His inner mouthspikes moved slowly, like when we Galactics—at least those of us who have lips—move our mouths, tasting a flavor.

"It is ancient Human metal. We are close to the Ruins. That, at least, is good." He looked at each of us, seeing our confusion. "Broodmother has mapped all of the ancient Ruins. We believe we have tunnels to all of them. My kind may be close." He balled his tail up and smashed the metal, like a dinosaur crushing an opponent with the bone hammer of its tail. We all jumped back, and an enormously deep gong reverberated out across the camp and through the ground.

Starbat swarms exploded into the sky from the darkness outside the camp's perimeter. Shrieking and glowing and pooping EVERYWHERE, they must have numbered in the millions. Turrets swiveled and focused on us. Guards drew their weapons, checked their scanners, and told us "stupid kids" to stop messing around or we'd pay.

We looked at each other with horrified grins.

If it wasn't for the threat of being incinerated, I'm pretty sure we all wanted Nonch to hit the flipping gravity well out of that metal thing again.

We could still *hear* the gong underground. "Do you understand?" he said, turning to us, "Human Ruins are old buildings. Strong. Huge. Many, most, are hollow and lead down under in Nem'. There are cities, with roads, tubes, tunnels, stretching across Nem', underground."

"Brilliant," Cri said, cocking her hip. "Shells, you know what you should do?"

Nonch tilted his head to her, orienting his sensor stalks to give my sister his full attention.

She continued, "You should smash that thing louder, and maybe my mom and dad will hear us and come to our rescue. Or, or...you guys stand with your backs to me, and I'll dig. Just make sure you cover the dirt so the guards don't see. Or..."

"Cri, why do you have to be such a *spike*?" Mieant said, annoyed. Nonch's sensor stalks dropped as the sarcasm hit him. "We're *scouting*. It's information. Maybe we can use...."

"*I'm a spike*? You've been a supreme butt-nova for the past three years!" Cri started out looking hurt, but as she spoke, her voice grew louder, and she got in Mieant's face. "Holding my hand doesn't mean you can tell me what to do, jerk!"

"HEY!" I interposed, stepping between them and grunting as I shoved each back a pace. *Sheesh. I mean. We're in a prison camp or what?* The two Lethian guards who had passed us were staring in our direction—no doubt blaming us for the white and green blossoms of starbat poop on their uniforms and looking for an excuse to do something prison-guardish. "C'mon," I said, "stick to the plan. We're on Human Ruins. We know one thing we didn't know before. Keep moving."

Cri looked down and sighed. Mieant pulled and straightened his tattered clothes and sucked in a breath.

I looked between them and said, "We good?" I waited until I got nods from both of them, and then continued. "OK. We're all really unstarred to be here. We're probably going to die." They frowned at me.

I continued, holding up my hands in a let-me-finish gesture. "I don't know what to do with that, except, uh, to try hard not to. We have nothing to lose." I put a hand on Mieant's shoulder. "We need information." I put my arm around my sister. "We don't know how much time we have.

"Focus."

I shoved them both forward, slapping their backs as I did. Banefire was rising, and in the morning light it became apparent where we were. Around us, a skeletal forest of twisted metal stretched toward the sky. Disturbed starbats screeched and circled and pooped their way back to their roosts. Behind the Ruins, one of the Mesas revealed its bulk in the morning light like a submerged rock that appears as a wave recedes. Banefire's light crested the horizon and colored the top of the mountain red. Dawn's light revealed the Storm Wall as an imposing purple, grey, black, and lightning-flecked barrier reaching up into Nem's atmosphere.

Why would Godwill have a base here? While the Mesas were huge, spanning kilometers, there were only three of them. If we were this close to the Mesas, might we be only a long walk from the farm? And if we were this close to the Human Ruins, did that mean we were close to the Human base AI told me to take shelter in? Could we be that lucky?

Sure. When gratchers fly.

38

As it turns out, except for the few ancient Human echo-y ruins sticking up from the ground, the camp wasn't exciting. It was just as Cri had said: a space three hundred or so meters long and three hundred meters wide. *Go Galactic creativity.*

That said, the camp WAS at the edge of the Human Ruins (which were interesting) and in the other direction, 'natch stretched out into infinity (which was not interesting). The camp was shoved into the Ruins like an iron egg in a metallic bird's nest. This deep in the tangled buildings, the struggle between the planet and Human architecture was evident. Grasses, flowers, and even some scraggly trees lined the ground, unsuccessfully trying to push aside the angry metal structures that blocked their precious light.

Starbats took shelter from the day, perching in the hollow Ruins and jostling each other for the best roosting spot. Geckomice no larger than my hand flicked about. Their whiskery noses protruded like thistle tips as they poked their heads around a struggling plant or a metal beam. They were as curious about us as they were intent on catching the myriad of insects hopping or flitting around us.

The insects, of course, were oblivious to the geckomice and the force wall. At one point, a geckomouse leapt from the edge of a leaf at a giant moth and caught it in clawed hands. Its arc carried it into the force fence, and the furry geckomouse disappeared in a *zzzzzushhh.* Nonch turned his head toward the smell. *I wonder what message he got from that?*

A low hum sounded from the east. It swelled with the pulse of anti-grav thrusters, and an NPD cruiser raced into view. As it drew near, the ship grew from a black dot against grey clouds into the potato-shaped ship that had visited our farm. Starbats launched themselves from their perches, their directions chosen at random. This time, they were even more irritated than during the earlier interruption. Geckomice scurried for cover, squeaking in rapid patterns only they could decode.

The insects just buzzed and darted and flapped louder.

Fire ran around my neck. My knees got weak for a moment, and I clutched my collar.

The cruiser touched down.

"Human!" Sarla shouted as she approached us, a small device in one of her five blood-red hand claws. Obviously, it was a controller that was linked to my collar. I collapsed to my knees, head to the dirt, hands pulling at the plastic circlet.

"Jurisdictor requires you." She held up the claw with the device, waved it, and pointed to my neck.

Out of the corner of my eyes, I could see my friends watching me.

Pain. I pushed myself to stand.

I reached out a hand, and Nonch extended an arm claw. Nonch's head, with its weaponry, pivoted toward me. I put my other hand on his mandible and pulled myself up. The cruiser's door whooshed open, and Godwill stepped out. My friends encircled me.

Seeing Sarla tense, I pushed through them. She seemed larger than my memory of her in the daylight. I walked toward her, hands at my side, and looked over my shoulder one more time. My friends huddled close to each other, a natural back-to-back formation. They were scared.

"It's OK," I said to them, one hand on my collar. "Nothing you can do."

"Ray...." Cri took a reflexive step toward Sarla, who, in response, arched her body and unfolded her sword arms like flower petals. I looked at her—my sister, who'd become so angry at me lately. Hope flickered that she just might still want to be my sister. That was worth protecting. She was important to me.

"Look around you!" I yelled, waving at the autocannons. *NOVA! WAS EVERYONE BLIND?* The closest turrets were tracking us with their molten red eyes. My friends followed my gaze. To my relief, Cri backed away.

"Ahh. Raystar of Terra," Godwill said pleasantly as he approached. He wore his formal NPD police uniform, and his black, pupil-less eyes seemed to stare at everything from the nothingness of his gaunt face. He came to a stop next to the Crynit. "Sarla," he said, "I will take the Human from here." Godwill gestured toward my friends and smiled. "Take our other guests to their enclosure. Be gentle with them. They all have important roles in the upcoming days."

Sarla flowed like a black waterfall toward my friends. In an eye-blink, she'd pinned Nonch on the ground, a blade claw pressing down on his head. Mieant was held around the neck with hand claws, a blade under his chin. Sarla's tail pinchers held Cri around the waist. I could see a thin trickle of blood where Sarla's sword-sharp chitin cut into her hips.

"Don't fight! Don't fight!" I yelled. "Wait for our time, yes?" I added this—I don't know why. *Sarla and Godwill could hear me.* The scent of 'natch wafted over us, and Sarla's head whipped toward Nonch. She cocked her head and slowly looked at all of my friends as they relaxed in her grip. Godwill laughed and shoved me roughly toward the two-story building.

Our smell communication had worked, and all Sarla had gotten was the smell of 'natch.

"Raystar," Godwill said, looking down at me as we walked. He grinned from bony cheek to bony cheek, showing his teeth. "This is a 'nova' day for me! That is how you kids say it?" He paused and then chuckled. "Although I doubt you'll share the same level of enthusiasm once we begin."

I spared a glance toward my friends to see them moving back toward the compound where we had slept.

"*Me*, Raystar. Pay attention to *me*. There is no help you can give them." And then he chuckled more to himself than to me. "And there is absolutely no aid they can give to you."

We reached the building. He opened the door and pushed my shoulder so I stumbled over the building's threshold. Two startled Lethian guards rose to attention and acknowledged us with a terrified, wide-eyed salute. Their overly enthusiastic fists slammed into open palms at chest level. Godwill ignored them as we walked by. The cacophony of starbats from outside silenced as the door closed behind us.

Godwill marched me down a hallway with white, reflective floors, walls, and ceilings. We arrived at a large, very out-of-place door. It was corroded and looked like it had been punched outward by whatever was on the inside. He made a gesture, and the building synth opened the door. It was a vault. The door was over a meter thick.

Stepping into the vault was an insane journey to a different world. The walls were stained, scratched, corroded. *This must have been where they'd taken me the first time I'd been tortured.*

"Move," Godwill commanded. I swallowed and walked down the stairs. My boots made scratchy sounds on the rusty metal. My fast breaths verging on hyperventilation, the swishing of his long military jacket, and the pounding in my chest were the only other sounds that could reach my awareness through my fear.

The stairway led to a room half the size of the building. Brown rust cracked underfoot like gravel. I frowned and snuck a downward glance. The weight of my kid-body pushed rusted material apart, and I was rewarded with a view of pock-marked Galactic alloy. *What could do that to Galactic alloy?* We reached the bottom of the stairs, and I blinked at the new surroundings.

What would he want a vault for?

Red stained the brown walls in patterns that looked like someone had decorated it with a hose. Some areas glistened in the pale yellow light. The room was sticky and hot and smelled like metal and offal. A rusted restraining chair, minus any sort of padding, sat under a spotlight in roughly the middle of the room. Dust motes floated in and out of the cone of light.

I swallowed as blind terror started elbowing plain-old fear aside for the captain's chair of my controls.

Around the spotlighted chair floated a wall of displays. Some showed readouts; others had what looked like news feeds on them. Next to the chair was a tub large enough for a Galactic my size. The tub extended out of a shiny new cylinder with a control terminal on one end. It looked like the tub could retract into the glass container. As we approached, the sound from the various feeds blended together in low, whispering, confidential voices.

At the far end of the room squatted a giant container half-filled with pink, sparkly liquid. It was covered with strange symbols, but the Convergence seal, a circle with multiple stars on the inside, was dominant. It was an old version of the seal. A retro version.

"Sit," Godwill pushed my head, shoving me toward the chair. I hesitated.

Pain stabbed from my collar into my spine and out through my back while radiating into my arms. I arched and sucked in a breath, too surprised to scream.

"*Mmmm*," he chuckled, low and deep. I turned to him, gasping. I was not going to survive this. Fear sent a tingle through my belly. I wiped my nose, and my fingers came away with my blood. It sparkled, little microarcs dancing on its surface but not turning into anything more than pretty white-blue flashes against crimson.

He snatched my wrist, his eyes wide, as he watched my corona dance over my blood. "Yes!" he exclaimed as he grabbed me under my arms and picked me up. His strength crushed my shoulders, and I was tossed into the chair. "Restraints," he called, grabbing an arm and a foot roughly and positioning them on the chair. The synth activated, and metal bands slid across my stomach, arms, thighs, and ankles and around my forehead.

"Why are you doing this to me?" I whispered. "What do you want?"

"I want *nothing* from *you personally*," he said. "Your body. Your DNA. You have not earned that. You were simply born with it. And just as luck gave it to you, luck has given it to *me*." He paused, statue-still, and regarded me with his pupil-less eyes. He slowly moved his head closer to mine as his lips peeled back into a grimace.

"Well, Raystar of Terra," he whispered. I could smell the caramel of his breath. "I humbly submit that I might have done a bit of planning, too."

He paused, his face close to mine. From the corner of my eye, I saw his hand move toward my head. I strained to track it—not that my seeing it would do any good, locked down and immobile as I was in this *nova-flipping* chair. I felt his fingers run though my hair.

"Raystar," he breathed, "You are beautiful." He let my purple bangs fall into my eyes. "You have no idea, little Human. You are my beginning."

Straightening, Godwill reached into his jacket pocket and pulled out a glass tube the length of my hand. It was capped on each end with dull grey metal, and through the glass, I could see a sparkling silver liquid.

Godwill stood above me, his mouth pursed in concentration. With one hand, he reached to my neck. His touch was warm, dry, and invasive. The collar clicked and he pulled it off, letting it fall with a crunch to the rusted ground. He ran his hand around my neck, pressed on my collarbone, and stopped over my heart. His black, reflection-less eyes looked down at me. He smiled, clearly mistaking me for a lab partner, and moistened his lips with his darting tongue.

Raising his other hand, he showed me the glass tube poised there like a knife. He jiggled it and smiled again at me. *Like we were sharing an old joke.* As he smiled, the grey skin on his face pulled taut, like a balloon over a skull. A needle the length of my little finger extended slowly from the part of the tube near the bottom of his hand. He put his other hand on my sternum and closed his eyes as he searched for my heartbeat. Which had increased to a thundering drumroll.

He lifted his hand from my chest. I couldn't breathe any faster.

Please. I want to live.

"Goodbye, Raystar of Terra."

I screamed with everything I had as he elevated the hand holding the syringe above his head and then hammered it down, driving the needle into my heart.

39

Buh-buh.

I gasped in recognition. *My heartbeat.*

I sucked in another breath of recognition. The hot, sticky air, the taste of metal, the smell of waste. But that last gasp, like the first, was filled with glorious oxygen. *Was I dead?*

No. I was pretty sure the place we go after we die didn't use body restraints or smell like a humidified gratcher pen. I was alive, which was good. I was still in Godwill's chair, which, not to belabor the point, was really bad. *Breathe. Calm. Focus.*

After a moment of drawing centering breaths, I wriggled my fingers and toes. The feeling of muscles clenching and unclenching was delicious. Braver now, I raised my head and popped open my eyes. As my stomach and chest muscles engaged, and as I lifted my head, unbelievable pain flooded through my sternum. A tidal wave of nausea made me snap my eyes shut.

Have you ever broken a bone? Bruised yourself really badly? Imagine that pain in your chest, right there in the middle, where your ribs come together. Add to that heart-rending ache the worst fever you can imagine, PLUS wanting to throw up AND being unable to turn your head. So, uh, if you did throw up, gravity would just make it run down your body. I hurt like that. Like I've never hurt before.

"I thought I was clear," I heard someone say as my awareness sharpened. *Godwill.* He was standing off to the side of me. I had no idea how long I'd been there. "I need the Convergence inventory of Human DNA reclamation solvent. ALL OF IT, LITTLE FOOL!" He paused. "Plans have changed. We will convert this population first." He paused again. "Remember, all of it. You will answer to worse people than I if you do not comply or are late. We have a small window before the 301st Battle Group arrives." The "fool" on the other side of the transmitter must have said the right thing, because Godwill regained his composure and closed the conversation with a stern "See that you do."

I knew he was approaching me, mostly because I could hear his panting. I tried to open my eyes, but my thoughts were too jumbled for my body to understand how to make my eyelids work.

"507 did not endure as long as you. But I will have you, Raystar," he said, placing a hand on my head. "Synth," he commanded, "elevate the chair."

Vertigo spun my world as the chair back elevated my upper body. My chest ached with renewed pain as the chair moved into its original position. I forced my eyes open. Godwill stood in front of me, with his head turned. From this angle, he looked even more skeletal. Small, deep, red blots on his combat armor looked like wet paint. To the right, where he was looking, the array of news feeds showed various scenes from around the planet. One screen showed something about Freela and Kaleren, Mieant's parents. I couldn't quite make out the words.

Other displays showed a body. *My body.* It was me, in fact, on the vid-screen; I knew that because when I wiggled a finger, the image on the screen wiggled a finger. Red tendrils reached out from MY heart. *Nova.* It was identical to what had happened when Dad and I had tried to fix the controller. *What was Godwill doing?*

Oh...no.

"Yes," he gloated, upon seeing my recognition. "Millions of your people, over eighteen hundred years, have been synthesized!" Godwill spat. "There are not so many of your kind left. Even fewer of you with the control gene. When we unlock your tech, *Homo sapiens* will not be needed, except as a chapter in our overcurious Recorders' history."

His hand gently stroked my hair as he continued wistfully, "It was only months ago when a Human boy was sitting right where you are. Artem, I believe, was his name. You would have liked him, I think. We found him in the Capitar system. The Humans in that system scratch out a living, well enough, I suppose. They try not to cause trouble, to get along, to be part of Galactic culture."

"But rumors about a purple-haired child who sometimes emitted clouds of sparks brought him to our attention." The sigh he expelled was that of remembering a lovely moment. "His parents, in their uniquely Human way, cared for him deeply. Imagine my surprise when they turned down my very generous offer of payment for the child. The extra hours of entertainment they provided left me grateful that they refused my offer."

My heart was crashing against my ribs. The pain, a pressure in my core, pushed my chest out, and I panted. His calm narrative sharply contrasted with the war raging inside me. Making sense of what he'd said gave size and scale to the game I was wrapped up in.

I flexed my arms against the metal restraints. *A game I was losing.*

Godwill continued, "I would have enjoyed converting you both at the same time, after giving you time to become friends. I even told him about you. Nothing like a little of hope before the end. You did not give that to Nurse Pheelios, did you?" His hand continued stroking my hair. "You should have paused, let her see her end. Given her a few seconds to contemplate her inevitable nonexistence. Nothing compares to the pleasure of watching another sentient become aware that their end is only seconds away."

Nova. This was insanity.

"I injected him with the reclamation nano," he continued, and then muttered to himself, "I do not know why we call it that. It is, in fact, a conversion solvent." Godwill looked down at me.

"It converts your DNA, your nannites, into a 'digestible' format Lethians can integrate. As you can see from the displays"—he waved toward the translucent displays floating against the brown and red background—"you are being converted. To soup, in fact." He pointed toward the tub. "You will go in there, where you will finish the conversion process."

"Unnngh," I managed. *I needed to survive. This madness needed to be stopped.*

"And let me tell you, Raystar, I have used the prototype of converted nano on myself! What an amazing power your kind have developed. I have access to your kind's ancient nanotechnology. Watch."

He raised his hand. As he did so, his body glowed. A nimbus appeared around him, purplish and much finer than mine. One hand was held flat toward the floor as the other pointed to the wall. A stream of sparks shot from his hand to the floor and started peeling off the corroded metal. He was consuming the floor, somehow powering himself with nonorganic material. A skintight smile pulled his grey skin, and he bared his teeth.

He turned over the hand, pointing to the wall, and made a clawing motion. Blinding purple-white ropes of plasma streaked from his hands and gouged jagged trenches in the far wall. The air filled with the acrid smell of ozone and metal.

"SEE?" he turned wildly to me, his black eyes wide and mouth agape in a craxy, emaciated grin. "I HAVE YOUR POWER!" He leaned in close and whispered, so the monitors, the rust, and all the other nonalive things in the room couldn't overhear his insanity. "And my people will have it too!"

I fought through pain to think. Puzzle pieces fell into place. The damage in this room—the rust, corrosion, and stains—must have been from Godwill using *his* nano. On others. There must be something wrong, though, because when *I* consumed something, I consumed it entirely. I'd consumed IT-ME, turned 'natch to ash, even vaporized parts of the lev-sled. Er. I mean, the assault tank. Nurse Pheelios existed one moment, and then she did not. There were no leftovers. How much of the rust covering everything in this vault was because of some problem? An imperfection in his "reclaimed" nano?

The synth chimed, soft and melodious. "Jurisdictor Godwill. We are under attack. Experiment 507 has returned. Commander Sarla has engaged, and per your orders, no guards have left the…."

Godwill struggled to calm himself. Sparks jumped around his mouth, eyes, and hair.

"Thank you. Let Commander Sarla know I shall be there momentarily."

"As you wish, Jurisdictor."

Godwill looked at me and sniffled. He lifted his sleeve, wiped a line of blood from his nose, and then gestured at the screen showing my body being "converted."

"I won't leave you alone for long, Raystar."

Sanity reclaimed, he adjusted his long jacket over his combat armor and straightened his sparkling hair in a gesture that reminded me a bit too much of me. The craxy Godwill had been replaced with the one I'd feared first. "If your brain hasn't turned into precious nano, we can talk about how you assassinated the Asrigards when I return. Humans won't be liked much by Galactics now. Enjoy your celebrity status."

He laughed, gurgling with a momentary lapse of insane pleasure, and swept away up the stairs.

I was alone with my breathing, the vids, the rust, and my internal war with the infecting nano. I could feel the battle inside me. I felt sick. My mouth was dry. I looked at the screen and blinked. The red had actually retreated, grown smaller.

I turned back to the vids. They were almost too soft to be heard. *Huh.*

"Synth, increase the volume." I guessed there were no specific instructions about using the compound synth, and that there were levels of clearance that were required for anything important. A news report was just beginning, and I remembered the reporter.

"This is Nyla Jax, of the Galactic News Network, reporting from the Blue River Educational Facility." Nyla was the young Lethian reporter who had been at the Greeting Ceremony. She looked nervous as the vid drones swarmed around her, each jockeying and shuffling for the best shot. One drone swooped near to her, and the draft stirred up leaves and mussed her hair. She brushed a strand of silver hair from her face, blinked, and continued. I noticed she had freckles. "Yesterday, only moments after Freela and Kaleren Asrigard, Co-Governors of Quadrant 4, announced the signing of the Human Inclusion Bill, they fell victim to what appears to be a gruesome assassination attempt." She looked seriously into the camera and continued. "Citizens of Nem', while officials haven't confirmed reports, the Co-Governors are not believed to have survived the attack."

Nova and great gravity wells. Mieant would never forgive me.

A picture of me flashed on the screen.

"What we know is that Raystar Ceridian, the adopted Human of Sathra and Nent Ceridian, appears to be deeply involved in the attack. Raystar, thirteen years of age, is the only Human on Nem.'" The vid of Mom wiping something off of my face and giving me an enormous *mwah* flashed for a moment as Nyla continued her narrative. "What could prompt this young Human female to try to kill the Quadrant Governors, especially after a pro-Human bill was signed into law?" Nyla emphasized the word "kill" and shook her head at the confounding question. "What we know is that the Human was not acting alone. We believe that the principal of the Blue River educational facility was a collaborator." The scene panned away as the vid drones rose like a cloud of flies to capture the second figure standing next to Nyla—Jurisdictor Godwill, in full NPD uniform.

"To help us make sense of this tragedy, Nem's newest Jurisdictor has agreed to join us for a public statement. Jurisdictor Godwill, what is the official view of the NPD?"

This interview was recorded. He'd come to the prison camp just after the interview! I winced, looked back at my body monitors. The red hadn't increased. I turned back to Godwill's interview.

He smiled warmly at Nyla and dipped his skull-head toward her, just as Storm-Wall thunder boomed and his slight bow became a reflexive duck. Nervously, they both looked up and then back at each other.

"Thank you, Nyla. This is a horrible event. It is clear that after 1,800 years, Humans—even Human children—cannot be trusted, despite how we have welcomed them into our Galactic civilization. The NPD is committed to tracking down and finding those responsible for perpetrating this tragedy. It is ironic that the very species the

Co-Governors were trying to save with their Human Inclusion Bill then turned against them. While we investigate this"—he paused, as if searching for the words—"Human Conspiracy, I will be managing the day-to-day governance of Nem.'"

Godwill paused, looked at Nyla, and then turned back to the vids. "Humans must be watched. If you have this species in your vicinity, please report suspicious activity to your local authorities." He turned his gaze down and then back toward the camera, because Lethians don't have pupils. "I am ashamed that any people belonging to our Convergence would need to be monitored, but Humans have proven their hatred for us.

"We do, not at this point, know the whereabouts of Raystar of Terra, Mieant Asrigard, Cri Ceridian, or Nonch of Broodmother Krig. I am hopeful that some group will come forward and claim responsibility for their absence, or that some citizen will help us locate the perpetrators. These are missing children first, after all."

Nyla nodded, her silvery bangs flowing with each bob of her head as she gave Godwill her focus.

"But more troubling is that we do not know the extent to which Nem's government and police have been infiltrated. Principal Entarch was thought to have been a loyal public servant, but she attempted murder. Clearly, she was turned by this Human Conspiracy. Glean swords were used to stab the Co-Governors. Who else has been turned? In order to protect our planet and our citizens, I am declaring martial law as authorized by the War Powers Doctrine. I have further directed that the 98th Battle Group take position in orbit. Soldiers loyal to the Convergence will, under my direct command, relieve existing NPD forces of their responsibilities until we identify the responsible parties and stabilize Nem.'"

Godwill smiled again at Nyla. Who blinked as his words—and their significance—registered.

For a moment, only the experian drones' antigrav engines whispered into their sound pickups. Nyla now looked at Godwill like he had turned into a giant, salivating legger. He pressed his lips together and stood with his arms behind his back.

Then her ambition overcame her fear, and she rattled off a series of questions. Her path to fame was established. THIS was going to be THE report that made her famous.

"Jurisdictor, you said, 'attempted' murder. Can you comment?"

"We will not comment on an ongoing investigation," Godwill said.

"Jurisdictor, Nem' is a small planet. Is martial law overkill?"

"Our Co-Governors were just attacked. We will pull this planet apart before we give up on justice."

"You mentioned the 98th Battle Group. Will Nem' be under military rule?"

"Nem' will be under NPD rule, enforced by the 98th under my direct command." Then he turned to face the camera directly. "Citizens of Nem', much has happened in the past few days. Even more will come to pass in the near future. The recent tragedy suggests that people and races that were our friends cannot be trusted. I want you to ensure that you make the officers of the 98th aware of any suspicious behavior. As your new Governor, I promise to use all of my power to find those responsible for these horrible events. In the meantime, remember that you are under martial law. There will be no further news, except at such time as I lift this ban. Thank you." Godwill gestured to someone off-camera.

Nyla pushed in front of him. "A Battle Group has roughly six million soldiers. Mixed with martial law, this looks like a military coup, Jurisdictor. When will the battle group arrive?" She glanced at something out of sight. Her eyes got big. "No way! This is not possible. You can't...." Two soldiers took her carefully by each arm and escorted her off-camera.

"Secure her," he said, facing the soldiers. As he followed their progress, he commanded, "Ms. Jax, kindly disable your vid drones." The images flickered, then vanished. She'd turned off her recorders. "The 98th is already here" were his last words before the images vanished.

"Scan stations for content," I said to the building synth. I didn't want to be alone down here. Screens flicked from static to static.

For the first time I could remember, the networks were silent.

40

The door at the top of the stairs slid open, and heavy footfalls thud-ded down the stairway. Godwill paused when he saw me.

"Incredible," he muttered, walking around me once and then stop-ping in front of the displays. He poked my head and then pressed down on my chest, where he'd injected me, as if expecting that area to be mushy.

He looked at the monitors. The red area had nearly vanished. Whatever my nano were doing, they were doing it better than what-ever he had injected me with. *Could I beat this?* Hope burned in my chest, and the nova of emotions that flared when I looked at Godwill went beyond fury.

"I suspected that additional solvent doses would be required. But this is remarkable," he muttered. He hesitated, then continued. "You are incredibly concentrated. Like source code. The boy, even with his DNA, took half a day. Those before him were harvested in minutes."

"Once 507's complete DNA is synthesized along with yours, we will have what we need"—he shuddered—"to be rid of your kind."

I blinked at this. "I thought Artem was processed?" I said, my mor-bid curiosity getting the better of me. Godwill returned my question with a blank look that lasted a mere second.

"YOU MOCK ME?" he exploded, his eyes twitching and bulging as he pounded a fist on the table. Strapped in as I was, I did my best to twist away from him. "507 escaped!"

He grabbed my throat and put his face near mine, spittle flying with each word. "But you knew that, didn't you? You and Artem have been in collusion since you met that day in the 'natch field! Your parents were sheltering him from me, weren't they? TELL ME, you miserable pupae. I will enjoy what comes next!"

He pushed my head against the table as he released my neck. I choked and sucked in as much of the metallic dungeon air as I could, coughing all the while. I had no idea what he was talking about.

But someone had escaped. Someone with less of the Human nano than I had. Which meant…wait. *'Natch field. That…creature…that had attacked Dad and me.*

Great. Flipping. Gravity. Wells. IT-ME. 507. Artem! He had been Human. HUMAN!

"Your next injection of Human Reclamation Nano Solvent will be here in two day-cycles. What an ignoble end for the last Human on Nem'. Synth!" he said into the air, "Release Experiment 508."

The restraints slid off of me. Without their support, I slipped off the chair and collapsed onto the crunchy, rusty floor. I stared at the jagged brown bits of corrosion lining the vault floor. Something made a soft *pat, pat* sound, and I realized it was blood. Mine.

I watched a red drop fall from my nose, splatter, and then spark, feebly.

"Put your collar on. Get up." He kicked my butt, and my elbows wobbled. I fell forward on my shoulder into the rust. Its taste was in my mouth, jagged and metallic. My arms flayed in front of me, and I pulled myself toward my collar. My knees were scraped. My hands bled from the sharp rust flakes on the floor. *Galactic metal didn't rust. This was clearly caused by Godwill's use of the Human tech.* Splayed on the floor, I required no effort to look pathetic and clumsy. I fumbled with the collar, buying time to think.

Unbidden, a small spark leapt from where my blood had dropped into the rust directly to the collar. The flakes where my blood had dropped melted, and I felt a tingle. I knew, at that moment, that if I let my hunger loose on the rusted byproduct scattered on the floor, it would have fed me. *Energized me.* The push of ravenous gluttony rose to my throat, and I fought to control it.

Fortunately, I had sheltered the spark from Godwill's sight. I took a pinch of the rust and the blood from my nose and rubbed it on the collar's connector, hiding the movement by pretending to fumble around. Not knowing what I was doing, driven by desperation, I willed my energy into the rust and into my blood.

The collar buzzed. I screamed as much out of surprise as it was to cover the sound. The rust sparkled and fizzed around the collar's leads. I closed it around my neck, and the seam burned hot. I hoped that Godwill couldn't smell the ozone and my seared flesh where it touched my throat. Luck was on my side; I was rewarded with a kick to my lower back.

"Get up, Raystar of Terra. Wearing the collar is the least of your concerns. Maybe I will let you take it off before your final session."

Groaning, I cinched myself back to my knees, then got my legs under me, until I wobbled to stand on my own. Impatient with my sluggishness, he pushed me toward the stairs, and my arms windmilled as I fought to keep balance.

"Then again," he chuckled, "Maybe not."

There was no railing, and I leaned heavily against the wall as I climbed one stair at a time toward the exit. My legs weakened with each step.

When I got to the first room, the one with the two entryway guards, there was no ceremony or parting words. Godwill simply pushed me through the door and into the evening shadows. Banefire was on the other side of the Mesa. I stumbled and sprawled onto the dusty ground. I lay there, watching the wind blow small pieces of dried leaves across the soil. Geckomice squeaked and scurried outside of the barrier. Starbats, millions of them, were crooning, flapping, and stretching themselves for their evening feast and preparing to launch themselves from their nests in the ancient buildings. *Get up.* I had to get up and tell my friends what I'd learned.

I was starving. No, really. Actually starving. The "nano solvent" Godwill had injected into me drew power from me in some manner. It must work the same way the industrial nano consumed a feeder cube to reconstruct our controller. In this case, *I* was the feeder cube. Whatever I was, whatever was in me, was resisting, fighting back, but this internal battle was about staying who I was or being remade into the universe-knows-what. And both sides were drawing energy from me!

I pushed myself to my feet and let the momentum carry me forward. Gravity seemed to pull me as I blindly turned left or right until I made it to our covered enclosure. My friends sat there, huddled in a circle.

Nonch had just flicked his sensor stalks in my direction when I stumbled into their light. "Raystar!" Nonch said, snaking out of my way to make room and guiding me to the ground. He wiped my face and chin with a rag that became red.

Cri took me in with a disapproving glare, but her eyes soon grew wide. I looked down at what had caught her gaze. The front of my shirt was soaked with my blood. I always bled before the storms. But now? With all of the power I'd been using, this close to the Storm Wall's epic release, something was very different. If the headaches followed, I didn't know if I could take that. *BIG IF.*

I frowned back at her. "This isn't my 'cry for attention', Sis'. I have information," I said bitterly, making eye contact with everyone, "that will make a difference."

"Of course," she said, dismissing my bloody, haggard appearance with a hand to the sky, "when don't you?" She scooched away from me and placed a hand on Mieant's shoulder.

Mieant lay curled on his sleeping mattress, like he was still asleep. The dim light couldn't hide his swollen jaw or split lip. His shirt was ripped across his shoulder, and his exposed grey skin was mottled with red, black and purple, knuckle-shaped bruises.

"Mieant," I sucked in a breath and frowned. "What happened?"

"The guards said it was supposed to look like a Human beat me. You." He opened an eye and shuffled on his back so he could see me. A cough shook his body, and I realized he was laughing. "But looking at you now, I realize how out of touch they are with reality. What happened to *you*?"

I told them.

When I'd finished, we stared at each other a long time in silence. Total silence.

"Well," Mieant said, in a small voice, "my parents are not confirmed dead." He looked at Nonch, acknowledging his earlier comments. "*That* is positive."

"We must escape tomorrow," Nonch said. "There is no choice. Raystar will die. We will be used for Godwill's plans. Then we will die."

"Autoturrets. Collars. Oh." Cri had re-engaged and began counting on her hands. "There are thirty guards," she said, raising another finger, "and they have guns." She met each of our gazes.

"Nevertheless," Mieant said, "they want us all alive, at the moment. We can use that. We have Nonch's smell signal. And maybe two of us, definitely three of us, can overpower a guard. Except for that monster, Sarla."

"Godwill made a mistake today," I said. Cri had been about to say something, and she glowered at me.

"He injected you with nanovirus?" Cri asked.

"No...."

"He beat Mieant to a pulp? Oh, and he framed us on GNN? Killed Mieant's parents?" she continued.

"No...he...."

"Oh, AND he left the autoturrets on? AND he took the keys to the NPD cruiser? AND he brought two entire Battle Groups here to support him as he takes over the planet? AND he...."

This was the moment of truth. *Had my nano fried the rust and broken the collar lock?* If not, our options were extremely limited. The circlet around my neck clicked open, and I handed the collar to my sister.

Cri turned the collar around and then looked down, her hair curtaining around her face and closing off her expressions.

I chucked her lightly on the arm. She looked away.

"I'm sure we're tracked by these things. How craxy would they get if we threw the collar over the force fence into the Ruins?" I asked, taking the band from her and refastening it around my neck.

The plan was simple. Jump the guard closest to the NPD cruiser. Cri, who was by far the strongest, would throw the collar over the fence, into the Ruins, thus pulling everyone toward the tracking beacon while we escaped on the transport. It seemed like our best chance.

"Raystar," Mieant asked, in such a tentative voice that we all stopped talking and turned to him. "Nonch asked me earlier which side I was on." He pulled Cri closer. "I want to escape. To find out what happened to my parents. To get us all to safety. On my honor, this is the side I'm on." He paused to clear his throat. "But what about you? What are you? When we were with Nurse Pheelios, you…did things."

I swallowed. I hadn't told *anyone* about that. We simply hadn't had time. And frankly, I didn't want to think about what happened. What I'd done was awful enough, even if it may have saved Mieant and me. What I'd felt was terrifying. Strength, power, hunger.

Godwill had been like that when he was with me. More than his usual arrogant self, I mean. I shivered, remembering the craxiness that had peeked out of him at that moment, perhaps a side effect of absorbing and using all the Human nano. If he'd been using this tech longer than I had, what could it have done to him? Was he even Lethian anymore?

Those red stains on the walls. They were not paint, and they were still wet. *Fresh.* Knowing what I had done with my powers and what I could do, I knew Godwill would be far worse. A million times worse. He enjoyed hurting people. And he was doing it with Human technology. I wasn't sure how, but he had to be stopped. And we had to get out of here. All of us.

I dipped my head toward Mieant, acknowledging his point, and looked at Cri and Nonch.

"Thank you for letting me tell the story in my words," I responded, looking at my laced fingers in my lap. I turned my gaze to each of my friends, and answered their concerned, serious expressions. "I ate her."

Nonch froze. Cri sputtered, "Twig, that's not even funn–*NOVA!* You're not kidding?"

I shook my head.

"It is as Broodmother has described," Nonch breathed. And then, more loudly, he said, "We were unsure if you had the power."

"*I* don't have anything! *It* has *me*! All this,"—I paused and waved toward the galaxy overhead—"is because of something that happened a long time ago."

"Nevertheless. You have the power over Human technology. Human weapons. You are one, yourself. If you are so integrated with the technology, how do you even know you are Human? It is what has troubled Broodmother about your kind."

"Could you," Cri said, rolling her four hands, "eat us?"

We sat in silence.

"Yes," I said, looking down.

"That's nova," she whispered, her anger and jealousy apparently on hold for the moment. I squinted up at her. Our thinking wasn't going in straight lines. We were all craxy insane. "I mean," she corrected, catching everyone's expressions as they regarded her, "totally horrible. But I saw her spark-out in the 'natch fields the day before school. Lightning claws, glowing eyes, super purple hair. *BZZZZZ-STH-BRA-WHAMP!*" We flinched as she mimicked my fight with IT-ME, sound effects and all.

"I went back to help your parents," I said to Mieant, in a small voice. "And you tried to help me in the nurse's office—we saved each other." Telling them about my powers was terrifying. *What if they left me? What if they didn't like me anymore?* I didn't want to be alone. I didn't want to die alone, in this horrible place.

"I'm not bad. I don't know what's happening." I said, looking at each of my friends. It was becoming harder to breathe. The fear of losing my only friends—my connection to my personal Humanity—made sucking in each breath hard labor. "I'm trying my best."

"Raystar," Mieant said, after a huge silence, "I am the only person that saw what you did for my parents. And to Nurse Pheelios. And yes, you healed me in that room. I don't know what you are, but I owe you two debts. And I trust you."

He reached across the space between us and put a hand over mine, where it rested on my knee. I stared at his long, grey fingers, his scraped knuckles, the tattered cuff of his once-beautiful shirt. Something rustled at my side as Nonch placed eight hand claws over our hands. It was his navy blue armored chitin, ending in many-digited, blood-orange hands. Cri wrapped our hand knot in her own red-skinned hands, covered with dirt and abrasions. Our thirteen-year old lives were most likely going to end horribly in the next several days.

But we'd face the future together.

41

Minutes later, after we'd all settled down for sleep, I was mildly surprised by a gorgeous smell of loam and sugar drifting lazily through the air. Slowly—very slowly—Nonch reared up and turned his head toward the force fence, snaking his lower body like he was targeting where to strike.

"Wha—?" I started. He put the soft part of his hand claws over all of our mouths.

"No sounds," he whispered.

I listened. Where were the starbats? The bugs? The other creatures? The night was silent. In the lull of the thunder, evening had snuck up on us. *Something* was out there, in the darkness.

We moved so our backs were all toward each other and faced outward into the darkness. The smell of death snaked through the air, until a constant, gentle breeze carried the Crynit's warning into the Ruins and toward what lurked outside the walls of our prison.

42

The morning air was paralyzed by the dark clouds lit from the inside by spiderwebs of lightning. Thunder rolled from one horizon to the other with such frequency as to be nearly continuous. Starbats rustled closer to each other and were muted, not wanting to attract the attention of whatever was up in the heavens. They peered toward the sky, twitching their angular heads this way and that, from within the shelter of the skeletal Human Ruins.

The lurker in the Ruins from last night was gone. Primordial memories of being hunted seemed to permeate the consciousness of every living thing, from insects and geckomice, to my friends and me.

In the night, I'd slid down and slept against Nonch's warm, armored side. He wasn't much of a pillow, though, and my unconsciousness had left me with my head at a right angle. His hard, banded chitin had imprinted small lines on my face. I rubbed the burn from my collar and sucked in drool from the corner of my mouth as I sat up. My nosebleed had stopped, and bits of crusted blood dropped to my shirt.

All of me raced to hurt. My neck was winning. My stomach was a close second. I hadn't eaten in over a day.

Nonch was in his sleeping ball. One sensor stalk extended vertically, twitching as it followed the sounds of a starbat or some other noise beyond my range of hearing. How everyone could be asleep during this thunder was beyond me.

I blinked as I took in Mieant and Cri.

My sister's long, black hair was over her face and shoulders like a lustrous, thick mop. Not quite hidden by her waves of hair, her face pressed against Mieant's chest. Two of her arms were casually draped over him. He was a good pillow, apparently, and her upper hand rested gently against his jaw. He'd encircled her with an arm and a leg, and they lay facing each other, breathing long breaths alternating with the other's rhythm. Mieant had pressed his lips against her forehead, and he looked…happy. Happy like his mother had been when I first met her at the school. Free from the perpetual frown that seemed to cloud the expressions of the Lethians I'd encountered, and that increasingly hovered on all of our faces.

The Lethian and Glean guards shifted at their posts, not noticing the two of them, not noticing us. Autoturrets, with their glowing hot barrels, swiveled, searching eagerly for destruction outside the camp. And the Ruins, a story of nearly two thousand years of Galactic war, a story that hadn't actually ended, hunched like broken people trying to forget the cause of their despair.

My sister and my ex-bully lay entwined on the concrete, their arms like force fields keeping the world out and each other's warmth in. I wanted to kick them. Or leave them alone. Protect them. But, mostly, scream about the unfairness of it to the stupid sky!

So I frowned and looked away.

Thunder pealed above, seemingly three meters away from our shelter, and shook the ground. I glanced back at Mieant and my sister. Their eyes popped open simultaneously. Black stared into gold for a serene moment. Her hand tensed around his jaw. Then they both looked toward me, their expressions morphing from bliss to horror.

"YOU!" Mieant howled, pushing Cri off of him as he disentangled himself. Her head was on his arm, and he lay on her long black hair.

"CREATURE!" Cri shoved him off with four arms. "OW!"

Nonch uncoiled and contemplated their clumsy scramble in opposite directions. "Mating," he said, tilting his head and waving six sword arms in different directions at our surroundings, "seems impractical, given where we are."

Mieant straightened out his ragged clothes, lifted his torn shirt back over his shoulder, and glared at his feet. The material, having already surrendered its life, fell back to its previous position and exposed his chest. Cri dusted herself off, one hand pushing hair from her glowing eyes, another straightening her shirt, and the other two patting dirt from her pants. She looked angry enough to take a swing.

"We were NOT mating," they said simultaneously.

My stomach cramped. I didn't want to think about not having Cri's attention, despite the rockiness of our relationship of late. I didn't want to contemplate what it would mean to have her interested in someone else beside me. We were supposed to be planning our escape. I needed food to survive. I needed my sister. Not love. This was all now, and urgent.

"Hey," I said, "Where'd you guys put the water?"

Cri glared at Mieant one last time and then turned to me.

"Ray," she gasped, her eyes getting large as she moved closer and grasped me by my elbows, shoulders, and around my neck. "You look like flip."

"Food." I nodded, feeling weak. There was a war inside me. I was winning for now, but for how long? She looked at Nonch and glared at Mieant.

"I'll stay with her." Cri waved a hand toward the starbats' nesting places. "See if any of the starbats died inside the compound. There's got to be something not Galactic-made." *Yeah, that would be something. Dead starbat. Yay.*

Nonch and Mieant exchanged a glance and hurried toward the perimeter. Mieant was muttering something about girls. Lightning raced across the sky, followed a boom that shook the ground once again. Cri looked up at the clouds, which had grown into bruised, purple-and-black monsters.

"They'll find you food," she said, punching my shoulder softly, "but it might be raw."

"What's with you and..." I nodded in the direction Mieant and Nonch had gone. Cri looked down. Then she looked back at me, her eyes big and vulnerable.

"It just happened. Last night, that thing that we all felt, out there," she lifted her chin toward the Ruins, "It was terrifying. We were sitting against each other..." She trailed off, keeping my gaze. "I'm worried about Dad. About them. What if no one comes for us, Ray? I don't want to die alone."

I frowned and looked at the dirt.

"I mean, yeah," she said, hurriedly. "We're all together. Mieant makes me feel good. I can stand this a bit more." She shrugged, looking up at me from a curtain of hair. "All we may have is now. Together. "

I didn't need this. *Now?* I was the lone Human on this planet. I felt hollow. Galactics got along just fine with other Galactics, except me. I raised my eyes to hers and shouted, "*I* am dying. We're supposed to be planning!"

My voice had grown loud. Which is why we hadn't heard Godwill and Sarla approach.

"Planning?"

Cri and I spun to face the Jurisdictor and the enormous Sarla. Godwill wore his combat suit from the day at the school. Melted, bubbly scorch marks streaked the suit's shoulder and stomach. His suit had been eaten away completely in other places along his calf.

Thunder cracked, deafeningly loud. Godwill's lips pulled back over his emaciated face, revealing white teeth and a red mouth. His black eyes bulged from his skeletal head. He grinned.

The starbats, unable to remain quiet, shrieked, and by the thousands, they exploded from their shelter in the Ruins. They flew in sheer panic, and in all directions. Sarla whipped her appendages around, and several of the big creatures tumbled to the ground in pieces. I watched hungrily as the bloody chunks rolled to a stop.

"My Commander is amused," Godwill chuckled, looking up at me. He smiled at the thunder clouds, closed his eyes and took in a deep breath like he'd just accomplished something. His matte-black eyes turned back to me. "Come, Raystar."

I put a hand on Cri, who had tensed beside me. Sarla could have bisected us without blinking. Technically, the huge Crynit couldn't blink, but that wouldn't make our evisceration any more difficult. And we were not even close to a match for Godwill and his stolen Human nanotech. Even with Mieant and Nonch. Godwill saw my look, my hand on Cri's arm and my other on my stomach, and narrowed his eyes before smiling again, broadly, to show his even, yellowed teeth.

"Once and for all, Terran, we shall be rid of your kind." He tilted his head and flicked a glance toward the bruised turbulence above us. The clouds were getting closer to the ground. "Behold, the 98th Battle Group approaches." He waved to the Ruins around us. "And we will have more than enough troops to recapture the boy, Artem."

Artem. *IT-ME*. Now that I knew they were one and the same, I wondered if that's who or what was watching us last night. If it was IT-ME who had damaged Godwill's combat suit. I stumbled as Sarla yanked me away from my sister. The Crynit's massive mandibles clicked. She flicked her head toward Godwill and said, in her husky voice, "Weak."

Cri pulled away, her eyes huge and worried.

Godwill leaned in further, looking not at me, Raystar, but at Experiment 508. He poked my chest, testing where he'd injected me yesterday. Was he thinking that somehow, I'd have become mushier? A corner of his mouth crept upward. "Bring her."

43

Sarla carried me gently toward Godwill's vault.

"Sarla," I said. She ignored me. I remembered what Nonch said to me in the library, and tried a different tactic. "Sarla, Crynits are brilliant, caring, and wise. Why are you helping Godwill?"

She shuddered, slowing, and lifted me to her orange eyes. She was terrifying.

"Explain."

"Nonch, Broodmother Krig's spawn, is my best friend." Upon hearing this, Sarla tilted her sensor stalks forward. "I'd do anything for him. I think he'd do the same for me. He asked me not to tell anyone this secret, and so I ask you not to break my trust, as I have done to his."

"Little creature, I could rend you limb from limb, make you tell me anything, without even breathing hard." Sarla laughed, but not unkindly. Her voice was surprisingly comforting. She'd only said a few sentences, but I liked it when she talked.

"Trust, Sarla. I tell you freely, and ask only that you keep my secret." Before she could comment, I continued. "Nonch told me he didn't want to be a Crynit. That Crynits were feared and only viewed as enforcers."

We stopped. She froze, and when I didn't say anything more, out of fear, she gently bopped my head with a sensor stalk that had the weight of a soft, heavy pillow. "Continue."

"What I know about your kind is that you are creative, inquisitive, loyal, and nurturing."

Sarla snorted and resumed moving toward the vault. "Are you not afraid?"

"Terrified. And yet, in the face of this"—I waved my hand weakly toward the camp, the guards, the autoturrets, the threatening sky, pretty much everything—"I persist. Because I believe."

She was silent.

"Sarla, help me, please." We were almost at the vault. "I know you think I'm just trying to save my life. I don't want to die. But this larger thing that's happening to us all is wrong! You don't have to believe me. Talk to Nonch!"

With a swish, she sped up, and we flowed past the guards at the front of the building. Sarla's armored hide rasped against the corroded Galactic alloy walls as she wormed her way down the stairs and into the metallic, foul-smelling heat of Godwill's rusty torture vault. She gently laid me in the chair, next to the vid-screens. The screens flickered to life. My body view showed a shrunken circle of red. I was still winning. My eyes scanned the room.

New, angry stains covered the walls. Fresh scars had been gouged into the floors and ceiling, from Godwill's lightning claws. I shuddered. Whatever gruesome thing happened here was just hours old. Godwill stood, his back to us, by the coffin-shaped collector that would be my home when I finally "liquefied." He was inspecting a new device, an upright holding tank, that was a much larger version of the containment unit we'd tried to use on IT-ME.

Sarla whispered to the AI in her language, and I turned my attention back to her giant, insectoid form. Straps slithered around my neck, wrists, ankles, and stomach.

"Stay alive, if you can," she said, leaning in close for a final look at me, "or die well. I...would not be unhappy if our paths crossed again." Like a black wave, she rippled away, exiting via the stairs.

A few moments after Sarla departed the room, Godwill turned to me. He held two syringes in one hand and smiled, gums showing. He patted the containment unit. "Do you know what these are?"

My blank gaze must have been amusing, because he grinned wider.

Nova. How in the great gravity well would I know? I wasn't going to give him the pleasure of watching me guess for real, either.

"A bookcase? Shoes? " I rasped.

The smile vanished and he flowed over to me, a fist pounding the chair above my head. I flinched, squeezing my eyes closed.

"IT IS NOT A BOOKCASE! It is your doom! Raystar of Terra!" With every "t" and "s" he uttered, flecks of spittle landed on my cheek. "That," he pointed, "is the culmination of millions of Human specimens being harvested, their DNA sorted, refined, concentrated. It is EVERYTHING we have."

"YOUR DOOM!" he screamed. "It is your end and our beginning! You, little Human, have sequences and aspects that not only complete the base genetic sequence, but also have other DNA codes that seem to point to avenues of Human knowledge we weren't even aware of. If we had found you centuries ago, we would not have needed to process the millions of other Humans. But then, the population of Humans today would be much greater."

His words hammered away at my guilt. *I'm special.* So special that I could have averted the deaths of millions of my kind, if I'd been born earlier, or surrendered myself sooner. I closed my eyes, processing what my guilt was telling me. *Strike a bargain? Sacrifice yourself sooner, and save more lives?*

I didn't ask for any of this. Godwill continued his gloat, droning on as I left my mind and returned to his words. "….With you finally processed, and then with 507 collected, the Human genome key will be assembled! To think, after 1,800 years, I will be the one to elevate my species…" He drifted off in the bliss of his dream, and as he did, his voice dropped to a purr.

There was no bargain to be struck.

"I have you to thank, Raystar." He moved back to the giant containment pod, and I watched him look at it with the adoration of a proud parent. He caressed it. "With the arrival of the 98th Battle Group, ancient Nem' will establish the final Lethian dominance over the

Convergence and all Galactics. We will inject our soldiers with this processed DNA, not only eliminating the need for Humans, but"—he pulled my hair so I could see him—"All. Other. Species. Crynits, Gleans, Char—everyone shall have their place in the Convergence redefined."

This was insanity on a Galactic level.

Something jingled. Godwill's head whipped toward the sound that came from the staircase. I craned my neck for a view. Sarla flowed into sight.

"Jurisdictor," she said, her husky voice carrying no threat, just co-operation. "You called me?"

He blinked at her. The Crynit's giant form was blacker than the shadows in the stairway. Her spikes, ridges, arm claws, and reflective orange eyes made her a nightmare of silhouettes blocking the entrance. "What?"

She flowed a meter closer. Sweet sugar and loam smells blossomed around us, drowning out the acidic, pungent smells of rusted metal.

"I thought you said 'Crynit,' which is your usual designation for me." *Great nova. She hadn't left.* She'd hung in the stairway…and had heard the entire conversation.

"Is that so?" Godwill's voice was low as he took two strides toward her. Lightning flickered around his head and hands. "Commander, I suggest you return to your duties."

They faced each other. After a moment or a year of stillness, Sarla dipped her head and backed up to and through the doorway. The vault door clanged shut behind her.

"Beast," Godwill muttered. "Vermin," he spat. "She will be the first." He ignored me as he strode up to the containment unit's controls. My eyes caught something bright by the stairway. It was a bell. That's what had jingled before. It was attached to a clump of green hair.

Nova.

Godwill returned to my side, intent on the injectors and their vials of Human Reclamation solvent. He did notice my gaze, however, and followed it to the hair. His tongue flicked out, wetting his lips. "This power we have, Raystar, is exquisite. You and Artem will be the last Humans in the Convergence who understand this," he said, leaning in close.

I could smell his breath, the sweetness of caramel, of meat. I looked at him from the corner of my eye, as I was unable to turn my head without the collar choking me. Tiny blood specks spattered his cheek; they were only noticeable when he drew in so close. "You know the feeling. The exquisite feeling of consuming someone. Of not merely ending their life, but unmaking them, molecule by molecule, until their self-awareness loses enough of itself to not recognize its end. And in that final moment of fear, they turn their soul's eye to yours, and ask you...to stop."

I did know that feeling. It repulsed me.

Godwill caressed my face. Smiling almost paternally, he dusted off flecks of dried blood from my nosebleed that were still stuck to my chin. With an almost dreamy sigh, he turned back to the matted hair and chime beads. "Jenna was delicious. Did you know that each individual has a unique taste? No, you wouldn't. You've only experienced the nurse." He frowned. "That must have been revolting. A Syllthan?" Wow. *The Syllthans weren't even good food.*

Godwill regained my attention with a pulled-back grin that suggested I should know something he knew. He leaned in. "Jenna's mate-to-be," he said, pointing to the beads again. "Darien. He yielded more energy, but much less flavor." Godwill shrugged. "Maybe I will be able to taste all of the races."

It was too much. *Did my ancestors know the potential for destruction they had created?* Jenna and Darien were spikes, for sure. But they were *kids*. They didn't deserve what he did to them. And, as if it mattered now, he had used them at Blue River to bully and manipulate other students. They were his own team!

I had absorbed Nurse Pheelios. Was I better than Godwill, because I had done it only once? Did my reason for doing it make me better than him? Or the same?

Unbidden, Mom's words came back to me. *We don't leave anyone behind.*

I thought of AI, and my face burned. I was going to die. Had I given back to the people in my life as much as they'd given to me? Nonch, Mieant, Cri—they were all here because of me. I wanted to thank them, to tell them how grateful I was. I wanted to protect them.

Godwill's hands were warm against my skin. This time, he lifted my shirt so my navel was exposed. He talked calmly the entire time, like he'd done this every morning with his eggs and gratcher steak. "With the last treatment, you somehow managed to isolate and neutralize the solvent. I cannot allow that to happen again. My preference would be to deliver it directly into your brain; however, that might terminate you, rendering you useless." He slid the needle in, and I screamed.

He rubbed another spot on my belly, probing to find the right spot for the next injection. I gulped in hot, metallic lungfuls of air as I tilted my head as far as the collar would let me, trying to track where the needle would go next. His hand went out of sight, and I felt the sting pierce my stomach. I screamed again, my throat hoarse.

"I'm distracting your defenses by making injections in two other areas. Your nano is not strong enough to contain all three infections. One of the three will get through. You simply cannot be that strong." He lowered my shirt and moved the nanocontainer tub over to my chair.

Six-millimeter-high walls ran along the perimeter of the chair, and at my feet was a x-tube that Godwill connected to the nanocontainer collector. *Soup. I was going to dissolve into soup and drain into a tub. Not a glorious ending.*

The monitors showed three red splotches in my body—the first one, above my heart; the second two, on my abdomen, on either side of my belly button. Red fingers now spread out from all three.

Godwill sat down on a chair and watched the screens with me. He stood, walked over, and poked me in each of the three injected areas, frowning. I had no idea of time, but he must have been growing impatient. My vision was blurry and a fever-chill crept from my insides out.

"Extraordinary," he said.

And then, suddenly, Sarla was back. Whatever tension had existed between them previously wasn't apparent now. "The Human is resisting all three injections. Take her to the enclosure. Have the cruiser ready. 507 may come for her as well. Two for one." Godwill commanded.

"Is the Human safe to touch?" There was a pause, a moment of crackling tension.

"Beast," Godwill said, in a low voice. "My command is your only concern, nothing else."

Lost as I was in my own feverish battle, I could still smell sugar and dirt as it infused each breath. That Godwill didn't even react spoke volumes about his one-track mind, or his ignorance. Or maybe he simply didn't fear Sarla.

It seemed like he should. Because the aroma of her hatred was overpowering.

I wondered, through the haze of pain and dizzying nausea, what Sarla was getting out of her alliance with Godwill. She picked me up with the care one might reserve for a newborn. Despite her massive, razor-sharp sword arms, she carried me so gently that I felt only a soft swaying as we moved as one. Through my chills, I couldn't help thinking that sleep would be nice. *A blanket, and warm sleep. That would be nice.*

"Why are you helping him?" I groaned. "Can't you see what he's doing?"

After what seemed like an eternity of swaying, Sarla returned me to the covered concrete square my friends and I had called home these last few days. "Take what peace you can find, little one," I thought I heard her say. Thunder rumbled and cracked continuously. I squinted at the flashes of lightning that were coming so fast, they created a strobe effect. My friends were not in sight.

The ground *thrummed* as she raced away. *Die. Dying. Did any of it mean anything?* Sleep might erase the pain in my heart, the stabbing fire in my gut. Life was effort. Right now, I wanted oblivion. Yes. I could feel my nanobots surging through my body, innocently responsive, waiting for an order. THE order to end myself.

Ray.

What was that?

I'm not your imagination. You're going to wish I was.

Someone was in my head. WHO THE FLIP WAS TALKING TO ME?

It would be too much to expect that you'd get any smarter over the past few days.

There was light, a flash of pain in my forehead, and bewilderment. I opened my eyes, and in a moment of clarity, looked around me, at the enclosure. There was no one here.

But you know what? It didn't matter. I didn't want to go to the darkness. I wanted to live. The biggest decision of anyone's life is the decision to live. *To be, or not to be.* I closed my eyes and could feel the three points of infection growing inside me, destroying me molecule by molecule. But I was…strong.

Stronger.

I want to be here.

I love my family. My friends.

Maybe myself.

I want to be here.

I closed my eyes and gave my nano the control, the energy, and the will they needed to win. I wanted to see the sky. The clouds. I wanted to wake up and take a deep breath of air. Drink a glass of water. Get a hug. Turn in my homework late. Be invited to the cool kids' parties.

I wanted to live.

44

"Wake her!"

"Really?"

Something slapped my jaw, making my teeth clatter. Weakness was getting old. I wasn't covered, and woke up exposed. The morning air held a chill that hinted at rain. Wind flowed across my face, filled my first waking breaths with the choking smells of burning chemicals. I wrinkled my nose, coughed, and tried to wrap my arms around my knees for warmth.

"That wasn't anything. Gleans are supposed to be strong."

Some idiot smacked the cheeky part of my face into the part of my brain that was listening to the conversation.

"STOP!" I shouted, springing to my feet. I waved my hands in front of me like a blind person reaching for furniture she knows is in front of her.

"What is wrong with you fools?" I demanded, rubbing my cheek and squinting at my surroundings. The concrete slab was reassuring underneath my feet, but the familiar grey, square boringness of the camp buildings instantly brought where I was depressingly back to me. I stood in a circle of my friends.

I glared at them, hand on my jaw, as I opened and closed my mouth.

Mieant was the furthest away. Guiltily, he held his palms down, as if only the floor was his responsibility. His long hair waved as he shook his head. His big, black eyes looked down, highlighting his lashes. Nonch snaked up beside Mieant, one claw arm holding a water cup and the others flat against his side. His sensor stalks were smooth, like flat hair; he looked like he wanted to be a billion kilometers away.

Cri, however, was right where she wanted to be. Two hands held her stomach, and for a moment, I thought she was in pain. Her other two hands were poised above me, like flips waiting to turn on their targets below. Cri's eyes glowed, and her hair curled into black whips in the rising wind. She wasn't in pain. I frowned. She giggled, not looking sane at all.

The molten red and orange pendant hovering in front of me stopped me cold. It was red hot, making the air shimmer around it. I didn't understand what I was seeing. The fist-sized, diamond shape from my past was not possible. *I'd flushed him. We'd looked for him. I'd given up hope. And he'd never floated before.*

I opened my mouth wordlessly, glancing first at Nonch and then back to the familiar metal form suspended in midair.

"I...."

I snatched him from the air and fell to my knees, dimly thankful that he'd cooled off fast enough not to fry my palms. Adrenaline surged through me, displacing the nausea and weakness. His metal edges pressed into my neck as I clutched him to my body. *AI!*

My friend was alive! Light and warmth fell over my mood, dispelling a large part of my guilt. *He wasn't dead. He was OK.*

He had come back to me.

I wasn't alone.

"UNIVERSE! YOU'RE BACK! I AM SO SORRY!"

"LET GO! Eighteen centuries go by, and teenagers are THE ONLY THING IN THE GALAXY THAT HASN'T EVOLVED!" This he said aloud.

I blinked, uncurled, and held him away from me.

I'm so angry, Raystar. You have no idea. NONE!! How could you do that to me?

265

I…was confused. Angry. Scared, I thought back. My friends were looking at us. Perhaps only Cri understood that we talked mind-to-mind. I didn't care. I hugged him, overjoyed at his return.

Nova, Ray, couldn't you let me finish my sentence, at least, before you flipping flushed me? Grief cracked his voice, and I winced at his pain.

I was so happy to have him back, so relieved to have him safe. But our reunion was….

Ray, TWO Battle Groups are coming. You think this 'natch-infested marble is going to drive them off by shooting nutrition at them? Despite the Glean protection, arguably the only force that could destroy the Convergence, these people are openly hunting you. Don't you see?

I didn't.

"I…." it was the best I could get out.

Gnnng, he said to himself. *Focus…* he said again, I think to himself. *I have so much to tell you. This isn't the time for this conversation.*

"Did you at least talk to the Elion, like I'd told you?" AI asked out loud.

Uh. No.

With a small grunt of, uh, sheepishness that captured pretty much everything else I felt I'd messed up on, I lowered him to the ground. I sat, cross-legged, a bit away from my friend.

I had completely forgotten about the Elion.

Nonch, Cri, and Mieant were still as statues, trying to puzzle together the verbal and nonverbal conversations between AI and me. Clearly, they sensed the craxy intensity of the exchange.

AI was covered in unrecognizable sigils. The hole where my leather necklace had woven through him was gone. Dust puffed outward in a three-meter circle as he shimmered, rising to hover with the tip of his diamond pointed toward me. *He'd changed.*

AI mentally huffed disbelief. *You forgot?*

In the silence between us, his mental eyes rolled as he snorted. I had the impression he'd dropped his hands to his sides and was looking around, exasperated, trying to find the clue I'd lost.

Thunder rumbled, and the chemical wind ruffled everyone's hair. AI's yellow scanner flashed over me, pausing on my collar, my heart, then my stomach. I heard him sigh, and then he verbalized, "You had all these years to destroy yourself horribly."

In a flicker of defiance, I shared my last few days with him. What I had been through. That should count for something. It wasn't like I'd been sitting on my hands.

Well, he started out in his old AI tone after listening to my story, *I trekked ALONE through kilometers of underground Ruins with that psychotic, reprobate nano-deviant from the controller trying to eat me at each turn, when…wonder upon wonders, I realized that floating through tunnels wasn't a practical form of transportation!*

Yeah. Wonder upon wonders. He was still a gravity-well filled jerk-head. I had no idea what a *reprobate* was, either.

MAYBE, he continued, *I could have JUST flown myself over legger-infested 'natch fields. Or I suppose the aircar would have been a way of getting around. Oh. I remember why I was doing this. My best friend flushed me down the loo!* At the last words, a small ruby star of anger glowed in the center of his diamond shape. My friends stepped back from his heat.

I remained where I was and glared at AI as the anger churned in my gut. I hadn't asked for any of this. I was a kid. You know, I do homework? Play video games? If someone expected me to handle this flip better than I'd been flipping handling it, I'd be happy to flipping give them my flipping purple DNA stuff and flipping introduce them to Godwill and….

Nonch swung three sword arms between us, nudging AI away. The beginning of a headache tapped at the base of my neck, and I felt a trickle of wetness from my nose. He positioned himself so we formed a triangle. My sleeve came away wet—not glistening, but instead glimmering, as electricity danced through the fabric of my shirt where it had absorbed my nosebleed. My friends leaned millimeters away from me. In the reflection of their eyes, I saw the beginning of a halo forming in my jagged, purple hair.

Nonch turned his weapony head to me.

"Pause a moment, Raystar-friend. I am gaining understanding. THIS is the defective synth you flushed down your sanitary waste recycler?"

FLIPSTICKS! That wasn't ANYTHING AI needed to hear! And I'd never claimed he was defective! My anger washed away like a receding wave, and I gulped. I was pretty sure that if I had called him defective, it was in an affectionate way. Like a nickname. Or something.

"It does not seem defective," Nonch voiced, oblivious to my giant eyes and minute head shakes that swished my bangs back and forth AND, IN PRETTY MUCH EVERY LANGUAGE, MEANT, "STOP!"

"But." Nonch turned his predatory head, his full intensity, toward AI. His sensor stalks flared. "*You* could have done more. Your secrets do not inspire trust, and in your keeping of them, you bring my friend harm."

A yellow beam washed from AI and splashed over Nonch. His feathery stalks rippled as if caressed by a light touch. "You don't want a piece of me, baby Crynit. Don't lecture me on my job. My beef is with our prima donna here."

Nonch and I traded skeptical glances. *Baby Crynit? Beef? Prima donna?* Nonch, confused, lowered his sword arms and looked at me. I sighed. "AI, meet Nonch and Mieant, and you know Cri," and I pointed to each in turn. "Friends, meet my, um, meet my oldest friend, AI."

"I want no confrontation," Nonch said, backing up a meter and lowering his claw arms, "but your presence and actions require explanation."

"Pfft," AI sighed. "None of your tiny, futuristic, alien minds could handle the—" Sucking in a virtual deep breath, he reined himself in and continued. "*Gnnng*, OK. I'm the advance party. The 'hooh-rah!' you hear when you open a can of whupass!"

He paused and snorted at our blank looks. "Never mind. I came up through the Ruins inside the camp perimeter. There's a world down there only Crynits really know about." He pointed at Nonch. We traded glances, remembering our friend's remarks about the underground Human Ruins.

"Uh, Sir." Mieant paused and looked at me, then back to AI. "How did you find us?"

AI muttered to himself and replied, "Asrigard, I got 'Eyes and Ears.'" He turned, glowed green, and shone a light on Cri's neck. "Those tattoos on her neck are broadcasting video, audio and location."

It didn't register for a second. So caught up with moment-by-moment survival, I'd forgotten about the tattoos Dad had put on Cri. My sister's jaw dropped. She slapped her lower hands over the tattoos. Joy lit up her face—and then instantaneously was replaced by panic. She covered the 'O' her mouth made with her upper hands.

Dad was brilliant.

"Nova," Cri whispered, looking at Mieant, "They saw US." Mieant's eyes got big.

"Yep. Everything and everyone in Cri's line-of-sight, from our nightmare-inspiring Sarla," AI continued, turning away from Nonch to Cri, "to you, Juliet, and your prissy Romeo over there."

He chuckled, and we all frowned. Our nanotranslators came up with nothing for "Juliet," "Romeo," or "prissy." AI continued. "We isolated your location based on the visual feeds and the initial route they used when they brought you here. It took much too long, but we found you."

We're neither forgotten, nor lost! My shoulders and neck tingled as his words sank in. Nonch's sensor stalks rose as he considered the implications of being found—of being re-connected with the people who loved us and, perhaps, the ones who protected us. Mieant stood taller.

Hope changes everything.

"Your parents are coming. I came to assess the landscape. Do triage." I touched my stomach, absently wondering where my pain had gone. He spun toward me. "You're the triage. That f–flipping Godwill injected you with an awful thing, Raystar. I've immobilized it, and I've healed you with what energy I can spare." He drew closer to me as he spoke. "But you have maybe two days before you turn into goo if we don't eliminate the infection."

Then, in my head, he said, *Ray. I can't do this anymore.... I can't watch what these people are doing to you.*

I looked at my friend, not understanding. Between his anger at me for flushing him, his disappointment in me, and something else, he was conflicted. And even stranger, I felt like I *should* know what he was talking about.

"Is it correct then, to believe that the Ceridians have a plan?" Nonch inquired politely. As he used pheromones as a secret language, he had probably inferred from my expressions that AI and I communicated via some alternate means as well.

"Why!" AI pivoted toward Nonch with a well-managed flourish (given that AI was a fist-sized, floating, diamond-shaped pendant). "Yes, my sufficiently courteous friend! In precisely one minute and thirty-two seconds, Sathra and Nent are going bring us home!"

One second earlier than expected, a six-meter-thick plasma-flower of destruction punched through the atmosphere at ground level, crushed the force fence, and sent dirt and debris skyward in a blinding, neon-blue flash.

Blue fire crashed across the field's barrier, melting three autoturrets within its heat radius. The concussion swatted AI to the ground, and we all did our species' version of head-over-butt tumbling as the shockwave pummeled us with brutal force. Nonch, of course, had a hundred feet and fared better; his sensor stalks swished like hair in a gust of wind. Starbats raged and again surged from the Ruins they'd just resettled. They were getting their exercise.

AI yelled something about schedules and precision.

Pfft. Life wasn't convenient for him either. Which somehow made me feel better.

I recognized the two guards who stumbled out of the vault building in various states of attaching their power armor.

The fence's autoturrets swiveled. I threw myself to the ground as their orange eyes pivoted over us and launched streams of glowing orbs toward some target on the horizon. Plasma balls flew like meteors, shrinking as they approached their distant purpose, and then flashed a brilliant white and lit up the clouds before Nem's atmosphere carried the *thump* of their explosions.

What was approaching over the horizon had an epic version of "returning" fire.

Ancient Human buildings lit up with staccato explosions as they got in the way of my parents' response. Structures that for 1,800 years hadn't received any attention, had minded their own ancient business, had fixated on their prior glory, crumbled in shock as their ankles were blown out by row after row of flowery energy blossoms. The titanic sound of metric ton upon metric ton of metal and kilometers-tall structures falling into each other like dominoes reached us seconds later.

The two guards who had eyed us just that morning as we'd explored the camp clasped the last segments of their armor on and rushed to assemble a heavy cannon. *Futile.* Their eyes grew moon-sized, so huge you could see the blaze of the fiery projectiles streaking toward them in their black sclerae.

I hoped they had hugged someone this morning before coming to work.

The camp was being razed as easily as a bully would shove over a little kid's sandcastle. Defenses were brushed aside as nova after nova vaporized their matter. Buildings flew in all directions and structures vanished in plasma's hungry orange fire. I'd never witnessed such power, such destruction.

But we were still alive. *Mom and Dad had great aim.* Shrapnel whirred around us, and through luck and reflex, we were not crushed, impaled, pierced, or beheaded.

A red sun streaked over our heads, incinerated a huge section of the prison fence, and blew a crater's worth of dirt skyward. Fence turrets that didn't immediately explode were thrown in twirling, fiery spirals that ricocheted off the Ruins before thudding to the ground. Starbats cried and swirled as their millions of nests in the Human Ruins were disturbed. I was sure those creatures would be starbatting about this for centuries.

The morning the gods fought.

Godwill, followed by Sarla, stepped out of the vault building. He was in the battle armor I'd seen him in the previous day. He pointed to us, and my friends dropped like marionettes with their strings cut. They writhed, screaming and clawing at their collars. My bet had paid off. I'd deactivated my collar, and while I was free, I didn't want him to know it. I followed my friends to the dirt, grasping at the plastic ring around my neck like I was trying to stop it from burning my head off.

"INCOMING! Cover your eyes and ears!" AI yelled from under the cot where he'd tumbled. Despite their pain, my friends complied.

The world turned white. Searing heat pressed down on my back. The *whump* that followed shoved us all at least two meters from where we'd lain.

Nova and gravity wells! Firing an atmosphere cannon at a target WITHIN the atmosphere was insane. After a millisecond of dead quiet, *thunks* and *clanks* sounded as gravity pulled whatever had been thrown toward space back to the ground.

I raised my head and looked back toward the direction of the heat, sheltering my eyes against the swirls of orange flame and black smoke. Not a bit of the NPD cruiser was visible. An enormous hole dripped molten metal into its glowing center, which was a pool of red lava. Godwill would not be able to follow us in the cruiser, at least.

My parents might be insane.

But they were OUR insane.

In the distance, a goliath approached. Mom and Dad's assault tank was becoming visible. It shrugged off the base's dwindling plasma fire like one brushes dust from clothes. The tank's forward shield was set to "obliterate." Air glowed crimson with shimmering heat as it pushed aside, melted, and burned whatever the hulking assault tank drove over. Millennia-old Human buildings crashed aside in slow motion.

The six-plus, meter-long twin barrels of the tank's atmosphere cannon swung toward us. Blue energy crackled at the dual muzzles. My eyes grew huge when they paused on exactly our position. The atmosphere cannons resumed their rotation a millisecond later, targeting the camp's remaining autoturrets. In a flash that lit up the ground, the sky, and the Ruins, their next shot cracked the air like a Galactic whip, and the ground behind us erupted in chunks. Wind, not to be left out of this contest of Armageddon, churned hot, acidic dirt into each of our breaths and blinks.

Smaller comets streamed toward us from the tank's eight other plasma cannons. Return fire lancing out from the prison-camp guards and the remaining autoturrets splashed against the tank's shields. The tank's autoturrets immediately targeted the sources and sent an answering string of orange light screaming back at the offending enemy. Oblivious to the lethal exchange, Godwill marched toward us, a skeleton made bulky by combat armor. His too-tight skin pulled his mouth back into a perpetual grin, and his bulging black eyes took in the destruction with what could only be called glee.

Backlit by fires blazing everywhere in the camp, he was terrifying. A purple nimbus pulsed around his hands and skeletal head, and a red gash on his cheek dripped silvery blood down his uniform.

Sarla was a giant, sinuous black form that wove and snaked behind him.

My parents would not reach us before they did.

My kid hands bled as I gripped stone and dirt and hauled myself to my feet. I poofed purple strands of hair from my face. I wasn't sure what would happen next, but being sprawled on the ground wasn't going to help.

Godwill, striding over debris, was at Cri's side in another eye-blink. He grabbed her ear and pulled her to her feet. She screamed, her four hands on his one that held her suspended, and her legs kicked wildly. Godwill made eye contact with me. In slow motion, he dragged his tightly held gun barrel from Cri's neck to her collar bone, tracing where the tattoo rested. She groaned, as much out of anger as of pain.

He smiled, daring me to come a step closer, as he pointed the gun to my sister's head and looked at her tattoos.

45

"Clever," he leered, "Clever, indeed." Godwill leaned toward Cri's face, and his pistol dug into Cri's collarbone as he lowered her back to the ground. She whimpered. "I know you can hear me, Nent. Sathra," he said, smiling calmly, looking at me as if he were sharing a drink with a friend at a cafe. "Nent, you missed defending your wife, years ago. Now you're letting your daughter die. Expensive lessons, Commander."

His words didn't make sense. Lightning cracked and clouds frothed as if a giant were blowing into them with a straw. The Storm Wall? I'd lost track of the days while in the camp. It couldn't be today. *That would be BAD.* In my state, the headaches probably would kill me. But this close to the Mesas, unshielded as we were, we'd be blended into mush by the swirling debris, tossed by gas giant-force winds, and fried by lightning. Or Godwill would kill us.

At least we had options.

I shook my hands out like an athlete and flicked them with a twist toward the ground. Blue lightning crackled around my fingers and coalesced into fiery orbs in my slightly curled palms. With my anger and fear, my active fight against Godwill's injections, and whatever AI had done, I could access my power more easily than ever. Energy surged through me. Control screens superimposed themselves on my surroundings, on me. But my displays were lit up with red instead of blue—it had to be the infection. My augmented vision showed the energy cell in Godwill's gun glowing like a small star.

"GODWILL!"

Ray! You can't do this! AI yelled in my head.

We are here because of me. Our circumstances are my responsibility.

I spared a glance at my friends. The active batteries on their collars also shone like stars.

Tiny, explosive stars.

I unclasped my broken collar. Godwill watched me, his eyes widening and his smile cracking, as I hurled the band toward the right side of his head. He was holding Cri with his left arm, and I wanted to keep his body between the collar and my sister. I flicked my hand, pulsing nanoenergy at the device. Godwill pivoted gracefully to the side. The collar exploded with a flash larger than its size would have indicated. Godwill's body armor protected him, but he'd had to release my sister in his dodge. She fell, writhing and holding her neck and her ear.

Time blazed by, but for me, everything was slow motion. I pivoted toward my friends, concentrating, and spread my hands wide. Lightning arced from my fingers to the bands of fire around their throats. I had a guess that my power was directed by my intention. *Help my friends.* The intensity of that thought gathered in my mind. My aura, now swirling around me, dissolved the collars' energy sources. Their circlets popped and fell from their necks. I felt a small rush. *I should have received huge energy from their collars' batteries, but I only felt a trickle!*

Godwill surged toward me and caught my shoulder in a vise-like grip. His armored fingers crushed against my tendons and bones. "At last!" he breathed, foul and deadly.

Free of her collar, Cri rose and kicked at his back. His power armor protected against energy attacks, but not kinetic blows. Cri's foot connected, and her strength became evident as he staggered forward, nearly dropping me.

Sarla rose behind Cri like a curling cloud of black smoke. The enormous Crynit's hide reflected the orange and blue of the fires around us, and she paused only briefly to point her five blade claws at Cri's back before falling into a strike, like a whale launching itself from calm water and then crashing down with inevitable certainty.

A smaller, midnight-blue form ghosted in front of my sister and intercepted the giant Crynit. They collided with a force I felt through the ground. Nonch's mandibles folded around Sarla's midsection, and his six arms kept her five longer blade arms from impaling Cri from five different, messy angles. Cri got the fraction of a second she needed to roll sideways and face Godwill from a new position.

Somehow, we'd become a team. Cri didn't even question that Nonch had her back; she focused on her target and assumed Nonch could do *his* job.

With Godwill's attention on Cri, Mieant attacked from his rear, striking the arm holding me. Mieant's knee came up as his elbow came down, meeting simultaneously at Godwill's forearm, above the armor encasing his fist. Something snapped. Godwill roared and released me—I collapsed. Mieant retreated in a flash as the wounded Jurisdictor spun to face him. Cri launched herself into a great arc, her lower hands and upper hands meshed together. Dual hammer strikes thundered on Godwill's back, whipping his head and audibly cracking his armor as he fell to one knee, then clumsily rolled aside into a crouch. He wasn't smiling anymore. Mieant and Cri circled on opposite sides of him, looking for an opening.

Our anger unleashed, we fought silently with the synchronicity of a pack of leggers. One of us distracted Godwill, the other attacked, then retreated out of range, while another darted in with a strike.

We were amazing. It was not enough.

Sarla simply dwarfed Nonch. Her hind tail pincers arched *over* her head to grasp him behind his first set of claw arms. Nonch hissed as Sarla, who, with a twist of her sword arms, ripped his front claw arms off and threw them into the flames surrounding our struggle.

Fury...cold, consuming, overwhelming, erupted in my heart. There was no going back. I streamed RIVERS of lightning at her. Waves of blue lightning, tinged with orange, washed over her so she was a black shape held in the light of my energy. Any restraint I had vanished at the sight of my friend getting hurt.

STOP! Raystar! Stop! The yellow light of AI's fear was lost in the orange and black of the fires around us. *I don't have enough power to protect you!* He shouted.

Augmented vision showed me Sarla's heart, brain, and vital organs. I saw into her body, where I needed to focus my attack. My first stream of nano knocked Sarla back, reigniting my hunger. This was *GOOD*. She was big. Convert her, and I wouldn't be hungry anymore and would have more than enough power to protect myself. But I frowned. My nano was orange, not blue or white as it had been.

I wasn't getting energy back like I had with Nurse Pheelios.

Sarla moved toward me. I jumped toward her, newfound strength sending me in a high arc. I concentrated my lightning in my fists as I landed and simultaneously punched. The Crynit was thrown through the air, landing and lying motionless fifteen meters away. That wasn't what I'd intended. My hunger was raging. I'd intended to devour her.

My power wasn't regenerating.

Godwill moved between Sarla and me. He spread his arms, creating a glowing shield around himself, and then reached out to me and grabbed my corona, my aura. And *began to feed off me.* I staggered and dropped to one knee.

The air around us was on fire, and the smell of burning chemicals was nearly overwhelming. Storm Wall thunder cracked, and bolts of lightning licked the ground like hungry leeches. Everywhere, the camp was in flames. In my peripheral vision, one of the tall, ancient spires tipped in slow motion, crashing to the ground with the scream of a million kilograms of metal twisting out of shape. Through the roaring of collapsing buildings, flames, and winds emerged the low *thrum* of approaching antigrav engines.

Sarla wasn't moving. She lay on her side where she'd fallen, amidst the scrabble of rocks and smoldering buildings. She was a distraction.

Godwill was the threat.

I reached into myself. There was power enough. My lightning claws extended, I lunged at Godwill, angling my blades slightly outward, funneling him toward my center. He grinned and lowered his shoulder into my charge. I brought my fist in with an uppercut at the moment of collision, hoping to drive my claws deep. We hit with a mini-nova and a billion-decibel *screech* as our energies collided, each trying to protect and destroy. I was flung six meters toward the approaching battle tank. Somehow, I landed on my feet and a knee, fist down, ready to charge again.

Blood gushed from my nose onto my hand, its electricity coursing through each splatter in an outline of white light. *The red heat of my life.* Godwill rose, gripping his ribs where my fist claws had torn the armor from his body. His bones were showing—white, pink, bloody. He looked down in wonder at his wound.

It should have been a mortal wound.

Sarla had been thrown, too. The giant Crynit warrior was lying off to the side, some five meters from Godwill. Her armor was cracked. She moved slowly, disoriented from the clash, her sensor stalks waving randomly as she tried to get her bearings. Mieant and Cri lay still on the ground where they'd been flung. Mieant had somehow wrapped himself around my sister protectively. Nonch had been tossed onto his back and was flipping over to his feet, although he looked disoriented from the blast, and I supposed the pain of having his arms pulled off. I snarled with my nano flaring to life around me.

Thunder roared just overhead.

Godwill looked up, stared hard at the sky, and laughed. I suspiciously followed his gaze skyward. Blood shone on his lips as, despite his wound, he struggled to his feet, threw both arms wide, tilted his head back, and screamed hysterically—defiantly—at the heavens.

Those weren't clouds.

He met my wide-eyed, open-mouthed gaze and activated his own nanotech. Lightning formed in the curl of his fingers. Still screaming, but now with laughter, he flung an orange bolt at my face.

46

Godwill's blast flower-petaled around my shield, incinerating the grass on either side of me and flaring upward like a wave crashing over a rock.

I staggered from the impact and was thrown on my back. Sucking in a breath that didn't have enough air, I blinked furiously and struggled to rise. What I saw above laid me flat again.

Realization paraded through my consciousness as my brain attempted to understand what my eyes were showing me. The Storm Wall towering up into the heavens surged and boiled around an impossibly large shape, striking it with lightning so fast that the "thing" was silhouetted in a coruscating, jagged cloud of blue light. Nem's Storm Wall hammered at the shape with such fury that thunder rolled constantly. The THING got larger, and I realized it was descending through the clouds! Steam billowed from its armored hide. Near to the center of the unimaginably large mass, kilometer-long blue flashes of electricity snaked across its belly.

It was a ship.

Static electricity danced over everything now: the Ruins, the wings of the starbats, ourselves. I readjusted my perspective dizzily as the behemoth oriented toward its final position over the Mesas.

It was so large, I felt like I was falling *UP*.

Clouds of dust streamed from launch ports and arced toward Blue

River. Except that wasn't dust—those were ships! With their atmosphere drives lit, they looked like swarms of tiny blue fireflies against the sky's grey and the gigantic ship's black underbelly. Another swarm descended toward us, growing from dust to dots then to actual shapes. *Thousands of ships.*

The 98th Battle Group had arrived.

The invasion force was here. NOW.

"Raystar of Terra," Godwill said, as his grin wrapped around his emaciated head and bulging eyes. I rolled to my stomach, getting my knees under me, and scrambled to my feet to face him. Microsparks poured over his body. His ribs were healed. He dragged Sarla behind him like she was a rolled carpet. Her body bent uncomfortably in the wrong direction. Her limbs waved; I could tell she was still alive, but that large chunks of her shell were missing. The proud, terrifying Crynit was a sack of wreckage.

Godwill was converting her essence to heal himself. He was consuming her.

"You have lost." He then leered at me and released Sarla; the part of her he'd been holding thudded to the ground in a cloud of dust. In two strides, the Lethian closed the distance between us. His nano snaked out in iridescent, airy tendrils of orange that circled my body and pulled me toward him.

AI? I called out for my friend twice and was greeted with silence.

Godwill grabbed my face, holding my cheeks in a vise-like grip and forming my mouth into fishlips. *Only Mom did that.* I swung, but my fist bounced harmlessly off of his forearm with a dull thump.

And then tentacles of nano formed a cloud around me. I tingled, I stung, and then I started to BURN as he sapped my energy until my corona sparked once and faded. He held me by my face as I writhed. I couldn't stop thinking about Nurse Pheelios. What terrible power my ancestors had created!

Godwill pulled me close, an insane snarl turning into a victory grin. "Who needs the solvent when I can consume you like this?"

The stinging was turning into fire. *He was eating me.*

White lightning streaked across my vision, slashing the ribbons of his nano that were consuming me.

Free from his grip, I dropped, gasping, and rolled away. Against the orange fires, black smoke, and dark sky, IT-ME—uh, Artem—walked toward us purposefully, his Humanoid form shrouded in a dense, white-gold clouds of sparks. The swirls of energy spun wildly before coalescing into comets that snaked in orbit around Artem's upper body.

Artem swung his arms forward as if he were in a pool trying to splash someone. His comets streaked toward Godwill.

"RAAAAYYYYYYYYYYSTARRR," Artem grated, raising a hand toward me. There was a flash and a wall of force that crushed me like a blindside tackle on the playground. I tumbled away from Godwill. *Where were my parents!?*

Their tank was plowing through the Ruins. It would not arrive for another few seconds, an eternity.

"No," Godwill muttered. "NO!" He took a step toward the silver figure and lifted his arm, palm out. His other hand reached behind him and made a grabbing gesture toward Sarla. Nano flowed between them and, upon contact, she writhed. I could see her matter flowing to him. I knew how that felt.

"407, I will have you this day!" Godwill shouted, releasing a torrent of silver energy that slashed toward Artem's comets. The two streams of light crashed into each other, largely cancelling each other out. Artem's halo flared into a bubble shield, but the force Godwill had released passed through its shimmering defenses and coated Artem's body.

"I AM NOT FOUR-OH-SEEVEN! I AM ARRRRTEM!" Artem screamed in his scratchy, bass-computer voice, flinging both arms toward Godwill. Lightning arced from Artem's fingers and stabbed at Godwill, who staggered, his own shields glowing, under the onslaught. Sarla remained prone; whatever power Godwill was throwing around came from her essence.

I felt fevered, empty, hollow. Exhausted.

Deep inside, though, I had a spark. A little left.

I touched my power, and energy coalesced around my hand. Red flashes mingled with my blue lightning. There was a war within me and a war outside, and I was losing the internal struggle. Concentrating, I balled my energy into an orb so bright it hurt to look at it.

Artem had reached Godwill and was trying to push his hands through his former tormentor's shield. Godwill was trying to do the same.

Revenge versus pride. Could either actually win?

Godwill's hand penetrated Artem's shield, sending ripples over Artem's defenses like a rock being thrown into a pond. The Jurisdictor's armored hand wrapped around Artem's neck and lifted him. For a moment, I saw the Human boy who had once been as he dangled in the Lethian's grip. Artem writhed, but Godwill was now consuming his essence and growing more powerful each second.

I released my energy, my last bolt of life, into the ethereal link Godwill had created to consume Sarla. The nano reacted instantly, connecting Sarla to me. Godwill shuddered, released Artem, and turned, his eyes wide. I pulled, using *EVERYTHING* I had to rip energy from him.

The injections he'd given me limited my ability to consume energy, but *this* particular power wasn't mine to take. I concentrated on flowing it through me into Sarla. *HEAL*, I thought, much as I'd done with Mieant's parents.

I wasn't going to consume anyone.

Artem took advantage of Godwill's focus on me. In a blur, he lifted Godwill above his head and hurled him ten meters into one of the camp's flaming buildings. He followed up with streams of glowing plasma, pulverizing the building as he marched toward the inferno and Godwill.

My connection with Sarla and her energy shattered. I staggered and dropped to my knees. I bowed my head, purple hair flowing over my face. I panted. *So tired, I just need a moment. A few breaths.* I looked up.

The swarm of dots from the Dreadnought grew into a squadron

of sinister assault ships. They would be here any moment. I looked around and realized that I was most likely going to die. We all were. So much of this was due to the genetic power I'd simply inherited. I was bone tired. Godwill had said that if I was dead, my DNA would be rendered useless. Maybe that was the way to end this. To save everyone. Die. I thought these things in a blink.

And then realized my death wouldn't solve anything. Not so long as that nanocontainer in the Vault existed. If that truly was the culmination of 1,800 years of "harvesting," then it needed to be destroyed.

Yeah. *Nova and great gravity wells. I had enough life energy to do that.*

It needed to be destroyed.

47

The burning building exploded. Flaming chunks of Galactic alloy arced skyward, like fireworks, against the darkness of the Storm Wall before gravity smashed them down against Nem's surface. Godwill, unharmed, stood facing Artem in the middle of the blaze. Artem had manifested an enormous, blazing sword, complete with orange fire that flickered along the length of the blade. Godwill crouched, his blue lightning claws emerging from each hand. If the two scariest beings in my thirteen-year-old existence weren't out to suck my DNA from me, or worse, I would have thought the flaming sword and lightning claws were ridiculously nova.

Alas.

My, uh, nemisi, nemeses (it's so rare that people have more than one nemesis, I couldn't think of the plural) circled, apparently evenly matched, as they searched for openings in the other's defense. I felt a familiar tingle. Both Artem and Godwill turned in my direction—but they weren't looking at me. They were looking past me. Mom and Dad's assault tank hovered to a stop not five meters from my back and blocked out the sky.

The tingles I'd felt were its shields extending their protective radius to encompass me, Nonch, Cri, and Mieant. Elation, relief, happiness—I should have felt these things. I should have crumpled to the ground and waited for my parents to get me, to protect me.

In their shelter, I would be safe. They, as always, would be my sanctuary.

But.

If the Foundationalists had really spent 1,800 years harvesting millions of my people to create the concentrated nano I'd seen in Godwill's vault, I wouldn't ever be safe. Humans wouldn't ever be safe. There would be NO sanctuary for anyone...ever.

That containment pod needed to be destroyed.

I took a deep breath, feeling my heart race as the insanity of what I was contemplating smashed into my consciousness. My fingers were scraped and raw, and my hands burned as I grabbed dirt and brick to haul myself to my feet. Blowing purple hair out of my eyes, I scanned the smoke and ruined camp for Godwill's vault.

There.

My first step toward the building was filled with fear—the second step, less so. By the third, anger at the cruelty and injustice of what had been done to my kind, and to me, energized my bruised muscles. *I was just a kid. What was I doing caught up in this eons-old war?* But I was in it, nonetheless. My fifth step was more sure. *The time for being a victim was gone.*

The harvested nanotech, created with millions of Human lives, HAD to be destroyed. If it was left intact, Humanity would be eliminated. I'd be dead.

By my tenth step, I was more determined and resolute. For once, sure of myself.

While my mind was willing AND focused, my body was still underfed, bruised, and unhappy with the situation. I tried sprinting toward the vault building, but only managed an ungainly half-jog, half-stumble filled with twinges of pain and sore muscles. Speed was important not only because of the thousands of ships pouring out of the Dreadnought, and not only because of Artem and Godwill, but also because if my parents saw me running through flaming Ruins, I was sure they'd try to stop me! I zigged through rubble and blazing detritus, noting that all the guards had fled upon the tank's arrival. I stepped over a hand that jutted out from under a piece of fallen building. *Not all of the guards had escaped, apparently.*

Sparing a glance back, I caught the tank's massive barrels pivot toward where Artem and Godwill clashed with their oversized blades. *No. Mom and Dad couldn't be that insane.* You don't fire something designed to take out spaceships at point-blank range. The atmosphere cannon *ZWUMPED.* Dirt erupted, burning buildings were scattered for hundreds of meters, and my field of vision went white. I was lifted and thrown halfway to the vault.

I *thumped* on clear ground like a sack of 'natch, winded, but not injured, and thankful I hadn't been impaled on the nearby mounds of jagged wreckage. The cannon blast had gouged a cavernous hole in the ground that glowed with molten rock and metal. Godwill and Artem were nowhere to be seen.

Light splashed against the tank's shield like rain, making soft pattering sounds as the Dreadnought's swarm of assault ships came within range and began firing. I was running out of time. The vault was twenty steps away. Several approaching ships noticed the little Human girl running toward the building and peeled away from the primary formation focusing on my parents' tank. And opened fire!

I was twelve paces from the door.

Dirt geysered nearly a meter from where I ran, and I staggered to the side trying to keep my balance.

Only three determined strides to the door.

No more blasts came. The ships were circling for another strafe.

I reached the closed door, gritted my teeth, and threw my adrenaline-fueled strength into the final distance, expecting to fly into the interior of the building as the door slid open.

I smashed into the door, windmilled backward, and landed on my side. I lay there, stunned. My shoulder was on fire.

The door handle gleamed in the darkness. *OF COURSE.* Because, you know, sometimes those things were used with doors. The ships were screaming in a tight circle, coming around for another shot.

Muttering bad things my parents would instantly ground me for, I picked myself up and pulled the door handle. The door swung open, and I stumbled inside just as plasma bolts tore up the ground behind me. *Who uses door handles?*

The hallway leading down to the vault was deserted. A blaster lay discarded on one of the desks. I grabbed it as I raced by, checking its charge. It glowed green—a full charge. But whether or not it held a charge, I was committed to my course. I just hoped that Godwill hadn't had the NPD remove the nanocontainer at the first sign of my parents' assault, or I'd feel like an even bigger moron than when I'd tried to shoulder the door open.

Plasma pistol held in front of me, like my parents had taught me, I sucked in a breath and stepped toward the vault. *All clear.* I entered and was greeted by steamy, rotting odors. I pointed the weapon down the dimly lit staircase. *No sound.* I stepped onto the stairs; the hairs on my neck stood on end as I reached the halfway point. I was too far from either exit to escape if someone sneaked up on me from the rear or ambushed me from the front. I hurried down the stairs, pausing at the corner for one last listen before crouching and peering around the corner.

Empty.

"Pppppllllllthhhhsss!" I exhaled in relief, straightened, and rubbed my bruised shoulder. Everything in the vault was as I'd left it. Something jingled at my feet. I looked down. Even the remnant of Jenna was as I'd left it—grim and sad.

The nanocontainer stood, quietly ignoring me. The chair and rows of virtual screens were sinister reminders of my powerlessness and Godwill's cruelty. I limped to a spot far enough away from the nanocontainer, where I had a clear line of fire.

Raising the plasma pistol, I flicked the safety off and heard a high-pitched whine, the weapon's battle cry.

I would be the one to redeem 1,800 years of Human oppression. Eliminate this threat and once and for all eliminate the discussion around access to Human technology. After I destroyed the container, I would be the only loose thread left. Sure, Godwill and Artem were made of the same stuff, but if Godwill was to be believed, I was the key.

OK, Ray, time to finish this.

I pulled the trigger.

48

Orange plasma bolts streamed from the pistol, splashing over the containment pod and washing the room with heat and fire. I raised my arm to cover my eyes and twisted away from the inferno. The rows of vid-screens melted and the chair became a slag heap.

But the nanocontainment pod remained untouched. It ignored my scowl.

Stupid shielded containment pod.

I fired again, aiming at different parts of the pod, squeezing off shots with furious abandon. The energy meter on the plasma pistol dipped to yellow, and my eyebrows were singed. I wiped sweat and burned eyebrows away from my forehead.

Nova. Great gravity wells. Flipping nova and great gravity wells and...auuugh! I raised my arm to hurl the useless plasma pistol at the pod.

"Raystar of Terra," someone said behind me. Surprised, I spun and fumbled the pistol. It flew through the air, landing with a crunch at the feet of the owner of the voice.

Sarla.

Orange eyes, huge mandibles, jagged, sword arms—the wall of intelligent lethality regarded me. Her bulk flowed into the vault and I backed up, terrified but resigned to my fate. I could see glistening skin in the areas where her hard shell had been absorbed by Godwill.

It looked incredibly painful. Panicked, I reached for my power, but I couldn't feel anything.

She scooped up my pistol, reversed her grip, and gently handed it to me, stock first. I stared until she shook the pistol impatiently for me to take it.

"If I wanted to destroy you, I could have just let you blast away in here until you cooked yourself. I did not expect truth from you," she said, waving an arm claw at the nanocontainer, "or honor."

"It needs to be destroyed," I said, and then looked down. "Maybe I do too."

She clacked her armor lightly, something I'd learned from Nonch to be equivalent to a laugh. "Little Human, you are a surprise. But we cannot eliminate the nanocontainer with that blaster."

We were a "we"? I looked up at her, my new sister in arms.

The building shook as something fell over upstairs with a crash; dust drifted down from the ceiling. A section of her armor slid open, and she pulled out a bulbous missile. "Tactical field nuke," she said, turning from me back to the device. Her arms and hands blurred with activity, and soon, she'd stripped the nuke of its engine and armor, leaving it a boxy, asymmetrical device. "Go upstairs. Make sure we can exit and are not ambushed. I will set the charge."

"Why are you helping, Sarla?"

"Human, I will not be psychoanalyzed while in combat. Get out of my way, or do not. I will be leaving quickly." She turned and approached the nanocontainer.

Right. I sprinted past her, up the stairs and through the corridor. Behind me, I heard a crash and the familiar thrumming of a massive Crynit. I spared a glance outside—all was clear. Not a hundred meters away, my parents' assault tank was taking fire from countless ships, its shield a glowing umbrella protecting it from the rain of fire.

"RUN, RAYSTAR OF TERRA!" Sarla bellowed from behind me. I heard her *thrum* up the stairs.

I ran. I had no accurate sense of time, and panic was creeping up on me. All I could do was keep my legs pumping.

Sarla's powerful hand claws circled my waist. Her speed was incredible, and we crossed the distance to the tank in a blink. She raced just past my parents' tank and did an abrupt right turn. Once behind the tank, Sarla came to a full stop in the time of a heartbeat, and the whiplash almost broke my back. My breath was squashed out of me as she curled into a protective ball with me at her center.

The ground shook, air was sucked from my lungs, my eardrums felt like they'd ruptured, and the heat was worse than anything I'd felt before. Silence, then noise, then more noise, then full volume. Sarla uncurled and I spilled out of her embrace. We were safe behind the tank, and protected inside the tank's anti-*everything* shields.

I rose, noting that the prison camp's ground was fractured and cracked like a dried riverbed. The camp was gone—completely vaporized. The nuke's ground-zero crater reached nearly a hundred meters in every direction, extending almost to where my parents' tank was positioned.

The only things standing were the assault tank and the structures behind the tank. Half buildings, vegetation, bits of fence—all were cleanly sheared off in a neat line between existence and nonexistence.

And then the rain of metal began. Countless attack craft had been flying either too close to the blast radius or too close to each other when the field nuke had literally shoved them through the air. They pounded to the ground in enormous shrieks of whining engines, exploding munitions and fuel cells, smashing metal, and blazing orange and black smoke. The battlefield paused in the aftermath of the bomb's destruction.

Sarla grunted, satisfied. "THAT, Human, is what was required to destroy the nanocontainer."

I surveyed the landscape. "Could it have survived?"

Sarla looked around, gently raised an arm claw, and gestured to the scenery around us, and then looked back at me. *Right.*

"Thank you, Sarla," I bowed.

"Raystar of Terra," Sarla said, dipping her head. "Courageous child. The scales are balanced. I would not have survived Godwill's attack without your intervention." She dipped her sensor stalks toward me. "I would welcome meeting you again. Tell my sister, if you encounter her, that she will know where to find me." And with that, she lowered her body so all her arms and legs touched the ground and raced toward the Ruins almost as fast as my dart could have managed. She wound her way through the burning brush at the edge of the skeletal Ruins, slid over several ancient stone blocks, and disappeared into the dark maw of a crumbling building.

49

Sarla was gone. In the time it took to inhale, the pattering I'd thought was rain increased to a steady, dull thumping. Flowers of color blossomed, lighting up the darkness around us. Orange light and blue shadows coincided with each thump and cast eerie shadows into the darkness.

The tank's protective shields shimmered above me in an umbrella of glowing veins radiating outward from each impact. Assault ships poured down a storm of orange fire in what had become a torrent. Behind the incoming meteors of destruction, a circle of hundreds of Convergence ships settled into position surrounding the camp's perimeter. Farther off, below the Convergence cruisers, troop carriers illuminated the dark ground with sweeping spotlights as they vomited squads of armored soldiers. My parents had planned ahead, but I was pretty sure they hadn't considered an entire Battle Group. *OR TWO!* Nearly every plan I'd made felt like it had been kicked into the gravity well when it met up with reality. Maybe it was the same for grownups.

"DAUGHTER!" the loudspeaker hailed me.

Mom? Dad? I couldn't tell whose voice it was, but the ramp to the side of the tank thunked down on the camp's dry ground. I blinked and lurched toward the cool lights of the tank's protective inside. The tank's autoturrets screamed their response to our skyward enemy in a blaze of golden dewdrops. I shrieked, crouched, and raised my hands above me, curling my fingers over my ears. The atmosphere cannon

ZWUMPED, shaking the ground and sending a house-sized streak of starlight at a medium cruiser. The oval, bristly ship paused as it took the hit—like it thought it might be survivable.

Fire blossomed from its side like speed-motion vids of flowers opening in spring, and then the ship lit the sky with its nova. Glean assault tanks were made to take and hold a position. *This was MUCH better than my hologram.* In a millisecond, the turret shifted with microscopic precision to its next target.

But I was beyond emotion. Cold. Is this what AI meant by "frosty?" I'd seen too much. Been through too much. "Too much" crushes you or, if you survive it, it makes you different. Good? Bad? I don't know.

The doors hissed open, and the tank's entry ramp slid from its belly to rest on the ground. Dad stepped out in full battle armor. Active weapon clusters mounted on his shoulders scanned the desolation with red sensor beams. His boots clanked as he stomped halfway down the exit ramp and took a defensive position, four plasma cannons aimed at nothing but ready for anything that needed to be annihilated. The golden Ascendancy seal on his chest plate shone against his charcoal armor.

Mom, dressed in her white combat suit, followed a millisecond later, her cape billowing in her wake. In two strides, she was halfway down the ramp, and with four arms, she swung me into an embrace. "Baby!" she whispered as she squished me against her chest. Pivoting, she rushed me inside the tank.

"Raystar," Mom breathed as the door slid shut behind us. "We have your friends…." Mom looked around. "We would never leave you. You knew that, didn't you?"

"I have the command," Dad called as he moved toward the cockpit.

Mom's face glistened with tears that shone against her purple scar. They glittered in the tank's white light on her red skin and matted, black hair. "MY RAY." She pulled me, squished me in her love.

Now that I was safe, emotions poured out. I sucked in a breath, and my thoughts clarified around my purpose. My destiny. *Mine.* I pushed away from her all-encompassing warmth to take in the tank's command center. Cri and Mieant were propped against a wall. Cri curled against Mieant, her arms folded across her chest. Mieant had his arms around her, and his cheek rested on her head. Right then, I hated their bond and the aloneness of my life, the isolating burden of my choices.

Nonch's feet didn't so much *thrum* on the metal floor as they *tacked*, like the drumming of a hundred heavy fingernails. He approached and kept pace with Mom by scuttling sideways, his head even with mine. His front claw arms, which Sarla had ripped off, were bandaged; otherwise, he was whole. I lay my arm on him, feeling the comfort of his warm shell.

"You live," he said simply, brushing my head gently with his sensor stalks. "I am happy."

I looked at him and was about to smile when Mom placed something cool against my arm. There was a hiss, and then a sting.

"For your fever, love." As I recoiled, Nonch pulled back and my numb arm flopped downward. But the fever in me still burned and pressed against the inside of my skull. To say I had overexerted myself was to say that there was gravity in a black hole.

"Peace, love," she said.

Peace. It was a concept you had to prove.

I wilted as whatever was in the injection coursed through my body, flooding me with near-overwhelming drowsiness. Mom kindly laid me in an empty command chair.

Words weren't coming. She pressed a thermometer to my forehead, scowled, and then continued. "I scanned AI. Our guess is he's containing the nanoinfection, but in doing so, he can't use any of his other functions. Dad thinks he can convert a power source from the hangar that should provide AI with ample energy to reactivate his higher functions while taking care of you. Mostly," she added nervously.

I had my family, my friends. *I was dying. AI had said that I had two days before I turned to goo. Then what? Would I end up like Artem? Or would I just end?*

I lowered my eyes at Mom and stared blankly at the Glean Creed emblazoned on her suit's breast. More than a creed, it was a to-do list: Peace. Love. Family. War.

We didn't have peace.

The 98th had arrived, and only Sarla and I knew Godwill's geno-cidal intentions. Would anyone believe me if I told them? Did I have enough life left in me to even tell my story?

Love.

What did that mean? Mom and Dad had come back for us. I wasn't sure they had a choice, given that both of their "daughters" had been kidnapped and the Glean Ascendancy knew it. Is love doing the things you have to do, or the things you *choose* to do? Maybe I didn't really know what that word meant.

Family?

I sighed. I was connected to everyone here. They were all I had, and in these past days, we'd stuck by each other. Somehow. But each of *them* had a family who would take them in, assuming we all survived this. I had been *given* to Mom and Dad as part of an agreement to keep me from falling into the wrong hands. I wanted, with all of my being, to belong. But I didn't even have a species on this planet to join.

In the dark part of my being, where thoughts lose their structure and I can only feel my way through the darkness, something ignited. It was a small flame, but its power source was clear: my resolve. *The past was gone. In the next few and last moments of my life, how would I live? How would I die?* I pushed myself out of my slouch and frowned. I would not be a victim anymore. Heat welled in my chest; I clenched my teeth. From now until my end, *I would happen to things.* Anger fueled my internal flame. The furious light of my purpose blazed away the darkness of my mind.

"Sathra, we have an incoming message," Dad said. "I'm transmit-ting to the screens."

The command center viewers flickered to life in a wall of icicle blue, casting cold shadows on me and my friends. Fuzzy pixilation gave way to clarity as the images resolved.

Godwill. But not Godwill.

His larger-than-life face, skeletal and gaunt, avalanched toward me, courtesy of amazing 3-D visuals, into the command center. Eyes wide, I turned my head and escaped from him into the accommodating gel of the command chair. Scars stretched diagonally from his right temple down across his left jaw. Redness from the newly healed wounds cut through his tight, grey skin. His long, black hair was shriveled and burned—even completely missing in some places, exposing grey-red patches of scorched flesh. His combat armor hung loosely; the melted breastplates testified to the extreme temperatures they'd been subjected to. His face was a picture frame of madness, and inside that frame, his eyes burned as twin flames of electric-white sparks centered in shadows so dark, so deep, they could have been voids in space. He was in a ship, I figured, noting the crates in the background—he was in some sort of cargo hold.

I gripped the arms of the command chair and turned to face him. *Was his violence the only truth? Was it now mine?*

Nova that. Fire and rage surged through me, and I met his gaze with my glare.

"Raystar," he hissed, raspy, almost digitized, as he leaned to glare at me with his pupil-less, space-black eyes. "You have destroyed my life's work, all that was important to me. Do not let me find your friends and family. Kill them before I get to them. Their suffering is my path to you…or don't." He smiled insanely wide, an abyss of teeth. "In the end, it doesn't matter." Then he whispered, "I am your Fate…and I am coming for you."

His image disappeared. The tank's life support hummed, and the occasional thud of a direct plasma hit interrupted the silence of the command center.

Peace. Love. Family.

The last mandate of the Glean creed surged through me. My mind burned with acceptance. Humanity's legacy, my inheritance, stood in my thoughts, robed in the phoenix's flames. My fate or my choice—it didn't matter. It was *mine*.

War.

END OF BOOK 1

Author's Note

I grew up reading C.S. Lewis, J.R.R. Tolkien, Edgar Rice Burroughs, and Philip K. Dick…wow, the list goes on. My imagination lit up when Gary Gygax exploded on the scene with his world creation system, Dungeons & Dragons. How cool was it to actually be able to dream up your own story, and then play it?

Now, with video games as immersive as they are, we have so many powerful ways of storytelling, imagining alternate realities, or simply just examining our own through different lenses. Raystar's journey is just beginning. I hope you'll join her as she discovers who she is, who her friends are, and what it means to be Human!

Acknowledgments

My deepest thanks go to:

- My dad, Karl, for getting me hooked on science fiction and fantasy at an early age.
- My mom, Indira, for helping me through all those late hours and teaching me how to edit in middle school.
- My brother, Bjorn, for serving as a sounding board and test reader.
- Kiran, my amazing kiddo, for being the prime reader, and for, after a sigh and incredible kindness, eventually saying, "I'll wait to read the final version."
- My amazing friends, who stuck with me through the doubt, duality, and crazy: Bill, Emma, Freya, Fu, Pete, Ronan, and Stew.
- Bruce, for actually planting the seed that I could, uh, write stuff, and for being patient, understanding, and forgiving with my writing cadence.
- Perrin, for her insight and sherpa-ness.

If I've learned anything through this process, it's that creativity isn't a singular thing; it happens as a synthesis, and there are simply too many people to list who have influenced the development of this story. But thank you ALL. I know I didn't do this alone.

And of course, thank you, dear reader, for your time and your belief—or for at least momentarily suspending your disbelief.

About the Author

Chicago is Kurt's base of operations. He sees humanity's hubris and ambition in every building that reaches towards the stars and draws inspiration and motivation from anything over fifty stories tall. Mix in having a passion for martial arts; being born in India; living in Sweden; and having great friends, an awesome daughter, amazing parents, and a tight family—and one might think he's content. Alas, since he was a wee thing, he's wanted to write science fiction and fantasy. So, pretty much, he's incredibly grateful for his typing speed and the fact that he doesn't have to use a pen.

CPSIA information can be obtained
at www.ICGtesting.com
Printed in the USA
FFOW03n0007170617
36702FF